PRAISE FOR RAIVENTON

"…Kevin and Raina dominate the pages with their carefully restrained passion and the ongoing threats surrounding them."
Indies Today

"Wow, this series just keeps getting better! … I read this book from beginning to end, losing myself in their world."
Archaeolibrarian Book Reviews

"The suspense, espionage, and intensity of the story kept me from putting this 5-star fantasy story down."
Reader's Favorite

PRAISE FOR WINTERSFALL

"…beautifully crafted and filled with vivid imagery, making
the experience of reading her novel similar to watching
someone paint a picture with sentences for brushstrokes."
Literary Lotte Reviews

"Their love story is swoon-worthy and steamy, and I
adored it!"
Julie from ONE MORE BOOK (Top 20 of 2021 pick)

"Very rarely do I read books like this that rise above the
romance elements and actually deliver in terms of storyline."
Shadow Girl Reviews

RAIVENTON

GEN-HEIRS: THE GUARDIANS OF SZIVERA

SARAH WESTILL

This is a work of fiction. Names, characters, places, and incidents either are the products of the author's imagination or are used fictitiously. Any resemblance to actual persons, living or dead, businesses, companies, events, or locales is entirely coincidental.

RAIVENTON

Gen-Heirs: The Guardians of Sziveria Book 2

Copyright 2021 by Sarah Westill

All rights reserved

ISBN 978-1-955293-03-7

Cover Design by For the Muse Designs

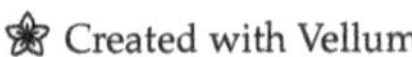 Created with Vellum

OTHER TITLES BY SARAH WESTILL

Levkaseon – A Prequel (Nov. 4th 2021)

Wintersfall

Raiventon

Kynhaven (Jan. 6th 2022)

Asherwick (June 2022)

Ericksen - A Wintervail Special (Nov. 2022)

For world maps and to stay up-to-date on the latest information, be
sure to visit www.sarahwestill.com

NOTE FROM THE AUTHOR:

Thank you so much for picking up this book! Please be aware this is the second title in an interconnected series. The characters are new, but elements of the plot continue from the previous title. I have done my best to keep you caught up, but please keep in mind a second book is a second book. Thank you, and enjoy!

Dedication and Acknowledgement

For Jerri Drennen
An amazingly talented author, who takes my manuscripts and makes them so much better. I am so thankful for you. For the time and effort you put into my books, and for the encouragement you give. I can't imagine my publishing journey without you.

WELCOME TO THE GEN-HEIRS WORLD

In the distant future, a major cataclysmic event not only reshaped the world as humanity knew it, but left entire lands uninhabitable. As generations of survivors struggled to endure a fight for territory and resources, humanity regressed into what became known as The Primal Years. A dark and dangerous time that lasted for centuries.

Slowly, civilizations formed in the new nations. Limited means of transportation and communication began to develop in a resource-poor world. Powerful countries arose known as Sziveria, Ruthenia, Italyssa, Westica, and Cairo. New cultures, with their own standards of honor, became global powerhouses.

By 830 Post-Cataclysmic Event (PCE), strong talents are now inherited traits, passed down through genetics. The recipients of an unavoidable hereditary legacy are known as Gen-Heirs. Trains, ships, carriages and if one can afford them, small magnetically powered vehicles move people. Radios are the only means of quick communication besides handwritten messages. Heated water is a luxury. Extreme drops in temperature and harsh arctic winds have forced most food growth indoors, in greenhouses. A dangerously lethal virus known as Human Rabies Syndrome (HRS) plagues the globe. The inhabited world is growing at a slow rate, each unique country striving to exist in harsher, cold climates, and those who survive have become ruthless in their quest to thrive in this new, forsaken world...

THE RANKING SYSTEM:

Guardians of Sziveria

Queen / King Elect
    Prince / Princess Elect
    Arch Guardian
    Prince / Princess
    Shield Guardian
    Master Guardian
    Primary Guardian
    Key Guardian
    Guardian (anyone who serves the realm)

Enforcement Services

First Prefect (FP)
    Master Prefect (MP)
    Prefect
    First Tribunii (FT)
    Master Tribunii (MT)
    Tribunii
    First Guardsman (FG)
    Master Guardsman (MG)
    Guardsman

Other Key Terms –

First Intelligence Office (FIO)
    Sziverian National Investigative Division (SNID)
    Haven City Enforcement Services (HCES)
    Medical Science Officer (MSO)
    Medical Science Investigator (MSI)
    Uninhabited Zones (UZ)
    Human Rabies Syndrome (HRS)

1

———

Haven City, Sziveria
   May 17th, 835 P.C.E (Post-Cataclysmic Event)

BITTER ANGER TORE through Kevin Merrick, the Master Guardian Raiventon. Not bothering to knock on his father-in-law's front door, he flung it open. He turned to the left, past the curved staircase leading to the second floor. A servant in green livery with large silver buttons rushed into the foyer, sputtering a protest. Kevin held up his hand and kept walking.

The dark wooden double doors to the Arch Guardians study were closed against intruders. Kevin ignored the bid for privacy and practically kicked them open, then slammed them shut with equal force. Henry Edmond, the Arch Guardian Synintel, leapt from his seat behind his massive desk. Recognition flared in the older man's eyes as he braced his hands on the surface and glared.

"Where in the arctic have you been?"

Kevin ignored the superior bite in Synintel's words.

"What was your daughter doing alone at Shield Guardian Enbrackon's house?"

Synintel smoothed a hand down the front of his long-sleeved maroon silk shirt, the buttons covered by a subtle seam of fabric. Nearing fifty, the Arch Guardian was fit, solid, knowing power came from presence as well as stature. His dark brown hair was liberally streaked with gray and neatly styled in the military standard he expected of those who worked under him. Of course, not all obeyed that unspoken rule. Kevin watched the faint motion of his hand with interest. The Arch Guardian was composing himself. He hadn't liked what Kevin told him.

"Enbrackon has taken an unhealthy interest in Lorraina these past few months. It's why I called you home." Slowly he returned to his seat. "How did you find out she was at his house? Are you following her?"

"No, I've no need to spy on my wife. She's an adult who can make her own decisions. I found out because the Shield Guardian kidnapped Guardianess Wintersfall."

Synintel's mouth actually gaped open. Kevin would have laughed if anger weren't still raw in his gut. "Did he harm her?"

"Why do you care?"

"She's an incredibly valuable asset. To lose her would be to lose our top sharpshooter. My other isn't exactly a team player."

Kevin fisted his hands at his side. "An asset? She's Sean's wife and as close to me as a sister."

"You saved her, correct?"

"Yes," Kevin ground out between clenched teeth.

Synintel nodded in approval and picked up his pen. "Good."

"What of Enbrackon?"

The Arch Guardian sniffled dismissively. "What of him?"

"Why was Raina at his house? And why hasn't he been

arrested for treason? I know as one of the top-ranking Guardians, and only fifth behind the Queen Elect, you can't possibly be ignorant to the discord and illegal behavior brewing in this country."

Synintel's pale brown eyes glanced up at Kevin before returning to the paperwork in front of him. His daughter had inherited those same eyes. "No, I'm not ignorant. As for why Enbrackon wanders free, I have no evidence. He's very careful. *They* have been very careful."

"Another reason we were brought home?"

"No, I already told you why you were called home."

Kevin frowned and recalled their conversation. "Because of your daughter's involvement with the Shield Guardian?"

Synintel sighed in impatience. "Yes. Now go home, do your job and keep her safe."

Kevin closed the distance to the desk and slammed his fists down on the surface. Ancient snarling bronze dragons on the front corners, from a world one could only read about, jumped and rattled from the force. They sat in the open, daring someone to have the guts to break into the house and steal them. A testament to how powerful the Arch Guardian considered himself. Kevin didn't really care. Let one fall to the floor and dent. "I *have* been! For four years, at your every beck and call. I've been to every city but this one. I've been where *you've* sent us, doing the assignments you've demanded. So, don't tell me to go and do my job."

A flush crept onto Synintel's well-shaven cheeks. "I married you to my daughter for one reason, one you agreed to. Keep her secure."

Kevin leaned forward. "No, you married me to her so you wouldn't have to deal with some sniveling fool of a son-in-law."

"A sniveling fool I certainly did not get. I have an impertinent one."

"Let me out of the deal and you don't have to have one at all."

The Arch Guardians eyes flashed. He gripped the pen so tightly Kevin was surprised the thing didn't burst in his hand. "You know she made the contract binding for life. Only death or infidelity. Are you ready to admit you whored around on my daughter?"

Kevin's jaw ticked and he took several breath's before he answered. "You'd love for me to say yes, wouldn't you?"

Synintel's grip on the pen lessened. "Not particularly. You really are the only one who can protect her."

"And how is your end of bargain coming along? Will I be keeping my Master Guardian rank?"

The little annoying sniffle Synintel gave when he didn't feel a question deserved his attention sounded again in the spacious office. "The next Endowment and Revocation Council meeting is in less than two months." His eyes took on a hard edge. "I'd suggest my daughter be well away from the Shield Guardian by that time."

Kevin straightened and crossed his arms over his chest. "Or what? You'll make sure your daughter is married to a baseborn? How do you think she'll take it? She already believes being a Master Guardianess is beneath her. I don't think she'll survive that blow. You have nothing left to threaten me with. I know you won't do that to her."

"And what of Primary Guardian Wintersfall?"

Kevin narrowed his eyes. A sinking sensation rolled in his stomach. "What of him?"

"His title is completely dependent on his staying in service for me. I'd hate for anything to change that situation."

"You'd blackmail me with that?"

Synintel raised a brow. "Would it work?"

How he loathed this man. "I never said I wouldn't keep her safe."

"Good. I never said I'd be forced to do anything to make sure of that."

Kevin flexed his hands, the tightness causing his fingers to ache. "Someday the puppet strings you hold us all by are going to break."

An arrogant huff escaped Synintel's lips. "That day is not today. Go make your presence known to society and to your wife. There's a soiree at Shield Guardian Gisburne's house. It'll be crowded, enough people to see you and talk about it. I'll make sure Kynhaven's sister is present too. She's the best gossip columnist in the city."

"I don't have an invitation."

Without looking, Synintel opened a drawer to his right. A second later an envelope rushed at Kevin from across the desk. "Now you do."

DAZZLING chandeliers glittered light over jewel-toned fabric and the mingling voices below. Lorraina Merrick, the Master Guardianess of Raiventon, took in the shuffling scene with little interest. If she weren't duty bound to attend at least five social gatherings a month, she'd stay happily sequestered in her gated home. But as the daughter of an Arch Guardian, she'd been bred into royalty, and royalty had to maintain standards. Her father ensured she understood her role from an early age. Duty, grace, and loyalty. Always be the perfect example of all three, at all times.

A server carrying a champagne tray offered her a drink. Champagne was rare, the grapes only grew in Italyssa with great care. The import showed the guests how wealthy, and how generous, their host was. Raina waved the server away with a flip of her hand, bow of her head and a kind smile. He returned the bow and moved on.

"Why so dull, darling?"

Raina snapped her attention to the male voice she hated to

admit she'd been dreading. She didn't have the energy to deal with Phipps Geier, the Shield Guardian Enbrackon tonight. He'd made a point to inform her at their last meeting that she wasn't pleasing him. As the wife of another man, she had no right to be anything to the Shield Guardian but the professional adviser he'd asked her to be.

But he wanted more. He'd made his desires very clear. He also wanted more *for* her. Over the past couple of months, she'd began to believe he could help free her from her father's shadow. The question was, how far would she go to make sure that happened?

Shoving the uncomfortable thoughts away, Raina turned to him with a smile. "Shield Guardian Enbrackon, what a pleasure to see you tonight."

Eyes so dark brown they were almost black sparkled in the crystalline light as he bowed over her extended hand. His shiny black hair was slicked back, revealing the smooth planes of a face he thought handsome. Raina considered him pretty. Dressed in the elaborate wealth he personified, nearly every finger glittered with a ring. Only the best fabric adorned his body in slacks purposefully too tight. A silver jacket with attention grabbing, red embroidery showed off his broad shoulders, yet hid his rounding stomach, was paired with a matching red silk shirt, and calf high, glossy leather boots. A gaudy diamond brooch at his throat completed the ensemble. The outfit, meant to make him stand out visibly in the crowd, accomplished the goal.

Enbrackon placed a fleeting kiss on the back of her hand, his hold lingering longer than socially necessary. "It's always my pleasure to see you. Why did you pass on the champagne? Truly is the best I've had."

"I don't enjoy alcohol."

He tsked and motioned for a server. The man appeared gracefully before them, lowering the tray for Phipps. Removing two glasses, he handed one to her. "Come now, darling. If you want to socialize with the top echelon, you have to make them comfortable. They drink. Champagne is harmless, I think you'll enjoy it. One sip won't hurt, now will it?"

"I don't think it'll hurt anything, I just don't—"

Phipps sighed and lifted her hand holding the flute nearer to her face. He leaned close so only she could hear his words. "Lorraina really, you can be so boring. I thought I told you boring just won't do. While you and I both know you are above everyone else in this room, they don't like to be reminded of it. And if they sip on wine, or champagne, or whiskey, while you sit with your hands in your lap, they'll hate you for it. You don't want to be hated, do you?"

A strange discomfort built in her chest. She stared at the bubbles in the golden liquid rising to the surface and slowly shook her head. "No, of course I don't want to be boring or hated."

"I thought not. See? What would you do without me? Now, take a sip and smile."

The thought of the sharp bite of alcohol hitting her tongue and settling in her mouth made her stomach roll. She swallowed and took a calming breath. "I don't think I can. I don't drink, everyone knows, and no one has cared."

Phipps cast her a dull stare over the top of his own glass. He took a heavy drink before lowering it. "They cared, they were simply too polite to say anything. Now, one sip. You'll see. It's more like bubbly, white grape juice. You like juice, don't you? No reservations to that?"

Why did he make it sound as though she were some purist no one could tolerate? She frowned at the glass. Was she? "Don't be silly, why would I have an aversion to juice?"

"Because you're holding its cousin like it's poison. Drink, Lorraina."

The dry, sharp scent of alcohol hit her nose before the

bubbles did. She wanted to both gag and sneeze. She quickly lowered the flute. "Not tonight, perhaps next time."

Phipps frowned, disappointment clear in the staunch line of his mouth. Again. "You said as much last time, to beautifully crafted red wine no less. Another cousin to juice."

Raina took a deep breath, staring at the champagne again. "The cousins don't seem to agree with me."

"Nothing ever does."

She lifted her gaze to his and caught the anger in the dark depths of his eyes. "Excuse me?"

He leaned forward again. His hand snaked around her upper arm, his fingers biting into the tender inner flesh. "I am tired of your excuses. I try to help you, but you won't listen. You won't even try. What do you expect me to do? Work miracles for you? You can't even take a tiny sip of champagne. Now, take a drink. You will save yourself the future embarrassment of falling flat on your face when you refuse champagne offered to you by a princess and insult the woman into slandering your name all over Sziveria. I know you don't want that. Someday, you'll be there. Get comfortable now with what you don't like."

Raina gasped at his painful hold and the image he painted. Of course, she could never refuse something offered to her by a princess. And if the Shield Guardian was correct, someday she'd be free of her father and could choose her own clients, which included princes and princesses. If someone wanted her to handle logistics for them, they wouldn't have to go through her father first as they did now. Phipps was right, she had to get past her discomforts if she wanted to move in the circles he promised.

She ignored the sting of tears in her eyes. With a shaky hand she lifted the rim of the fragile glass to her mouth. And still she couldn't. Despite his words, despite his physical pressure, her mind refused to let the substance pass her lips.

His grip tightened until she bit back a cry. "Take a drink."

"I—"

"How thoughtful of you to get me a glass, my dear."

The deep, smooth voice raced up Raina's spine like silk. *Kevin.* Not sure she heard correctly, she turned as Phipps released her so suddenly, she swayed. The flute seemed to magically disappear from her fingers just as a gentle hand steadied her.

"Are you feeling okay?" Kevin asked.

Raina took in the dangerously handsome man standing before her. His stormy gray eyes looked her over with concern. She had to look up, way up, to see.

"I thought you were a dream," she breathed out.

Kevin raised a dark blond brow. "If that's not the best a husband can hear when he sees his wife, I don't know what is."

She shook her head and blinked. Now was not the time, or the place, to relive a dream she now believed was a memory. "No, I... never mind. You're home."

Once again she looked him over. Dressed effortlessly in black leather shoes, finely spun black wool pants and coat, and a gray silk shirt matching his eyes, he looked far more casual than the rest of the men in the room. Yet far more alluring. The simple style accentuated his lean, well-built frame. He'd done nothing special to flaunt his wealth other than wear luxurious fabrics. Nearly a foot taller than her five foot five inches, and inches taller than all the men in the room, he commanded attention.

And he was her husband.

His hair was short, and not styled. In fact, she couldn't help but smile at how finger-mussed the strands appeared. She had a sudden urge to tame his wayward mane. A close-cropped beard shades darker than his hair brought out the angles of his high cheekbones, strong jaw and perfect nose. As for his mouth, she dared not look at his full lips for more than a glance. If what she feared were correct, she'd come much too close to begging for his kiss nights ago.

If the faint smile turning his mouth were any indication, her examination amused him. She flushed, turned and faced the crowd. "How long have you been home?"

The sensation of his hand settling into the small of her back made her shiver. He leaned close, which had to be a feat, and murmured, "What? No Master Guardian Raiventon this time?"

She gasped and turned so quickly she found her mouth a mere whisper from his. Oh mistake, big one. Breath hitching in her lungs, she grasped the supple fabric of her gown's skirt to keep from grabbing his jacket. "The other night, it wasn't a dream, was it?"

He didn't move away. The hum of conversation around them faded, and she wondered if perhaps she shouldn't take a step back. "No, it wasn't a dream."

Then she remembered Phipps. She touched a hand to her mouth and turned. He was gone. "Where did Shield Guardian Enbrackon go?"

Kevin straightened, handing the champagne off to a passing server who likely wanted to hear their conversation more than be of service. "He knew what was best for his safety."

Wide-eyed, she turned her attention back to him. His face was set in hard, deadly lines. The gray of his irises grew dark until they were slate. Raina blinked. "Excuse me?"

Then, like a storm, the sun returned and he smiled, all traces of lethality gone. "Why was he so intent on you drinking the champagne?"

"Y-you were eavesdropping on our conversation?"

"No, I was watching you continue to refuse the drink as I walked across the room. He wouldn't let you. Why?"

"Oh." She didn't know whether to be flattered or not that he'd only had eyes on her, and so intently he'd understood her turmoil. Then a sliver of panic set in. What was she supposed to say? Working as he did for her father, Kevin would never understand, or sympathize, with her need for freedom. "He was just sure that I'd, um, really like the champagne. I've never tried any before."

"Does he own the label?"

Confused, Raina tipped her head to study him. Once more his handsome face caught her off guard. At least her father hadn't married her to some short, fat man. No, he'd found the best looking one in all of Haven City, shackled them together, and then made sure the man never set foot in her house again. Blinking, she realized she was staring and she'd forgotten the question. *Darn it*! "Does he what?"

Kevin raised a perturbed brow and repeated himself. "Does he own the champagne label?"

"No."

"Then why would he care so much if you tried it?"

Aggravated, Raina huffed. "Why don't you ask him?"

"I would have, but he slinked off like a bad cat. Now I'm asking you."

Her mouth fell open. "Are you always this persistent?"

He leaned closer to her. "I don't know. Are you always this evasive?"

Heat climbed up her cheeks. If social graces didn't dictate she be the complete picture of respect to her husband, she'd be defending her right to privacy. The realization made her blush further. Less than five minutes and he'd managed to rile her to the point of causing the gossip tongues to begin whispering. "I need some air."

When Raina made a move for the open greenhouse doors, Kevin caught her elbow and gently steered her the opposite direction. He slid her arm around his and leaned close. "Unless you want all the guests in this room thinking you welcomed your husband home in the garden, I suggest we leave as we're expected to. Everyone is aware of how long it's been since I was home."

The flush of her cheeks turned to fire. She quickly glanced to the floor and would have put space between them if Kevin's hand hadn't slid over hers and tightened to keep her near. His fingers were warm, rough, and calloused. Nothing like Phipps soft, carefully manicured hands. Raina glanced at his hand and noted the small collection of scars running along the back and frowned. What exactly did he do for her father?

Out in the vast circular vestibule, guests wandered in from the front door, the salon, game room, or dining room. Raina took a deep breath and smiled as they walked past. Several women waved when she caught their eye.

They waited on the bottom step for the carriage to be brought around. Kevin allowed the carriageman to help her inside, though refused help for himself. He leapt in so swiftly, and with such little movement to the vehicle itself, Raina couldn't help but gasp. Once the door closed, she glared in the darkness.

"We could have stayed longer."

Kevin settled into the shadows, his long legs stretching as far as they could to her side. "We could have, but no one would have believed it. Your father insisted we make an impression tonight no one will forget. He even made sure Miss Dandridge was present for a firsthand experience to write for the gossip column in the morning."

Raina let out a low, very unladylike, growl. "So, when my father snaps his fingers, you bow too, do you?"

"And you don't?" The words were quiet. No condescension, no mockery. Almost defeated.

The steam left her and she slumped back against the seat. "Of course I do."

Though if she had her way, she wouldn't be under her father's control much longer.

• • •

Tantalizing shafts of silvery light brushed across Raina's face whenever an alley opened enough to let the full moon shine into the carriage. Kevin studied her in the quiet. Raina's rich brown tresses were elegantly braided and held in place as a crown by an assortment of simple ruby pins. The gentle angles of her face were beautiful in the shadowy depths. Softly arched brows, a heart shaped mouth, with a bottom lip just full enough from the top to make them entirely too kiss-able, and a small, rounded nose.

Her petite frame and delicate features made him wonder if pixies really existed and he happened to be married to one. In comparison, he was a giant, towering over her by a foot, at six foot five, and more than double her weight. But the crimson silk flowing effortlessly over her curves reminded him that while small, she wasn't lacking. Firm, subtle mounds rose beneath the elegant material, drawing attention to her flat, narrow waist and the gentle flair of her hips. Breaking with fashion, she didn't wear pounds of fabric beneath her skirt, only enough to keep her warm.

No, what troubled him about her appearance was she'd matched the embroidery color of Enbrackon's jacket. Kevin wanted to ask if it'd been done on purpose. If he'd noticed, others had too. He wanted to snap and demand the answer. But he couldn't. They'd spent hours together in their four years of marriage, not weeks or even days. She didn't know him any better than he knew her. Asking questions of her wasn't his right. Not yet.

"How long this time?" she asked, so quietly he almost missed the inquiry.

Kevin knew exactly what she asked. "Not sure, he didn't give me a time table." That wasn't entirely true, so he added, "Probably two months, maybe less."

Her sharp intake of air was audible. "Two months?"

"Is there a problem?"

"No, of course not. I'm just… shocked. Father has never

let you remain home for longer than a single night before one of his men knock on the door. Sometimes you didn't even stay that long." Fabric rustled and heavier shadows fell across her face and torso as she angled to face him. "Do you know why?"

"Why he's letting me stay home?"

Even in the darkness, he caught her nod.

Because you're playing with a wolf and I have to make sure you don't get eaten. Kevin shrugged. "Who knows? Maybe he's ready for grandkids."

The gasping choke she made had Kevin smiling wickedly. "I can't believe you just said that."

"Can you think of another reason he'd keep me home?" He was giving her an opportunity to come clean on her own, if she recognized it. The faint fidget of her shoulders and thighs told him she did.

"No, not really. Maybe he's allowing you to have a break?"

And she didn't take the chance. Great. He heaved a heavy sigh. "Maybe."

She squirmed again, the motion amplified by the gentle rock of the carriage. "Were you really in my room a couple of nights ago?"

Kevin's gaze swept over her, lingering on her mouth, to the gentle curve of her collar bone that invited his attention lower to the soft swell of her breasts. He'd come so close to feeling all of her against his body. Dangerously close. He had to breathe against the hot pierce of desire at the memory. "Yes."

"Men really broke in?"

"Yes."

She released a shuddered breath. "There was no evidence. Not even your bed was unmade. I didn't think it'd been real."

"I've been in the house every night since."

Even in the dark he could tell every muscle in her body tensed. "Really?"

"Yes. You didn't think I'd leave you alone in danger, did you?"

"Well I… I didn't think it was real. My father would have sent men to patrol the exterior if you'd asked."

"Why? I'm your husband, I can take care of my house."

She chuckled lightly. "But they're trained."

Kevin couldn't stop the bark of laughter, and when he ran her comment back through his mind, he laughed harder. "Yes, I'm sure they're very skilled."

"Why do you laugh? My father only hires the best. You know that. They wouldn't let any harm come to us."

Thankfully the carriage arrived at the house, saving Kevin from an argument he couldn't win. To be fair, Raina wasn't at fault for not knowing exactly what her husband was capable of. Kevin was in no hurry to enlighten her. The Guardianess Raiventon took her position in society seriously. Knowing just who she was married to likely wouldn't go over well.

Kevin helped her from the carriage and then followed behind, watching the edges around the house closely. Satisfied no threats lurked, he took the row of stairs two at a time. A bright trail of light across the wide brick porch preceded the front door opening for them.

Portly and shorter than Raina, Mrs. Taft held the door in both hands, beaming at her Guardianess. Her silver hair was piled high on her head in a stern bun, her dark green uniform with an ivory apron was immaculate. "You look as beautiful as when you left." Her dark blue eyes moved past Raina when she noticed her mistress wasn't alone. She gasped, her hand flying to her ample bosom. "Oh my! Master Guardian Raiventon! We were not expecting you. Oh my, I don't have your room ready, or your place setting at the breakfast table, or—"

Raina set her hand on Mrs. Taft's shoulder. "It's okay, he's been home a couple days. No need to fret."

Her mouth opened and closed like a beached fish. Pink darkened her cheeks. "Well, my goodness, how could we be so remiss! I'll have those girls' heads for their negligence."

Kevin shook his head as they entered the house. "As Guardianess Raiventon said, no need. I leave before anyone is awake most mornings. If I'd wanted special attention, I would have called you for it." Kevin cast her a sideways smile. "I'm just grateful you remembered me at all."

She waved her hand and laughed. "Forget you? Silly man, that's unlikely. We'll be sure to have everything ready for you now, whether you're here in the mornings, afternoon or evenings, makes no matter. You're home."

"Thank you," he said, giving her a respectful bow.

Mrs. Taft returned the gesture and then closed the front door. "Tabby is upstairs waiting for you, Guardianess."

"Thank you, Mrs. Taft."

Kevin waited until the robust housekeeper disappeared into the breakfast room before following behind Raina. "Tabby?"

With her fingers trailing up the rail, Raina headed upstairs. "Tabitha, Mrs. Taft's daughter and my Stylist Elite." She paused and he took a moment to take in her beauty. The diffused warm light from the few candles still lit washed over her delicate features. "Will you be needing a valet?"

Kevin grunted. "No, I can dress myself."

She stepped down until she was at his height and then playfully tossed a hand through his hair. Kevin's breath caught at the sensation of her spirited touch on his scalp. Her pale brown eyes danced playfully. "You could use one though, do something with this hair."

Blinking, he reached up and touched his head. "What's wrong with my hair?"

"Other than it goes any direction it feels like? Nothing at all."

Frowning, Kevin looked her over once more. Nothing was out of place. Remembering the last time he'd seen her, the sleepy mess of her hair and the way her thin silk nightgown had pooled around her knees had him almost falling to his. "Do you want me to change it?"

Her lips parted slightly and her hand fell to her side. The tip of her tongue darted out, wetting her bottom lip. Kevin took a small step back before he did something stupid, like kiss her.

"No, not unless you want to. I think the disheveled look will grow on me." She cast him a soft smile and then turned and continued up.

Kevin watched the sway of her hips and the way the gown molded to her rear with each step up, before sliding into place again. The cut of his pants suddenly became too tight and he sighed. Two months... he had to make it two months.

2

After cancelling all her meetings for the day, Raina sat behind her desk and pretended to be busy, while simultaneously trying to spy on her husband. Since her desk sat a solid thirty feet from the double doors to her study, and the corridor to the other side of the house was narrow, and dim, she found herself rising and craning her neck to catch even a glimpse of him. Not exactly stealth. Sighing at her pitifulness, she plopped back down in her seat. She hadn't seen him this morning, and she hated to admit she wanted to.

A melodious bell sounded seconds before Mrs. Taft came rushing from the back of the house to answer the door. Raina rose and waited to see who their visitor could be. Since Kevin was home, she wondered if he'd have callers.

"Raina, my lovely, where are you?" a woman's sing-song voice called. "I read the most delightful thing in the paper this morning, I just had to come by."

Happiness swelled in Raina's chest and she practically ran into the corridor to greet her best friend. "Patricia!"

Patricia Welsh, married to a Ruthenian royal, and niece to the Queen Elect of Sziveria, squealed in delight when her cobalt eyes fixed on Raina. Her mess of blonde curls bobbed about her sweet, round face. "Oh, there you are!"

They exchanged quick cheek kisses in greeting, Patricia holding Raina's hands tightly. "I'm so happy to see you."

"Well, of course you are, silly. Though I must say I'm a little upset I had to read about your husband being home." Patricia pouted and swayed, the supple light pink cashmere of her dress whispering.

"I was writing to you first thing this morning, I promise."

"You know how long I've been dying to..."

The words died in her friend's throat. Kevin strolled from the room Raina had designated as his study four years ago, and had never been utilized until now. Bare foot, he wore light brown pants and a navy blue cotton shirt, untucked, the long sleeves rolled to below his elbows. With every step the fabric pulled tight to his muscled frame. From his thighs to his broad shoulders, there was no doubt the strength in the man's body. He sniffed as though he were tired and still waking up, and disappeared into the breakfast room. The women stood motionless.

Reappearing, he held a steaming cup in his hand, raising it to his lips. He took four steps before he realized they were still staring at him. The cup lowered and he raised a brow. The harsh morning light cast his handsome face in sharp angles. The stormy gray hue of his irises looked pale in the bright sun streaming in from high windows. Tousled locks of hair hung over his forehead.

"Good morning, ladies."

Patricia's grip tightened until Raina grimaced. When Raina realized her friend was going to remain speechless, she smiled at Kevin. "Good morning, Master Guardian "

He inclined his head to them and then disappeared into his study.

Visibly slouching, Patricia raised a hand to her chest. Then she fanned herself. "Goodness, I had heard rumors, but I was *not* prepared for that."

Raina bit her lip and ushered her friend to her study. "He will hear you."

"Good, let him." She craned her neck over her shoulder. "Maybe he'll walk back out."

In her office, Raina grabbed both doors, taking one last glance down the hall before closing them, hating to admit she wouldn't mind another look herself. Sighing at her ridiculousness, she pushed the doors closed. "You are married. What would your husband say?"

Patricia snorted. "Get a good look and then come to bed, my apple blossom."

Raina couldn't believe the crassness of her friend. She'd never seen the playful side of her. "He would not!"

Patricia nodded, a devilish gleam in her rich blue eyes. "Oh, he would."

Pink fabric fluffed up around her friend as she fell back into one of Raina's many overstuffed chairs, positioned in comfortable meeting locations around the room. Raina always let her clients, or guests, choose where they wanted to convene. Patricia had chosen a view of the greenhouse in the far right of the spacious office. Raina settled down in a chair adjacent to her, an empty round table large enough for a refreshment tray between them. In a few moments, Mrs. Taft would bring in tea and an assortment of breakfast meats and biscuits. Raina's stomach grumbled at the thought.

"I'm not so sure I want to know this side of your relationship."

Patricia fanned herself again. "How are you not pregnant? I mean, really."

Raina flushed. She'd never told her closest friend her husband had never been to her bed. Some things couldn't be trusted not to be repeated no matter how close the relationship appeared to be. A juicy morsel such as that would be whispered to the first person who listened. Raina rubbed her forearm in discomfort and said what came to her mind. "He's only been home a couple days."

"Well maybe that preposterous Shield Guardian Enbrackon will be seen around you less."

"Shield Guardian Enbrackon is helping me build a client portfolio that well outmatch anyone else in the city. I'm grateful for his help," Raina bristled, thankful when the sharp knock she'd been expecting sounded.

Mrs. Taft entered with a small tray, placed it between the women, and then departed. Raina realized she should have asked if her head housekeeper had checked on Kevin, but then remembered he'd declared his being an adult and capable of caring for himself. He likely wouldn't appreciate her mothering him. Though, as she chewed a biscuit, she had to admit she didn't know what he'd appreciate at all.

"How long did it take you and William to become comfortable together?" Raina asked more as an afterthought while she mused.

Patricia swallowed her bite and took a sip of tea before answering. "Not long, but William was determined since we had to share a room on the ship to Ruthenia for the summer months." A wicked smile twinkled in her eyes over the top of her cup. "He didn't want a bashful wife for the long journey." She set her cup down. "Are you and Raiventon not comfortable?"

Raina worked her bottom lip between her teeth. How did she word the problem without giving too much away? "He's been gone a long time, I'm not sure how long to expect him home this time."

Patricia leaned across the distance and patted Raina's knee. "You both will be fine. Just keep jumping in his bed like you must have last night, and the rest will work itself out."

Tea snorted up Raina's nose and she coughed. The liquid

burned in her sinuses and she waved tears away. "Patricia! I had no idea you were like this!"

Her friend shrugged. "I didn't know I could be, but after seeing your husband, and reading Miss Dandridge's article, I know there's no way you're an innocent."

What had the woman written about them? Raina chanced another drink to hide her whimper.

KEVIN PINCHED the bridge of his nose in agitation. Lines of numbers, notes and shorthand only his wife understood stared back at him from an open file. Early in the morning before anyone stirred, he'd decided to see if Raina had any files on Enbrackon so he could gauge for himself the level of their relationship. She did, and the information made very little sense to him. Sighing, he snapped the folder closed, stacked it with three others, and tossed them in the drawer to his left.

A deafening shriek had him leaping from his chair and taking the quickest route from the study, over the desk. He skidded into the carpeted corridor and came to an abrupt stop. Raina stood outside the vestibule, the morning paper clutched in her hands to the point that if she held any tighter, the thing would disintegrate in her grasp. Bright red splotches covered her neck and chest and fanned across her cheeks.

"This can't be happening. This isn't happening to me," she breathed out. The paper shook in her grasp. "No, no, no, no."

Kevin crossed his arms and propped his shoulder against the wall in front of the stairs. He knew the problem. Cora Dandridge had followed the Arch Guardians orders, likely all too happily. "How bad?"

Her gaze shot up, her pale brown eyes wild with anxiety. "How bad?" She shook the paper at him and shrieked again, *"How bad?"*

In mock surrender, Kevin held up his hands. "I didn't write the article."

Tears gathered in her eyes and Kevin straightened. Was she going to cry? The angry red flush on her skin began to dissipate. She stared at the paper and shook her head.

"I can't believe he'd do this to me."

"Who?"

She looked at him again. "My father. You said he made sure Miss Dandridge was at the event last night."

"Yes, he wanted to make sure everyone knew I was home."

The flush returned, along with her temper. She crumbled the paper, stalked up to him and threw it at his chest. "Well, everyone knows, all right."

Kevin took the paper at the same time he grabbed her upper arm before she could stalk up the stairs past him. She glared at his grasp and tried to yank free, but he held firm.

Her spine straightened and if she'd been able to look down her nose at him, she would have. She certainly craned her neck far enough to try. "Get your hand off me, immediately."

Anger hit him fast and hard. He hauled her up against his body, ignoring her supple curves along his thighs and torso, the way her belly pressed between his hips. "Listen closely princess, only two people have earned the right to give me orders, and you aren't one of them."

A short gasp escaped her parted lips. If he weren't less than two months from having to lie to get out of a marriage she didn't deserve to be in, he would kiss her. His pulse pounded in his ears and his senses demanded to know how she'd taste. How she'd feel pulled tighter to him. How she'd move in desire. But only a fool would tease himself with what he wanted and walk away, and Kevin wasn't a fool. He released her so quickly she stumbled back.

He held up the paper. "I didn't write the article, so don't

blame me for it. Take it up with your father if you're that upset."

Irritation flashed in her pale eyes. "Don't treat me like a child."

"Then lose the tantrum and stop acting like one."

For a moment, she simply stared at him, spine straight, shoulders back in defiance. Her firm, petite breasts pressed tight against the navy fabric of her dress. Kevin continued to fight the urge to haul her back to his body and change the direction of her passion. Raina took the paper and then slumped down onto the nearest stair. The crumpled pages went slack between her hands. He let out a breath he hadn't realized he'd been holding.

"Do you know what she said?" Raina asked, her voice low with defeat.

Kevin sat beside her. She had to scoot over, but even then, their hip and thighs touched through fabric. He half smiled at the juvenile thrill. "Doesn't sound like I want to."

"Oh, nothing bad about you. No concern there."

"Why would she write something bad about you?" He clasped his hands between his knees.

Raina's shoulders rose and dropped in a curt motion, the paper rustling in her grasp. "Who knows why she writes any of the drivel she does. I must have done something to make her angry, because I've never read one of her articles with so much venom."

Kevin considered his options. On one hand, he knew how witchy Cora Dandridge could be. She was after all her brother's twin, and Mason could be ornery with the best of them. However, she took her job as a journalist seriously. Even when she was assigned the gossip section by an Arch Guardian... she wouldn't write an outright lie. So that left Kevin wondering if he should ask the hard question. He decided he should. "Does she have reason to?"

"Have hatred toward me?" Raina scoffed. "I don't see

why she would, since we don't exactly move in the same circles."

"But she knows me."

"Knows you how?" Raina asked slowly, a hard edge to her words.

Kevin raised a brow. "Is this jealousy coming from a woman who wore matching clothes with a man who wasn't her husband?"

Brilliant red bloomed across her cheeks. The paper creased in her hands again. "Don't be absurd. Who you keep company with is none—"

"Is completely your business, or have you forgotten?"

She blinked. "Forgotten what?"

"That you made our contract binding for life, barring death or infidelity."

"Oh, yes." She licked her lips again and Kevin quickly looked at the wood floor beneath his feet.

"Why did your clothes match Shield Guardian Enbrackon's?"

Raina snapped the paper, attempting to return it to a folded state. But she'd wrinkled the thing so many times it'd never fold normal. "I have no idea. I hadn't even noticed until I read it in the article."

"You didn't plan for the similarity?"

She glanced at him and then quickly went back to trying to straighten the paper. "Plan? Goodness no, what would people say?" Then she laughed, a sarcastic, sharp sound. "I guess what they did say, hmm?"

Kevin hated to admit he was relieved. Either the Shield Guardian didn't have his claws in as deep as Kevin feared, or Raina was that naïve. "Did she just talk about you two?"

"No, that was a highlight to get to the part about where I must be quite good. One man seduced, the other man I left with… and stayed with."

Now Raina's reputation lay in assumed tatters for the

vultures to pick at. How he loathed the society he'd been forced into. However, no matter how mad he wanted to be, his little wife had dug her own hole. She was just now forced to look up from it. An unexpected protective urge tightened in his chest and he frowned. He didn't have to leave her there.

Kevin knocked his thigh into hers and then stood. "Come on."

Brows drawn tight, she met his gaze. "Where?"

He offered his hand. When she did nothing more than stare at his outstretched fingers, Kevin sighed. "I don't bite."

Cautiously, her hand slid into his. The gentle sensation of her touch meeting his caused Kevin's breath to hitch. He hadn't been expecting skin like silk, or warmth close to sitting near a fire. Would she feel similar underneath all the layers of clothing she wore? Kevin shook the thought away. He'd never know.

Using him as an anchor, Raina stood with ease. She didn't pull free. Instead, she seemed to inspect their joined hands.

"You're very strong." The words came out more as an observation than anything else.

"You aren't used to strong men?"

Frowning, Raina turned his hand over in hers and delicately traced a scar running the width of his palm. Kevin inhaled deeply through his nose, but didn't snatch his hand away. He should. But he couldn't. Her tender touch left him mesmerized, and more than a little aroused. The subtle, very feminine scent of peaches and flower blossoms filled the space around him.

"Not like this. None of the men I meet are built like you, nor do they have scars. Did you have a hard childhood?"

Kevin pulled away, fisted his hand and dropped it to his side. "No. I had a very happy childhood." *It's adulthood that's been beating me.*

"And the scars?"

Kevin shrugged. "I work under your father. Occupational hazard."

Her frown increased. "Doing what, exactly?"

Before he could stop himself, Kevin stroked a finger down her cheek. "Ask me again when you're ready for the answer."

She opened her mouth then snapped it shut and nodded.

Kevin dropped his hand. "Are you more comfortable in a carriage or Ariot?"

The small vehicle only big enough for two people, was run by a magnetic engine harnessing the power of positive and negative attraction. Expensive, not many Sziverian's were able to own one. A lack of resources made them a rare commodity, used mostly by those willing to show off their wealth, or were used by the government.

Raina stared at him thoughtfully. "You have an Ariot?"

"Yes."

She tilted her head in confusion. "Why? I don't even own one. Not that I like them, they're far too cramped for me. I feel squeezed and unsafe when I ride in one."

"Because your father wanted me to, so he made sure I have one," he answered as if the reason should have already been known. "So, which is to be?"

"A carriage, why?"

"We're going to see a friend."

A COLD, misty rain left everything gray and gloomy. The perfect accompaniment to Raina's mood. She rested her hands on her legs and watched buildings go by. Water seeped like tears over the edges of partially dry brick and stone. They'd been riding for longer than Raina expected.

"Who is this friend?" she asked, wondering if he were always so quiet. He hadn't spoken much on the ride home last night either.

"Primary Guardian Kynhaven."

Raina tried to place the name. "I don't think I've met him."

"Likely not. He doesn't attend social functions unless he's dragged to them."

"How do you know him?"

"We work together."

"Why am I going with you then?"

Kevin's smile was more predatory than kind. Raina shifted slightly in her seat. Who was this man she'd married?

"So you can talk with his sister."

Raina sighed with irritation. "Why would I want to do that?"

The carriage slowed before an imposing, two-story granite mansion. A wide porch and equally wide steps covered with an arched stone awning made the imposing structure seem more approachable. But the steep, angled, rich rust-colored roof in the dreary light took the feeling of welcome away. The carriage rolled up to the side of the house to a well-kept stable area with a second story.

Kevin jumped out before anyone could open the door for him, and then offered his hand to Raina. Butterflies danced in her stomach as she reached for him. She'd held lots of hands in her life, from simple assistance like Kevin extended now, to more intimate actions, like a fluttering kiss across her knuckles. None of them caused her to *feel* before. Had made her heart race and a warm tingly sensation spread through her body. All from a simple, rather innocent touch.

If holding his hand made her all breathless, she wondered what a kiss would do. The idea was a dangerous one. When he kept her hand after she was free of the carriage, she didn't protest. She tried to convince herself it was due to the rather nasty article that had practically painted her an adulteress. If anyone watched them, they'd see a woman with her husband who didn't believe the rumors. But she'd be lying to herself. The modest affection from him comforted her. Made her feel close to a man she wished she knew.

Being married four years to a stranger hadn't been something she'd anticipated when her father arranged their contract. Though, looking back, she didn't know why she expected less. Arch Guardian Synintel seemed to live to control every aspect of his daughter's life. Her marriage was no different.

The front door opened before they even reached the first step. A footman dressed in plain black pants and a pressed gray long-sleeved shirt appeared in the doorway and executed a neat bow.

"Master Guardian Raiventon, I was unaware you were expected."

"We weren't. Are they home?"

"They are. I will inform them of your presence."

"Thank you."

The footman executed another curt bow and then disappeared into the house. By the time they walked inside, a gorgeous woman with long, black hair was practically running down the stairs. The muted blue silk gown she wore billowed behind her, showing off every curve of her figure. Her unbound hair flowed wildly around her shoulders. Modestly applied makeup brought out the planes of her face, from her full cheeks and lips to the perfect arches of her brows.

"Kevin," she said with a grin, her silver eyes dancing. "I guess my article made a bigger impression than I expected. You forgive me, don't you?"

Raina gaped. *This* was Cora Dandridge? She didn't know why, but she'd always imagined the journalist to be a short woman with glasses and crazy, dull hair. Not a voluptuous beauty who was a good four inches taller than Raina and made her look, and feel, like a twig. Then again, with Cora's reputation as a flirt, who managed to succeed in her conquests more than she failed, the woman's attractiveness shouldn't have shocked her at all.

"I have nothing to forgive." He glanced down at Raina. She tried to pull her hand free, but he wouldn't let her. "My wife however…"

What did he expect her to say? She was the daughter of an Arch Guardian. Diplomacy having been bred into her from the cradle. "Miss Dandridge is entitled to her opinions."

Cora slowed when she reached the last two steps, her fingers trailing like a lover's caress over the banister as she slid her foot to the last stair. Each move was calculated, seductive without effort. Raina tried to stifle the onset of jealousy. Even in her dreams she couldn't make herself move with such outward grace.

"Opinion? Darling Master Guardianess, if all I wanted to do was write opinions, I'd be working for *The Havener*. My editor requires research and honesty, and our readers expect it."

Raina straightened her spine. "Then your research was lacking."

Cora looked from Raina to Kevin and then back. "I see. Enlighten me." She motioned to a room on the left.

Kevin released Raina's hand and the immediate cold surprised her. When he didn't follow, she glanced over her shoulder. He'd already walked away, heading down a long corridor opposite the room they entered. Raina had the unfortunate sensation of heading into a viper's pit.

Cora continued through a simple library to a small study. However, the journalist surprised Raina by sitting in front of a gently burning fireplace and motioning to a chair across from her, not behind her desk where she'd have all the perceived power. Raina sat and folded her hands primly on her thighs.

Cora eased back into the seat, her arms on the rests, legs crossed. "Tell me, how do I have you wrong?"

Raina straightened until the small of her back ached. "Excuse me?"

Annoyed, Cora waved a hand and sighed. "You came here all bothered about my article, therefore something I said offended you. What part do you feel I lied about?"

All of it. But she couldn't admit that. No one but she and Kevin needed to know the true condition of their marriage. Just the thought of the seductive woman across from her aware of how available her husband was had Raina squirming in her seat. Even though their contract practically made infidelity a capital crime, at this point, Raina couldn't fault the man if he wasn't faithful. The thought however, made her feel ill. The revelation wasn't something she had time to dwell on. Cora Dandridge stared at her expectantly.

"I haven't been seduced by Shield Guardian Enbrackon."

Cora's eyes widened. "Oh?"

"We have a professional relationship, nothing more."

Cora regarded her for a moment, her foot tapping in the air. "Guardianess Raiventon, I think you believe that, honestly, but that's not what the rest of society is seeing."

Raina's stomach dropped. "What do you mean?"

Cora's foot stopped. "Have you really not been listening to the gossip around you these past few months?"

"I haven't heard any."

Cora laughed, a musical sound meant to draw attention rather than genuine emotion. "You're joking."

Unamused, Raina frowned. "No, I'm not. Our relationship is strictly business and no one has implied anything to me otherwise. At least until I read your article this morning."

All traces of humor left Cora. "Then you haven't been paying attention, you silly girl."

Raina gasped and blinked in shock. "Excuse me?"

Cora slammed her hands on the arms of the chair and then stood. She paced in front of the fire, the elegant folds of her gown flowing like water around her legs. "For at least three months everyone has been whispering behind their hands about your secret love affair with the Shield Guardian while Kevin has been absent. You've been seen going to his house alone. He arrives at yours well after your last client has left for the day. Do you deny any of this?"

"There has been no secret love affair!"

"And the visitations?"

Raina wanted to deny them but realized she couldn't, nor was she able to give the reason why. Not without giving away a secret that wouldn't really exonerate her in the end anyway. "Were all business related."

"That is not what Haven City sees, or says. If you want your relationship with that vile man to be professional, you best start changing its parameter's and fast."

Vile man? Everyone seemed to have a rather negative view on Enbrackon. All he'd done for her was try to help. Well, most of time. "I don't understand."

Cora rolled her eyes. "Don't see him when you aren't accepting clients. And do not, under any circumstances, be seen at his house alone again. I can't fix what you've done. But your husband is home now. Before you could get away with it, loosely. Now, the vultures are watching. Do you understand?"

Raina closed her eyes against a sharp, heavy pressure in her chest. "Yes."

"Good. Because if you hurt my friend, I will write an article about you that makes the one released this morning seem like a daisy field."

3

Kevin sighed as he took a seat in Mason Dandridge's study, across from the Primary Guardian Kynhaven's desk. Mason barely glanced up from the sketch he worked on, his fingers smudging coal on the wide, cream colored sheet. His long black hair, the same length as his twin sisters, was pulled into a neat pony tail. Dressed in black, likely to keep from ruining any other clothes as he worked with the charcoal medium, he looked big and imposing in the small, messy space he called his. The rest of the house was very much Cora's.

"What brings you here?" Mason asked.

"My wife needed an education only your sister could give."

Mason raised his head. "Oh? I'm not sure I want to know."

Kevin laughed. "Strictly a society based lesson."

Mason scratched at his bearded jaw. "For an Arch Guardians daughter? You'd figure she'd know the layout by now."

"Apparently not when it comes to the evil ways of gossip."

Mason raised his chin in understanding. "Ah. Did you make it past the society pages this morning?"

"I didn't read any of the news, why?"

Reaching across the desk, Mason grasped a folded newspaper and then tossed it to Kevin. "I think you'll be very interested in that."

Kevin rose to catch the paper before it could flutter into sections between the desk and him. Mason already had the page folded to the article of interest. *Conflict Rises in Italyssa.* Curious, Kevin read the short and to the point piece, on the edge of his seat by the end. He bit back a curse and met Mason's grim stare across the desk.

"Yeah, that's about how I felt too," his friend stated, attention returning to his art.

Kevin read the report again. "Could just be a coincidence."

"Could be."

"Or could be the exact same formula we're seeing here in Sziveria. Kidnap kids, distribute drugs, increase overdoses, rise in violent crimes… to what extent do people ignore it? In Italyssa they stormed the House of Absolute Law demanding to be heard. Four people died, making the national government look thoughtless and uncaring. They played right into their opponent's hands."

"And considering Italyssa is the most peaceful country in the inhabited world, doesn't bode well they were aggravated to the point of crazy."

Kevin tapped the folded paper against his thigh. "Wish we knew someone in Italyssa who could answer questions, then we'd know if the descent into chaos went a similar path to the one starting here in Sziveria."

Mason rested his forearms on the desk, a coal pencil perched in his right hand. "Why, though? What would they have to gain?"

"You're the strategist, not me."

Closing his eyes, Mason shook his head. "We need more than our two brains for this level of thinking."

Kevin laughed. "Just different approaches to an age old problem."

"Yeah, the 'we don't like how people above us are running things, so let's shove them off a cliff and see if we can do better' problem." Mason tossed the coal pencil away, sighing. "I *hate* that problem."

Equally frustrated, Kevin shook his head. "Rarely works out."

"Only works out if the new leader isn't as corrupt as the old one," Mason agreed. "And always takes at least a decade to unravel, *if* it's caught in time. If it's not... I can't believe this crap is happening in our country!"

"No country is immune to betrayal or pure selfish ambition."

"I know, but this is home, and it's supposed to be safe when I come back to it." If the complaint hadn't reflected Kevin's own internal toddler, he would have laughed.

Footsteps sounded in the corridor. Kevin twisted in his seat as the ladies appeared in the doorway. Cora swept in with her usual regal grace. Raina stopped short the moment she looked past Kevin to Mason. Amused by her hesitation, Mason waved his fingers in a non-threatening manner and then went back to his drawing.

Cora laughed. "Your brutish ways are catching up with you again, dear brother."

"I know. I can't seem to leave my reputation behind me," he mumbled with a head shake.

A rich flush bloomed across Raina's cheeks. She toed into the study, looking anywhere but at the people within. Then her steps faltered again when she noticed a detailed sketch of ragged trees, a shoreline with gentle waves, and the ruins of a building so old no one knew if it was post-cataclysm or pre. *Ravenna* was written in quick cursive along the bottom.

"This is amazing," Raina stated, rising on her toes to try to get a closer look. Kevin couldn't help but smile at her attempt to gain height.

"Thank you," Mason replied.

Cora joined Raina at the sketch. "I have a larger one in my room from the Korean Islands you should see. Mason said when the region is stable again, he's going to take me."

"Don't remind me of another revolution gone south."

Cora raised a brow, her arms crossed over her chest and faced her brother. "Another?"

Kevin lifted the paper and then handed it to her. "Not reading your employers work? Italyssa is under conflict."

The brow arched higher. "Really?"

Kevin waved the paper to make his point. "Really."

Cora slowly accepted the news. "You know," she began, scanning the article, "Jonathon is promised to the heiress for the Italyssian shipping empire, Sun Wind Trade."

"Jonathon Hunter?" Kevin asked, wondering why Cora used Key Guardian Asherwick's name and not his rank. Then again, he probably didn't want to know. Once Cora went to a first-name basis, the poor fool wasn't long from her clutches.

Cora nodded, her expression turning as grim as Mason and Kevin's had at reading the information.

Mason shot a glance at Raina, who had moved down to the next framed sketch. A rocky cliff face with *Ruthenia* scrawled along the bottom.

"I think Sean is going to have to invite Asherwick to our team meetings. We have to be able to gather somewhere safe and his basement is the only place we can."

"I'll talk to him, but I'm sure he won't disagree."

Mason retrieved the pencil he'd tossed aside in frustration. "Does he need *someone's* approval?"

Kevin almost snorted at Mason's attempt to keep Raina oblivious to the conversation by not mentioning her father.

"No. He doesn't. We're on home soil and allies are Sean's to make."

"That's good to know. Glad I don't need permission for who I befriend." Mason glanced past Kevin to Raina and then shook his head. "Apparently it's just for who we marry."

"WHAT DID Primary Guardian Kynhaven mean by his words?" Raina asked on the ride home.

"Which ones?"

Raina frowned as she studied Kevin's calm demeanor. He hadn't looked her direction the entire ride, not even when he spoke. She knew they weren't far from arriving. The privacy of the carriage awarded an opportunity for discretion not always found at home.

"The ones about marriage."

That managed to shift his attention to her. She fidgeted under his stormy gaze. "The FIO seems to take a great interest in who we're to spend our lives with. Mason is currently the only one on our team not married by their command."

Raina wasn't sure how to take the information. "You weren't contracted to me by the FIO. My father made the arrangement."

"And your father is who gives the orders for my team. He's one of the three leaders at the First Intelligence Office. You can call it whoever's will you wish, his or the FIO's."

The hard edge to his words let her know the topic of their marriage wasn't one he wished to discuss at length, and she wondered why. Knowing her father, Kevin wouldn't have been able to refuse if he'd been given the order to marry her, and she wouldn't put it past her father to do so. Sighing, she was thankful when the tall, wrought iron fence line for their property came into view.

Once inside, Mrs. Taft met them at the side entrance and ushered them into the quaint breakfast room. Used as the personal dining room when not entertaining, the first course for lunch waited to be served.

"We weren't sure when you'd be home, so Mr. Ferkas prepared a cold lunch today," Mrs. Taft announced.

"That is fine, Mrs. Taft. Thank you," Raina said.

The housekeeper unfurled Raina's napkin and gently laid it in her lap and then made sure all her utensils were in perfect order. Raina nodded her appreciation. Kevin beat Mrs. Taft to the task, placing his own napkin in his lap and scooting his chair in so she couldn't crowd his space. The first server arrived with their salads. They ate in silence. Within seconds of finishing, their plates were swept away and a new one placed before them. Raina bit her inner lip to keep from laughing at Kevin's bewildered stare as the servers departed.

Raina pushed the cool, creamy sauce around on the spiral pasta before her. "You look as though you've never been served food before."

"Outside of a restaurant, I haven't, and even then it's just one plate of food."

Raina cocked her head and regarded him, fork poised over her bowl. "Really? Your family didn't hire a chef?"

A chuckle escaped his mouth. The short burst of laughter transformed his face from handsome, to downright devastating. The fork slid from Raina's fingers to the bowl with a harsh clink and she jumped.

"No, we didn't," was all he said with a shake of his head and attention on his food.

Thankful her little slip didn't seem to be noticed, she picked up her fork and focused on the meal rather than the man who made her heart race with a simple smile. Since Raina didn't trust herself to look his direction again without staring, she kept her gaze on her food, or out the window.

Kevin departed without a word when he finished. The room seemed somehow larger with him gone. Empty. Raina frowned, turning in her seat as he disappeared across the corridor and into his study. He hadn't even been home a full day, and already his presence left a distinct impression. Knowing he wasn't going to be dragged away by Synintel's men in green livery made her awareness of him stronger. Then again, how would Kevin's presence interfere with her personal plans for her future?

Chewing her lip, Raina pushed her bowl away and rose. She hadn't considered the implications with him home, and the direction she'd taken to secure clients not under her father's control. Since Kevin was ultimately owned by Synintel, she had to assume he'd take a negative view to her plans.

Fisting her hands at her side, she stalked to her office. If that turned out to be his *official* position, she'd deal with him the same as she'd deal with her father. On her own ground, with her own terms, and with a profitable client base at her fingertips, a reputation she'd built on her own. Then again, if what Miss Dandridge had implied was true, her future endeavors may already be unraveling.

Raina turned the moment she entered her office and stopped at the wide window overlooking the immaculate greenhouse gardens. Fruit trees blossomed in the dull, gray light. A faint green haze crawled up the glass along the bottom edges, adding a surreal feel to the artificially warm environment. She should have gone out and walked the calm, winding, brick paths that had been laid to maximize the space and tranquility.

A few windows were open at the top to allow birds and pollenating insect's access to the outside world if they wished to venture farther. A fine mist of rain swirled in the air, but not enough to do much more than dampen leaves higher up. The natural sanctuary could have helped distract her from the brutal truth laid at her feet.

Taking a deep, worn-out breath, Raina wrapped her arms around her waist. A faint knock pulled her from her depressing mood. Straightening her shoulders and touching her hair to make sure she appeared put together, she bid the person to enter. A sliver of disappointment surprised her when Mrs. Taft entered and not Kevin.

"A note has arrived for you with instruction for delivery on receipt."

Raina drew her brows together and held her hand out as the housekeeper approached. "Thank you."

Once Mrs. Taft departed, Raina popped the wax seal on the envelope. A not so pleasant sharp, musky, masculine scent wafted up to her. Raina wrinkled her nose. Only one person ever perfumed their correspondence. Shield Guardian Enbrackon. Normally, excitement preceded one of his letters, but today she almost considered not reading. Even in notes, he managed to take an emotional toll on her.

Breathing in slowly through her nose, ignoring the strong cologne, she pulled the folded note free.

My Dearest Lorraina,

I knew the moment I read the society pages this morning that you were distressed. Of course, you should be. Miss Dandridge was out of line with what she said. We both know Master Guardian Raiventon stole you away last night, and you didn't go of your own wishes. How could you have? We had so much left to discuss about your new client. He's most eager for you to get started on his import schedule. I told him how swiftly you were able to get my last import delivered. He was highly impressed. Please let me know the moment we can meet again. You know I miss our time together, and count the breaths until I can see you.

Yours always,
Phipps

An uncomfortable sensation settled in Raina's chest. Her first reaction was to take the letter to Kevin. At no point in the night had her husband forced her to do anything, unlike the Shield Guardian. And yet... the Shield Guardian described as different an evening as Cora had. Confused, Raina went to her desk and sat. She set the note down and stared.

If she took the letter to Kevin, he'd ask about the client Enbrackon mentioned and Raina couldn't afford to have questions asked. Not yet. She only had the Shield Guardian and three other clients he'd referred her to, not nearly enough to count herself successfully free of her father's reins.

Spreading her hands on the desk, she took a calming breath. No, she'd keep the situation contained. The silly man was being his usual arrogant self. Despite that character flaw, she needed him to reach her goal. She'd deal with his superiority as she always had. By ignoring it, alone.

THE MUTED PATTER of rain against the study window was the only disruption in Kevin's otherwise blissfully silent study. And he didn't count the soothing thrum of water to be a distraction. Earlier in the afternoon he'd personally asked Raina's chef to prepare his meal all at once and have it delivered to his office.

Not that he didn't want to dine with his wife. But knowing a server hovered outside the door, listening to every word they said, waiting until their silverware lifted the last bite, was too much for his cautious self. The people outside his house had enough to say, he didn't need the ones within saying more.

Gathering together his empty plate and utensils, he stood. The house was silent, except for a few hushed voices from the kitchen. They quieted once Kevin entered with his plate. Mrs. Taft stared at him as if he'd grown a second head.

"Guardian, I would have been happy to collect that for you," she stated, rushing across the kitchen to him.

Kevin shook his head. "No need, I'm perfectly capable of carrying my own dish. I won't hurt myself."

The housekeeper laughed. "No, I don't suppose you will. Can we expect this to be a regular thing from you?"

Kevin returned her smile. "Probably."

"And Guardianess Raiventon?"

Kevin shrugged. "Guardianess Raiventon has her schedule, I have mine."

Mrs. Taft bowed in acknowledgement and turned away. "I'll ask her anyway, tomorrow."

The words made Kevin pause before he left the kitchen. Part of him wanted Raina to say she would join him in the privacy of his study, and that surprised him. Rolling his shoulders to send away the unfamiliar need for companionship, Kevin went into the corridor and listened. Except for a lightly burning lamp outside the vestibule, and the light spilling from his study, the house was dark. Having learned the schedule his wife didn't seem to deviate from, he knew Raina had already retired to her room upstairs.

Kevin flexed his fingers and glanced up the stairs. He needed to find the letter Raina had received this afternoon. Without being told, he'd already guessed who'd sent it. Unless he could deduce the nature of her relationship with the Shield Guardian, he was useless in protecting her from whatever the crook had planned.

Though, after seeing how easily Enbrackon manipulated her at the ball, Kevin worried she'd ignore any protests he threw her way. She had no reason to trust, or listen, to him. Of course, if she caught him snooping around her office, she'd definitely ignore anything he said, no matter how pure his motives were.

Deciding to wait until he was sure she wouldn't be back down, he returned to his study. He'd always hated this part of any task. The waiting. A situation he seemed to find himself in daily now. His team had been brought home when they'd failed in a mission weeks ago, only to learn an unknown threat was creeping through the population in Sziveria. They couldn't gather intelligence without raising flags about what they knew, and they couldn't act on anything without more evidence. Existing in the waiting was it, for now.

Two hours later and with nothing but rain falling to break the silence, Kevin decided it was safe to venture into Raina's territory. He'd also returned the files he'd borrowed earlier in the day, not knowing when she'd need them again and not wanting to raise her suspicion.

In her office, he didn't light any candles or lamps, simply used the silvery gray light filtering in through the many large windows. Raina's office doubled as the library, taking up the entire left side of the house. Her massive oak desk was the focal point of the room. Unlike her father's however, it was free of anything more than neatly stacked files and paper-work. No displays of wealth or power greeted her clients.

Caressing his hand along the cool, polished wood, he rounded the desk. He found the small, handwritten note in the second drawer. A strong, pungent wave of cologne assaulted his nostrils before he even flipped the envelope open. Dropping the letter as though it'd burned him, Kevin glared. If any of that stench touched his hands, he'd be stuck with the smell for hours. Interesting tactic the Shield Guardian used, surround Raina with his scent, as well as his words.

Kevin dug around in a drawer and found a letter opener. Using the edge, he carefully pulled the letter free and opened the scented paper. By the end, his jaw clenched along with his fists.

Not caring she'd find the letter different than she'd left it, Kevin opened the second drawer and used the opener to push the papers over the edge. They fluttered into the dark wooden space before Kevin closed them away with a harder shove than necessary.

Kevin glanced at the hall clock on the way to the stairs. Shortly after eleven. Good, Raina should be well on her way to sleep and he wouldn't have to answer any questions about a late night. Wasn't as if he had anything of great importance to do. He was standing in his ranked property. Unlike Sean and Mason, he didn't have a city of people to worry about.

The stairs creaked under his heavy weight, something he was able to avoid if he felt like putting energy into his upward progress. He didn't. On the landing, Raina's door cracked open and Kevin paused, his hand on the railing.

"Oh, it's you." Raina opened her door until the light from inside cast her in a warm halo.

Kevin tried his best to keep his gaze on her face and not on her very sheer, backlit nightgown. A petite frame did not mean a lack of soft, seductive curves. "Yes, just me."

She picked at her nails nervously, glancing back into her room. Kevin almost bolted back down the stairs in case she decided to call him on his bluff and actually invite him to her bed.

"I was thinking of going for a walk in the greenhouse. I can't sleep." She turned to face him again. "Would you care to join me?"

"Are you going to put more clothes on?"

Her hand flew to her chest and he knew her face was likely a charming shade of pink. "Y-yes, a robe."

Kevin smiled. "Then yes, I'll walk with you."

She disappeared. Kevin went to the middle landing and waited. When she reappeared, she had on a thick, pink, floor length wool robe tied at the waist. The fluffy outerwear swallowed her small figure, hiding any hint of woman beneath. Kevin tried to convince himself that was for the best, and ignored the disappointment.

Careful with each step, Raina walked down. Her small feet peeked out before disappearing beneath waves of fabric.

Knowing she expected his arm when she reached him, he offered. With a small smile, she wrapped her hand around his forearm and in silence they made their way to the greenhouse.

The humid, warm air moved faintly with the cooler breeze from a few open windows. Summer was winding down, but until the first full frost, most households chose to keep a few windows open to the outside for their conservatory eco-system to thrive and grow. A good groundskeeper would seek out any unwelcome intruders come dawn.

Kevin breathed in the thick air, subtly scented with decaying vegetation and fragrant fruit blossoms. "Do you often walk at night?"

"Yes, unless it's too dark from clouds or a lack of moon. No one can bother me at night."

Her bare toes made Kevin smile. He should have taken his boots off. He bet the cool, slightly damp brick felt nice under foot. "Lots of sleepless nights, then?"

Her grip on his arm tightened for the slightest moment before relaxing. "I have trouble not over thinking things. I keep myself up most of the time."

"Such as?"

When she remained silent except for a heavy sigh, Kevin kept their pace slow, his frame relaxed beside her. Being strangers made for strained conversation in the best of circumstances. In the dark, completely alone, the vulnerability seemed to be getting to his petite wife. Since he understood all too well, he was more than comfortable to let her ease into a conversation at her own pace.

The silvery light of the moon brightened the longer they walked. Crickets singing their slow night song, and a few frogs seeking a mate added to the calm atmosphere. A break in the trees allowed the near full moon to wash a section of path in bright light. Raina stopped in the muted glow and angled closer to him.

"Can I ask you a question?" she prompted, her gaze looking past him, into the shadows they'd left behind.

"Of course."

She lifted her gaze, the pale light making her eyes seem almost gray. "And you'll answer honestly?"

Now Kevin had the honor of being uneasy. But, if anyone deserved an honest, unreserved answer from him, Raina did. "If that's what you wish."

Another deep, slow breath escaped her and she nodded. "I do."

"Then ask."

"What did my father do to make you marry me?"

Kevin drew his brows together. The pale light washed over the subtle texture of her face, bringing out her pixie nature. He had the strong urge to smooth his thumbs over her brows and caress her cheeks. More than anything, he wanted to taste her lips. Drawing in a ragged breath he quickly looked away.

"That's not a simple answer," he said.

"I didn't expect it would be."

Kevin drew them back into a slower pace, deciding movement might help ease the rise of anger coiling in his stomach. Being reminded of how they both were pawns in a master's hands was never something he liked to dwell on. And he was sure she'd have her own fury once she knew the truth. "How aware are you of the generation clause for ranked inheritance?"

Her hands clasped over his forearm, bringing her close, their hips nearly touching with each step. "Not too much. Something about a rank having to be in the family for a generation to be inherited without question, correct?"

Kevin nodded. "Yes, close. First the heir has to prove they can occupy the seat, or can serve in a Guardian role with the required Genetic Heir abilities. They either prove a logic-based talent through testing, or a touch-based talent fit for a Guardianship. Once that's established, if the rank hasn't been held for a generation, then it has to go before the E&R council to be approved. My father only held his rank for six years before he died."

Raina's steps slowed to a near crawl. "My father is on the council."

"Your father basically runs the council."

"And he threatened to have your rank revoked?" Disbelief laced her words.

"Not so much threatened as implied everything my father did would be wasted, if I threw away the chance to marry the most sought-after daughter in the country."

Raina snorted with derision. "I wouldn't have gone that far."

"He could have married you to anyone. Literally." Kevin stopped and forced her to face him. "You're one of what, six women in the country who can marry a prince, correct? And not just one of Sziveria's, but one from any nation, making a peace treaty almost a sure deal."

"Well, yes, but his plans didn't go quite the way he expected. In the end, he just wanted me..."

When she failed to find the correct word, Kevin helped. "Safe."

"Yes, safe. When he contracted us, a princess from Ruthenia had just been kidnapped, and two daughters of a politician from Gaula had been ransomed and murdered. I wasn't even allowed to leave our house for three months without a full armed guard. I still can't even..." She took a deep breath and fluttered her hand as if waving away a bad memory. "He's still nervous."

He's nervous for other reasons. Kevin caught himself before the words tumbled out. "What better way than to lower you on the food chain."

She grasped his arm again and tugged him back into a

walk. "So, he dangled your newly acquired, not quite approved ranking, and you agreed."

"I didn't really have much choice. I could have let my father's legacy die with him, but then I'd also be giving up my commission with the FIO. At the time, that actually seemed more important than the rank."

"I see. And now?"

Kevin shrugged. "Now it doesn't really matter. The Endowment and Revocation meeting is happening in a couple of weeks. Your father has made sure you won't be affected if he doesn't rule in my favor."

That made her stop again. "What do you mean?"

"When we married, your father transferred my ranked property to this house."

"But the house is mine." She blinked, her hands sliding free from his arm. "I mean, my father willed it to me."

Kevin's stomach clenched at the innocent bewilderment on her face. He stroked a knuckle down her cheek. "You won't lose the house, princess. It'll revert back to its owner. Your father is anything but stupid. He knew what he was doing."

"I don't understand. If the house is yours now, how will I get it back?"

"In less than eight weeks, when your father doesn't cast his vote to allow the ranking to remain with me, he'll expect me to do the honorable thing by you."

Raina stepped away. Her fingers pressed to her temples and she closed her eyes. "I'm sorry, I'm trying to understand. If he doesn't vote for you, and others agree, you'll lose your rank and the house, and so would I. How could that change?"

Kevin looked at her with expectation. She was smart, surely she could figure out her father's plan on her own. Her jaw dropped and horror filled her eyes.

"He's going to *kill* you?" she practically shrieked.

"No!" Kevin held his hands up and shook his head. "No, he won't kill me. Come on, Raina."

She visibly relaxed with a sigh. Kevin wasn't sure how to feel. He supposed pretty good since she didn't wish him dead.

"Well, that only leaves…" Her eyes shot back to him with a glare. "An affair."

"Real or imagined, the confession will have the same results," he said quietly.

A different wave of shock crossed her features and she took another step back. "No," she whispered, her head shaking. "No, that's not right. He'd never force you to do something so terrible, to ruin yourself and lose everything."

Kevin wished he had her rosy view of the world. Then again, his jaded one kept him alive and composed when the worst happened, or needed to. "I won't have anything to ruin once I'm a regular guy."

She scoffed and waved her hand. "You could never be a regular guy."

Kevin squared his shoulders and stared at her. "What is that supposed to mean?"

With a pointing motion from his head to his feet, she said, "They could strip you of everything you've earned in life and I have a feeling you'd still be you. Kevin Merrick. Nothing would change. And there's nothing *regular* about you."

The sudden urge to kiss her was more than Kevin could ignore. Reaching across the distance, he wrapped his arm around her waist and hauled her to his body. The fluffy padding of her robe cushioned the space between them. Kevin wanted to tear the ridiculous layer off. Before she could protest, his lips touched hers. The flutter of her mouth under his was a tease, an appetizer for something he dared not taste. He allowed himself one more gentle kiss before slowly releasing her.

"You're making a case for me to defy Synintel," Kevin whispered.

Her hands pressed into her belly and she shyly met his stare. "Has he really asked you to lie and walk away?"

"No."

"Then how do you know he will?"

"Because he hasn't said he won't."

Unease and something he couldn't, or didn't want to, identify shone in her big, beautiful eyes. "Will you be able to?"

Kevin looked her over. The moon shone off the glossy, layered lengths of her light brown hair, her lips parted softly, begging for another kiss from him. A strange shift slid through his chest to his heart and he fidgeted under the intensity of her stare. "I don't know."

4

Raina waited like the dutiful daughter she was expected to be outside her father's office doors. A footman stood blocking the way in. No one had ever barred the entrance before. She wondered what had brought about the new orders.

The overly large silver buttons on the man's rich green uniform glinted in the sun streaming through a nearby window. For the past four years Raina had come to loathe her father's distinct service attire. One of them always showed up to collect her husband within hours of his arriving home, ensuring she stayed married to a stranger. But not right now, and if she were a braver woman, possibly never again.

The unfamiliar sense of desire Kevin had awakened with his simple kiss was something Raina needed to explore. If she were willing to challenge her father for her career, she better be willing to challenge him for her marriage. She took a deep, grounding breath to ease the anxiety growing within.

As if he heard a cue she hadn't, the footman stepped aside and swept the door open. Raina nodded curtly and brushed past. Her father didn't bother to rise from behind his desk, merely cast her a glance of annoyance. Dressed in charcoal gray and deep red, colors meant to intimidate, his large imposing frame made her steps slow as she crossed the room. He shook his head in irritation and sighed. Childish repentance at disturbing his work time had her clasping her hands in front of her and sitting primly before his desk on the edge of the chair.

"You know how busy I am, Lorraina. What do you need?" he inquired, reaching across the desk for a sheet of paper.

Raina swallowed against the nervous dryness coating her throat. "I had an interesting conversation with Master Guardian Raiventon last night."

He quirked a brow, but still basically ignored her presence. "Not a deep enough one to refer to him as anything more than his rank, I see."

And had Raina used Kevin's first name, her father would have sneered at her apparent familiarity, along with what that might mean. Keeping calm and careful not to show any outward emotion, Raina continued to regard her father. "Since you used the inheritance clause to force him into a contract with me, I wanted to make sure you'd be voting in the affirmative at the E&R meeting."

"Sent you to ask the dirty question. I didn't expect Merrick to be a coward. Perhaps I should reconsider his constitution."

Raina bristled at the insult. "He's unaware of the purpose to my visit."

Synintel waved a flippant hand. "Don't worry daughter, you won't be left a commoner."

"I can't be a commoner, I'm a Gen-Heir. Your genetic heir."

He sighed. "You know what I mean. Of the lower-class."

"Kevin already assured me of that."

Finally, her father looked at her. "Did he, now?"

"Would you really strip his rank?" She tried to keep her voice even, but the faint crack of worry wouldn't be denied.

"I think the question, dear daughter, is would he really do

that to *you*? Make you live well outside your comfort or station? No. There are many reasons I chose him, his honor was one."

"Where is your honor? Has he not earned what his father has, and then some? He works for you, does he not?"

The Arch Guardian sighed again, as if she were the small child who used to sit before him so many years ago. "Lorraina, you don't understand how things work. You're my daughter, and really, a Master Guardian is below you, we both know it. But Raiventon is... unique. And when the threat against you is over, naturally your marriage will be too."

Raina couldn't stop her incredulous gasp. "Threat against me? Father, won't that be never ending?"

"In one sense perhaps, in another no."

One of the dragons snarled at her from the desk corner and Raina had the urge to throw the heavy bronze beast at her father. "You and your riddles. They're as meaningless now as they've always been!"

"And your husband's impertinence is rubbing off on you. I won't have you speaking to me in such a manner, Lorraina."

She went to hang her head in remorse the way she would have done when she'd lived under his roof. But learning Kevin had the backbone to stand up to her father and walk out provided much needed courage. She stood. "Then I'm finished speaking. But know this father, if you take away Kevin's rank and *his* home, you take away mine too. I made that contract for life. I won't let him tell a lie that will cost him everything his family worked for just because *you* want to have *your* way."

Anger flared in his pale brown eyes. "You silly little girl, you never did grow up. One day you'll see the world for what it is. I hope by then it's not too late. Your *husband* will do exactly as he's told, when he's told to do it, regardless of how you feel about the matter. Now stop concerning yourself with things you can't change and don't understand."

Raina fought tears, her hands fisted at her sides. Anything she said would fall on deaf ears. Turning on her heels, her lavender gown billowing around her ankles, she stalked from his presence. At least she knew her father hadn't changed even a little. Now, more than ever, she wanted out from underneath his control. And her reasons why doubled in importance.

"Tell me again why we need to be here?" Katria Blackbain, Primary Guardianess of Wintersfall asked her husband, leaning in a little closer than social norms dictated acceptable.

Her husband, Sean, glanced down at her, his jaw shifting to hide a smile Kevin knew his friend was tempted to give. "Because you refuse to do anything else social and I don't want us to look like cowards hiding in our house."

Katria heaved a sigh of annoyance and rolled her eyes. "Fine."

To hide his own smile from his bickering friends, Kevin glanced around the ballroom searching for Raina. She'd spotted her friend Patricia when she had entered and immediately departed for her. Across the distance of the room he finally saw her. Their eyes met for the briefest of moments before her attention shifted to Katria standing next to him. A small frown crossed over her features.

Not wanting to give anything away, Kevin kept his expression neutral. Katria turned toward him. The inky black length of her hair fell in cascading waves down her back, adorned with small glittering flowers. Their rich purple matched the shimmery silk of her violet gown. Her startling blue eyes fixed him with displeasure. Apparently since her husband wasn't biting, she'd see how far she could rile Kevin. Their little sharpshooter was in one of her moods tonight.

"Where's your wife? I'm beginning to doubt you actually have one."

Kevin laughed and shook his head. "Just for that, I'm going to make you wait. And maybe even guess."

Exhaling in a dramatic fashion, Katria wrapped her arm around her belly and rested her elbow on it, tapping her chin in thought. "Let's see, too condescending, not pretty enough, too short, not old enough, too… something. Maybe her? No."

Kevin crossed his arms over his chest and fought another wave of laughter, wondering if the *too short* woman had indeed been Raina. Once again he found his attention drawn to her. The cream gown accented with glittering navy beads hugged her curves. A braid curled into an elegant crown atop her head, small white crystals in each fold sparkled in the warm light. Simple makeup brought out the pale shade of her eyes and the curves of her cheeks and jaw. Everything about her was beautiful.

"Your husband could tell you," he said.

"What's the fun in that?" Then all traces of humor left Katria's face and Kevin followed the direction of her stare.

Sean let loose a low curse only the three of them could hear. "Well, there goes my good mood."

Shield Guardian Enbrackon sauntered in from the arched entrance to the social room straight for Raina. The cream jacket he wore glittered with dark blue beadwork. Navy slacks and shirt, along with cream-colored boots completed his flashy outfit. Kevin clenched his jaw and fisted his hands. Katria shifted back, her already pale skin turning a sickly shade. In a protective motion, Sean stepped forward, sheltering her.

"I should have given in and let her bring a gun," Sean said with a shake of his head.

Kevin frowned. "That would have been unwise."

"Probably, but satisfying."

Since the statement was true enough, Kevin didn't argue.

"He likely didn't know you'd be here, or he wouldn't have shown."

"I don't know. He's an arrogant scab."

Raina had taken a large step back when she'd noticed the Shield Guardian, the shock on her face genuine. Kevin flexed his fist. "She didn't know."

Sean raised his brows. "That he's a stalker? How could she not know? Maybe she'll figure it out now."

Kevin's frown intensified. "Can you tell me anything by what you see?"

"I think you'd know her body language better than I would."

Yes, one would think so. And yet Kevin knew much less than he wished where Raina was concerned. Especially her body. What he could tell, he didn't like. Enbrackon crowded her space, isolating her from the group of women she'd been conversing with. Slowly, he forced her to walk nearer to the greenhouse doors, his perfectly styled head low to hers, whispering words. Raina's frame was tense, her steps compulsory. If Kevin didn't do something quick, they'd be out into the greenhouse and he'd be forced to make a scene.

"I need to borrow Kat."

Sean stared up at him. "For what?"

"Chess."

"Chess?"

"Yes."

Sean glanced at Raina, who'd managed to stall the progress. The Shield Guardians hand raised to her elbow and with a not-so-gentle tug, they were walking again. "Ah."

Kevin offered Katria his arm. "What do you say, Kat? Do you want to play?"

"Anything to leave this room," she answered.

Leaning over, Kevin whispered, "Act like I said something entirely too charming."

She looped her hand onto his forearm, her brilliant blue eyes wide with mock fascination. "You? Charming?"

"Aren't I always?"

"Yes, I'm so enchanted when I'm being flipped and land hard enough to have the wind knocked from my lungs," she muttered.

Kevin laughed and led them from the room. "I'll remember you like it."

"Please don't." She stepped in closer to him. "Why are we disappearing together?"

"To catch a cat, we must play mouse."

Katria glanced over her shoulder. "Which one are we hoping to catch, exactly?"

"The pretty one."

A frown creased her forehead. "They'd both be considered pretty."

Kevin chuckled. "My wife, Kat."

That caused Katria's steps to falter. Kevin grasped her upper arm to keep her upright. "*She* is your wife? But she's so much smaller than you!"

Kevin purposefully didn't look over his shoulder. "Yes."

"Did you teach her to fight, too?"

The sudden image of Raina locked in battle with him, sweaty, her body pressed in close to his, dressed in the same tight black clothing Katria wore to their workouts had Kevin's breath hitching. "No," he somehow managed to get out.

"Probably a good thing. She would run circles around you."

Kevin had no doubt. Because he'd let her.

THE SECOND KEVIN disappeared with a beautiful raven-haired woman on his arm, Raina stopped paying attention to any word Phipps spoke. She had chanced a glance at the good-looking man they'd left behind. He was tall, but not like Kevin, his hair two shades darker than her husband's, though considerably longer. Even from across the room she could make out the intense amber of his irises, probably because he wore a shirt not much different in shade. Like Kevin, he was incredibly fit. Something that stood out among the languid men and women of their society.

"Lorraina," Phipps barked. "Did you not hear me?"

"Yes, of course I heard you. And I told you, I'm waiting on a radio transmission to see if my plan to get the cargo here sooner is feasible."

"Of course it's feasible, we already discussed the method. You just need to use your smart brain, which we're paying good money for, to see to it. The cargo *must* arrive by the date I appointed."

Raina despised when he used events to try to strong arm her professional decisions. Even more than she despised the stout cologne making her itch to sneeze. "I told you we can discuss this tomorrow afternoon, when I'm accepting appointments."

Two couples walked into the room, arm in arm, laughing. Neither of them her husband and the siren he'd left with. Where were they? She worked her bottom lip. More importantly, what were they doing?

Phipps crowded her space, backing her into a table, making sure she had no exit. "I don't need an appointment to see you. I'm your best client, the only client capable of making sure you have the means to support yourself without father-dearest's help or hand. We will discuss business whenever I feel inclined."

Anger rose inside her. Raina wanted to snap that he could keep his *business* to himself, and she didn't need him. But the lie wouldn't make much impact, so she kept her mouth shut and nodded. Another small group crossed under the arch, none of them faces she wanted to see. Images of Kevin kissing the woman in ways she wanted him to pay attention to her had her stepping free from the Shield Guardian the moment he gave her space. When he reached for her, she quickly side-stepped him.

"We've discussed all I dare tonight. I'm sure you don't wish for any of your trade partner's secrets to be overheard."

He frowned. "No, I don't suppose that would be good."

Too stressed to care about how he felt, Raina put more distance between them. "Excuse me, I must go find Master Guardian Raiventon."

Before he could reach for her again, she melted into the crowd, hoping he wouldn't be bold enough to pursue her. People would already be discussing the mistakes she'd made tonight, separating from her husband early in the evening and speaking to Enbrackon, who somehow matched her again. She'd consider the implications of his attire later, after locating her wayward spouse.

Would anyone be discussing his disappearance with a woman other than her on his arm in the morning? Likely not. As Synintel's daughter, she was held to a standard no one in the room could truly understand. One she'd been failing miserably at holding even herself to.

As she slipped through the throng of guests, head held high, weariness settled on her shoulders. She wondered if being thrust into the lower class would really be such a terrible thing. Is that how Kevin had grown up? He'd said his childhood had been happy. Raina wasn't really sure what a *happy* upbringing entailed, but she figured better than hers.

Shaking her head against the negative direction of her thoughts, she searched through the rooms open to guests. Both the game room and dining hall yielded empty results. For once thankful she was on the smaller side, she easily managed to make herself inconspicuous enough to disappear into the shadowed parts of the house. To make sure everyone knew where they were, and weren't allowed, the lights had been extinguished in the upstairs and back portion of the sprawling mansion. Though now she wished she'd worn something other than cream, a beacon in the otherwise dark areas.

Nerve's dancing, Raina reached for the first door she came too. She eased it open and poked her head in. Heavy breathing and a flash of red hair in the available light had her quickly closing out the couple with a grimace. Oops. At the next door, she hesitated. What if she found Kevin with the woman in the same way?

No, if he hadn't been unfaithful in their less-than-intimate marriage, he wasn't about to start at a hosted event. Which begged the question, what was her husband up to? Raina's fingers hovered over the knob. Taking a deep breath, she let the door fall open. Muted lamp light lit one corner of a vast three-story library. Beneath one of the lamps, Kevin and the woman were engrossed over a game of chess.

Or so she thought until she heard the woman fuss. "Wait, wait, I thought that one moved in the shape of an 'L'."

"No, that's this one," Kevin replied patiently. "How has Sean never taught this to you?"

She shrugged. "I don't know. He never played when we were on assignment. Now? Well..."

Kevin held up his hand. "Forget I asked."

Raina stepped into the room. Kevin glanced up and set the piece he'd been holding back on the board. "I was wondering when you'd finally appear."

Unsure of how to respond, she went to open her mouth, but the woman twisted in her seat. Raina gasped at her startling shade of blue eyes. With her black hair and pale skin, she was beyond compare.

"Oh, thank goodness," the woman said, her body visibly relaxing.

"I wasn't so bad of a teacher," Kevin grumbled.

Laughing, the woman turned back around. "You're an

amazing teacher, you know that. But this," she waved her hand over the board, "is not something to learn in one sitting. Like fighting, it takes practice and multiple lessons."

Raina raised a brow. Fighting? What were they talking about?

"Do you have your check-mate?"

The deep voice behind her made Raina jump. She spun around and then took a hasty step back as the handsome man she'd seen across the ballroom sauntered into the library. He was much larger than he'd appeared from a distance. Though calm in demeanor, there was no mistaking his air of authority.

Kevin relaxed further back in his seat. A black marble chess piece flipped between his fingers. "I do."

"Good. Then I can have my wife back."

Finally, Kevin looked her way. Neither his dark gray eyes nor guarded expression revealed anything concerning his mood. She found herself fidgeting.

"Raina, I'd like you to meet Sean and Katria Blackbain. You may know them better as Primary Guardian and Guardianess Wintersfall," Kevin stated, still not rising from his seat.

More than a little shocked, Raina's attention returned to the man. Everyone knew of the various scandals that had plagued the Wintersfall rank for generations, all of them atrocious. She'd never met anyone in the family personally, her father would have none of it. The well dressed, relaxed, commanding man wasn't the image she'd had in mind at the Wintersfall name.

Sean helped his wife rise, his amber eyes dancing with laughter as he looked Raina's direction. "That's how I expected you to stare at me when you found out we were married."

Raina flushed and quickly looked away. She clasped her hands before herself demurely, embarrassed she'd not only been caught staring, but apparently with the shock she'd felt.

"I was raised so far from Haven City, that wasn't a concern." Katria brought his hand to her chest and smiled. "Besides, I loved you as Sean, before I knew you were Wintersfall."

"No you didn't," he correct quickly.

"Yes, I did. I think I know when I fell in love with you."

Raina pressed her lips together. She didn't know whether to be concerned or charmed by their banter.

Sean's jaw flexed. "Yes, at your fathers, after I—"

Katria raised on her tiptoes, wrapped her arms around Sean's neck and pressed her mouth to his. With a growl, he pulled her close. Smiling, Katria broke their kiss. "Take me home."

The raw hunger in Sean's gaze as he stared at his wife stole Raina's breath. She'd never seen a husband express desire for his spouse before. At a woman he courted sure, or even at a woman he intended to woo into his bed as a lover. Not even Patricia's husband looked at her with such intensity. In their world, passion and marriage didn't exist.

"I will take you anywhere," Sean said.

Katria released her hold and then took his hand, pulling him to the door. A wicked grin turned up the corners of her mouth. "You know exactly where I want to go, husband."

Kevin laughed and waved an exaggerated goodbye. "See you tomorrow."

The couple made a hasty exit, but not before closing her in the library with Kevin. The chess piece still flipped and rolled between his fingers, his other hand thrummed the armrest. He motioned at the seat opposite him with the piece.

"Sit. You look like a monster is going to jump out of the shadows."

Unconsciously, she glanced over her shoulder and then rolled her eyes at the ridiculous action. There weren't any monsters in the room. Not unless she counted the handsome beast sitting in front of a chessboard.

Raina took the seat, her gaze transfixed on the way muted light cast Kevin's face in both soft and hard planes, defining angles and textures that made her want to crawl across the table and trace his lines. She settled for focusing on the tallest piece on the board, her fingers outlining the ridges of the cool white marble.

"Do you play?" Kevin asked, still too composed for her to know his mood.

She shook her head. "No, my father does, but he never taught me."

"That surprises me. I'd think he'd want his daughter to have a clear understanding when it comes to a game built on logistics."

Raina wanted to hide her distaste at her father's view of his daughter, but the hurt was too raw, too bitter. To him she was weak. Something needed protection that could only be provided through marriage. Most people were able to test the waters of a relationship with a year-long contract, see if the bond was a good fit with the safety of being exclusive for a set length of time. The security measures were put in place during the height of the Human Rabies Syndrome epidemic, since HRS was transferred via sex during its inactive phase. The simple option had never been one Raina could entertain. "If my father had his way, I'd have married some distant prince to secure a better future for Sziveria. I'm lucky he let me train in my genetic ability at all after tests confirmed my logic-based talent. Once any prospective husband learned he'd be marrying a highly educated wife, he wanted nothing to do with me."

The piece paused mid flip between his fingers. "I didn't know he'd offered you to anyone else."

Raina clenched her jaw, hating the rise of humiliation she thought she'd managed to get over so many years ago. When she'd discussed their marriage in the greenhouse, she'd been too embarrassed to share her side of the story. Since she already made the mistake of telling how undesirable she was, she didn't see how mentioning more could hurt. "Twice."

"And they said no because you're intelligent?"

"One, the other because I wasn't pretty enough."

"Was he blind?"

If his tone hadn't been genuine, Raina would have thought he joked. She glanced at him and smiled faintly at the sincere questioning in his eyes. "No."

Kevin sighed and resumed playing with the black marble. "They both were fools."

A faint flutter in her chest had her breath hitching. Did he think she was pretty *and* valued her intelligence? She didn't have time to dwell on the notions before he asked another question.

"And then to me?"

She slid a small piece forward with a ball on top. When the marble moved without effort, she tipped the stone up and noted a glued fabric swatch on the bottom. "Sort of, it was all very strange. A little over four years ago something happened. My father acted strangely for weeks. He wouldn't come out of his office for any reason except to sleep and bathe. He dispatched footman after footman with letters. I thought we'd gone to war and no one else knew yet. Then he simply announced he'd found me a husband and handed me the contract to read over."

"And you made two changes."

"Yes." Raina's attention went back to the tallest figure on the board. "Did you make any?"

"I wasn't permitted to."

Startled by the information, Raina snapped her gaze to his. "How could that be? Legally you had every right to make changes as I did. I always figured father handled the negotiations with you instead of myself."

He gave a cold smile. "You assume I had rights in the matter."

"You must hate me," Raina whispered before she realized she'd thought the words.

Kevin sighed heavily and set the chess piece down with equal weight. "I don't hate you. Your father, yes, I have a healthy amount of that emotion for him. But you didn't exactly have a say in much, either. I imagine the changes to the contract were to piss him off more than me."

"Yes," And now Raina worried her act of defiance may have led to Synintel's decision to dissolve Kevin's rank. She wondered if he'd still reserve his hate for her father alone if he figured that little tidbit out. Needing to change the subject, she pointed to the small piece she'd moved forward. "What is this one called?"

"A pawn."

"What were you holding?" She glanced at the oddly shaped black silhouette that reminded her of a horse's head.

"A knight."

Raina worked her bottom lip and moved to the tallest. "And this one?"

"The king, also the weakest piece on the board next to the pawn. Capture that piece, checkmate, game over."

She touched the slightly shorter piece beside the king. "This must be his queen."

"Yes, and she's the strongest piece on the board. She can move any direction she wishes."

The beautifully carved white marble seemed to glow in the pale light. "Must be my father's favorite piece."

Kevin shook his head, leaned forward and set a black pawn in the center of the board. "That's your father's favorite piece."

Raina stared at the small, insignificant cut stone. *A pawn.* Her gaze flitted to the row of them, neatly line up, ready for their master to send them forward as sacrifice to keep the more important, more maneuverable pieces in play longer. While she wanted to rail against the fact that she was one of the ones thrown forward for sacrifice, she couldn't ignore the truth any longer. To her father, she was one of the important pieces, lined up in the back, waiting for the next move.

Her husband was the pawn.

Suddenly, the game lost any appeal it may have had. She pulled her hands away, not wanting to touch another piece. "Why did you come in here?"

Kevin shifted the pawn back into line. "Shield Guardian Enbrackon matched you again. The less time you stood in his presence, the better."

"Why didn't you just join us?" she challenged, squaring her shoulders.

The stormy depths of his eyes lingered long enough to make her shift in the padded seat. "Because I can't get within a foot of him."

"Why?"

"He'd end up a twitching puddle on the ground."

The imagery both confused and amused Raina. The gruff, entirely masculine delivery did something else to her. "I don't understand."

"All the better Trust me."

Raina glanced over her shoulder at the closed door. "We should probably return to the event."

"For what purpose?"

Because it's expected of us. But she hadn't exactly been meeting expectation the past couple months. The reason would sound hollow even to her ears. "People will talk."

"People always talk."

She flattened her hands on the chair's arms and rose. "True, and I'm tired of being their topic."

"Then stop giving them so much to discuss." His words were more suggestion than order.

Still, they rubbed Raina the wrong way. She stalked over to him and stopped at his knees, hands fisted at her side. Sitting, he wasn't taller than her. In fact, if she straightened, she'd be able to look down at him for a change. "I have nothing to defend against baseless gossip. If they want to speak, nothing I do will change the lies."

He lifted her arm and caressed the distance to her hand. The warmth of his touch slid up her forearm. Without resistance, her palm opened at his urging. The tips of his fingers glided along the sensitive skin and up to her inner wrist and then back. The undemanding touch was sensual and riveting. Rational thought fled her mind.

Raina's pulse quickened and her breath echoed in her ears. What was he doing to her? A strange sensation built deep in her belly. With a gentle tug he pulled her closer and she didn't object. A mild pressure at her back eased her forward, sinking into his waiting embrace. Her knees settled into the spaces beside his thighs. Straddling his lap, Raina tried not to be overwhelmed at the intimacy of their position. The breath rushed from her lungs as his chest met hers.

Tender at first, his lips brushed across hers. Raina closed her eyes. The subtle, clean scent of Kevin invaded her senses, heightening her awareness of him. His tongue slid along her bottom lip and with a sigh, Raina accepted the invitation. The second her mouth opened and his tongue caressed hers, everything changed. A sharp, intense sensation burst to life at her center and she whimpered, rising on her knees, her hands grasping his strong shoulders, desperate for more.

Kevin's hands pressed into her back, forcing her down onto the hard mass behind the buttons of his pants. Primal pleasure tingled as her center settled over him. Too many layers of fabric bunched between them, but somewhere in the part of her mind that still held to lucid thought, she knew she could do nothing about that. Not here. His mouth slanted over hers, possessing, claiming, pulling her deeper into a kiss she hadn't known existed.

Under her hands, every muscle in his shoulders drew tight and his mouth tore from hers. Breathing heavily, he relaxed his hold and put some distance between them. Confused, Raina stared at him.

"Wh—"

"We've been discovered, my dear."

Heat crept into her cheeks and she chanced a look over her shoulder. A man and woman quickly exited the library. The woman's giggles carried to Raina a second before the door closed again. She drew in a shuddering breath, unsure if she should be embarrassed or not.

"I suppose we should leave. They'll have plenty to say now," she said.

Kevin helped her rise, straightening the front of her dress while she adjusted the corset style top. "Yes, and none of it will be a lie."

Shocked, Raina stopped in her adjusting. "Is that why you kissed me?"

"Would you be upset if I said yes?"

She blinked, unsure how to take the question. "Would I? I should think so."

The smile he offered was less than kind. "Yes."

5

—————

Kevin tried to convince himself the callous answer he'd given Raina had been for the best. Because any other answer would have brought her right back into his arms and *that* would have been a disaster. His wife's unexpected passion had blindsided him. Until he could figure out how to gather his self-control, he needed her anger. Right now, he had it.

But he didn't want anger.

No, he'd much rather have Raina. *All* of Raina. A dangerous desire he couldn't afford.

She sat in silence across from him in the carriage. Only the occasional kick from her foot dangling in the air from her crossed legs let him know she was still awake. Kevin wondered if he grabbed that foot, slipped her shoe off, and caressed his way up her calf, if she'd stop him. His fingers twitched to find out. His teeth gritted against the swift logical reminder she wasn't his to touch.

In a couple weeks Synintel would passively demand Kevin do the honorable thing and release his daughter. Since Kevin wanted nothing more than to be free of the spectacle of high society, and the restrictions and obligations brought on by holding a ranked Guardian position, he'd give them a one-finger salute and gladly bow his way back home. Something he couldn't do if he claimed Raina as his wife. She deserved better. And she definitely deserved better than he'd be able to give after they stripped away his rank.

Finally, the house loomed in the shadows of night. Kevin jumped out before the carriage came to a complete stop, needing distance from Raina before he did something truly stupid. He didn't do the honorable thing and wait for her, offering his assistance from the vehicle. The moment her hand touched his, she'd be back in his arms, and the only place they'd go from there would be upstairs. To a bed.

Growling in aggravation, Kevin slammed the side door open and closed it just as heavily. The kitchen area was empty and not a sound echoed in the house besides his booted foot-falls. A single lamp burned on the switchback to the second story, lighting the stairs enough to make them safe in the darkness. Kevin ignored the steps and went to his study.

Once inside the small space Raina had designated his in her sprawling house, aside from his bedroom, he leaned against the closed door and took several slow, centering breaths. If he'd been in his own house, he'd be punching and kicking out the pent-up emotions. Here he had nothing to help ease his inner turmoil. The five a.m. workout he conducted daily with his teammates wouldn't come soon enough.

At his desk, he sat, then pulled a clean piece of staff paper from a drawer. Staring at the perfectly straight, evenly spaced lines, he thrummed his fingers on the desk. If his mother had had her way, Kevin's Gen-Heir ability would have been music. But in his second year of secondary education at Sziveria Royale Academia, an aggressive assault on him had unlocked his true talent. The poor idiots who'd attacked him hadn't stood a chance.

Within weeks of the fight, he'd been pulled from the school and sent to a military training facility. Two years later, he was on Sean Blackbain's team with Mason Dandridge. Katria had arrived into the fold years later, and the Guardian Intel Team had been complete.

Everyone needed an escape though, and his first love still called. After drawing the elegant curves of the clef on the first set of staff lines, Kevin pushed negative thoughts away and focused on the notes drifting through his mind. He hummed the first line, writing in a language that hadn't changed for millenniums.

After the first few pages, it became painfully apparent he'd actually need a piano to make sure the pacing and flow of notes were in harmony. But that'd mean sharing a part of himself he rather enjoyed keeping away from others. A secret oasis for his battered body and soul.

Shuffling the partially constructed sheet music into a neat stack, he slid all the papers into the desk drawer. A dull ache settled in his shoulders, and he stretched as he stood. At some point, he'd have to decide when his body was too old, too scarred, too jaded to fight for a cause that was rarely his own. But he was only twenty-seven. The First Intelligence Office still expected at least a decade more, regardless of how he felt about the matter.

If Synintel did what he planned, Kevin could walk away from their summons as well. The only reason he aided now was to keep from going crazy of boredom in the Hall of Laws. Each ranked Guardian either served as a commissioned civil servant to one of the many branches of military or law enforcement, or served their peers as a vote from a seat. Since being on commission also allowed Kevin to simply be Kevin Merrick, not Raiventon, he'd jumped at the opportunity to use his skills and travel. Guardian ranks held no place in the military or law system.

Until Raina's responsive kiss shifted something deep inside him, he wondered if being the Master Guardian Raiventon wasn't all that bad after all.

He scoffed at the absurdity. If a kiss had him rolling over like a dog, what would actually *touching* her do, let alone sharing her bed? The prospect didn't bode well. He crossed the room, hoping his far too delectable wife was safely closed in her room.

Kevin froze the second he opened the door to his study. Someone waited for him. An energy of expectation thrummed in the air. The breathing the person tried to hide echoed in the stillness. Darkness blanketed the house. Silently he took a step back into the recess of the doorway and waited. Like fire through his veins, the familiar onset of adrenaline forced his eyes closed, unlocking his genetic ability. Neither touch or logic-based, Kevin's genetically inherited talent was in a class all its own.

A high endorphin rush made most people jumpy, on edge and prone to erratic response. Kevin reacted in a different manner. Every sense heightened, from hearing to smell. Muscle memory became a rapidly triggered response, a flash of motion most would never perceive. His body tense, his mind would soon process movement at a rate that appeared to make actions slow. He usually knew an aggressor's move before they did by the micro gestures they made before committing to an attack.

A flare of silver from the left came in warning. Kevin crouched low. Air shifted above him. Shadows moved enough to give him perspective. Fisting his hands, he sent a hard punch up with his left hand, connecting with the sensitive tissue between a man's legs. When the man bent over, gagging, Kevin threw his right fist under the opponent's jaw, snapping his head back. The body slumped to the floor, muffled by fabric and the carpet runner.

Harmless, the knife clattered to the ground where Kevin left it. He waited, listening. Patience his ally. Two masses lurched forward. At the correct second, Kevin leapt and executed a split kick. The two men flew through the air. One landed on a table, splintering the wood, the other into a wall, bouncing forward.

Kevin engaged the invader still upright against the wall. A solid hit to his diaphragm and another to his temple. Before the man landed on the floor, Kevin was atop the intruder attempting to rise from the busted table. With a simultaneous knee to the assailant's breastbone and punch to across his jaw, Kevin eliminated another threat.

"Kevin?" Raina's uncertain voice drifted down from upstairs.

Kevin glanced at the banister. The moment of distraction cost him. A slice of fire spread across his shoulder blade and the back of his bicep. Hissing, Kevin spun and kicked the knife from his attacker. "Do not come down here! Stay upstairs!"

"But—"

Frustration made him hit the man who'd likely cut Kevin's back and arm open hard enough to send teeth flying. *"I said stay!"*

The slamming of her door echoed. Kevin made quick work of what he hoped was the last attacker, swiping his legs out from under him with a head hit on the way down. No one even flinched or groaned as Kevin quickly checked for weapons and made sure they remained unconscious. Minutes later he held two pistols and three knives.

He shoved a gun in the back of his pants, threw the knives into a deep vase near the stairs, and then cocked a round into the chamber of the second pistol in his grip. Last time the attackers had remained solely downstairs. Since this time they had no way of knowing where in the house he was located, he wasn't risking any intruders hiding out.

After clearing the remaining first story, he kicked off his shoes before silently creeping up the stairs. He searched every room, closet and alcove. When he reached Raina's room, he found the door locked. Staying calm, he gently tapped on the door.

"It's me, open up," he said evenly.

The door cracked open. Kevin waited until he was sure she was clear before pushing it open completely. She gasped and pressed against the wall beside the doorframe when he entered, gun leading.

"What's happening?"

"Anyone in here with you?"

She sputtered and then managed, "No! Why would you think I'm not alone?"

Confident her room was safe, he lowered the gun. "I was attacked downstairs."

"What?" Her eyes widened and she grasped handfuls of her nightgown. "Again? Are you okay?"

Just to ease his mind, Kevin checked her closet. She padded after him. "I'm fine."

"What are they after?"

Then he turned and crossed the distance and checked her dressing room. She followed. "I'm not sure."

"What are you looking for?"

When he turned, she slammed into his chest. Kevin gripped her upper arm with his free hand. "I needed to make sure you're safe."

Raina's beautiful eyes stared up at him with an innocence he wished he could remember having. "Oh."

The word came out on a breath, teasing his already high-strung senses. Unable to resist the temptation, he pressed a quick, fleeting kiss to her lips before releasing her. "Stay upstairs."

The soft falls of her feet chasing after him followed to the stairs. "What are you doing?"

"Taking out the trash."

· · ·

RAINA DASHED around the landing to the room across from hers. For the second time in less than a week, someone had broken into her home. Kevin had simply told her of the first attack. This time she'd heard for herself. At the window overlooking the long sidewalk to the gated entrance, she saw the evidence as Kevin dragged two unconscious men away from the house by their ankles. Their heads bobbed along the paved walk, their limp arms dragging. At least she hoped they were merely unconscious.

Kevin left the men just outside the gate and then returned. The lithe, predatory way he made his way back to the house sent a shiver up her spine. Before tonight she couldn't imagine him taking on intruders. Now she'd seen him carry a gun like an extension of his arm and move with a strength and grace she hadn't noticed before. Or hadn't wanted to.

Rubbing her arms, she stepped away from the cold window. Once again she wondered what Kevin's role was with the FIO. She wandered back to her room, leaving the door open. Minutes passed. Unsure what else to do, she sat on the edge of her bed and waited.

Soundless, a shadow crossed by her door.

A spike of adrenaline coursed through her veins, flushing along her skin. She reminded herself Kevin had checked upstairs. But surely she would have heard him on the steps? Several of the boards were loose and creaked under any weight, even her own, and he more than doubled her in size.

Rising from the bed, she tiptoed to the wall beside her door. Her fingers wrapped tightly around the wooden frame. For a moment she waited, listening. Silence continued to reign. Slowly she edged into the hallway and then to the railing overlooking the stairway. Peering down, nothing but darkness greeted her. She glanced to her left and noted a faint, shadowy light under Kevin's door. She frowned. Had he passed by her door?

Raina worried her bottom lip between her teeth, contemplating whether to go to her room, or to Kevin's. She had questions, and if she were honest, she was a little scared to be alone. However, if she continued with that same honesty, she'd also admit being alone with him wasn't wise.

A faint pulsing sensation still thrummed at her center. An awakened need she hadn't known existed nor understood. All she did know was Kevin's passionate kiss caused the stirring. What if he kissed her again? What would happen? More importantly, was she ready? Raina closed her eyes. No, not yet. While Kevin wasn't the enigma he'd been a week ago, she still knew so little about him. Husband or not, a stranger wasn't welcome in her bed.

Never mind the kiss had seemed to mean considerably less to him than to her.

With resolve, Raina squared her shoulders and walked to his door. She'd ask her questions, keep her distance, and then leave. Her fingers trembled as she reached for the knob. The door fell open, revealing Kevin's back. His shirt slid free of his muscled shoulders. All of Raina's carefully laid plans floated away when she spotted the dried blood that had at one point ran down his back and arm.

"You're hurt!" Not considering the repercussions, she rushed into the room, reaching for his injuries. "Why didn't you say anything?"

He hissed as her fingers touched just outside the wound on his shoulder and he shied away. Raina immediately withdrew.

"They aren't serious, I'll be fine."

The calm way he spoke opened her eyes in a different way. The dim, moving light of the lamp on his nightstand etched a myriad of scars in harsh relief across his back, arms and sides. She wanted to force him around to see if his chest was equally adorned. Unable to stop, she traced a long, thin white line from his shoulder to his hip. Tears stung behind her eyes.

"What has my father done to you?"

"You should be more concerned about what I'm going to do to you if you don't stop." The husky spoken statement left a promise that sent every nerve in Raina's body on full alert.

Slowly, Raina lowered her hand. She glanced around the impersonal room. Not a rug on the floor, or a painting on the walls. Only a large four poster bed, dresser, desk, two chairs in front of a cold fire and a book shelf with three empty shelves adorned the otherwise spacious room. Furniture she'd picked out four years ago for him when he hadn't done the task himself. She hadn't understood then he wouldn't be using the room. The space still wasn't his. Nothing *felt* like Kevin.

Sighing, she went to the desk and grabbed the chair. Kevin remained like a statue. Raina dropped the chair behind him. "Sit."

He glanced over his shoulder his gray eyes dark in the moody light. "What?"

"I said sit, let me take care of those cuts." When the only reaction to her request was clenched fists, she added, "Please."

With a heavy exhalation, he planted himself in the chair. "I have a medical kit in my chest on the other side of the bed."

Raina went to the chest. Inside were neatly folded clothes, some worn books, loose sheets of paper and a canvas bag that she assumed was the kit. She made sure before removing the bag and closing the top.

"Take out what I need while I go wet a washcloth to clean off the blood," she said.

He accepted the bag. "I can take care of myself, you know. Been doing it for over a decade."

"I can't imagine how you'll clean the cut on your shoulder. Unless you have eyes in the back of your head?"

The sound of his faint chuckle followed her into his bathroom. "No, even I can't watch my own back."

Raina wetted a washcloth, hating the water would be so cold, but she figured in the amount of time it would take to heat, Kevin would probably change his mind about allowing her to help. Cold water would do. Back in the room, she paused a moment, taking in his strong frame. The muted, shifting light danced off the muscled plains of his arms, shoulders and back, defining the smooth ridges. Even sitting, he was almost taller than her. If she were to walk to his front, he wouldn't have to bend down to kiss her, and she wouldn't have to rise on her toes… The temptation had her closing the distance to his wounds.

"Seems you did a decent job to me."

He shrugged. "There were only five, and they weren't coordinated."

Gently, Raina began cleaning away the dried blood. The canvas of violence painted on his body tore at her heart. She stopped cleaning. "What do you do for my father?"

A small glass jar appeared over his shoulder. "Put this on, it will keep them from getting infected."

The heat of his skin burned through her fingers as she smoothed the silky cream along the injuries. Why did he keep ignoring her question?

"Do they look deep?" he asked over his shoulder.

"No."

He grunted in reply.

The desire to kiss his shoulder near his neck and taste his skin came over Raina so strongly she had to take a deep breath. His subtle, clean, masculine scent invaded her nostrils and made her all too aware of how little clothing they both wore.

What is wrong with me?

Pressing the back of her hand to her forehead, Raina tried to find rational thought. Never in her life had a man affected her in such a profound, disturbing manner. Enbrackon always brought a tremor of fear, and a tinge of guilt, but nothing more. Other men who'd entered her space, kissed her cheek, or hand, even touched her wrist intimately, had elicited little more than annoyance.

Desperate, she wanted to ask Kevin if he were having a similar issue, but then he'd know how deeply he'd affected her. And the risk of him having such knowledge wasn't an option.

A man's power over a woman could be measured by his control of her.

The moment Raina allowed Kevin to know he had such control would be the moment she lost any she might have had. It was the very reason she'd never allowed the Shield Guardian more than a touch to her elbow or a kiss to her knuckles. Currently Enbrackon held all the cards of her career. He wouldn't have anything else.

Steeling herself against the effects of touching Kevin, she smoothed more salve on his bicep. The muscle twitched and tightened beneath her gentle caress. Raina's pulse throbbed through every part of her body. "Okay, all finished."

His hand appeared over his shoulder and Raina set the small jar on his open palm. Against better judgement she took a step forward until the heat of his naked back radiated through the thin silk of her nightgown. Closing her eyes, she lifted her hands, intent on smoothing them along the tops of his shoulders, wanting to know with a need she didn't understand how his skin felt beneath her fingers.

"You need to go." The deep, hoarse words penetrated the fog of her mind. They weren't spoken in anger, rather in a strained manner that once again held a promise she knew she wasn't ready to collect on.

Or was she?

No. Quickly she turned on her heel and strode from his room without looking back, knowing if she did, she'd change her mind.

6

Only when Kevin was sure he could occupy the same space with Raina, regardless of the size of the room, and keep his hands and mouth to himself, did he venture to her office. The door was open, her last client having left over an hour ago. A half hour later her assistant had also departed, leaving the house quiet and almost empty feeling.

Kevin had checked every window and door lock into the house, finding nothing broken and no signs the locks had been tampered with. Raina's office was the last remaining room for him to check.

After a restless night and a workout that did little to ease the frustration of the break-in and the sensual torment following, Kevin found himself in a poor mood. And Raina didn't deserve the venom he'd likely direct her way. While his control slipped toward nonexistent thanks to her, she was blissfully unaware of the havoc she created within him. He'd barely made it through her doctoring his wounds without hauling her over his lap and finishing what they'd started earlier that evening.

While Kevin had never been a love-them-and-wake-up-before-they-do kind of guy, he could in fact count his lovers on one hand, he'd never felt anything close to the way Raina made him feel. Impatient, hungry, almost obsessive with need to know more of her.

When she'd traced a scar down his back, the pain of his wounds had all but disappeared. Not to mention when she'd stepped so close to him last night, the heat of her body and swell of her breasts brushing his back, he'd almost leapt out of his skin. How she could set fire to his blood with barely a touch?

Shaking off the uneasy thoughts, Kevin convinced himself he was not a coward and could face his pixie wife, and gently rapped on her office door. She stood behind her spacious desk. Three maps overlapped and she had a folder open on top of them.

Dying sunlight streamed in through the wide windows behind her desk, casting her in a beautiful hazy orange glow. Several locks of light brown hair had worked free from the bun atop her head. In the vibrant light they appeared almost red. When she finally glanced up, her hand froze over the folder and her lips parted. Blinking, she quickly looked back to her work.

"What can I do for you, my Guardian?"

Kevin raised a brow. *My Guardian?* Were they back on formal grounds? Perhaps that was for the best. "I wanted to know if your stylist locks the door when she leaves for the night."

He crossed the distance to the windows on the right and carefully checked the locks and edges. All looked untouched.

Raina's pale gaze watched him cross the room to the next set. "Yes, she's supposed to. Why?"

"There isn't any evidence of forced entry. I wanted to know if those who attacked me last night could have just walked in."

She straightened, turning his direction when he reached

the windows. "I certainly hope they didn't, but you're more than welcome to ask Tabby."

Kevin headed to the oversized window behind her. "Would she lie?"

Raina considered the question. "Perhaps I should ask. You might intimidate her."

Since he knew his effect on most people, he didn't disagree. He inspected the latches behind her desk and the edges of each frame, frustrated when the results were the same. When he turned around, Raina took a step back. In her haste she bumped the desk, shifting the maps and sending papers fluttering off the other end. One large step separated them.

The wise course of action would be to leave. He'd seen all he needed to. Raina's hands gripped the edge of the desk with such intensity her knuckles were white. Jaw clenched, she stared at him in a mixture of cautious awareness. Kevin reached across the space. His finger caressed along the smooth, silky skin of her jaw to her ear, where he tucked a wayward lock away.

"What about you, Raina? Do I intimidate you?" he asked softly.

The straight, long navy skirt and matching vest style top she wore over a crisp white shirt were meant to give her a professional appearance. At one point in the day, her traditional hairstyle had been immaculate, capturing the essence he was sure she'd hoped to achieve. Now, with her arms reaching behind, pressing her breasts against the shirt and vest until the buttons strained, and her hair a wild mess around her face, Kevin wanted nothing more than to clear the desk of the rest of her work and see just how far she'd let him go.

Her gaze flickered to his mouth. "I'm... no."

Kevin took a small step forward, closing half the distance between them, leaving enough room that if she wanted to bolt, she could. He wouldn't stop her. "You don't sound very convincing."

She pressed further back, practically forcing herself onto the desk, but a flash of defiance lifted her chin. "Do you want me to be frightened of you?"

"Of course not." Kevin chuckled and shook his head. "I'm pleased you don't react like most people. I seem to annoy you more than anything. The only other people that are at ease with me took a year or two to be comfortable in my presence."

Some tension left her shoulders and relaxed her frame. "You don't annoy me."

Kevin took another small step forward. She didn't shift this time. Good. Though he really shouldn't think so. If she knew what was best for her, she'd be scared. And if he knew what was best for him, he'd be leaving. "Could have fooled me."

"Somehow I doubt you can be fooled."

Ah, but she was making a spectacular fool of him now. Kevin closed his eyes and leaned in close enough to her neck to inhale her sweet, floral and peach scent. When he opened his eyes, his gaze locked on the maps. The delicate yet heavy sensation of her breathing across his ear told him she wasn't immune to his nearness.

"What are you working on?" he asked.

"What?" Her voice was weak, almost confused.

Kevin resisted the urge to smile. Stepping to the side of her, he pulled a half-hidden map free. "You use maps to plot courses or for something else?"

"Um." She turned around. Her slender fingers traced over the lines of the map as though she were attempting to ground herself. Kevin gritted his teeth at the memory of that same feathery touch over his back. "I don't plan routes unless I'm directing for a shipping fleet. Usually, I use existing fleets to move goods for my clients. I need the maps so I can locate where the fleets are and plan how to move commodities efficiently."

"Do you often direct a fleet?"

"No, I don't like to. There are too many factors. Weather, tidal shifts, port schedules. I much prefer to route the goods themselves. Most fleets staff a Gen-Heir logistics expert to manage plotting. I work with them if it's an unusually large delivery that may require an entire ship for cargo space."

Kevin looked over the maps. She'd made notations along coastal cities and others well inside land. Kevin pointed to one. "What are these?"

"Rail stations. They move cargo faster than anything else on land. I have to get cargo to a railhead and then to the nearest port city that has one of the fleets I'm contracted with, whichever one has an outbound ship with space available."

"And there aren't maps with the rail routes on them?"

"There are, but they're usually outdated. As more and more areas are being developed closer to the Uninhabited Zones, they're finding preserved lines from before the cataclysm to repair and utilize. Some countries are even able to have more than one line, and competitors don't like to occupy the same map. It's easier for me to make my own."

Kevin stared at the three maps, one for Westica, one that covered Cairo, Ravenna and Thanzia, and another for New Columbia. "Mason could consolidate for you."

"Do you think he would?" The hopefulness in her tone had him glancing at her.

"He draws maps for us in almost every city we go to."

Her attention still on the maps, she slid a new one forward. "Is that what he does on your team?"

"No, he's our strategist."

The tip of her tongue danced across her bottom lip. "And Primary Guardian Wintersfall?"

Kevin turned and propped his rear against the desk, crossing his arms over his chest. "Besides our leader, he's also our Medical Scientist and a Sympath, so if we need answers…"

Raina gasped before meeting his stare. "A Sympath? I've never met one before. Can he really experience other people's emotions as his own?"

"Yes, when he touches them. So, now you can say you've met one."

"How does his wife deal with him being gone so much?"

Kevin worked his jaw and glanced out the window. The dying ball of the sun shimmered brilliant red, casting long pink shadows across the immaculate side yard. Warm light reflected off the greenhouse windows. Soon any trace of warmth would leave when the suns last rays died under the horizon, leaving behind a cold so intense frost would form within in an hour.

If he told Raina about Kat, he'd have to tell her about himself, too. Sean and Mason were safe, they didn't actively search out and sometimes kill people. That dreadful task was left to Katria and less often, Kevin. Granted, on Kevin's end they were *usually* trying to expire his life first.

Kevin doubted her lack of fear regarding him would remain if she knew how lethal the man she'd been forced to marry was. For some reason, that bothered him. From what he'd observed, she was different with him than around others. Off guard. He didn't want anything to change.

He could answer one thing. "She's on the team too, they travel together."

Raina's mouth dropped open. "What does she do?"

Kevin shook his head. "You will have to ask her."

"Does she travel with you?"

"Normally it was just her and Sean. Mason and I would meet them wherever we're assigned."

She faced him, bracing her hip against the desk and her palm flat on the surface. The faint wisps of light still peeking over the horizon cast every curve of her face and body in harsh relief. Kevin turned his attention to a safer view of the floor. A fluttering touch brushed from his knuckle to his wedding band.

"You never took this off?"

The gold band glinted as he lifted his fingers from his bicep. "Nope. And I refused to pretend to be married to anyone else either."

"Why?"

Kevin shrugged. "Made Synintel's job that much harder." He gave a sardonic chuckle. "And it pissed him off."

"Did anyone have to pretend to be married often?"

"Not really. Only Sean and Kat, which ended up being ironic since they were in fact married the entire time and didn't even know."

Raina gasped sharply. "*No.*"

Kevin couldn't help but grin, remembering the shock on their faces the day Voklane handed them their very real marriage contract. "Oh yes. I wish I could say I felt bad for them, but we're all so close I just thought it was hilarious."

She slapped his arm and he winced. With a cry of alarm, Raina grabbed his elbow. "I'm so sorry, I forgot!"

Kevin rubbed the tender flesh beneath the cut. "I'm fine."

Her frown said she didn't believe him and the worry in her eyes warmed his heart. "Still, I'm sorry."

"Don't be. Kat would approve of your retribution in her honor."

"She's important to you, isn't she?" Raina joined him with her back to the desk, her gaze at the window and the last bloom of colorful streaks painting the sky in a gradient of orange, purple and gray.

"Who, Kat?" he asked, looking over long enough to see her curt nod. How exactly was he supposed to explain his odd, almost sibling relationship and trust in a woman whose genetic ability was looking through a scope and pulling a trigger? "They're all important to me. Sean and Mason are like brothers, and whenever we worked together, Kat was a cousin, or my ward. For Mason, she was usually a cousin or sister. With their straight black hair and light eye color, they never would have been believable as anything else. I came to see her as family too."

And they were, one strange, deadly family. Kevin sighed.

"Do you think I'll have a chance to get to know them, before…?" Her words died and she turned back to the maps.

Kevin finished for her. "Before I have to leave again."

Yet another reason he had to keep his hands off her. Even if Synintel decided to let the Raiventon rank stay in Kevin's family, he'd just send his son-in-law off for another four years. Rolling his neck to ease the tension in his shoulders, Kevin straightened.

"I'm sure they'd all love to know you better. I will see what I can arrange."

When he headed around the desk and then for the door, her almost anxious words stopped him. "Where are you going?"

Kevin glanced over his shoulder. "I want to look at the doors again, make sure I didn't miss anything. You'll speak to your stylist soon I hope?"

She nodded. "Yes. She's probably upstairs waiting for me."

Waiting to change Raina into something more comfortable since no more guests were expected. Kevin quickly left his wife's office before images of her undressing could creep into his mind. The desk was still too tempting an option…

ALONE IN THE DINING ROOM, Raina stared at the full plate of food a server had set on the table before she'd arrived. The moment she'd sat, he'd removed the warming lid with a flourish and disappeared. At least from her view. Looking at the open doorway and into the empty hall, she realized the reason why Kevin had closeted himself away in his study for meals. If he'd been sitting at the table across from her, their entire conversation would have been for someone else's ears. The lack of privacy wasn't something she ever considered, or had been bothered by.

When Kevin had walked into her office earlier in the evening, the huge room had suddenly seemed so much smaller. And when he crowded her space, he hadn't touched her. Not once. Raina didn't know which was worse—his restraint, or her disappointment.

Even now she wanted to see him, hear his deep voice wash over her like silk. Wanted him to stir something in her she hadn't known existed before him. She knew she played with fire, in more ways than one. Yet the woman in her, too long denied, yearned for the man just outside her reach.

Raina stood and went to the swinging door dividing the small dining space with a large, formal dining room. Sure enough, the moment she peered around the edge of the door, her server peered back with grayish blue eyes. She smiled warmly, but didn't enter the room.

"Are there any more courses this evening?"

"Two, my Guardianess."

"Please bring them, and Master Guardian Raiventon's as well, and you may be dismissed for the evening."

"His Guardianship already has his full meal."

Raina kept her shock to herself. "Very well, then please bring mine, and you may retire."

He performed a quick bow, his dark brown hair falling over his forehead. "As you wish, my Guardianess."

In the dining room, Raina bunched her fingers into the fine-spun cotton of her dress. A simple lavender gown made for comfort rather than entertaining, had a discreet floral pattern woven along the hem and bodice, with a row of impossibly small buttons up the back.

If she asked Kevin to join her, would he accept? Worrying

her bottom lip between her teeth, she edged for the door, convincing herself if the answer was no, her feelings wouldn't be hurt. Out in the hall, she paused again, took a deep breath and then turned past the stairs to his study. The door was firmly closed.

Raina raised her hand to knock, but Kevin's muffled voice from the other side beat her to it. "You can open the door."

Snatching her hand down, she stared at the light polished wood. How had he heard her when she hadn't made a sound? At least, she didn't think she had. The knob creaked in her hand as she turned it and let the door fall open by its own weight.

Kevin stared at her from across his desk, his plate off to the side, a black pen poised in his hand, ready to write. He still wore the same clothes from earlier, a simple maroon button up shirt rolled halfway up his corded forearms, and light brown pants. No shoes. Raina wondered if the man had something against them.

"Yes?"

Raina straightened her shoulders in anticipation of rejection. "I wanted to know if you'd join me for dinner."

"I don't much care for the extra company."

Her guess had been correct. She held in a triumphant smile. "I dismissed the server for the evening, it'll just be us." Then she added a bit of truth to her request. "I eat by myself every meal. The other morning was nice, when I didn't."

Kevin pushed his seat back and picked up his plate. "After you."

Pleased her effort paid off, Raina led the way back to the dining room. The second course of her meal waited beside the first. She noted all of Kevin's food had been on one larger plate. A second set of silverware wrapped in a dark green linen napkin rested on the table near her seat.

After pulling out the chair nearest to her, and sliding a little closer, Kevin set his plate on the table and sat. Raina joined him and pulled her plate forward. In comfortable silence, they both ate. Since Raina often had her means alone, the quiet was normal.

"What did your stylist say?" Kevin asked.

Raina pushed a small pile of raw tomatoes in a sauce along the center of her plate. "She swore she locked all three of the bolts at the back door before leaving for the night. She said she wasn't used to you being home yet and forgets I'm not alone, and she'd never leave me in that type of danger."

"Don't you have a stylist's quarters off your dressing room?"

Raina nodded, pushing her near empty plate away. "Yes, but Tabby married a couple months ago. She refused to live in the house. Something about it being too quiet at night."

Kevin coughed and Raina realized they'd been left with nothing to drink. She stood and glanced around the room. She wasn't sure where her server may have left a beverage. Kevin motioned her back to her chair, still coughing.

"I'll go look for something." He left and returned moments later with a pitcher of water and two glasses. After pouring both cups, he sat and took a healthy drink. "I guess the break in routine made them forget about drinks."

Raina chuckled, wrapping her fingers around the cool glass. "This house is nothing but routine. My father set the schedule when I first moved in, I don't think it's changed even by a minute in the last four years."

"Do you want it to?"

Surprised by the question, Raina turned her attention to him. "I don't know, I never really thought much about it." She gave a little insecure laugh again while she sipped at her water. "I don't know what I'd change."

Kevin shrugged, easing back in the chair he'd angled toward her. One long leg stretched out, brushing past her ankle. "Sleep in for fifteen more minutes. Have dinner earlier or later. It's your house, they're your staff."

Frowning, Raina sighed. "Not really, all the staff in the house with the exception of Tabby, are my father's. He still pays them and they report to him for orders."

A rivulet of condensation rolled down the edge of Kevin's glass. He traced the droplet. "I see."

"Is it too fanciful for me to feel like we're two people stuck in a prison of my father's making?"

His dark gray eyes met her stare. "I can think of worse prisons to be stuck in."

Heat bloomed across her cheeks. She turned her focus back to the safety of the water. "I doubt you are attacked anywhere else you've lived."

"Neither you or Synintel hired those men." His foot nudged her ankle. "Unless you *really* don't want me here."

She gaped at him. "I would never… I don't even know…"

He reached across the space and grabbed her hand, still damp from the death grip she'd had on the cup of water. "I was teasing. Does no one tease you?"

Blinking, Raina stared down at his hand, larger than hers, with long elegant fingers. "Who would?"

"Your friends?"

In relaxed, lazy motions, his hand intertwined with hers. He brushed along her sensitive palm and slid his fingers between hers in a constant, seductive motion. The butterfly sensations were having an odd effect on her. She couldn't look away.

"Friends?" While she counted Patricia a friend, the woman rarely teased. Only recently having shown a playful side Raina hadn't known about. No one else would dare do anything more than be completely respectful to her. Well, except Cora Dandridge. She'd been decidedly unfriendly. Anyone else had too much fear of the Arch Guardian and his powerful reach.

"Yes, you know, those people you can be comfortable around."

"I know what friends are," she said with a frown. But dare she admit she could count only one? His fingers weaving and sliding along hers distracted her to the point she almost snatched her hand away. "They don't tease. And somehow I don't think you'd take your friends pestering you."

She had a suspicious feeling he was *teasing* her in an entirely different way with his touch.

Feathery light, his fingers shifted from her palm to her wrist, and then brushed along her forearm. Little flips danced low in her belly. She found herself perched on the edge of her seat in anticipation. The cool, polished wood under her arm allowed her to focus on something other than his maddening caress.

"Depends on my mood."

Desperately she wanted to ask about his current mood, but she didn't know if she was ready for the answer. He leaned in close until his knees touched hers. Raina kept her gaze fixed on a lighter strip of wood next to her arm. The caress continued up her skin, past her elbow, fluttering briefly at the sleeve of her dress before moving on to her shoulder. Everything in her went into not biting her lip and ignoring his presence drawing closer.

Yes, she'd wanted this, but the overwhelming sensation curling at her center had started again and she found herself scared. Maybe being a dormant woman was okay. She'd gone this long without knowing what all the fuss was, or wasn't, about. Then Kevin's fingers were tangling in the long hair at the nape of her neck and he applied a strange pressure that forced her head toward her shoulder, baring the tender flesh below her jaw.

Her eyes closed as the whisper of his breath slid across her skin. The warm, moist tip of his tongue glided along the pulse thrumming with the same intensity as the one in her ears. Raina swore she felt him smile a second before his lips touched where he'd licked. He kissed up her neck, to her ear and across to her jaw. She wanted to scream *kiss me already*! But ladies didn't demand.

"Guardianess Raiventon?"

Raina jumped an inch from her seat at the sound of her stylist elite's voice echoing from the stairs. *The schedule*! How could she forget? The time had arrived for her to change into her sleeping gown for the night. Perhaps there were changes she'd make after all…

Sighing heavily, she opened her eyes. And found the seat across from her empty. Gasping, she grabbed her chair and searched the room. Where had Kevin gone? And how had she once again not heard him make a single sound? Or felt him withdraw from her presence? If curses were allowed to come from her mouth, Raina would have spoken one.

The only evidence she hadn't imagined the entire encounter was the still moist spot on her neck where he'd given her the most intimate experience of her life. Leaving her to wonder what else the man knew how to do.

7

—————

Jonathon Hunter, Key Guardian Asherwick, opened the top folder on a small stack he carried the moment he closed the front door. A nagging sensation that he'd missed a vital note in one of the cases currently under his investigation bothered him the entire ride home.

Several lamps burned in the entry hall. Every door was open on either side, revealing dark, empty rooms. His younger sister, Ramsey, must be upstairs, brooding into one of her books, or doing whatever else she did. Since she rarely left the house, he wasn't sure how she spent her time, only that she managed to occupy it fine without him.

Jonathon passed by the stairs to the left, heading to his study at the back of the house. He flipped a page, frowning as he read a witness testimony. So lost in the page, he passed by the open library door, failing to note the bright light spilling past the doorway.

"Jonathon."

He froze. Only one person in the entire world spoke his name as though it were a lyric in a song. Sylphine Seartavos, the stunning Italyssian shipping heiress. And the woman everyone believed Jonathon intended to marry. Snapping the folder closed, he took two steps back. A fist tightened around his heart the moment the library came into view. Pasting on a grin, he sauntered through the door.

"Well, if it isn't my bride-never-to-be. I didn't know we were expecting you."

The warm, dancing glow of the lanterns shimmered along Sylphine's sun-streaked, dark blonde hair and cast her richly tanned skin in a deep golden hue. The sheer covering over her lavender to midnight purple gown reflected the light, making the fabric appear alive with each sultry step she took. The silk left much to the imagination, falling over her full breasts and tapering just enough to hint at the voluptuous curves of her stomach and hips. Little bells around her wrists and ankles announced each step before she even took the next.

"You know I can't resist showing up unannounced. I have to make sure no one is claiming you in my absence, don't I?" Her remarkable tourmaline blue eyes danced with mischief.

Jonathon chuckled. "What rumors have you heard now? I can safely say they're *mostly* false."

One high arched brow rose and a smile teased her full, naturally pink lips. "My Jonathon, if you're attempting to make a woman jealous, I have to admit you may be succeeding."

"Ah, but not enough," he said with a wink.

She laughed, a graceful, sing-song sound that never failed to stir something too deep in him to admit. "True, yes, not enough."

Jonathon let out a sigh of discontent. "Pity, and here I thought I was just a smidgen closer to actually *being* the envy of every man who's seen you, not just in my own imagination."

She waved a hand, the light catching off the detailed silver promise band fastened around her wrist. The stones set in the center, the same color of her eyes, sparkled with blue-green light. Raised flowers on a woven vine accented the beautiful craftsmanship. "You tease. I can't believe you imagine much of anything about me."

If Jonathon didn't have great practice at keeping his mouth closed when shocked, his jaw would have dropped. *Woman, you have no idea the direction of my imagination when it comes to you.* "Best you keep that theory."

A suspicious glint replaced the playful gleam in her gaze. "Now don't be one of those I have to hide from because they think to be able to conquer me. You are supposed to be different."

Jonathon smiled at her perfect, yet not perfect, Sziverian. Since he could say maybe five words in Italyssian, he was impressed with her knowledge of his language. "Conquer you? While conquest certainly sounds like a fun game to play where you're concerned, I think all that would happen is a white flag surrender. And not from you."

She threw back her head and laughed. "Oh, it's only because you've sworn to never be my husband do I let you get away with speaking to me in such a manner."

"It's the only reason I dare."

"I can see now how the rumors concerning you are only mostly true, Jonathon, dear."

Jonathon winked. Two could play the endearment game, and he enjoyed the banter more with her than anyone else he kept at arm's length. "Well, Sylphine-love, your beautiful promise band has kept my own conquerors at bay. So once again, thanks for the proposal."

"One day you will have to tell me why you wish to remain alone."

Jonathon inclined his head to her. "And you will have to do the same."

The twinkle returned to her eyes. "Ah, secrets we shall keep, then."

"The worst relationships have them." He tucked the

folders under his arm, a flash of light catching his attention in her hair. Time to switch to a safer subject. "What's in your hair?"

She twisted her head as if trying to see behind herself and then giggled when she realized what she'd done. "Blessings from my family. They are part of my nation's culture for their daughters."

Jonathon wanted to step closer and examine the myriad of colors woven intricately throughout the thick, softly curled lengths of her hair. But the last time he'd tried to get closer than five feet, she'd practically run from him. A recent phenomenon he worried was the true reason she'd asked for a fake engagement. The professional interrogation he'd given his sister shortly after assured him no one needed to disappear in a manner only an investigator could guarantee. Whatever had happened to Sylphine had been of her own doing.

"Like the charms ladies wear here in Sziveria?"

She shook her head. "No. On each birthday a female relative presents the daughters with a *Naenzi te kordelka*, meant to ensure her beauty for her future husband. Once she's married, she no longer receives any. Since I am twenty-three this year, I have many more than most in my country."

"Do women marry young in Italyssa?"

"We marry when we fall in love," she said simply. Jonathon didn't miss her fingers toying with the silver band on her wrist. He wisely chose to ignore the unconscious gesture. "Age has no bearing providing the family approves of the union and the parents feel the couple capable of providing for a family. However, traditionally, a woman doesn't usually marry before her sixteenth birthday."

"So, they're to make you pretty?"

A beautiful flush swept across her cheeks. "They are to make me desirable."

Jonathon looked over the varying sizes of beads, ribbons and small feathers, then furrowed his eyebrows. Then to the woman herself, who was already irresistible. He wasn't sure how trinkets in her hair could increase that. "How?"

She picked at her fingernails and bit her lip. "Are you sure you wish to really know?"

Files in hand, he dropped them against his thigh in a dramatic rush. "Well now, yeah, I do."

"Have you ever been to Italyssa?"

"No."

Her eyes widened. "Really? I am sad for you."

"You'll have to take me some day."

"I would love to."

"Stop stalling."

The perfectly sculpted curve of her jaw shifted, drawing attention to the high sweep of her cheeks. Yes, the woman was breathtaking. The fact that her skin tone was a solid two shades darker than his, and she had a figure most women in Sziveria failed miserably at attempting to duplicate, only made her all the more appealing. There was no one like her in his country.

"Fine," she practically snapped, her intense teal eyes flashing.

She inhaled deeply and as she exhaled lifted her hands high above her head. Then, before Jonathon had a chance to brace himself, she was a flurry of movement, sound and color. The beads on her ankles and around her wrists jingled and chimed. Each rapid movement of her feet rising and falling echoed in the sensuous rhythm of her hips and up through her shoulders.

The gown he'd only thought was loose until her full curves danced within, strained the fabric across her breast, hips, belly and rear, no longer leaving anything to his imagination. And when she spun, not once, or twice, but three times, her hips rolling before each twist, her hair flew out in an arc of rainbows and texture. The light shimmered and danced, mesmerizing, demanding equal attention for its contribution to the seductive play of female movement.

When she stopped, one hand rested on a hip, one foot braced on her toes and the other hand in the air, Jonathon almost sank to his knees. His body remembered to breathe, while his heart pounded so hard he was shocked he wasn't in pain. Well, the discomfort pressing against the front of his pants didn't count. Hopefully she wouldn't look down.

"Desirable, huh?" Jonathon scratched under his chin at the day's growth.

"Yes."

He waved the folders in a curve before himself. "All the women in your country learn… that?"

With a sighing chuckle, she returned to the desk at the back of the library. "Italyssa is a country of wind, water, light and warmth. There is movement in everything. The men and women of my nation are born dancing. We have a dance for every stage of life, from birth to death."

Jonathon stared, not daring to follow, not trusting himself to stop once he reached the desk. "The men dance like that, too?"

"Well, they are a compliment to their female partner. I don't think I could explain very well, not with how a dance is here. At home, the woman sets the pace, the…" She waved her hand around, her eyes looking to the ceiling in thought. "Ah, yes, the mood, the energy she wishes those around to see. He must be an extension of her."

"Does a woman dance with a man before she decides to marry him?"

Sylphine lowered herself behind the desk. "Sometimes."

The single spoken word held an edge of incompletion. "Why?"

Another alluring flush bloomed across her cheeks. "An answer I'm not ready to give."

"Fair enough. How long are you staying?"

She shrugged and pulled a folder closer. "When my father says it's safe to go home. I think it's safe now, he disagrees."

"If the situation were reversed and Ramsey could be away from internal conflict, I'd send her somewhere safe too. Your father is simply being cautious."

"I have traveled and resided in countries deeper in turmoil than the small annoyance of people, who know nothing of how things are handled, rebelling. If they knew how hard our enforcemen are working to figure out what's going on, they'd be thankful, as they used to be. But whispered lies have made them uneasy, distrusting. Foolish." She shook her head, a sadness crossing over her striking face. "Sadly, I fear it's reached the point that any reminder given would simply be viewed as a lie to appease rather than the absolute protection it provides. My country may be in for a sad future if something can't be fixed, and soon."

Uneasiness swept through Jonathon, dispersing any lingering desire. "We're facing a similar problem here. I have no idea how to stop the descension into chaos before we reach the state Italyssa finds itself in."

Her jewel toned stare narrowed. "For how long?"

"I don't know, months. I've only now begun hearing people whisper about nothing being done."

"Well, our whispers have become shouts. If history is any teacher, soon there will be blood."

Jonathon sighed. "I hope you and your father can help avoid that outcome."

"I, as well. He may not have the political power, but he a lot of people respect him on our island."

A rapid, sharp knock sounded on the front door. Since Jonathon was never officially off duty, he couldn't ignore the intrusion. Pointing the file at Sylphine as he walked out, he said, "By the way, if you ever dance like that again, you *will* marry me."

She winked. "Promises, promises, Jonathon, dear."

"I mean it. Consider yourself warned, Sylphine-love."

Her chin propped on her hand thoughtfully was the last thing he saw as he left the library. Let her wonder how much he meant the words. If he knew she'd touch him, he'd make her put those Sympath abilities to the test. But a small part of him wondered, after learning how much emotion she was capable of feeling, if her distance wasn't due to her gift. Or perhaps, unlike Sean Blackbain, who used his to an advantage, Sylphine felt herself cursed.

Jonathon opened the door and then stared in shock at the man who towered over him by almost five inches. "Master Guardian Raiventon, is everything okay?"

"Yes, sorry to bother you so late. I'd have written, but I'm a little nervous about messages being intercepted."

Jonathon's lips twitched. "I can see how an interceptor would have that problem."

"Yes, much like an investigator doesn't trust the security of his home to another person."

Jonathon inclined his head and stepped away from the door, motioning for Kevin to enter. "You would of course be correct. What can I do for you?"

Kevin closed the door after he walked through. "I've had two break-ins recently. I can't find any evidence someone did anything but walk right through a door, which doesn't make any sense since they're always locked. Usually in triplicate. I was wondering if you have time to come look everything over. I'm not an investigator, I'm thinking I must be missing something."

"Anything stolen?"

Kevin shook his head. "No, nothing. They were personal attacks on me."

That piqued Jonathon's curiosity. "Why?"

"Wish I knew."

"I'll take a look tomorrow morning, before I go to Division."

Kevin held his hand out. "Thank you, I appreciate it."

"Sure. Can't really say no to the man married to Arch Guardian Synintel's daughter, can I?"

Kevin rolled his eyes, reaching for the door. "You could. If I thought doing so wouldn't bring down a ridiculous amount of wrath, I'd say you should."

"Well, I'm not worried about the wrath, not from you."

Kevin laughed. "And I'm not worried about it from him."

ARMS CROSSED OVER HIS CHEST, Kevin braced a shoulder against the wall while Jonathon crouched down and slid his hand over the edge of the front door for the third time, a heavy frown on his face. Black slacks pulled tight across Jonathon's thighs, while his pale gray shirt barely caught the glow of the rising sun. The golden threads on the black Haven City Enforcement Services field jacket with his last name and rank stood out in stark contrast, stressing their importance for anyone who cared.

"I don't see anything. There's no indication of locks being picked, no sign of stress on the wood for any of the frames or the doors." Jonathon sighed and shook his head, standing.

Kevin worked his jaw, his attention on the brass door-knob. "They used a key."

"I hate to say you're right, since it seems to mean someone has a key who shouldn't, but it's the only explanation." Jonathon ran a hand through his short, dark hair, bracing most of his weight on his back leg. "I guess the biggest question now is how long is your enemy list, and who would be trusted enough to get inside."

"Inside to have access to the keys?"

Jonathon raised and dropped an arm. "Access to the keys or access to staff that uses the keys, take your pick."

Kevin tapped his fingers against his bicep in thought. Most of Raina's genteel client base couldn't care less about him. And since they were all vetted by Synintel, only one stood in stark contrast to the others. Shield Guardian Enbrackon.

Up until a week ago, Kevin hadn't even known of the man's existence. Now he loathed the wretched Guardian with almost everything he had. Kidnapping the woman he felt as close to as a sister ensured the animosity. Then the team had learned someone was eradicating witnesses, falsifying records to make their deaths look like suicides rather than murder. Since Enbrackon was the Shield Guardian over Haven City Enforcement Services, Kevin was more than a little suspicious of Enbrackon's involvement. Now there was a real chance Enbrackon had weaseled his way into obtaining a key to Kevin's house. The thought made him flex his hands in rage.

"If you weren't a thief, how'd you get a key?" Kevin asked, more out loud to himself than an actual question.

"If asking the lady of the house to part with one wasn't an option?"

"Correct."

Jonathon shrugged. "Most of the wealth in Haven City doesn't know the meaning of the word no and thinks they're a gift to anyone below their station. Seduction is usually the best method of getting what one wants within any home. Be it information or thievery."

"Thievery through staff is common among the rankings?"

"Sadly, yes. A high-born woman sees a necklace she likes on hostess, she uses her body with a footman to get said necklace two weeks later. A Key Guardian who runs a small bakery chain tastes the recipe from a Primary Guardian who owns one of the highest grossing pastry shops in the city, and uses the Primary Guardianesses stylist elite to obtain the recipe for him. Sometimes the thief receives some sort of compensation for the effort, sometimes not, depends on the perceived emotional involvement."

Kevin grunted. "Love."

"The idea of love, anyway."

The sarcastic reply had Kevin lifting a brow. Clearly the topic of relationships wasn't something Jonathon cared for much. Kevin couldn't really fault the man, he probably saw more romance gone wrong than anyone else in the city.

"Did you check pockets?" Jonathon asked. "See if anyone had a key?"

"I didn't find anything, which is why I suspected a break-in."

Jonathon looked at the door again. "What about their boots?"

"What about them?"

"Did you check there? I have found boots hold a lot more than socks and feet over the years," Jonathon said with a weary frown.

"No," Kevin admitted on a sigh. "I didn't even think about checking their boots."

"I bet you would have found your mysterious key."

Kevin turned on his heel and left the vestibule. He quietly sought out Mrs. Taft. Raina was with a client, her first of the day. Soon her next would likely arrive, and Kevin wanted his personal inquiry within the house conducted before gossip had a chance to sneak out.

In the formal dining room, Jonathon stood beside Kevin while Mrs. Taft escorted all the household staff to stand in a line along the far wall. When the last employee took position, Jonathon stepped forward and walked slowly by the fidgeting members. He backed up twice and then kept walking.

Kevin did his own searching from further away, taking in the slight differences in uniforms that spoke of their assigned areas within the house, be it in the kitchen, household chores, or gardening duty. Most of the women wore sensible hair-styles, ponytails or buns, while the men had close cropped cuts. Kevin wondered if that was Raina's doing, or the Arch Guardians.

Jonathon returned, but kept his back to the group when he spoke. "Two of the women are wearing jewelry they likely can't afford. One is a ring, the other is wearing a bracelet, necklace, and hair clips."

"Ring could be an inheritance." Kevin kept his voice low.

"Could be."

So that left the woman with more on her person than she would likely be able to obtain on her own. Kevin searched the line again and spotted the young housekeeper. The gold bracelet studded with amethyst glinted in the sun streaming through the tall window behind her. She played with an amethyst teardrop necklace on a silk choker. Little purple flowers clipped around the dark blonde bun atop her head made Kevin sigh.

Her green eyes laced with flecks of gold widened when he approached. Kevin stared down at the large stone still rolling between her slender fingers. "The rest of you may be dismissed."

Mrs. Taft made quick work of clearing the dining room, but lingered when everyone else had gone. Since the staff was technically under her charge, Kevin didn't argue her remaining. However, the young woman was about to find out how much the goods she'd traded for her mistress's safety were truly worth. Her position in the Raiventon household was finished.

Kevin reached up and pulled one of the amethyst flowers free. "At which point did he obtain the key from you? With the bracelet, the necklace, or the pins?"

Her face lost color and she stepped back, only to hit the wall. "I-I don't know what you're talking about."

"Twice now a group of men have been able to step foot in this house well after the doors were locked. When did you give up the key to make sure that could happen? Before your lover parted with a small fortune in amethyst, or after?"

Panic set in, and her golden-green eyes flicked past Kevin to Jonathon. "I didn't give anyone a key to anywhere."

Annoyed with the lies, wishing he had Sean's magic touch, Kevin glanced over his shoulder at Jonathon, who held a look of disgust on his face. "You can tell the truth, or Master Tribunii Hunter can take you to the HCES office and ask more questions there."

Her gaze darted back to Jonathon. She licked dry lips and swallowed. "I only provided him a key to th-the servant's house."

Kevin snapped his attention to Mrs. Taft. "Do they use the same key?"

Mrs. Taft shook her head, dark curls sliced with gray bobbed around her round face. "No, my Guardian."

Flexing his jaw, he looked back to the young maid. "Try again."

The hold on the amethyst around her neck shifted from caressing to a white-knuckle grip. "I didn't want to give it to him, but he said I must not trust him if I couldn't make sure he could see me whenever he wanted, regardless of the time of day. I told him he couldn't just sneak into the house and find me, Guardianess Raiventon would see, or suspect, or someone else would."

Tears welled in her eyes and she sniffed. "He said I meant everything to him and he just couldn't bear the thought of not being able to see me whenever. He wanted to make sure I always wore what he gifted to me, so he knew I felt the same."

"Who said?" Jonathon asked, stepping forward.

Her gaze dropped to the floor, a tear sliding down her cheek. "Shield Guardian Enbrackon."

Kevin slammed his hand against the wall above her head.

She jumped and squeaked.

Turning on his heel, he walked past Mrs. Taft. "Get her out of my house. Immediately."

Lips set in a harsh line, Mrs. Taft nodded. "Without delay, my Guardian."

Out in the hall, Kevin held his hand out to Jonathon, despite feeling completely uncivil. "Thank you for your help."

Jonathon accepted and returned the offered shake. "Of course. I'm a bit concerned and shocked that Enbrackon is coming after Synintel's daughter."

Kevin frowned, but chose for now not to correct Jonathon's assumption. The less he knew, the better. "I'm not sure of the game yet, but he's definitely playing at something."

"Let me know if you need any more help."

Kevin shook his head. "You've done enough. I'm not going to risk anything more from you. Enbrackon holds the power to end your career with one pen sweep, not to mention your life with the same stroke. And we both know he has a Medical Science Investigator writing fraudulent death certificates."

Jonathon let out a huff of annoyance. "Don't remind me of that last one."

"I don't want you to be the next to go."

"Fair enough. Good luck."

Another thought had Kevin holding his hand up. "I do know another way you can help though. Cora mentioned your promised is from Italyssa."

"She is."

"Good. What can you tell me about the conflict?"

"Not as much as she could tell you."

Kevin raised a brow. "Do you think she'd meet with us?"

"I can ask. Ramsey insists she stays with us when she's in the city. Her father will send a message when he feels it's safe for her to return home."

"Please do. If we can find similarities, maybe we can get a little ahead of whatever is happening before a similar fate befalls our nation."

Jonathon's dark blue gaze narrowed. "I agree, so long as she stays out of danger."

"I'll tell you how to make sure neither of you are seen entering Sean's house." Kevin laughed and added, "Just be sure to wear shoes you don't care about."

The deep, rumbling sound of Kevin's laughter took Raina by surprise when she opened her office door for her client. Her assistant, Janice Halsley, also appeared shocked, if her leaning forward to look into the hall was any indication. The client cleared his throat in obvious displeasure, and the two women swiftly cleared the doorway. Raina muttered an apology, but didn't bother with seeing him out, far too curious about what had her husband so amused.

The next client on her list had yet to show. Not abnormal for the wealthy merchant, who figured a late entrance was fashionable and showed how important he was. She glanced over her shoulder at her assistant. "Will you please make sure Mr. Willingham's files are prepared, Miss Halsley?"

Janice's short auburn hair slid into her eyes when she nodded in understanding, grasping a thick section of her dark blue skirt before stepping into the corridor. "Of course. I'll also make sure Guardian Tillabrook's files are ready, since his appointment follows."

Janice's attention to detail was one of the reasons Raina continued to give her assistant raises. She didn't need someone else stealing the talented young woman away. Well, Raina wasn't sure if she could truly consider her *young* since Janice was twenty-one to Raina's twenty-three. "Thank you."

Kevin shook a man's hand. Slightly shorter, but similar in build, the man had neatly cut and styled dark hair and held himself with an air of authority Raina had come to recognize in those who served, and therefore held a certain amount of power over those who didn't. As usual, Kevin was barefoot with the sleeves of his untucked dark orange shirt rolled halfway up his forearms. At least his slate gray slacks didn't appear to have been picked up off the floor.

The man seemed to notice her before Kevin, his deep blue gaze passing her direction before offering his hand to Kevin once again. They shook and then the man turned, nodding to her with a polite greeting, and left behind her client. Raina barely had a chance to recognize the Enforcement Services emblem on his jacket.

"Why was someone from HCES here?" Raina asked, rubbing her arms against a sudden chill.

"Because I asked him to come."

Raina glanced at the closed front door. "Why?"

Kevin raked his hand through his already unruly hair on a sigh, leaving more dark blond strands sticking out in odd places. "I needed help figuring out how the break-ins happened."

"Did you?"

Frowning, he turned and headed down the side hall to his study. Raina had to practically run to keep up with his much longer strides. Why was he walking away from her?

"You won't like it," he called over his shoulder.

Raina paused. When he disappeared into his study, she took a deep breath and followed. "Would anyone care to learn how their home was invaded?"

Perched against the corner of his desk, long legs crossed at the ankles, arms folded over his broad chest, his relaxed appearance made him seem less imposing than normal. Raina entered the office and then hesitated at closing the door. They were married, but she knew for a fact now, having been caught alone with the man on multiple occasions, it wasn't exactly *safe* for her.

"Everyone can hear, or just you," he said, as if reading her thoughts.

Not wanting to look the coward, Raina closed the door. She then designated a perfect square around herself. If she remained in her spot, and he remained in his, all would be well. Squaring her shoulders, she met his stare. "What have you learned?"

"First I need you to answer a question, honestly."

"Have I lied to you?"

The set of his jaw shifted and his lips thinned. "No, but I don't want you to evade either."

Oh, you mean like what you've been doing? This time it was her turn to frown. "I will do my best."

He took a deep breath and then asked, "How long has Shield Guardian Enbrackon been your client?"

Raina drew her brows together in a frown. "What does he have to do with anything?"

"How long?"

The no-nonsense way he snapped the question made her spine straighten. "Around five months."

"And did he ever arrive early or stay longer than your business required?"

"I don't understand."

Kevin's mouth flattened into a straight line. Raina's fingers twitched to smooth across the unhappy expression and bring back the full, kissable lips she much preferred. She bit on her bottom lip and reminded herself of her designated square.

"Did you ever notice him staying longer than he should, or arriving much sooner than necessary for your meetings?"

She worked her bottom lip a bit more in thought. "I normally wait at my office door for my clients to enter or exit. If he arrived early or stayed late, I wouldn't know. But why would he?"

Kevin's shoulders rolled and he shifted his hips along the

table. The graceful, fluid movement conveying unease left Raina's throat dry. What was wrong with her? A simple, normal action left her wondering if she closed the space between him and demanded a kiss, if he'd laugh or give in. Closing her eyes against the sudden fantasy, she blamed her lack of sleep. Rest hadn't quite found her since Kevin's embrace, and she doubted a repeat would help matters. No, she needed to keep herself, and her daydreams, far from him. Resolved, she met his curious stare.

"Well?" she asked when he continued to study her.

"I'm trying to decide if you'll believe what I say or not."

His honesty shocked and infuriated her. "Why wouldn't I believe you?"

He shrugged. "Why would you?"

Because you're my husband. She opened her mouth to say just that, then clamped it shut. While she'd had four years to get used the idea of being a wife, the man standing across from her was little more than a stranger. For all purposes, she knew Shield Guardian Enbrackon better. And Kevin acknowledged the truth, even if she hadn't. Uncomfortable, Raina shifted her weight and crossed her arms over her chest.

"I guess I'll decide after I hear what you say."

"One of your housekeepers has admitted to giving Enbrackon a key to the house."

"Why would she do that?"

Kevin heaved a long sigh, unwrapping his arms and then grasping the edge of his desk. "Because he was showering her with gifts."

A muffled knock sounded behind her. Raina ignored the likely summons. "Why would he give her anything? She's my employee."

Kevin arched a brow. "And because she's your employee, someone can't give her nice things?"

Raina waved her hand, annoyed. "That's not what I meant. How could they possibly know each other well enough for him to give her something? My housekeepers are not to be seen by my clients, so they work odd hours downstairs."

"Then he made quite the effort to not only seek her out, but to seduce her as well."

The knock came again, louder, but the shock of Kevin's words made her ignore it again. "Seduce her? You must be mistaken."

"She said it herself."

Anger burned hot enough to make Raina clench her fists. Whether at the conniving housekeeper, or that the Shield Guardian could have seduced someone under her roof while spouting emotions for her, she wasn't certain. Surely she wasn't such a bad judge of character? "Then she was lying."

Kevin reached into his pocket and withdrew a glittering amethyst flower pin. "The small fortune in jewelry says otherwise."

Ignoring her designated square, Raina marched forward and snatched the hairpin from Kevin's fingers. "Then she was mistaken in his identity. Why would a Shield Guardian seduce one of my housekeepers, and for a key no less? What purpose could he possibly have?"

"How do you think he knows what you'll be wearing at a function you both will attend?"

Raina fisted the pin, disregarding the bite of the stones against her palm. "He didn't sneak in and look for himself, I assure you."

"I have no doubt of that, since he already had a spy in your midst. And the key wasn't for him, but for the men he sent. Twice."

Processing Kevin's logic, Raina glanced past him, to the blank wall beyond his desk. The evidence was strong, and yet... She shook her head. "He has no reason to send men to my house, to harm either of us. I can accept the spy rational, he has matched me twice now. But needing entry into the house to hurt one of us doesn't fit. He's the First Prefect, the highest-ranking enforcer in the Haven City Enforcement Service. Risking his career, and his Guardian rank, by seducing a housekeeper for a key makes no sense."

His fingers wrapped around both her wrists, gently pulling her forward. "Why are you defending him?"

Because he's the means to my freedom. Months of hard, demanding work, accomplished without her father's knowledge, would be wasted if Kevin's suspicions were correct. Raina couldn't afford the outcome. Enbrackon had made it clear he had the social connections she needed to move out from underneath the Arch Guardians control. So far, he'd proven right. "I'm not. I'm stating the obvious. He'd never risk such an action, not with his career."

The darkening of Kevin's eyes was the only indication her words had affected him. His touch remained light, his thumbs caressing the sensitive inner flesh of her wrists. "Perhaps he felt the risk worth the outcome."

Despite the distraction of his touch, Raina somehow managed to think past the maddening sensations traveling from her wrist straight to her stomach. "I don't see how you or I injured would benefit him."

His touch caressed up her arms to her jaw, where his attention focused on her mouth.

Raina forgot to breathe.

"That is the question, isn't it?" Kevin urged her closer until she stood between his knees that she hadn't even realized he'd parted. He leaned forward. "Am I the first man to have kissed you?"

The heat and strength of his presence flowed over her, overwhelming her senses and turning her mind to mush. "Yes."

"Guardian or Guardianess Raiventon, please answer!" A muffled voice begged from the other side of the door.

Before Raina could blink, Kevin slid away and was

halfway across the room. The haze quickly cleared. With the return of her higher thought functions, a rush of heat swept her cheeks over how quickly he managed to make her senseless. Along with the embarrassment came a clarity to his question. Why would he ask if he were the first man to have kissed her? Unless he believed someone else held the distinction.

Opening her palm, she glanced down at the pretty purple bauble. Fury hard and swift made her foot stomp. She bit her tongue to keep from screeching like a banshee.

Her rich burgundy skirt swished around her ankles as she turned on her heel. The second he opened the door, Raina rushed past, grabbing the elbow of her assistant. She looked back just long enough to snap a livid glare at her husband. She would have flicked the hairpin at him for good measure, but his suspicions made her hold onto it. Despite being the means to her freedom, Shield Guardian Enbrackon had some questions to answer the next time she saw him.

8

———

"He has more sway over her than I do," Kevin admitted with a heavy sigh, throwing a rock into the pond he and Sean walked around. The flat stone skipped three times, leaving smooth ripples in the water before disappearing into the inky depth.

They were just two friends taking a casual stroll in Atherton Square. Nothing suspicious, and no means of plotting anything beyond life. At least that's what they hoped if anyone had bothered to follow either of them.

Sean tore at a leaf he'd picked up at some point. Little pieces floated away with each step. "He had Kat in knots after only a few minutes with her."

"She was drugged."

"His words were toxic."

Kevin met Sean's amber gaze, recognized the seriousness in them and frowned. As they continued along, Kevin searched the bank for another suitable skipping stone. "If I knew what hold he had on her, maybe I could figure out why he's so important. As it is, she always seems more annoyed by him than pleased to be in his presence."

"At least you know it's not seduction then."

Rolling a stone between his fingers, Kevin focused on the cool, smooth surface. "Of that, I can thankfully be positive."

The crisp, evening air blew hair around Sean's face. "Do you believe he's tried?"

Kevin nodded. "I do. And I think he relishes in the fact everyone believes he's succeeded."

Sean tossed the rest of the leaf and rubbed his hands together to finish cleaning them. "Except you're still married."

"Well, no one said I wasn't a fool." Kevin flicked his wrist, sending the stone skidding along the water's surface. He smiled. Five jumps before sinking.

Sean sighed. "You aren't a fool."

"No? Then explain why I agreed to marry an Arch Guardians daughter to save my rank, only to be forced to give it up to save her honor? And she doesn't even trust me." Kevin shook his head, kicking at a cluster of rocks near the shore of the pond.

"You joke."

"I wish."

Sean let out a long strong string of curses. "Every time I think it's treason to hate that man, he gives me no reason to feel loyal." He sighed again. "And you're going to?"

Kevin reached down for a stone, inspected it, discarded it and chose another. "What choice do I have? His nomination and subsequent vote is out of my hands. If he doesn't go in my favor, I'm back to where my family started. In a poor fishing village not even within Sziveria's legal jurisdiction, only their protection."

"It'd serve him right if she went with you," Sean growled.

"And we both know she doesn't deserve such a fate."

"I'll leave that for you to decide. I don't know her well enough."

Continuing along the edge of the pond, they both nodded to an elderly couple enjoying the mild late summer evening.

"Tell me you wouldn't have sacrificed more for Kat, even before you knew you loved her."

Sean clasped his hands behind his back. "Point made. Though I should warn you, I loved her before I knew what the emotion stirring in my chest even meant. That particular train tends to hit fast and hard."

Subconsciously, Kevin rubbed the center of his chest. While he couldn't deny his desire for Raina, something he'd been fighting since the first moment he saw her standing noble and fearless at her father's desk to sign their marriage contract, love wasn't something he could afford to have for the pixie. Once she claimed that part of him, he knew he'd never get it back. "Noted. By the way, I've told Asherwick how to meet with you without anyone knowing he's at your residence. He's supposed to be bringing his promised, who's from Italyssa. I'm hoping we can compare timelines and methods for the uprising."

"I think I'd rather figure out why the First Prefect for Haven City has gone after my Interceptor. Twice."

"At least he hasn't gone after your wife again."

"The only reason he still lives."

Kevin scoffed. "That, and he hasn't as of yet harmed mine. Enbrackon's not the only one who knows how to hide a body. And if he keeps playing games, those who hold *his* puppet strings are going to learn the hard way."

ALONE IN HER STUDY, Raina twisted the simple gold band on her ring finger in thought. The dying rays of the sun cast long, pink shadows across her empty office. Four years ago, she'd fought being offended at the unadorned band. Women of her station often had prominent bands ornamented with sparkling gemstones to show off how much more their husband loved them. Station and perceived wealth through all things shiny hadn't changed in the history of humanity.

As she fingered the smooth, modest surface, she realized the ring signified everything her husband was. Deceptively uncomplicated. Only recently had she also realized his wedding band matched hers. Another uncommon act. One that made hers more valuable than any other she'd ever seen.

And the more she turned the newly discovered treasure around her finger, the more she realized she wanted, no *needed,* to trust her husband with the plans for her future.

Fear however, was a fickle friend. At any moment a man dressed in the Arch Guardian Synintel's green livery could arrived at her door and whisk Kevin away for another four years. Then where would she be? Absolutely nowhere. Stuck, with only her father's handouts and no accomplishments to claim.

A subtle rap sounded on her open door, disrupting her thoughts. She glanced up from her hands to Mrs. Taft's concerned face. "My Guardianess, Shield Guardian Enbrackon is asking to see you."

She straightened in the oversized chair she sat in, her feet hitting the floor. "He's here? Now?"

The frown on the head housekeeper's face intensified. "I'm afraid so. Would you like me to tell him you're no longer accepting visitors?"

Raina licked her dry lips and thought quickly. If she sent him away, he may take the prospective clients he'd been dangling in front of her away. However, if she accepted him after hours again, the speculation, which had finally begun to die down, would return. Maybe she could compromise, meet him the vestibule and convince him to return during her regular hours.

With a plan, she rose. "I will see him where he waits."

Mrs. Taft nodded. "Very good, Guardianess."

The older woman followed dutifully behind. At the spacious vestibule, Enbrackon paced like a caged animal. For a moment, Raina considered hanging back and having Mrs.

Taft take over. A heavy, uncomfortable sensation washed through her at seeing the Shield Guardian, one she'd never dealt with before and wasn't sure how to handle.

Kevin's suspicions made her steps falter. *If* he were correct, the Shield Guardian had been sneaking around her house, seducing one of her staff and spying on her. And she couldn't call him on even one of the accusations.

As with all upper-class, anything said against them by anyone lower than their rank was often waved away. He'd deny every complaint. Since most cases *were* fraudulent, the accusations often amounting to little more than blackmail, they ended in a decent handout to keep the lies out of the gossip section. Unless the maid had solid proof her paramour was Phipps, the Shield Guardians denial meant innocence. Raina had no doubt he'd deny right up to his pretty, dark brown eyes.

Relaxing her shoulders, she forced a smile. "Shield Guardian Enbrackon, I wasn't expecting you this evening. I'd be happy to see you in the morning, before my first scheduled client."

His frame visibly loosened when he met her gaze. "I'm afraid an acquaintance of mine has had an emergency arise. His firm is unable to help on such short notice. I told him not to worry, I had the best logistics expert in the country able to help without any notice. You won't let me down, will you? Tomorrow would simply be too late."

Raina clasped her hands in front of herself and took a deep breath. "I don't see what I can do. Logistics takes time to plan accordingly, not to mention all radio signals are down until dawn."

He waved a hand while reaching with his other into his jacket pocket. Folded papers emerged. "You know I have access to a twenty-four-hour signal."

Surprised, Raina raised a brow. "The emergency is that great?"

"A shipment of medicine from Imperial Qu'in to Ravenna. It's already a week delayed, and my dear friend received word they're running dangerously short. If the shipment can't be routed, people *will* die."

"And a firm really denied such a need?"

Phipps shook his head and heaved a sad sigh. "Personal comfort is often met before the needs of others. I knew you'd have a different view. Besides, the fact that the shipment is due past a week shows their ineptitude, does it not? Why waste more time?"

Why, indeed? Raina looked away from him, focusing on the potted plant near the door. Kevin had left over an hour ago and had yet to return. Her assistant had left before that. Mrs. Taft, and Tabby, were the only staff remaining in the house. Raina was positive Mrs. Taft only remained because Kevin had yet to return. Though her very professional housekeeper would never admit it, knowing one of her hired staff members had put the Guardianess of the house in danger was a personal upset. Mrs. Taft wouldn't leave until Raina wasn't alone, even if she had to sleep in an upstairs room after her daughter left.

While Raina didn't want to contribute to another nation's growing disaster, she also didn't want to contribute to her social one. "My assistant is gone for the day. I can send word for her to arrive early and we can address the shipment if you'll leave me with all the pertinent information. We can have instructions to relay to Imperial Qu'in the moment the first communications station is open."

A frown darkened his face. "My friend and I would rest much better tonight knowing the medicine is already en route come the sun's rising. I know a frightened nation would be too."

Raina glanced nervously at Mrs. Taft, whose stern expression matched her no-nonsense uniform. "Would you mind helping me with the Shield Guardians emergency, Mrs. Taft?"

Phipps stepped forward, the papers clutched in his hand. "I don't mind helping, no need to put another person out."

Mrs. Taft's smile was anything but warm as she snatched the papers from his hand. "Helping Guardianess Raiventon is never a chore, Shield Guardian. And while not her assistant, I do believe I'm more familiar with her needs."

Red bloomed across the Shield Guardians cheeks. His shoulders squared and his chest filled with air. "Master Guardian Raiventon must not be much of a man around this house if his female servants behave in such a manner." WIth a swift flick of his wrist, the papers were back in his control. "You will *never* speak to me out of turn again, or take something from my hands without my express permission, is that understood?"

Too stunned by Phipps condescending treatment toward one of the few people Raina trusted in her life, she couldn't even sputter a protest when he grabbed her arm and all but dragged her down the corridor to her office. Her feet stumbled. With a rough yank, he hauled her against the side of his body, his hand wrapping possessively around her waist. When Raina went to release his hold, he tightened to the point of pain. Once they were inside her office, he freed her. And firmly shut the door, and Mrs. Taft out, with a swift click of the lock.

Raina put distance between them. The sun's rays had fully died, leaving the room bathed in the delicate blue light of twilight, visible, yet strangely difficult to see in. With an ease that alarmed Raina, Phipps went to the oil lamp beside the door, locating the matches on a small shelf beneath without asking for their location. As if he'd already known, had already lit that very lamp before. The match flared to life.

"I asked for your help in good conscience. I did so politely. I will not be so polite again. Do you understand?" Light burst from the lamp the second he touched the flame to the wick. His dark stare made her stop in the center of the room.

Unsure what to do, she nodded.

He shook the match out. "Good. We've come so far my dear, I'd hate to have to undo all our good intentions. Now, be a good girl and pull out the map of Imperial Qu'in. I don't have enough time for further pleasantries."

Raina thought quickly, glancing to the shelves that held her neatly rolled maps. She'd never been locked alone in a room with a man before, and Phipps certainly wasn't the one she ever wanted to be unaccompanied with. "Qu'in is eight hours ahead of us, it's currently two in the morning there. I don't see what help I could be for another four to six hours."

Before she could scramble away from him, Phipps grabbed her arm and forced her around the desk. "Let me worry about the time. You do your job that I, and my acquaintance, are going to pay you handsomely for."

The moment he released her, Raina put space between them again. "Why did you lock the door?"

"I don't want to be disturbed."

"My husband won't stand for it."

His dark eyes betrayed nothing, but the harsh line of his mouth showed his displeasure. "Raiventon doesn't concern me. I can have him in handcuffs and charged with any number of offenses before you sputter a protest. And trust me, he'd likely deserve all of them. You know nothing of the man your father forced you to marry, or you'd never have signed a contract binding you to him."

Raina's heart pounded and she swallowed against panic. While she didn't trust his words against Kevin, she had no doubt of the threat. Enbrackon was the one man who could draw up trump accusations and make sure they stuck. At least until her father, or another higher-ranking official, stepped in. As the First Prefect of Haven City Enforcement Services, only a higher-ranking Guardian with the First Intelligence Office, or Sziveria National Investigative Division could interfere.

Without another choice, Raina went to her maps and pulled free Qu'in's and Northern Africa's. The Shield Guardian laid out the papers he'd been carrying. He lit both the mounted lamps behind her desk, bathing the space in workable light. Fading pink tendrils still clung to the low clouds in the sky. The Shield Guardians threats against Kevin may frighten her, but she somehow doubted they'd concern her husband. Hopefully once the light died completely, he'd be home. Not too much longer…

Laying the maps out, she secured them with heavy brass holders. "I'm assuming the papers contain all the information I need to properly fill out the shipping manifest?"

"They do, along with port information and the final destination."

Raina shifted into professional mode, a safe, familiar place. She reached for the papers and looked over the information, comparing it with the maps laid out before her. Three times she checked the destination. "Is this city spelled correctly?"

The Shield Guardian shifted closer. "Yes."

Raina frowned. "It's not on my map of Ravenna."

"Oh, it's not a city, it's a camp."

"What's the nearest city?"

He moved closer still, until his hip touched hers and the sharp, pungent scent of his cologne invaded her space. "I believe it's written below. See, right here."

Raina swallowed and tried to focus as his hand slid around her back to touch the paper under her right wrist, brushing her breast in the process. Revulsion slithered along her spine.

"Yes, I do see, thank you." Moving would bring his hand entirely in contact with her breast, so she stayed still.

"Good. There's a rail line that runs to the camp from that city."

"That will help. The camp needs the medicine the most?"

"Yes. Half will be offloaded at the dock. The other is to be taken to this camp. They are distributing to the poorest areas of the nation, the ones that cling to the edge of the Uninhabited Zones, where land is cheapest to purchase or work."

The words seemed planned, rehearsed. Raina forced away unease. "What is the problem that the ship isn't able to make port in Ravenna?"

"There is no ship. That's why we need you. The shipment is large and no one has had the available room. You've never failed in securing a means for transport, regardless of the size."

Raina chewed on her bottom lip, overlooking the map. She opened her top drawer and pulled out a binder of the carriers and known transport companies. "Imperial Qu'in is still a very primitive country, their exports are marginal. As a result, most trading companies don't export from there, and their ships are small."

"Again, why I'm here."

The clipped tone of his voice made her stiffen in wariness. "I need space to work."

His hand left the page, but didn't leave her, settling on her hip. In caressing lines, he rubbed from her upper thigh to her side. "You know I've said it before, we'd make an amazing team. We could rule this city."

Uncomfortable by his forward touch, crowded and on edge, Raina gritted her teeth. "I thought you needed this route completed without delay."

He sighed. "Someday soon you will see the error of denying me. But you are correct, I do need a plan."

Only when he stepped away, did Raina allow herself to become lost in the puzzle that was routing and plotting efficiency. Looking between two maps and two lists, she solved the problem with an ease her father had attempted to recruit before her sixteenth birthday. But sending troops proficiently to their death wasn't something Raina had any interest in.

After writing out the plan in step-by-step instructions, she handed the paper to Phipps. "The shipment will need to be transported via rail from Imperial Qu'in to Vativarsa. From there, Alexandria East Shipping has a near empty vessel. If you secure space quickly, it can sail with the medicine once it's loaded. I can't handle any of the routes for you this time of day."

A smug sound escaped from Enbrackon. "Now, that wasn't so hard. Why couldn't the other firm see the solution?"

Raina shrugged. "I don't know, I don't work for them."

"I will handle the routes."

"And the manifest?"

He waved a hand. "Already done by the other firm."

"Vativarsa will require a new one."

"I will be sure the person in Imperial Qu'in is aware new documentation is needed."

Raina glided her fingers along the drawn coast of Ravenna. "I will have my assistant bill for a consultation fee."

"Don't be absurd. Full fee as if you did all the work, it's the least I can do, or rather my acquaintance can do. You saved lives, after all."

Before he could gather any of the papers up he claimed contained everything she'd have needed to get the job done for him, she picked up the one nearest to her. A shipping manifest for destination from Imperial Qu'in. But not for Ravenna. The location listed was Italyssa. As if she'd seen nothing strange, she reached for another and stacked the remaining pages for him. With hands that were steadier than her pounding heart, Raina handed him the sheets.

"Sulphur and silver compound. Is there an infection in Ravenna others need to know about?" she asked mildly, hoping he believed that's all she'd seen.

He shrugged, using the desk to straighten the papers before refolding them. "I have no idea, I only know of the importance of making sure the medicine arrives."

Slowly, Raina inched around the desk. His dark eyes fixed on her and she froze.

"I need your official route recommendation, Guardianess Raiventon."

"Since I'm not handling the assignment itself, I can get you the documentation tomorrow, during normal hours."

"Now. Alexandria East will need your logistics code for the manifest to show you set up the transit."

Dread flowed through her, forcing her to swallow. Her gaze flitted to the door. Stronger, and likely faster than her, Phipps would have her pinned to the wall before she was able to unsecure the lock. She didn't want any involvement with whatever Enbrackon was doing with the shipment he'd forced her to plot. In fact, she wasn't sure she wanted much to do with him anymore at all. She couldn't be free from a prison cell.

"But I'm not setting up transit, you are. They can leave it blank. As a private consumer, your colleague—"

"Acquaintance."

"—can make the inquiry and then purchase the space."

"He's a business making the purchase on behalf of Ravenna, who is in turn purchasing the medicine from him. As a company, he must utilize a third, neutral party, to secure the means of distribution. You know that. I need the code."

To safeguard against one country hoarding resources already scarce worldwide, many allied countries had gone into agreements that once their country's needs were met, the assets would be shared. A neutral third party kept businesses and their allies trustworthy, checking market conditions, value and additional shipments of the same resources. The use of logistics codes allowed other analysts to identify each other on the reports, and to know where to look because they usually specialized in routing specifics commodities. While Raina didn't, she managed whatever someone brought to her, knowing who specialized in what *did* make her job easier.

Raina gritted her teeth and kept from fisting her hands. Technically, Phipps had her code already. It was located on the dozens of manifests she'd filled out for the shipments leaving Sziveria ports she'd arranged for him, and on the route recommendations he'd been given duplicate copies of. One for his records, one to file with the manifests. If he really wanted to use her code, he could. The only reason she could think that he'd need paperwork for this farce of a job left her cold and more than a little scared. He needed the paper trail.

"But I'm not securing anything, you are. I simply advised."

Anger rivaling his earlier mood returned, turning his cheeks bright pink and making his already dark eyes black. She gasped as he snatched her wrist and yanked her forward so hard her hip slammed into the corner of the desk. Her desk chair appeared behind her knees, hitting the backs of her legs and forcing her to sit.

"Fill out the damn paper, Lorraina."

"O-okay."

Phipps released her wrist and stepped away, his focus on each small movement she made. Raina was careful to keep them minor, reaching only for what she needed. Her wrist and hip burned, as did tears threatening to spill down her cheek. Being treated like a bad child was a wholly unpleasant experience.

The paper trembled slightly when she lifted it from her desk drawer, along with a pen. She quickly filled out the sheet, hesitating at the code box.

"Don't even think about lying, I *do* have your number and will compare them."

Raina resisted the urge to hum in fear. After filling out the correct information, she handed him the paper. All the sheets disappeared into his jacket.

Raising her chin to show annoyance, she stated, "Now, if that will be all, I'd like to retire for the evening."

A predatory light entered his gaze. "But we're all alone, without the threat of intrusion. How could I possibly let the potential slide from my grasp?"

Before she could rise, he had her pinned in the chair, a hand on each chair arm. Raina pressed herself into the leather, trying to put distance between them in vain. His mouth crushed to hers at the same time his hand fisted around her breast. She whimpered and turned her face away. His tongue slid along her cheek, leaving a wet trail to her ear. In painful squeezes, his fingers dug into her tender flesh.

Terrified, Raina grabbed his wrist and tried to pull his hand free. He subdued her attempt, gripping her forearm and forcing her touch to him. The hard evidence of his arousal ground against her palm. Bile rose in her throat. His fingers bit into her flesh as she tried to wrench her hand from his crotch. She pressed her other hand into his hip for leverage, but he didn't budge or release her.

"Do you see how much you make me want you? But then, you've always known, you've always teased. You don't have to pretend anymore. Why waste the energy?"

"No, I-I haven't," she denied. "Please stop."

The grasp on her arm tightened to the point of agony. Holding her hostage, his fingers moved to hers and covered them, forcing her to grip his length through the fabric. His grinding turned to outright thrusting and she bit her lip as a tear slid down her cheek.

Breath escaped his lips in harsh puffs. He continued to squeeze her breast as he pumped into her hand. "It's okay to admit it. We're alone."

The tip of his tongue snaked into her ear. She grimaced and fought the heave of her stomach. His fingernails dug into the flesh of her hand as she continued the useless struggle to get free. What else could she do? Bite him? Kick, maybe? She didn't fight, she never had the need, so she wasn't sure what to do. The bulge in her hand grew thicker while his thrusting increased. His labored breaths became rougher into her ear. All the while she was helpless in the role he'd forced her into.

Using her free hand and both her feet this time, Raina shoved firmly against Phipps. The action took him by surprise. He tumbled back onto the desk. Raina scurried into the chair, the skirt of her gown bunched beneath her feet. She grasped the back of the chair for support and attempted to keep balance so the thing didn't topple over, sending her through the large window behind her.

Fury turned Phipps' beautiful face into ugly, harsh lines. His fingers arched like claws reached for her. Panic quickened in Raina's stomach. No matter how she looked at her situation, she had nowhere to go but through the glass to get away from his reach. Shock registered on the Shield Guardians face a split second before he was yanked off his feet and across her desk.

Paper tore and fluttered. The heavy brass holders thumped to the floor. Without stopping, Kevin dragged the Shield Guardian across Raina's office and into the corridor as if the man weighed nothing. Not once did he look over his shoulder. Phipps' feet attempted to gain traction on the carpet, his arms flailed at his sides. Incoherent words sputtered from his mouth.

Raina scrambled out of the chair. She kept a safe distance from her client-turned-aggressor while Kevin rudely showed him to the door. But he didn't open it, rather he hauled Enbrackon up and shoved him hard against the solid wood surface. Gasping, Raina's steps halted and she grabbed the edge of the wall, hiding from view.

"If I catch you in my house again, you won't live to leave," Kevin's deep voice threatened. An odd shiver raced down Raina's spine and made her fingers tighten on the corners edge.

A smug expression entered the Shield Guardians gaze. "You can't threaten me. I'll make sure you're holed up in a cell so deep not even the Arch Guardian will be able to find you."

Kevin released Enbrackon with a sudden step back. The man crumbled to the floor in an embarrassing heap. "I'm not threatening, Enbrackon. I'm giving you the benefit of a warning. You won't get a second one. Stay away from my wife."

Kevin didn't wait for Phipps to move from the doorway. He opened it, shoving the man along the floor. He hauled the Shield Guardian up again, and threw him outside. Then, with the swift turn of two locks, his gray eyes, darker than the worst thunderstorm she'd seen, settled on her.

9

———

While Kevin wanted to be furious at more than Enbrackon, he knew he couldn't blame Raina for what happened in her office. Yes, he could fault her for being foolish enough to see the predator after hours, but not for what transpired. He had to keep reminding himself she was okay with each slow step closer to her cowering body around the corner, and each deep, centering breath.

The second he opened his arms, she rushed into his embrace. Closing his eyes, Kevin let the warmth of her ground him. She was safe. Her hand fisted in his shirt behind his back. Her face pressed into his chest. Kevin's fingers threaded into her bound hair, forcing pins free until the silky tresses flowed over his forearms.

Though shorter than him by a foot, somehow her body managed to fit perfectly against his. Every inch of her pressed into him. Despite the proof of her condition, he had to hear it from her. "Are you all right?"

A faint tremble flowed through her body and Kevin tightened his hold. "Y-yes."

Leaning back enough to see her face, he gently molded his

hands to her jaw. He searched her pale brown eyes glistening with unshed tears. "He didn't hurt you?"

Her fingers tightened in his shirt, pulling it snug across his shoulders. A tear slid down her cheek as she closed her eyes. "No."

That single streak of liquid heartache was enough to break him. Kevin sank to his knees, making her slightly taller than him. Unable to keep her hold, she released his shirt, her hands coming to his biceps. His fingers delved back into her hair, as he rested his forearms on her shoulders. Closing his eyes again, he brought her forehead to his.

"I am so sorry I wasn't home."

She sobbed, her grip tightened on the underside of his arms. "I am such a fool. I fear I have made a mistake I don't know if even my father can fix. I am the one who needs to apologize. I didn't listen to you, or even Synintel. I trusted the wrong viper."

"Have I ever given you reason to believe I didn't have your best interests in mind?"

She shook her head. "No, but I believed my father owned you, so you had *his* before mine."

Knowing he shouldn't, but unable to stop himself, he confessed, "You are the only one who owns me, princess. I will do anything for you, and your father knows it."

"Why?"

Kevin sighed, his fingers gently curling in the softness of her hair. "I don't know."

In a timid flutter, her lips brushed across his. Kevin froze, knowing he should take the innocent kiss and nothing more. But his body wouldn't listen. Before he could rationalize the insanity of his actions, his mouth captured hers, demanding entry. Without hesitation, she opened for him, her tongue sliding along his with the same urgent need coiled deep inside his stomach. Her sweet scent surrounded him, made him breathe deep even as he struggled to remember how.

Her hands slid from his arms to his neck and hair. A desperate whimper escaped from deep in her throat. Kevin sat back on his haunches. Without urging from him, she straddled his lap. The skirt of her gown pooled between them and flowed in waves around their legs.

For long minutes, Kevin allowed himself the beauty of her innocent passion, of knowing she was unharmed by the evil that had almost taken Sean's wife. And if they'd been anywhere besides the very public vestibule, he'd make her forget the frightening moments locked away with the Shield Guardian. But somewhere Mrs. Taft still wandered the house, and her daughter as well since Raina had yet to retire.

Regretfully, he broke the kiss. She blinked and frowned. Kevin smiled, smoothing hair he'd managed to make a terrible mess of away from her beautiful, flushed face.

"We aren't truly alone."

The pink deepened on her cheeks and she pressed her lips together. "You seem to make me forget I'm a lady."

He gave her a quick, chaste kiss, before helping her stand. "That's probably because I don't know how to be a gentleman."

Her frown intensified. "You're more of one than the man you just threw out."

"I think the criminals he arrests have more honor than he does." Balancing on the balls of his feet, he stood, pulling his shirt free from his pants to hide the evidence of how badly he did *not* want to stop what she'd started.

She worked her bottom lip between her teeth and glanced down the corridor. "I believe you may be correct. And if he had me do what I think he did, he may very well be able to show up with a certificate of custody for me."

Dread mixed with anger. Kevin's hands fisted at his side. "What did you do?"

Tears gathered in her eyes again. "I think I may have helped him steal medicine from Italyssa."

Thinking quickly, Kevin brushed past her and walked with strides faster than she could match to her study. "When can he set it into motion?"

"He has access to a twenty-four-hour signal from the HCES offices. As for if anyone in Imperial Qu'in is able to receive this time of day, I have no idea."

Thankful she'd gone into professional mode as quickly as he had, he glanced over his shoulder. "Imperial Qu'in? They're barely able to maintain their rails, let alone a radio signal. They don't have the knowledge or resources. I doubt any station is manned for more than a handful of hours a day."

"I know, and I think they have only one at a port city. Everything else must be sent via regular correspondence. I'll know for sure when I look at my maps, I have stations marked."

Regular correspondence, otherwise known as a letter by courier. "Is the radio station at the port where the ship you sent will embark from?"

"No, I recommended sending the supply by rail to Vativarsa and boarding an Alexandria East ship."

"Bound to?"

"Ravenna."

Kevin picked up the maps that had slid free when he'd yanked Enbrackon across Raina's desk. "Show me everything."

Raina took him through the steps the Shield Guardian had asked of her, pointing out the critical cities and destinations.

"And you think he'll take the documentation to HCES tonight?" he asked.

"I don't know. His urgency could have been fake. Would he risk using the radio for such a purpose from the Enforcement Services?"

"Why not? He runs the place, no one would question him using it."

She closed her eyes. "I tried everything to keep my name from anything once I realized what he was asking of me."

Kevin focused on the maps and ground his teeth. "I hate to tell you this, but I doubt this is the first time he's asked you to do something unethical." Shaking his head in aggravation, he sighed. "How could your father have ever approved him to work with you?"

"He didn't," she said so quietly Kevin almost didn't hear her.

"What?"

Raina slid brass holders across the maps to their corners, her gaze averted. "Shield Guardian Enbrackon approached me to help several of his acquaintances who were having issues with their logistics firms about five months ago. I was tired of my father only sending simple, easy jobs my way and was ready for a challenge, and the freedom securing my own clients provided. I accepted their offer."

No, please, please tell me you weren't so foolish.

An unfamiliar sense of panic welled in Kevin's chest. He wanted to shout at her, to grab and shake her until her intelligence returned. Though after what he'd walked in on, he figured maybe she understood her mistake now. Splaying his hands across the maps, he took a deep breath.

"Do you know why your father always chose your clients?" he asked.

"Because he wanted to keep control of me, as he always has." While calm, her voice betrayed her frustration.

Kevin shook his head and closed his eyes for patience, or rather understanding. "No, he did it to keep you safe. As an individual you aren't held accountable by fair trade laws like a firm. You aren't audited yearly to keep your honesty maintained. If someone wants to do something illegal, they go to an individual, who isn't on record."

"But I have a personal code."

"Yes, Synintel assigned you one so he could keep up with

your clients, make sure they weren't using you for nefarious purposes. However, when he had one assigned, it allowed you to take on large cargo loads, not just something that takes up a corner. Essentially, you became an undocumented, yet registered means of moving anything anyone wants."

A hiss of air turned his attention to her. Pale, she leaned heavily against the desk. "How is it you know that and I don't?"

"Because you've never worked for a firm and your father handled your affairs. You just utilized your Gen-Heir ability and didn't worry about the bureaucracy."

Meeting his gaze straight on, she pulled her bottom lip into her mouth. She imparted a quick bite before releasing it, leaving a glistening sheen that drew attention to how much fuller it was from the top. Kevin's pulse quickened, remembering all too well how those lips felt across his.

"But you do."

He looked back over the maps. Either that or make her forget being upset by kissing her again. Only this time, they had privacy. "I do what?"

"Worry about bureaucracy."

"Live and breathe it." Then he amended, "Not as much as Sean, though."

Understanding widened her eyes. "My father wasn't controlling my clients. He vetted them."

"Yes. For a man who organizes strategical teams around the world, he sucks at communication."

Raina laughed, though the melody was more sad than happy. "I think he communicates very well for what's important to him."

Kevin faced her and traced his fingers along the smooth curve of her jaw. "Raina, you're more important to him than you realize."

"As an asset, yes, I'd agree."

Sorrow and irritation had him shaking his head. How

could Synintel love someone so much he'd ruin lives to keep her safe, and yet drive her so far away she didn't even know her value to him? "No, as a daughter."

She scoffed and pushed his hand away. "I already told you he tried to marry me off to the most powerful men he could find, making sure allegiances to this country were solidified if the unions had been successful. My entire life was lived by a schedule he dictated, still is if I'm to be honest."

"In a palace you'd be safe, and treated like the princess I'm sure he always saw you to be."

Her jaw clenched and when she faced him again, the defiance in her eyes almost made them glow. "Why are you defending him?"

Kevin pushed his hand through his short hair. "I'm not so much defending him as hoping you see a different side to your father. The side of Synintel I know is a tough bastard who gets jobs done the only way he knows how. Brute dominance. However, where you're concerned, he prefers a gentler route. He smothers because you matter. Remember the chess board?"

She nodded. "Yes. And I remember thinking I was behind the line of pawns."

"You thought correctly. And no one was supposed to be back there with you that he didn't expressly permit."

A shuddering gasp escaped her lips. Focusing on a place on the map only she could see, her arms wrapped around her small waist. "And I made myself a pawn and set myself in the middle of the board, wide open for anyone to capture."

Gently he tugged her into his arms, pleased when she offered no protest. Once again, he found his restraint tested. The curves of her breasts and hips pressed against all the right places, made him almost forget he was honor bound. So instead of focusing on how right she felt in his arms, he focused on how to ease her fears.

He rested his chin on top of her head. The delicate scent of her had his senses going into overdrive. "Hey, nothing is going to happen to you. I swear."

"You can't swear when you don't know the extent to which I'm in trouble. Not even I know that."

Kevin glanced down at the map, his hold tightening around her. "If you'll let them, Sean, Mason, and Jonathon can help."

She stiffened. "I'm not sure if I really want anyone else aware of my incompetence when it comes to judging character. Obviously, I've mistaken Enbrackon's."

Kevin softly traced her spine through her dress with both hands, from the nape of her neck to the subtle ending arc of her back. Slowly she relaxed into him again. His fingers explored all the sensual curves she had to offer in the process, smoothing along her shoulders and hips. Idly, he wondered why he tortured himself so. The feminine heat of her skin and shallow breath caressing across his chest told him she was far from immune to his sensory play.

"They won't judge you. They can tell us what Enbrackon and the others may have been planning, and how deep they've involved you. The choice, however, is yours."

Her hands settled on his hips behind his back, squeezing. Because of his touching or his words, he didn't know. "I've only made one decision completely for myself that I'm aware of, and I made the wrong one."

Kevin slid his fingers into her hair. He cradled her against his chest, wishing he could rescue her from negative choices. But he couldn't. "You have to decide on your own. I won't do so for you, Raina. Ever."

And he meant the statement.

If her future rode on anything he had power over, she'd be the one to speak life into the choice. No matter how much it cost him.

• • •

KEVIN'S WORDS barely penetrated the haze of Raina's brain. His hands had gone back to their magical caressing. In lazy strokes, from her hair, to her hips, his masculine touch teased over her back, setting a fire with each light touch. How a man with unbridled strength could touch her as though she were porcelain, distracted her more than his confession.

Trying to ignore the bewilderment his caresses caused, she forced herself to concentrate on his offer. Of everything she knew concerning her father's hand-selected teams, he only chose the best, and the most trustworthy. Sean Blackbain's team was at the top.

Raina only wished she knew what everyone's role was, so she'd know exactly how they'd judge her. Because despite what Kevin said, they would. Stupidity was stupidity, no matter who was on the other side. And she'd been most stupid. She figured admitting it was half the battle.

Now she just had to find out how deep a grave she'd dug herself, and if there was any chance of climbing out.

Easing back, she looked up at Kevin, who seemed somehow taller. Even if she stood on her toes, she'd barely reach his shoulders. "Will your friends say anything to anyone?"

"No, of course not. Especially since they know I can kick their butts, and will, if they put you in any danger."

Raina frowned. "How will I be in danger?"

He heaved a heavy sigh, his chest rising and falling dramatically against hers. "Are you sure you want the answer to that?"

The serious frown he directed at her and the concern in his storm-colored eyes, made her wonder if perhaps this wasn't something she should remain ignorant to. Then again, if she were honest, she'd admit ignorance had put her in the mess to begin with. That and her own misguided dreams. "Yes, I want to know."

"So far, whoever you've worked for has managed to get

away with whatever they've needed from you. Once they realize you know, you won't be any use to them anymore because you won't be compliant."

Raina processed the statement. His steady graceful motion on her back kept her calm, allowed her to focus on something other than panic. "Does this mean I should be cooperative if I'm asked to do something more?"

His hands paused and his frame stiffened. "Enbrackon won't show up here again."

Raina thought back to the words he'd spoken to the Shield Guardian. "You think your threat will be enough to make him give up whatever I was able to do for him?"

"Not a threat, a guarantee. Threats may or not may not be carried out. There is no *maybe* to what I told him. He appears on this property, he doesn't walk away."

A shiver raced through her. Kevin's gentle onslaught returned, along with his words making her all too aware of his size and strength. She found herself wondering again what role her husband played for her father. And when he'd finally tell her.

"What about a letter?" she asked.

"Have they ever written before to ask you to do things for them?"

"No, Shield Guardian Enbrackon only informs me in a letter if something will be necessary soon, but he tells me everything in person."

Kevin grunted. "No risk of an ink trail that way."

She gave a sarcastic snort. "Right, because I burn all the paperwork when he leaves."

"Has he ever asked you to?"

"No."

"And up until tonight you've suspected nothing?"

"Everything has appeared legitimate."

He was silent for several long moments. Raina resisted the urge to lean further into him, to inhale his subtle, earthy scent. In the stillness, with the steady rise and fall of his chest, and the solid muscle hidden beneath a layer of fabric, she found herself imagining how his skin would feel under her hands. He'd already done the hardest part, untucking his shirt, leaving the temptation easily within grasp.

"Will you let us help you?"

The words broke through her musings, and just in time. She'd actually been reaching for the edges of his shirt. Thankful he couldn't see the sudden flush of her cheeks, she glanced at the maps. "I trust you, so I'll trust them. Yes, let's see what they can discover."

If she came out looking an even bigger fool, so be it. At least she'd know how badly they'd used her.

Kevin's arms wrapped around her, hugging her to the chest she'd been aching to explore. "Thank you."

"What will they need?"

"Anything you can give them. Maps, files, any notes Enbrackon wrote that you did save, even if you think they're insignificant."

Raina scrunched her nose. "I need my maps for all my clients. I didn't make any special ones."

"But you've marked specific locations that will be in the files that aren't on other maps, correct?"

"Well yes, but—"

"Mason will transfer the information and then get your maps back to you. And as he works with your version, he'll also be redrawing them as I promised he would."

The prospect of having single maps of regions with all the information she needed, up to date and condensed into only a handful of sheets, had her smiling for the first time that evening. "I can't wait to see his work. If they're half as good as his art, they'll be the best maps I've ever owned."

"And I bet it'll put you even further ahead than your competitors." He pulled back from her until she met his stare. "Why don't you work for a firm?"

"My father wanted me to stay in the house."

A frown tensed between his brows. "Exactly how much of your life does Synintel control?"

Raina focused on one of his shirt buttons, her finger brushing along the smooth, round surfaces. "I will answer that only if you answer in kind."

"I thought I already had answered." He grasped her hand while his other rested low on her hip.

"You told me how he tied us in marriage. Not what hold he has over your life now."

He lifted her hand and brushed the sensitive tips of her fingers across his mouth. "You're how old, twenty-three?"

She tried to keep her focus on a button, but when the heat of his breath caressed along her fingers, her gaze slid to his mouth. Oh, mistake. Somehow she managed to answer. "Y-yes."

"And if over the past couple weeks I've been home my assumptions are correct, Synintel runs your household, with the exception of the housekeeping staff, which is run by Mrs. Taft, who is likely paid by Synintel. He sends you all your clients so you don't have to leave the house, or worry about being used for illegal dealings. I'm also assuming he chooses the social functions you attend, am I wrong?"

The short whiskers on his chin rubbed against the center of her fingers and her lungs seized. She blinked to try to remember his question. "H-he sends me a list each week, with the invitations."

"Interesting. He's been sending mine as well."

"He seems to have an insatiable need to control every aspect of my life."

A needy ache pulsed in her stomach and flowed to her center. Her lungs continued to fail. What was he doing to her?

"And you, princess, seem to have an insatiable need to rebel. I'd recommend another direction, but since you've been doing it long before I came along, I don't think my words will have much influence."

Currently, she figured he could have any power over her he wanted. She'd deny him nothing. Still, for some reason she wanted him to understand. "Is it not in human nature to be stewards of our own destiny? I've never been able to make any decisions for myself. Not even my genetic inheritance was mine to decide. I was born with a gift, nurtured into it for uses my father saw long before I could understand. My first rebellion against him was denying him what he'd hoped to use for Queen Elect and country."

"And what would you have done if the choice *had* been yours?" His fluttering kisses moved from her fingers to her wrist.

"Um..." She inhaled shakily and blinked. "I don't know. I wasn't allowed to explore anything beyond logistics once the test confirmed that was my ability. Besides the standard education that is, reading and arithmetic. Geography, cultural studies, and world history took up the time I had left after having to study map legends, trade routes and commodities movement."

Kevin lowered his head, his sensual play moving down her arm. Raina's lips parted and she closed her eyes. A bigger mistake than looking at his mouth had been. Every breath he took, every shallow movement of his chin, sent ripples of sensation along the sensitive skin of her forearm. The playful stroking he'd done in the library so many nights ago had nothing on this.

"No thoughts of art or music?" The question teased like a caress across her flesh.

"A flippant waste of perfectly good time." Supporting herself suddenly seemed an insurmountable task. She sank into his warm strength, thankful when his arm snaked around her waist and held her.

"There is much to be learned about cultures in their art and music, not to mention about oneself."

Raina sure was learning a lot about herself at the moment. Like how a simple touch could ignite a fire so deep inside she'd surely combust any moment. Or how the hard evidence of desire pressing into her belly didn't repulse as it had when attached to Enbrackon, but rather excited. A deep urge to shift her weight against the bulge had her staying perfectly still.

"What about you?" she found herself asking, even as he slowly turned until her low back met the edge of the desk.

"Music."

"Music? That's your Gen-Heir ability?"

"What my mother wished for me, but turns out no. If I had a choice, I'd wish it for me too."

The longing in his voice broke through the clouds in her mind. She pulled back and met his smoky stare. With trembling fingers, she slid her hands along the curve of bearded jaw. The trimmed hairs tickled her palm. "You hate what you do so much?"

He closed his eyes, his arms wrapping around her as though she were a lifeline he needed to be grounded. "No, I don't hate it. I just know someday..." He sighed and shook his head. "It doesn't matter."

"Of course it matters." Raina's fingers clenched, forcing his eyes open. "What?"

"Someday I won't walk out."

Raina stared at him, not understanding. "Won't walk out of what?"

"Whatever Synintel sends me into."

A tingle of unease slithered along Raina's spine. Was he speaking of death? She glanced back at the neat buttons in a row down his shirt front. "Is that why you won't tell me what you do for him?"

He shrugged and she dropped her hands, splaying them across his chest. "Partly."

"What's the other part?"

"How you'll look at me when you know."

Shocked, Raina met his gaze again. "Excuse me?"

He stroked a finger lightly down her cheek, a sad smile in his eyes. "Trust me. And I'm not ready for that. I may never be."

Raina wanted to deny his statement, to assure him nothing he did as an order from her father could change who he was. But before she could utter the words, his mouth was on hers, demanding, taking the second she opened for him. He lifted her from the floor and set her on the desk before she could even comprehend the motion, as though she weighed nothing. Every cell in her body flared to life in a single moment, wholly aware of a man in a way she'd never been before.

The folds of her skirt glided up her legs. Cool air shivered across her skin, a sensation quickly forgotten as his fingers brushed the outside of her exposed thigh. His large form edged between her knees, forcing them apart. Raina fisted her hands in his shirt, his tongue doing all sorts of wicked within her mouth.

Somewhere in her rational brain, she realized his hands were on her bare skin, touching places unexplored and venturing into territory destined only for him. Which meant… Pulling her mouth free, she quickly went to work on the infernal buttons of his shirt. Despite shaking fingers, she managed to get enough of them free to slide her hands across the hard planes of his chest to his sides. The heat and mixed texture of his skin, sometimes smooth muscle, sometimes rough scars, sent an excited tremble through her body.

A low, primal growl sounded deep in his throat. Once more his mouth claimed hers in possessive passion. When he drew closer, forcing her legs completely apart, settling the most intimate part of himself against her, she didn't stop him. His hand slid over the top of her thigh, creating a teasing path to her center. A sharp breath caught in her throat. Anticipation the likes of which she'd never experienced before had her giving a short whimper. Somehow she *knew* she wanted him to continue.

Her fingertips pressed into his side until her nails demanded what she couldn't voice. Almost agonizingly slow, Kevin's touch moved past the flimsy barrier of her silk underwear. Gently, he sought her with an intimate touch. A cry of pleasure escaped her throat and she pulled her mouth free as he caressed her inside and out in playful, tender strokes. Pressure began to build.

Every thought aligned on his very skilled hand and the burning need he drew from within. Her nails bit deeper into his skin, a silent plea, though for what she wasn't sure. She wanted to both lie back and crawl deep within him... or maybe have him crawl deep within her. The two warred with each other, leaving her sitting perfectly still and waiting with a need robbing her of air.

Kevin's mouth found her throat. She let her head fall back, giving his tongue access. He rained kisses from her jaw to her collar bone, while his touch increased in pressure and urgency between her legs. Sharp pleasure exploded from her center, gaining momentum until she cried out in both wonder and delight.

When the tendrils of heat faded and she could draw a semi-normal breath, she managed to ask, "What in the world did you just do to me?"

His forehead touched to hers, his breathing as erratic as her heartbeat. The haze of desire he'd woven around her had made her unaware of the effects she'd had on him. A new rush of need coiled deep in her belly. She found herself seeking him again, pressing into his warmth and the dizzying masculine scent that was his alone.

"You have no idea what you do to me, knowing I'm the only man to have ever made you *feel*." The sensual words caressed along her cheek, to her mouth, where his lips gently brushed kisses.

Her hands traveled up the contours of his chest to his shoulders. She continued, emerging from the confines of his shirt to stroke up into the short lengths of his hair and the back of his neck. A sense of boldness swept over her. Somehow she knew she'd pleased him by more than his confession.

She wrapped tightly against him, her thighs pressing into the outside of his, hugging him close. "There's more though, isn't there?"

His fingers slid along her slickened flesh until she shuddered from an aftershock of pleasure. Then, much to her disappointment, he withdrew, wrapping her in strong arms to his torso. "Yes, there's so much more. But not here, not tonight."

Frustration and confusion welled up inside her. She frowned, pulling back enough to see his face, set in grim lines. "Did I do something wrong?"

His eyes closed and he gently smoothed his hands along the sides of her jaw into her hair. "My beautiful princess, you did everything all too right."

"Then I—"

His whispering kiss stopped her before she could say what he demanded be spoken before he came to her bed. He pressed his forehead to hers, his breath falling ragged across her mouth. "No. Do not say anything more."

The frantic beat of her heart still pounded in her ears and at her center, pressed intimately enough to him to know he definitely desired as much, if not more, than she did. "Kevin..."

"No," he said again, more forceful, his fingers tangling in the length of hair at her neck. "I have immense control, Raina, but it's sorely being tested right now. You have no idea what your father has done. I will literally be damned if I take away your choice to decide if forever is really where you want to be with me. Once you're mine, you're mine always, do you understand?"

There are many reasons I chose him, his honor was one.

Synintel's words echoed in her mind. She licked her suddenly dry lips and nodded, not trusting herself to speak the same agreement. If he believed she'd regret a life in his arms, she had to trust the reason. But as he pulled away from her, leaving her cold and alone, she had to wonder what could possibly be so terrible he'd walk away from forever with her too.

10

———

"Brother, you *promised!*"

Cora's whine barely tore Mason from the work laid out before him. Her glossy black hair was swept into an elegant braid. The silvery gray of her eyes was emphasized by feathery pink accents at the creases of her lids and thick, black lashes. Her simple gray gown was meant to ease nerves rather than entice, meaning she expected to do something work-related soon.

"Promised what again?" he asked.

Huffing, Cora placed her hands on her very full hips, pushing one out to the side in a manner that most men found endearing. Being her brother, he found it highly annoying.

"To go to the luncheon with me at the Forstmaus residence."

Mason screwed his face in discontent and traced the long line of a yard stick across the expanse of paper covering his desk. "Key Guardian Forstmaus?"

"Yes." Cora crossed her arms over her chest and tapped a foot. "I really needed this luncheon. She has refused to sit with me since the Julinas scandal, and I need her testimony for my article."

Lifting a brow, Mason regarded his frustrated twin. "Would that be the scandal where you disappeared with the hostess's husband, or the one where you were found with the host's brother-in-law?"

A bright flush blossomed across her ivory cheeks. "Hostess's brother, promised to her best friend."

Mason raised his charcoal pencil. "Ah, yes, that's right. The best friend wasn't Key Guardian Fortmaus, was it?"

Her foot stopped tapping. She shifted her shoulders and looked to one of his drawings on the wall. "No... her sister."

Sighing, Mason returned to laying the foundation of a map, the latitude and longitude lines. "And my sister needs to learn seduction is an art, not an obsession."

"I do believe I've mastered that particular art."

"You mean worn it out," Mason muttered, applying another sweeping line.

"We can't all have high moral standards like you, brother," she snapped, her silvery eyes flashing.

"No one ever said I did. I just don't want to end up a mindless rabid animal. I'd rather prefer if you didn't either."

"I told you..."

Mason waved a coal darkened hand. "Cora, I don't care how careful you are, you have no way of knowing about the secret lovers. If you find it exciting to dodge bullets, I can have Katria stand you in the middle of her range. You're playing with the same odds."

She worked her jaw. "You're just embarrassed by me."

"No, that would be our mother."

A flicker of shame crossed over her beautiful face. "About the luncheon."

Sighing again, Mason stopped before applying another line. "What about it?"

"I need you."

"Why?"

"She has a..." Cora waved her hand in the air. "Thing for

you. If you're there, she'll likely answer my questions so she can stare at you and drool. My saying I'd bring you was the only reason she extended the invitation. I can't show up alone."

"I'm working."

"Not work mother would approve of."

"We're such a disappointment to our matriarch."

"Truly is sad. I weep for the perfectly plotted future we've destroyed."

Mason hid his smile and shook his head. "You're terrible."

"Says the man who's broken her heart not once, but three times over refused contract promises."

Annoyance at the reminder of his mother's many failed schemes to see him married and continuing the Kynhaven held rank, and Dandridge line, had him growling. "I'm not marrying some nit-wit with a pedigree to keep lines pure. No such thing. We're a country built from many nations on the brink of extinction. Some have been rewarded, many have not. Reward does not equal good breeding. *If* I marry, she'll be of my choosing."

"Of that, we agree. Now, lunch."

Mason held up coal-stained hands and offered a look of mock apology. "Little dirty sis, sorry."

She found a discarded ball of paper and launched it at him. "You are so infuriating!"

"Take someone else. With the donkey she's married to, I doubt she'll care who's sitting next to you."

"She wanted you."

Mason tsked and settled another line across the paper. "Many do, they're always so sad. I can't please them all."

Another paper ball bounced off his shoulder. "Oh come off it, you don't please any of them."

Leaning on the desk, he pointed his pencil at her and glared. "I'll have you know I can be *very* pleasing if I wish to be."

"Sure, I'm extra satisfied with my brother's attention at the moment. I can only imagine how your lovers have fared."

Mason grimaced. "I wish you wouldn't. That's just gross and wrong."

A shriek of frustration sounded before she stomped her foot. "How did I get stuck with you as a twin?"

"I don't know, bad genetics?"

"I swear, I—"

A throat clearing stopped her words cold. Mason glanced up to see their butler in the doorway. "Yes, Tybalt?"

"Key Guardian Asherwick is here to see you, with the lovely Miss Seartavos. Do you wish them to be shown in here, or the parlor?"

Mason glanced down at his smudged clothing and blackened hands. "Here is fine, at least I'll look in place. Thank you."

Tybalt bowed quickly and retreated. The flush returned to Cora's face and she quickly glanced at her simple gray cotton gown, chosen for an interview, not to impress. Mason flexed his jaw.

When he spoke, his words were laced with warning, and anger at knowing the direction her thoughts had headed. "I will be the one who is swearing if you attempt to challenge Miss Seartavos. She's a foreign heiress, Cora, not someone you have to compete with for the affections of a man."

Tybalt reappeared and with a sweeping motion of his arm and ushered the hesitant couple into the small, disorganized space that served as Mason's study. Jonathon entered with a quirked brow, while his promised stopped in the doorway, her gaze leaving nothing unseen.

"My, I have heard artists are colorful with their space." Her words were musical and elegant, like the woman speaking them. Mason didn't correct her assumption he was an artist. Neither did anyone else.

He did however find himself staring, and had to quickly

ensure his mouth wasn't hanging open. A gown that faded from brilliant pink at her shoulders to rich red around her feet, enveloped and moved like water around her voluptuous frame. Sun-kissed hair fell in graceful waves around her shoulders and face, pulled back at the sides and adorned with ribbons, beads and small colorful feathers. Her vivid aquamarine eyes were a startling shade against her golden skin. Bracelets decorated her wrists, but none more prominent than the thick silver promise band, ensuring everyone knew she belonged to someone.

Jonathon motioned for her to come the rest of the way into the room, closing the door behind her. "I think, Sylphine-love, it's more this particular artist doesn't like anyone in his space to clean it."

"Correct," Mason said, putting his attention back to the paper before him, where his eyes were safe, and not on the woman whose beauty was almost painful to look upon.

"Ah, much like you and your office at Enforcement Services," Sylphine said with laughter.

"Yes, exactly, and I haven't misplaced a case yet, so there must be something to be said for messy work spaces."

Her beautiful eyes twinkled as she took a seat Jonathon waved to before the desk. "I will have to trust your judgement."

"My judgement has never been in question. Yours however..." Jonathon laughed when a pretty blush swept up her cheeks.

Despite the play between them, Mason noticed neither touched the other and Sylphine never reached out to greet Mason. When Jonathon did, Mason wiggled his very artistic hands. Jonathon nodded and then took a seat beside his bride-to-be. Mason snuck a sideways glance at his twin, who'd for the first time in her life managed to become a wallflower. Whether intentional or not, she made no move to change her situation.

"So," Jonathon began, leaning forward and grasping his hands between his knees. "You said you had some files for me to look over?"

Mason set the pencil down and wiped his grungy hands on his pants before reaching for the stack of files Kevin had left for him. "Yes. These are files of men who've been working with Enbrackon for shipping through Guardianess Raiventon. Kevin suspects they've all been fraudulent. None of us are sure how to go about proving that."

Jonathon sighed and accepted the stack. "That's more an Investigative Division thing than what I handle. I'm local violent crime."

"And see, that's why you're here." Mason gave a shallow smile. "However, I know you have a particular interest in the unknown shipment that went missing. I think some answers might be in those files."

Jonathon flipped open a file. "I think we can agree we all have an interest in that *missing* shipment. But what makes you think someone Guardianess Raiventon worked with was involved."

"Off record?"

Cora's back straightened. Mason shot her a glare that said what his mouth didn't. *This applies to you too, sister.*

Jonathon glanced up. "I figured by now any conversation with you and the rest of Wintersfall's Guardian team is off record."

"This is really off record. I told you I don't want to drag you into anything that could cost you your job. And this is definitely one of those things." Mason braced his hands on the desk and fixed a serious stare on Jonathon. "You can tell me to continue or allow you to remain blissfully unaware."

Jonathon heaved a long sigh. Sylphine angled closer to him, but made no gesture to reach for comfort. "I see." He slid his gaze to his beautiful promised and quirked a smile. "Still thankful you came with me?"

"And miss all the excitement? Your sister is like one to me, but I have not figured out how she remains cooped up in your house day after day. I need sun, and the, how do you say..." Her forehead scrunched in thought as her hand waved, considering a word beyond her reach. Then she smiled. "The hum of conversation, even if I am not part of it. Continue. You are brave, you will be fine, regardless of what Primary Guardian Kynhaven has to say."

Mason raised his brows.

Jonathon rubbed his fourth finger across his temple. "How can I argue with that? Apparently I'm brave, so on with it."

Mason quickly shared the details of Raina's likely assistance in the theft of medicine bound for Italyssa.

Distressed, Sylphine touched her hand to her chest and gasped. "Why would she do this?" Hurt and horror danced in the Italyssian heiress's eyes.

"She didn't do it of her own free will." Mason held his hands open, hoping she'd understand. "In fact, had her husband arrived even two seconds later, I think Asherwick would have a new case to handle and we'd not be having a civil conversation about it."

Somewhat placated, Sylphine relaxed in her seat. A mask of calm settled over her face. "Do you know why they wished to steal medicine from my country?"

Mason crossed his arms over his chest. "As a means of payment maybe? I haven't had an opportunity to study her maps, they may give me some insight."

Jonathon turned a paper and didn't glance up when he added to the conversation, "Comparing shipping manifests will yield greater results."

"Likely," Mason agreed. "But I can't be seen at the records department asking for manifests. None of us can, too risky. Know anyone on the inside that'd be willing and who's trustworthy?"

Slowly Jonathon shook his head, attention still on the file

before him. "No, not at records. Mostly old cranky widows who work there. While I'm sure most of them are trustworthy, they don't like to do more than what's required. I ask for documents well before I may actually have use for them."

"I know someone." Cora had the undivided attention in the room. She smiled. "Not an old biddy, and not someone who will run their mouth. And, I'm there all the time asking for any number of odd documents. I can throw some manifests into my queries. Just make sure they aren't any you want to draw attention to right away. I recommend saving the trouble makers for when you're sure they'll be worth the potential fallout."

Jonathon frowned. "The files could be flagged."

Cora inclined her head. "Yes, and depending on who flagged them, an inquiry must be reported."

Mason met his sister's stare. "Can you ask if they're flagged before they're pulled?"

"Maybe." Cora tapped a finger against her chin. "I've never worried about it before now, but this particular friend has no interest in seeing me in trouble. Won't hurt for me to see before I hand over the list."

Mason clapped his hands in anticipation. "Excellent. Maybe we'll finally start to have some answers."

11
———

"You are unusually quiet my dear friend, what's wrong?" Patricia laced her arm through Raina's and matched her steps along the winding path in the sparsely populated park. The fabric of their skirts, hers a blue floral print, Patricia's ivory, swished together, joining the skittering leaves across the brick path before them.

Uneasy about venturing out of the house after Enbrackon's attack, Raina had almost sent a denial to her best friend's request for an outing. Instead, she'd insisted they go to Quinton Park, closer to the outskirts of town than the very popular Atherton Square. Patricia had replied a walk was to be *seen*, but she'd indulge her friend this once.

A short distance behind them, Raina was keenly aware of Kevin's attendance. She had to resist glancing over her should every few seconds.

Patricia seemed to sense her distraction, her hand tightening on Raina's forearm. "Of course, I'd be rather preoccupied myself if my sinfully handsome husband were behind rather than beside me. We aren't the only women here you know, but I think you'll be the most popular before we leave.

Every lady will be fairly thankful you dragged him along with you, I must say."

The teasing elicited a laugh from Raina. She patted her friend's hand and sighed. "Let them look, I get to see him anytime I want. I'm afraid he'll never leave my side again."

"You say this as though it's a bad thing!"

Again, Raina laughed. The urge to sneak a glimpse over her shoulder finally overtook her. Kevin leaned against a tree, arms crossed over his strong chest, pulling a dark green shirt tight across his shoulders and biceps. Leaves danced around his booted feet on the lazy wind. An unfamiliar longing to be in his arms rather than on her friend's made her look away before she yielded to the temptation and fled to him.

"Do you miss your husband when he's away?" Raina couldn't help but ask.

"Depends on how long he's been gone." Patricia glanced behind her quickly. "I should think you'd be used to being away from Raiventon, though. Has he received orders to leave again soon?"

"No, but we've never had this much time together. I'm afraid I will miss him more than I can bear when he's gone," she confessed on a whisper.

A trio of women walked past slower than necessary and Raina realized with a frown they were rounding the corner and nearing her husband again. The women were unhurried, no doubt hoping to gain his attention. Jealousy slithered through her, hot and unwelcome. She clenched her jaw and ignored the pointless emotion.

Patricia's fingers tapped a drum beat on Raina's arm. Birds fluttered off into the brilliant blue sky, catching her attention before she spoke again. "I have found writing to William when we're apart helps ease the long distance. Perhaps you and Raiventon could begin such a tradition, too."

"Perhaps." Raina glared at the women who'd slowed to a

mere crawl past her husband, giggling and batting their lashes. For a moment his gaze slid from her to them. Raina raised a brow.

Heaving an exaggerated sigh, Patricia pulled Raina to a bench overlooking a gently sloping hill into a maze of houses and shops below. Patricia sat and pressed her hands onto her thighs. "What is really going on, Raina?"

"Nothing, I'm just trying to sort everything out is all." Nervous energy had her pacing before her exasperated friend. Raina didn't care if she looked crazy to the onlookers strolling by in the slightly chilled afternoon air. "My mother died when I was only nine, and my father wasn't exactly a fountain of information when it came to relationships or marriage."

Patricia's blue eyes softened and she held her hand out, wiggling her fingers in invitation. The steady breeze toyed with the golden curls piled atop her head. "Then allow me to answer any questions you have. I promise you, Raina darling, I won't breathe a single word to another soul."

Desperately, Raina wanted to trust her. The only person her father had ever allowed her to befriend, she figured if Patricia were going to betray her, she'd likely have done so before now. Still... Enbrackon's cruelty and unexpected character flaws were too fresh in Raina's mind for her to think anyone, beyond the man leaning casually against a tree to make sure she was safe, could be reliable. And there was no hesitation in Raina's mind, she trusted Kevin without a second thought.

Raina pulled on Patricia's hand. "Let's walk again. My confusion with my marriage is likely from not knowing what to expect at any given time. I'm used to being alone. I think maybe he is too. We're getting accustomed to each other's habits, and I'm sure that's never an easy thing."

Rising, Patricia laughed. "Oh, yes, habits can be quite shocking, let me tell you."

"I don't think I want to know," Raina said quickly, giggling. "Let Brentwood keep his secrets."

"I wish you trusted me more."

The quietly spoken confession made Raina stare. "I trust you more than anyone else in society."

"But not enough to tell me what's *really* bothering you." Patricia patted her arm and began walking again. "It's okay, I'm patient. Eventually you'll need a confidant, we all do, and I'll be here. After all, no one else knows when I kissed my first boy in a greenhouse at fifteen, or accidently dyed my hair blue, or when I threw up in that potted tree at the Dresner's dinner two weeks ago. You have shouldered my secrets, dear sister, and I will shoulder yours."

"I was worried at that event. Did you ever discover what made you sick?"

Patricia shook her head, frowning. "No, I'm still not sure. William has his suspicions, but he said I have to figure it out first." She shrugged. "I don't know what he expects me to figure out."

Raina considered what Brentwood would want his wife to conclude and shrugged, drawing a blank. "I'm sure it'll come to you."

Her friend came to an abrupt stop, yanking Raina's arm. "Apparently my husband *has* decided to come to me."

Frowning, Raina searched through the sparse grove of trees to the street beyond, where riders, carriages, and small Ariot's intermixed in a slow parade. One looked grossly out of place. The carriage was ivory, with bright blue gelding, a large crest on the door, and light gray horses with blue ribbons in their hair and over their reins. After all, a royal of Ruthenia had to travel in such a fashion that everyone knew of his presence. Since Brentwood was an emissary for the Ruthenia Nationals, it only heightened his need to announce his importance.

"Does he not trust me to get you home well?" Raina asked, her frown increasing.

"I think it's rather we're in one of the most remote parks in Haven City." Her displeasure was sharp in her voice. "It's my trust in question, dearest friend."

Giving a firm tug, Raina sent them back on their walk, now toward the garish carriage. "I imagine his ride home won't be too pleasant."

"No, especially since he's grown accustomed to certain benefits when we ride home together."

The playful manner in which Patricia spoke the words had Raina searching her friend's indignant face. "What do you mean?"

The heated flush on Patricia's cheeks increased. "Oh come now, Raina. Surely you can't tell me with a husband like *that* —" She waved Kevin's direction. "—you haven't had an exciting ride home... or two."

Raina considered the last carriage ride she took home with Kevin and shook her head. "No, not really. I was rather mad at him last time, actually."

Patricia pulled her to stop again and then forced her to turn until they faced each other. Her blue eyes serious, Patricia grabbed Raina's shoulders. "Allow me to give you a small piece of marital advice. Your carriage is one of the most private places you will get with your husband. Use it wisely, as often as you're able. There's a reason they put curtains on all the windows and the carriagemen and drivers are *outside*."

"My house is very private after seven at night. We're completely alone."

Patricia blinked. "Are you serious?"

"Yes. You aren't?"

"No, not really. My stylist elite sleeps in the room just off mine, and William's valet sleeps in quarters adjoined to his closet."

Raina bit her bottom lip. "I'd say I'm sorry, but you have

control over that."

Patricia raised a brow and glanced at her husband's waiting carriage. The door had yet to open. "Indeed." Giving a quick smile, Patricia dropped her hands and stepped away. "I have enjoyed our walk. It's peaceful here and I don't have to worry about gossip. Can we meet here again, soon?"

Surprised, Raina simply nodded. Patricia brushed a quick kiss to Raina's cheek before flouncing off through the trees to her waiting husband. The door opened moments before Patricia stopped on the sidewalk. If the quick flutter of hands and bright red of Brentwood's face were any indication when he stepped away from the carriage to his wife, Patricia had already given him an earful. Raina bit her lip to keep from laughing.

The couple disappeared into the carriage and a footman dressed in navy blue and ivory promptly closed the door behind them. Seconds later the carriage ambled off. Raina moved her focus from the road to her husband, who still leaned casually against a tree. The small group of women who'd been attempting to gain his attention continued to try. An urge to walk right up and kiss him had her feet stumbling forward.

A small smile crossed Kevin's lips. He straightened. The women giggled and chortled, edging closer. Much to their disappointment, however, his attention wasn't directed at them. Breezing past without so much as a sideways glance, Kevin walked with predatory grace down the wide brick path. Raina stopped, heart in her throat, unable to look away.

When Kevin reached her, he took both hands in his and lifted them to his mouth, placing teasing kisses along her knuckles. His gray eyes danced with a mischievous light that made her pulse race. Raina rose up on her toes, desperate for his lips to be somewhere other than her hand. Slowly, he shook his head, the whisper of his beard brushed along her skin.

"No," he whispered against her fingers.

She made a noise of protest. His thumb traced the line of her bottom lip, sending a quiver of heat through her stomach.

"I never want you to regret any intimacy between us, no matter how small. And trust me, princess, you'd regret your very public show of affection about a second after we stopped."

The group of ladies glared at Raina. She cut her eyes right back. For the first time in her life, she wanted to stoop well below her station and shout taunts at them about who her man belonged to. "Apparently they missed the gold band you wear."

"More than likely they didn't care."

She turned her attention back to him. "Excuse me?"

He kissed her hands again before releasing one and bracing the other on his forearm. "They don't know my lady owns me for life. Most husbands aren't too discriminatory since they'll be out of a contract and looking for a new lover in a year or two."

Wind tugged at Raina's hair, playing with loose tendrils around her face. She worked her bottom lip between her teeth. "I will admit I never considered your feelings on our life contract. Then again, I assumed you would have changed it if you cared. I didn't know you didn't have an option."

She urged him off the path. A sudden need to know how he felt about their marriage welled up inside her. Slipping her hand into his, she met his slate gray eyes. "Do you care? Do you wish I'd placed a limit on our years together?"

His gaze moved past her into the shadowy woods. With a tug, he pulled her into their depths, just far enough to award their words privacy, but not enough to lose complete sight of the park.

"I wish," he said, his hands on her upper arms, turning her to face him. "That you'd had more information before you made such a rash decision."

Raina nodded in understanding. "Then my father wouldn't be able to force you to lie."

Kevin sighed, his hands gently rubbing her arms. "He won't be forcing me to do anything."

Memories of his touch, the passionate way he kissed, swept through her and sent a shudder of desire curling to her toes. Was she alone in her feelings? Confused, she stepped away. "You'd leave our marriage just like that? Because he tells you to?"

"No, I'd walk away because it's the right thing to do. You don't understand what you'd be giving up. The life you'd be living is so far beyond your comprehension, and not fair to even ask of you." Despite the distance she tried to put between them, he crowded closer with each word until the heat of his body brushed against hers. "As for your question, no, I don't care about the contract length. Five years, fifteen, twenty, forever. I'd do them all with you if I had the choice."

Tears burned behind her eyes. She fisted her hands to keep from grabbing his shirt in denial. "Everyone has a choice."

Kevin cupped her jaw and pressed a tender kiss to her forehead. "Yes, when they know the depth of their decision."

Raina leaned into his strong chest. Her cheek rested on the silk of his shirt. The heat of his skin radiated through and his faint clean scent surrounded her. "You are like my father, speaking in riddles. Do you think me so weak I couldn't handle whatever it is?"

Gently, his thumbs caressed the pulse in her throat to her collar bone and back to her jaw, sending a delightful shiver along her spine. "Not weak, but a princess deserving what she's always known. I won't be the one to take that away from you."

Raina grasped his wrists and straightened. "But you wouldn't be, my father would. *He* has made the threat and he'll have to be the one to stand by it."

In a fluttering caress, his lips touched to hers. "No, by

refusing his order, I'd be the one changing your fate."

A strange clenching sensation pained her chest. The thought of Kevin disappearing from her life not just for months, but forever, caused a physical reaction. "What if I can't let you go?"

Kevin drew a sharp breath. Then his head snapped toward the park. All emotion disappeared from his handsome face. Raina opened her mouth to ask what was wrong when a scream echoed.

"Don't move," Kevin demanded. Grasping her shoulders, he positioned her behind a large, sheltering tree and squeezed.

Her pale brown eyes grew wide and she tried to see the park beyond. "But…"

Another sharp scream disturbed a flock of birds above them, sending them squawking and skittering through the trees. "Promise me, Raina!"

She nodded, her lips drawn tight, her skin pale. Kevin caressed her cheek to her jaw and pressed a quick kiss to her mouth. He wanted to do so much more, not knowing what he'd be walking into, but there wasn't time. A new wave of screams erupted, multiples, not one. Breaking into a run, he cleared the trees. Stopping at the edge of the wide path, his gaze swept the park.

Two blood-soaked bodies led his attention to the trio of women who'd been intent on gaining a response from him. They had hold of one of their friends, shrieking in panic while another woman wrenched the young brunette free with strength her small frame should not possess. *Human Rabies Syndrome.* Kevin let loose a string of heavy curses, sprinting across the distance to them. He had seconds before one of the other girls, too close to flee, became the infected's next victim.

With only the brain capacity to distribute the virus through her bites, the diseased female didn't notice him behind her. More times than not however, in their rabid need to spread the infection, they killed the victim. All the better since no cure existed and within weeks the poor prey turned into the same mindless killing machine.

Kevin took the situation in quickly and formulated a plan. Leaping into the air, he landed against the small woman's back. The moment his chest touched her, he switched his momentum, yanking as he wrapped one leg around her thighs, the other around her hips. He snaked an arm around her upper arms, the other under her chin. His weight, more than her tiny frame could handle, immediately toppled them backward. The ground rushed to meet his back. He ignored the sharp jarring of his spine and ribs.

Teeth gnashed and fingernails clawed at his forearms and biceps. Fabric protected some of his flesh, but not enough. Fiery pain spread from his arms and hands. He pushed the pain to the back of his mind, knowing it'd only get worse. Slick blood mixed with saliva pouring from her mouth coated his forearm wrapped around her neck. The body of the victim fell across the women. Her friends sobbed and dragged her away.

Kevin ignored their frantic pleas. He tightened his hold on the infected. Gritting his teeth as she fought with an inhuman strength to find some part of his anatomy with her mouth, he jerked her neck. He pulled with enough force to not only cleanly separate vertebra, but also break the spinal cord. Her body went limp, but her mouth continued to snap. Only a brain injury could kill her.

Unable to do anything more than bite her teeth together, she was neutralized until a containment unit arrived. She had another two to six hours before the virus ran its full course and her body died completely without assistance.

His name being screamed forced him carefully out from under the tangle of lifeless limbs. Staggering to his feet, Kevin held his hands out in front of himself. Raina made a run for him, her eyes wild with fear. Her navy print skirt flowed out behind her, clutched tightly in her hands.

"Stop," he snapped, taking slow steps away. "Don't touch me."

She froze. Tears gathered in her eyes and went to look at the viciously snapping woman on the ground. Kevin stepped to block her view.

"You're bleeding."

Kevin glanced down at the deep gashes on his arm that had held the syndrome victim. Small rivulets of blood flowed down his forearm and dripped to the brick ground. He carefully kept his arms apart and from touching any other part of him. "I'll be okay." He hoped he wasn't lying.

"How could you do that?" she asked, still holding onto her skirt as though it were a lifeline. The wind teased her hair that had come free from its bindings. "How could you risk yourself for so many strangers?"

Kevin blinked and looked around. Parents with two young children were fleeing the park. An elderly couple collapsed on a bench, aware the threat was over, but weakened by the excitement. The group of friends still huddled over the one he hadn't been able to save. "How could I not?"

She went to reach for him again. He quickly sidestepped her. "You could have been hurt worse than you were."

Sighing, Kevin shook his head and motioned for her to follow. "No, the chances of that were unlikely. Syndrome victims are fast, but they're uncoordinated and easily subdued."

Raina fell in step beside him, but thankfully made no attempts to touch him again. "You sound like you've done this before."

"Unless there's a gun or a knife, it's the only way to neutralize one. I don't carry either."

If his enemy did, and he needed to make use of one, that was a different matter.

Kevin waved when they reached the road. Raina's carriage appeared among the crowd of transportation. The driver leapt down the moment he was able and opened the door for them. Kevin entered first to ensure minimal risk in contaminating Raina, instructing the driver to go to Primary Guardian Wintersfall's residence instead of their own.

Inside the carriage, Kevin braced his forearms on his thighs, careful not to touch any part of the interior. Droplets of blood soaked into the dark green carpeting. Raina sat carefully, pressing into the far corner, her gaze fixed on his injured arm.

"Does it hurt?" she asked softly.

He flexed his fingers, assessing the pain as tendons moved under his skin. "I've hurt worse."

A small choking sound escaped her lips. She looked away and out the window, but not before he caught the sheen of tears. Kevin focused his attention on the blood slowly oozing down his fingers. If she struggled with a simple removal and injuries from an HRS victim, how would she react when she learned he could take down seven armed men with a knife wound in his side? He imagined not well. Another check mark in the *She has no idea who she's married* column.

The ride to Sean's was made in silence. Kevin instructed Raina to get out first when they arrived. Davis, the butler, was waiting with the front door open, calling to Sean. Once inside, Raina stepped to the side, hands clasped before her, a testament to her father's training of when she should and shouldn't be seen or heard.

Sean rushed out of the library, Katria steps behind. "What's going on?" he asked, alarmed.

"HRS victim at Quinton Park," Kevin answered, holding up his injured arm and the other well away from it.

Sean hissed, hands fisting at his sides. "And you brought that crap into my house?"

Kevin raised a brow. "Yes, I did. And why would I dare do

such a thing?" He inclined his head in mock thought. "Oh yes, that's right, because maybe you're my MSO!"

The reminder forced Sean to relax, his gaze shifting to Kevin's visible wounds. "Sorry. Go to the greenhouse, Kat and I will meet you there."

Kevin made his way past the stairs and the library door to the side door leading to the greenhouse. A work in progress, the once beautiful paths were torn up, the bricks stacked neatly along the far wall. Old root balls and leaves were being thrown into a massive pile in the center to be burned. Over a decade of neglect had made the conservatory a clean slate, a project Sean still hadn't decided what to do with.

Raina found a row of benches along the nearest wall. Kevin had to bite the inside of his cheek to keep from laughing while she inspected each moss and dirt coated seat, finally choosing the cleanest looking one to perch herself on. Moments later, Sean and Katria appeared. Sean carried two buckets of water, his white shirt sleeves rolled up past his elbows. Katria carried a crate of supplies, her midnight hair tied back into tight ponytail, the sleeves of her black gown pushed to her upper arms. This wasn't the first, nor would it be the last time, this couple had to work together to get him healthy again.

"Hold your arms out to the side, palms facing out," Sean instructed, setting the buckets down.

Kevin did as instructed.

"Kat, his shirt buttons."

Katria set the crate down. Before Katria could walk around him though, Raina was on her feet.

"I'll take care of that," Raina said quickly, keeping clear of Kevin's extended arms as she came around him.

Kevin didn't miss the secret smile that passed between Sean and Katria. He had his own if he were honest. Raina didn't look at him, her fingers trembling as she undid each button, having to tug on the fabric once she reached his waist.

"Is either arm contaminated that you know of?" Sean asked, a pair of scissors in his hand.

"Left." Kevin glanced at the soaked fabric and smeared blood, wincing. "All of that is from her."

Sean sighed and muttered a curse. He slid the scissors into clean fabric at Kevin's shoulder. The cool, blunt steel of the bottom blade brushed Kevin's skin. Sean cut around his entire arm. He handed the scissors off to Katria before carefully pulling down, turning the fabric in on itself, drawing the silk off his arm. Holding the dangerous section well away from his body, Sean went to the burn pile and tossed the scrap.

"Everything goes onto that. *Everything.* I'll burn it tonight."

Raina finished the buttons and stepped away, her cheeks brilliant red. Kevin kept his mind far from where he wanted it to be, finally allowing himself to focus on the burning ache of his scratched skin. Sean decontaminated his uninjured arm, then disinfected himself at the greenhouse faucet with Katria's careful help. The entire process was slow. No one wanted to end up the rabid equivalent of a mythical zombie.

Everyone in the conservatory was dealing with one of the two sole ways to become infected – blood and saliva during the end stage. The other was sexual intercourse during the dormant stage. One of the top reasons people married in a contract for the minimum year. Being sexually promiscuous was deadly. Keeping a safe partner for a year was a better bet.

Once clean, Sean cautiously cut the fabric away from Kevin's injured skin, never allowing any single part to touch damaged tissue, flinging the patches away the second they came free. With skill and precision honed from taking care of too many injured teammates, Sean had the wounds inspected, cleaned, disinfected, coated with salve and bandaged. Only after the cuts were closed off from contagion, did Sean allow Kevin to remove the rest of his ruined shirt with Raina's help.

"Take a shower the second you get home," Sean ordered,

handing him a bottle of iodine and a jar of silver salve. "Clean it all again before you go to bed, and twice a day after that. Bandages for three days. If it starts to look infected, come back." He looked at Raina. "Help him."

She nodded. "I will."

Kevin glanced at Katria and with a sharp nod at the house. Katria responded with a small jerk of her chin and then smiled at Raina. "Come upstairs with me. I'll get some of Sean's clothes for Kevin."

"Thank you," Raina said with a relieved sigh.

Kevin waited until they were well out of hearing range before turning to Sean. "Do you think I have to worry about being infected?"

A heavy frown settled across Sean's face. "I don't think so, but you know as well as I do, if she drooled while biting and holding her victims, getting her saliva mixed and on her hands, she could have when she scratched you. I'm not going to lie, you *could* be at risk. But, the chances are slim."

Kevin pressed his lips together and focused on the empty door his wife had walked through. "Symptoms are a common cold, right?"

"Yes, a fever, coughing, runny nose, fatigue. It's why we can't pin down the sick. The second stage of the virus is mild and deceptive."

"Two weeks?"

"At the most." Sean clapped him on the back. "You know, if you carried a knife, this wouldn't be a problem. It's why I do. I learned too young you need to be armed against that particular threat. Brain can't function without a blood supply."

"Yes, perhaps I need to amend my rule." After all, he no longer had himself alone to worry about. If he turned into a raging lunatic, he'd take out everyone in the house, his wife included. Suddenly saving a park full of people seemed an unwise decision if it cost Raina her life...

12

Gray light slowly illuminated Raina's room. She stared up at the textured tiles of her ceiling. They appeared flat and drab in the shadow-less light, echoing her heart's condition. Sleep continued to evade her. Two weeks had passed since she'd last seen Kevin. When they'd arrived home, he'd gone to shower as instructed, and she'd went to check messages. When dinner time arrived, she'd found his study and bedroom empty. How she missed the footman in green livery coming to collect him, she wasn't sure, but she must have.

Normally she'd roll back over, wait for sleep to claim her again until Tabby arrived to dress her for the day. But anger had her hands fisting in her sheets. Fourteen days and not a word. Fourteen days of existence in a hollow routine she'd come to despise. Her reality had returned to life before Kevin. Had she meant so little to him? He couldn't even say goodbye when Synintel called him away.

A tear slipped down her cheek. She blinked in shock and wiped it away as she threw the covers off. Sitting on the edge of the bed, she glanced out the window. The first rays of light crept over the horizon, turning the gray sky pink and velvety orange. No one would arrive for several hours to help her dress or begin her work. Her pillow and plush mattress held the same appeal as her desk.

Pushing tangled hair from her face, she rose, determined to get through the day without thinking about the man who seemed to have taken her heart when he left. While she wanted to be shocked at the revelation, a sigh was all she could muster. Since the moment he slipped her wedding band on her finger, she'd been lost to him. She didn't realize how much until the precious gift of time had been given to them.

Now... she closed her eyes and forced breath in and out. Now she'd simply exist, knowing she was as alone in her heartbreak as she'd been in blossoming love.

Summer crept ever closer, the final shackles of ice and occasional snow flurries over the ocean would dissipate to nothing, leaving the waterways of the world north of the Northern Boundary wide open for trade and transportation. She'd have plenty of work to keep her occupied.

After brushing her teeth, she donned her fluffy robe over her long silk nightgown. With no one else in the house, padding around shoeless and in nightclothes wouldn't matter. Then again, she'd have to care, which at the moment she didn't. Wallowing in a shallow pool of self-pity felt too good to return to being the Master Guardianess Raiventon for the sake of her staff. Maybe after Tabby worked her magic, Raina would force herself into a sense of normalcy.

Downstairs, she slowly compelled her feet to move to her study. Hands shoved in the warm pockets of her robe, she stopped in the doorway and stared over the empty space. Weeks ago the idea of work was exciting, the possibility of a future of her making. Freedom of choice and decisions. All of her work had turned out to be an illusion, lies woven by a master. And her marriage, it seemed, had been the same. Whether the illusionist had been her father or her husband, she didn't know.

An unwelcome moan sounded deep in her throat. She

leaned against the doorframe and closed her eyes. No one could see her like this. Not even when her mother died had she been allowed to show the depth of her sorrow. Statuesque at her funeral, gracious at the reception following, no one had seen anything more than the perfect daughter of the Arch Guardianess. They could see no different now.

Raina rolled her body until her back rested along the frame. The edging dug into her spine. She ignored the discomfort, instead focusing on the warm light seeping over the edge of houses beyond, spilling through the large windows to brighten her work space. She closed her eyes and took a long, deep breath.

Today would be no different than yesterday, or the day before. She'd smile, radiate charm and finesse. If Synintel asked any one of her clients how his daughter appeared, they'd have nothing more to say than she was the epitome of his genes. While Kevin had never expected, or even demanded, that she be his lady wife, her sire required no less. And with Raiventon gone, she was once more solely accountable to the Arch Guardian.

Just because life sucks right now doesn't mean I have an excuse to show weakness. She brushed away the fresh tears that slipped free, latching onto sharp bitterness. Her heart burned with anger and she sniffled away the sting of new tears trying to break free.

The faint click of a door closing made Raina gasp. She wiped her eyes and quickly headed for the stairs. Self-pity had been a bad idea after all. In such a hurry to get out of sight, she didn't notice the looming figure heading straight for her. Raina collided with a wall of muscle. Strong hands grasped her upper arms to keep her from falling backward.

Blinking, Raina looked up and found herself staring into stormy gray eyes. Her first reaction was to throw her arms around him and show exactly how much she'd missed him.

Her second, much stronger reaction, was to forget she was twenty-three years old and raised a lady.

She shoved him away. Hard.

Stunned, he didn't react when she did it again with enough force to cause him to lose his balance. Since he hadn't released his hold on her arms, she fell with him, sprawling across his chest and legs. The seething anger she'd been fostering since before she went to bed bubbled over. She straddled his stomach, her feet anchoring his thighs, her hands pushing his shoulders into the floor.

"Where have you been?" she demanded, punching his shoulder.

He opened his mouth to answer.

Raina cut him off, pushing the heel of her palms into the hollows of his shoulders. "Two weeks! I thought for sure my father called you off again, but here you are. So he didn't. Which means you just left me alone, without a single word." Hitting him again she shook her head in denial. "Why? Why would you do that?"

She grabbed his injured arm, looked it over, noticed not even scabs remained and glared at him. Hurt pierced her heart. She released the hold on his arm. "I was supposed to take care of you."

Trembling in her frustration, she scrambled off him and resisted kicking at his ribs. She shrieked in an unladylike fashion, fisted her hands, and stormed up the stairs. She stopped at the landing, stalked down a few steps and pointed an accusing finger at him.

"You won't let me be your wife for anything will you? Not in your bed, not to care for you, not even to bother to tell me where you disappeared to for two weeks." Heat exploded in her cheeks and she clenched her hands until her nails bit into the tender flesh of her palms. "Or will you not be lying when you tell my father you've been unfaithful?"

Kevin rose slowly from the floor, straightening the maroon cotton button up shirt he wore. Before he could open his mouth, she waved a hand and again spoke before he was able.

"Don't bother. If it wasn't worth telling me two weeks ago, it's not worth telling me now."

She realized too late turning her back to him had been unwise. On the landing a strong arm snaked around her torso and his hand clamped around her mouth. With a swift jerk, she found herself pressed against his chest. Her head fell back to his shoulder. Dark and furious, his gray eyes met her equally upset stare.

"Well, aren't you a fountain of emotion this morning," he murmured.

The warmth of his breath teased the hair near her ear. Heat from his body surrounded her, making her all too aware of the strength at her back and holding her. Tense, she grabbed handfuls of her fluffy cashmere robe, refusing to give him the satisfaction of touching him. She'd already embarrassed herself enough by pinning him to the ground.

"Now it's my turn to speak."

While he didn't release her, his hold loosened enough to make her feel held instead of hostage. His hand slid from her mouth, but his thumb began to trace the bottom of her lip, his gaze shifting. Transfixed by the simple, yet intimate motion, Raina continued to watch his handsome face, silent. The early morning light softened the angles of his cheeks and bearded jaw, made his storm-colored eyes seem almost black in their intensity.

"I was gone, princess, because Sean couldn't guarantee I wouldn't become infected. I couldn't risk you, not even if there was less than a one percent chance I contracted HRS."

A shiver raced through her body as her anger fled. The hurt however, remained. His thumb traced from her lip to her chin and fluttered along her jaw. Her thoughts struggled between focusing on the trembling his touch drew deep in her belly, and the frustration she tried to continue to hold onto. "You could have told me."

He shook his head. "No, you would have insisted I stay."

"As if I could make *you* do anything." Maintaining an even, butterfly wing pressure, his touch smoothed from her jaw to the hollow of her throat. Raina closed her eyes and resisted the urge to relax against his strong frame.

"My dear wife, you are the *only* one who could."

Raina turned her face away and stared at the wall of the landing. She tried to make sense of his words, wanting to rail that if he spoke the truth, they'd not be sleeping in separate rooms. But they did. Clearly her ability wasn't as strong as he claimed. "You could have written me a note, sent a message. Something. Anything. *Two weeks*, Kevin."

"That's the maximum time for the virus to go from dormant stage to final." With a sigh, he loosened his arm.

Reluctant to be free of his strength and presence, Raina slowly stepped forward. When he didn't join her on the landing, she turned to face him. Nearly level with him, her breath caught. She could kiss him with the same ease as she'd done the last time she'd been so bold. Only now she had a little more experience thanks to him. The compulsion was so strong she bit her lip and glanced down at her toes peeking out from under her robe.

"And you still could have written. The virus isn't contagious on paper."

"Very true, I could have." His index finger pressed under her chin until she met his gaze. "I'm sorry. I'm not used to someone worrying about me."

The apology and confession took her by surprise. "What about your team? Surely they care about your well-being."

His lips quirked into a smile, making them all the more enticing. "Knowing I'm alive is usually enough."

"It would be enough for me too," she whispered. "They often know more about if you're alive and well than I do."

"Raina."

Her name on his breath sent warmth spreading through her. She cupped his jaw and slid her fingers into the silken bristles of his beard. Giving into temptation, she pressed a lingering kiss to his lips. "Please don't leave me without a word again, it's all I ask. Promise me."

"I promise."

A door closing soundly echoed in from the back of the house. Chipper female voices floated from behind the walls. She wanted to say more, to confess what his absence had done to her heart, to her body. But soon they'd have an audience. With great effort, she let her hands fall and stepped away.

"I'm going to hold you to that, Master Guardian Raiventon."

"I expect you to, princess." Then a mischievous smile graced his all too handsome face. "Though if I get tackled to the floor by you when you're that angry, I might be tempted to ruffle your feathers more often."

13

"Guardianess Raiventon, it's beautiful!"

Frowning, Raina turned in her chair and glanced over her shoulder to see what her stylist elite fawned over. Glittering jewels fell between her fingers and over her palms, catching the warm glow of the lamps lit all over the dressing room. Large sapphires accented by smaller diamonds in a tiered, flowing pattern comprised a necklace and made Raina's breath catch.

Gripping the back of her chair tightly, Raina stared at the jewelry. "Where did that come from?"

Tabby glanced behind herself at a shelf with a small silver box. "I don't know, it was sitting on your bed, no note. Master Guardian Raiventon must have left it for you."

A knot formed in Raina's stomach. She held out her hand and Tabby let the gems slide onto her palm in a heap of wealth. She inspected the necklace, frowning. "I don't know. I think he would have given something this lovely to me in person."

Or rather not at all. She couldn't help but look over her simple wedding ring in comparison to the expensive piece she held in her hand. Kevin didn't strike her as the type to spend money so frivolously, even for her. And she also didn't think the outlandish display was his style. She chewed on her lip, letting the jewels fall onto her dressing table.

"I don't think I should wear it until I ask him."

Tabby pouted. Then with a grin she disappeared into Raina's vast closet. When she returned, she carried a dazzling royal blue gown with ornate beadwork on the off-shoulder bodice and along the flowing hem of the skirt. "Look! This will be absolutely stunning paired with it. Oh please, Guardianess Raiventon, please? For me? I haven't been able to adorn you in gems of that caliber the entire five years I've worked for you. You never want to wear anything so glitzy."

Raina chewed on her lip some more and picked at her fingernails. "I'm just not sure I should."

"Why? Who else could have possibly given you such a gift?"

The dread in Raina's stomach intensified. Considering the alternatives, she shook her head. "You're right of course, no one."

And to make sure her stylist didn't formulate any conclusions, Raina took a deep breath and agreed to be adorned with the necklace. An hour and a half later, Raina was clothed, and styled. Tabby fluffed out the bottom half of her gown and then stood back to admire her handiwork. She clasped her hands tightly to her chest and sighed.

"You are so beautiful, Guardianess Raiventon."

Raina looked herself over in the mirror, noting the simple curls piled atop her head, and a few left to cascade around her shoulders. She'd never been one for the towering hair loaded with baubles that had become high fashion. Thankfully, Tabby never pushed the style on her. Modest makeup colored her cheeks and eyes, accenting her fine-boned features. The gown highlighted her narrow waist, the figure-hugging top filled out enough of her breasts to make them appear fuller than they were. Sapphires and diamonds drew the rest of the attention to her neckline, sparkling any direction she turned.

"Yes, you have outdone yourself tonight, Tabby. Thank you."

Tabby curtsied in acknowledgement and then began cleaning the dressing room. Raina headed to the stairs, passing a curious glance at Kevin's open door and dark room. Downstairs, Mrs. Taft waited with Raina's thick black cloak. She swept the plush fabric around Raina's shoulders and helped settle it over her gown.

"Master Guardian Raiventon said he'll meet you at the theater."

Raina frowned at the information. "Did he say why?"

Mrs. Taft shook her head, fussing with the clasp of the cloak. "No, he simply said to tell you he's alive, healthy and he will see you at the event."

Wanting to simultaneously laugh at Kevin's kept *promise* and roll her eyes at his clear mockery of same said promise, she settled for sighing. "Thank you."

A footman waited at the door to escort her to the waiting carriage. She'd gone through the same motions for all the excursions she had to attend alone the last two weeks. For the first time in a long time, she'd actually been looking forward to attending something on her husband's arm. Once again though, she'd be walking in alone. Tamping down the disappointment, she fingered the cool stones around her throat. Perhaps Kevin had gifted the necklace to her, knowing how she'd feel.

Cool misty air swirled around her feet and toyed with the loose curls around her shoulders. Soon the chill would only be present during the early morning hours when summer came fully into season. Then open carriages with blankets would come into season, along with romantic night rides. Raina wondered if Kevin would take one with her. The thought made her smile.

The threatening rain drizzled by the time Raina arrived at the Haven City Performance Theater. A sprawling, intimidating structure complete with spires and gargoyles. The builder had had a mild obsession with a period in time called Pre-cataclysm Gothic style. A few other prominent builders in the city had become enamored with the dark designs.

Inside the lobby, instead of lamps, candelabras and high chandeliers cast a dull glow over everything, leaving heavy shadows. The low murmur of conversation and melancholy music drifting from a second story balcony added to the gloomily crafted environment. Raina paused at the wide entryway. Not a bright color in sight. Her vivid royal blue outfit seemed like a beacon among the crowd of blacks and grays with a few darker shades of reds and greens.

"A program for you, Master Guardianess," a low voice whispered behind her. Something brushed her fingers. She grasped a piece of paper. "Brave of you to arrive alone."

Gasping, Raina spun around. The program fluttered in her hand. Guests milled about near the door, some arriving, some going to get fresh air, in the huge open lobby. No one stood staring in triumph at having scared her. Turning back around, Raina searched, her pulse racing. Whoever had spoken the ominous words had vanished without a trace.

Raina shook off the odd greeting and slipped further into the lobby. She made her way to the huge staircase off to the right leading to the second story seating tier and private viewing boxes. She wondered if she could leave a message for Kevin at the ticket counter, and then go home. Anxious, she knew she'd spend the evening looking over her should every chance she could. There wasn't a reason to stay. Taking a deep breath, she lifted the hem of her gown and slowly pushed through the crowd to the waiting usher at the base of the stairs checking tickets.

No, she couldn't flee. Why someone felt the need to frighten her, she wasn't sure. Perhaps Synintel had made a new enemy. Wouldn't be the first time she found herself on the receiving end of something meant for him. And her father had provided the tickets to the performance, which meant she was perfectly safe.

She found her box, a thickly shadowed space with four elegant chairs, and watched the other patrons milling between the seats, aisles, and socializing. Aside from the ghostly lighting, dark colors, and eerie music floating in the air, the pre-performance mingling appeared normal, mundane.

"You shouldn't have stopped helping *us*," a voice whispered.

Raina swung around in her seat, gripping the padded, wooden backing. The dark velvet curtain fluttered, but no one stood behind her. Heart in her throat, Raina leapt up and grasped the heavy fabric, flinging it open. An empty corridor greeted her. Stepping into the hall, she saw a couple disappear around a corner into another box. Taking a bracing breath, she backed into her box, the all but forgotten program crinkling in her hand.

Frowning, Raina glanced down at the paper and relaxed her hold. Thick printed letters came into focus. Blood drained from her head until she swayed and collapsed in her seat. The paper trembled in her hand... No, the program wasn't real, it couldn't be real.

In Memory of Kevin Merrick, Master Guardian Raiventon
Born...

Raina scanned the dates in a flash, born twenty-seven years ago, and according to the paper, died today. Her heart clenched. Not real. Could *not* be real.

Raiventon is survived by his wife, Lorraina Melody Merrick.
Survived. As in alone, without him.

Panic clawed at her stomach until she struggled to pull in a normal breath. She snapped a glance over her shoulder, but only the curtain, now unmoving, greeted her. Attention forward, she attempted to breathe normally, but only harsh gasps escaped. She had to leave. She had to find Kevin.

Raina escaped the balcony, narrowly avoiding running into a small group passing her box. To keep from tripping down the stairs in a flight for the lobby door, she grasped fistfuls of fabric. The program— no not a program— memorial paper, crinkled against her palm.

Her heart echoed in her ears. She shoved her way through the crush of people gathered in the lobby, not caring how rude her actions were. Only when her first name was shouted near her ear and a hand grabbed her elbow, did she respond with a flinch and stop. Her gaze caught concerned amber eyes. Warm fingers slid to her wrist.

"Are you okay?" Sean asked.

Raina tried to grab at his jacket, but his hands caught hers. "Where is Kevin? Do you know where he is, right now?"

"No, I don't. Why?"

Raina released the paper into his hand. Frowning, Sean straightened the sheet.

The necklace shifted along Raina's skin. Blinking, she moved her attention from Sean to his wife, who stared at the collection of gems hanging from Raina's throat. Raina realized Katria was touching one of the large sapphires.

With wide eyes, Katria met Raina's stare. "Where did you get this?"

"My stylist said she found it on my bed, in a box," Raina whispered. "Why?"

Katria's hand fell away. Her mouth turned into a hard, straight line. "I almost died the night this necklace was stolen from us."

A startled cry escaped Raina's throat. *Stolen?* No… no she couldn't be wearing something stolen, let alone something someone almost killed to take. Had Katria not reached out to steady her, Raina would have stumbled back into the crowd.

"Calm down and breathe," Sean instructed gently, taking

hold on her forearm again. "Just breathe. It's going to be okay. We'll figure out what's going on, I promise."

"W-why would someone do this?" Raina managed to exhale out.

Troubled frown still in place, Sean slid his attention over the crowd. "I have my suspicions, but they won't be discussed here."

Slowly, he transferred Raina over to his wife, who gently took Raina's hand in hers. Sean slid his thumb along Katria's jaw. "Take her home, I'll be along in a couple of hours."

When Katria turned, holding tightly enough to Raina to force her to follow, Raina dug her feet into the floor. "No, I have to find Kevin. I have to know he's all right. He's supposed to be meeting me here."

Sean shook his head. "He's not coming to the performance, he never was. You weren't supposed to be here either."

The news made Raina's anxiety increase. She struggled to get free from Katria. "What are you talking about? My father sent the invitation, along with the schedule. This was our event tonight."

"Someone tampered with what your father sent. I don't know where Kevin is tonight, but I promise I'll find him." He held up the paper. "Whoever handed this to you did so only to scare you. Go home with Kat. You'll be safe there."

Confused, Raina allowed Katria to guide her through the throng of people and out into the wet night. Inside the carriage, Katria knelt on the floor and removed the top of the bench seat. She pulled out a rifle and a pistol, setting both on the floor with casual ease. Raina grasped a handful of fabric and stared at the metal gleaming in the streetlamps shallow light. The carriage lurched forward and began its bobbing journey down the brick road.

Katria fixed the seat and picked up both the weapons. In the thick darkness, Raina couldn't see the woman's features.

"Do you know how to shoot?" the Primary Guardianess asked coolly.

"No, of course not."

"Of course not," Katria repeated, her words light, as if she were smiling. Heavy metal landed in Raina's lap between her clasped hands and she gasped. "If the vehicle stops suddenly and the door opens, just pull the trigger. Okay?"

Breath lodged in her throat, Raina managed to squeak, "Okay."

Every flicker of bright light and overly harsh bump had Raina jumping in her seat. The gun in her lap felt too heavy, bringing forth a primal sense of fear she didn't know what to do with. Ignore, or give in? She couldn't bring herself to touch the cold, lethal steel, she couldn't even bring herself to look at it. And all the while her mind repeated the mantra that Kevin was alive, healthy, not the recipient of a bullet from a gun like the one on her lap.

When the carriage slowed, Raina's heart leapt into her throat. Katria sat forward, her attention out the window.

"We're home," Katria said. Her hand remained wrapped around the rifle, the barrel pointed up, stock positioned on the ground near her feet.

Raina didn't realize she'd been holding her breath until she sucked in air. Then she noticed *home* wasn't her home, but Katria's. "Why are we here?"

"Where else would we be?"

Katria didn't give Raina the chance to answer, opening the carriage door the moment they came to a stop. She leapt out, rifle tucked against her thigh, her hand held up in a motion that stopped Raina from following. Then Katria's fingers waved forward and Raina bit her lip.

The gun thumped to the carriage floor when she rose, causing her to leap back against the seat. Her head bumped the back of the carriage. She grabbed at the ceiling and bench to keep from teetering over. Good grief, she was being pathetic. Closing her eyes to steady her nerves, she took a deep breath.

Davis waited patiently at the open door. He raised a brow at the rifle in Katria's hand, but had no other outward reaction. When both the ladies were safely inside, he closed and locked them in. "Will you be needing anything, my Guardianess?"

Katria looked in question to Raina, who shook her head. "We're fine, thank you, Davis. I'll call if we change our mind."

"You'll be in the library?"

"Yes. Sean will be home with Kevin in... I'm not sure when, but they'll be here."

Davis bowed and then left them. Raina stood in the small foyer, unsure where to go. Katria disappeared two doors down into a dimly lit room. The last time they were at Wintersfalls, the emergency had been too great for her to take in the intimate home. A breakfast room that opened into a formal dining room was on her left. A sitting room, and another room with a closed door were to her right. Wide stairs led up to a hallway that branched in both directions.

Compared to most ranked Guardians, the home was small. But as she glanced around, Raina couldn't help but notice how comfortable the space felt. The couple had made the dwelling theirs with small touches of warmth from the landscape paintings, to the deep earthen shades of the painted walls.

Raina went to what she assumed was the library and came to a stop inside the two-story room. Floor to ceiling bookshelves lined the front half of the area. A large fireplace provided warmth to the space. Stairs leading to a loft were flush to the left wall. Papers littered a large, mahogany desk at the back. Blankets covered the couch, and one of the chairs in front of the desk. Books were piled on every small table in the room. Cozy and lived in, the space immediately made Raina feel at ease.

"You can wait here, unless you want to change into something more comfortable too? I'm sure my clothes will be a little big on you, but I never can stand to be in these gowns any longer than necessary." Katria tugged at the black satin gown she wore with a scowl.

Raina smiled at the offer. "Thank you, but I'm fine. I'm used to wearing them." She reached up with shaky fingers and unclasped the necklace. "Here."

Katria captured the cascade of gems in her palm. "Thank you. I'm not sure I'll ever be able to wear this again. Sean can return it to the Winters Fall Lake house when we go."

Before Katria could disappear completely, Raina called out, "Why did you bring me here?"

"Because Kevin would hand us our heads on a platter if we let you go home alone after this." She held up the necklace, letting the light capture the faucets in the beautiful stones.

"My home is safe," Raina felt compelled to defend.

"Really? Because someone managed to separate you from your husband tonight with great ease, and to make sure you faced the woman who was almost murdered the night this necklace went missing. A woman who is very capable of making sure *you* didn't walk away."

KEVIN HAD JUST WALKED into the bustling gallery of the event where he'd promised to meet Raina, when he spotted Sean heading across the room for him. Every nerve in his body wanted to rush to his friend and demand what had happened, because something was clearly wrong. But years of training in enemy territory to maintain an upper hand, no matter the cost, kept him calm. In control. Pulling on the bottom edge of his jacket, he eased along the crowd and met Sean halfway.

In a low, composed tone only Kevin could hear, Sean said, "Raina is safe, she's with Kat."

"Do we need to stay here for any amount of time?"

"Without our wives, I think it would appear odd."

Kevin raised a curious brow. "Then why show at all?"

Sean gave a predatory smile. "Who says we did?"

"Figments of imagination, hmm?"

"Well, I can't be two places at once, or even three, can you?"

Kevin chuckled, heading for the greenhouse, where they'd disappear into the night. Wouldn't be the first or the last time they appeared only to vanish at an event. "Who have you enlisted to help spread the sightings?"

"Asherwick's promised is feeling secluded. He's taking her to several houses tonight. Mason and Cora will also, at the same time, be speaking of just having seen us as well at a previous engagement."

"I wonder what people will think, our being so popular."

"Probably that someone else was mistaken for us, so where were we really?" Sean asked.

"Indeed."

"Don't worry, whatever someone had planned tonight will appeared to have failed, because it did," Sean said.

Kevin swept into a shadow with Sean close behind. The humid, earthen air hung heavily around them. Above, rain gently pelted the sheets of glass. Out in the night, a faint wind blew, chilling the already cold air further. His jacket soaked through quickly. They walked down the street away from the house to a hired carriage Sean had waiting.

Water puddled at their feet and on the wooden benches they sat on across from each other. Sean shut the door firmly and then rapped on the roof to let the driver know they were ready to leave. The steady clop of hooves and wooden wheels treading along over brick covered any conversation that could have escaped to the driver.

"Someone gave your wife gifts tonight," Sean said, leaning back against the rough wood of the hired transport.

"And I'm assuming sent her to the wrong event as well."

Sean nodded. "Correct."

Kevin kept from slamming his fist into the thin wooden wall beside him. "Damn. I thought I handled the spy in that house."

"Or perhaps Synintel has one in his. After all, she said the schedule had the event on it." Then after a brief pause, Sean asked, "Does he really schedule her life?"

"Sadly yes, and none of that changed with my being home."

Sean tapped his fingers on the seat. "You don't check what she receives?"

"I haven't, no. Mine usually arrives in a stack with other mail. I've always assumed Raina's match. I won't make the mistake again." Kevin rubbed the bridge of his nose, a sudden ache forming between his eyes. "What were the gifts?"

"Your Memorial pamphlet and the necklace stolen from Katria weeks ago."

Kevin snapped his attention to Sean despite the fact that he only caught glimpses of him in the passing streetlights. "My memorial?"

"Yes, someone printed that you died tonight."

Kevin clenched his jaw and held his arms open. "*Not* dead."

"I already noticed. I think that was done for Raina's benefit. To what purpose, I don't know."

"Or a warning to me," Kevin theorized. "They have after all, failed twice. Perhaps this is a warning the third time they won't."

Sean sighed.

"And the necklace is from the night Katria was stabbed?" Kevin asked.

Sean nodded.

Kevin cursed. "That is definitely a message my wife isn't any safer than yours was."

"Or an attempt to fracture our team," Sean said in contemplation.

Annoyance flashed through Kevin. "Who would be foolish enough to think either of you would place the blame on myself or my wife for Katria's injury, and your stolen property?"

"Someone who doesn't truly understand team dynamics."

"And the complete confidence that comes with them," Kevin mused.

Sean nodded. "Someone who plays in the shadow world, where no one can be trusted."

Kevin completed the rational. "So why would anyone else's life be different than theirs?"

"A good thing they think that way. We finally have something to put us ahead."

"Until they realize their mistake." Kevin rubbed his face, trying to ease exhaustion.

"Who says they will?" Sean leaned forward, bracing his hands between his knees. "Raina went home with Kat, seeming of her own free will, but she wasn't happy. The only staff in my house at this time of night is Davis, who once I walk in the door, will disappear to the staff quarters behind the house. No one will witness what happens in my home after I walk in the door. Raina can even leave alone, looking distressed."

"No, she won't leave alone," Kevin practically growled, his hands fisting on the seat beside him, angry Sean would even suggest something so foolish. "Too dangerous. If someone is watching, someone could also be waiting for an opportunity."

Sean held his hands up in defense, sensing Kevin's irritation. "She wouldn't be *alone* Kevin, you'd of course be waiting in the carriage for her." Sean chuckled. "The way you're acting, you'd think this was my first assignment, a complete novice at how to handle danger."

"You know better than anyone how helpless you can feel at the thought of your wife being in jeopardy."

"Yes, which is why I know better than anyone how to alleviate said risk." Sean leaned forward and spoke softly, "We've been speaking of trust. You trust me. Remember that."

Kevin took a deep breath, knowing his friend was right, knowing when the worst had happened, Sean had placed his entire trust in Kevin and his ability to save Katria. When the tables were possibly turned, Kevin could do no less. "You're right, I'm sorry."

"I know you're stressed. Instead of the danger being in my house, it's in yours."

"Seems to have been all along," Kevin said more to himself than to Sean.

Sean patted Kevin's knee in brotherly comfort. "We'll get it sorted out, one way or another."

They stopped in front of Sean's house, but only Sean hopped out, appearing to pay the driver, and also left instructions to venture on another five blocks to let Kevin out. Once well enough away from Sean's for anyone to see him, Kevin exited the carriage, paid the driver an additional amount, and then walked on foot a few more blocks. Hands shoved in his pockets, he ducked into a narrow alley, weaving between dozens of houses.

Kevin ensured no one followed. He stopped every couple houses, waited, watching. In the patter of rain and gentle rush of wind, listening was impossible. Confident he was alone, he slipped unnoticed into an abandoned greenhouse. The house had long ago began to crumble into disrepair, but the exterior wall connected to the greenhouse remained in solid condition. Using his foot, Kevin opened the secret door once installed by one of the many lovers of the former Guardianess Wintersfall.

The underground passage was dark, wet and held the musky odor of mold and decaying soil. Kevin ran his fingers along the damp, uneven brick wall, knowing each winding curve and irregular surface of the dirt floor. At the end, he opened a door into the shadowy underground room the team used for training. A single, long burning lamp glowed beside the door.

After gently closing the passageway, Kevin bounded up the long staircase that led to the second floor of Sean's house. The upstairs was dark, silent. He found the small group where he expected, in the library. They sat in silence. Raina stared at the floor, her hands clasped tightly in her lap. Katria was curled on Sean's lap on the other side of the couch. He stroked her back in lazy motions, sending her into a peaceful calm.

Sean met Kevin's gaze, but remained silent. Kevin took the hint, holding his finger to his lips when Raina's stare shot his direction. Relief mixed with need flashed in her pale eyes. She rose from the couch and rushed across the room so fast he had to catch her. Faint tremors wracked her small frame. A wave of fierce protection stole through him, forcing his arms around her weaker body, holding her close in the safety of his embrace.

"I was so scared," she confessed into his chest, her hands fisting in the wet fabric of his shirt.

He pulled her into the foyer so their conversation wouldn't disturb Katria's descent into slumber. Sean obviously wanted his wife to get some rest. Since Katria needed a full night's sleep to function properly, or she'd fall asleep anywhere she sat, Kevin understood.

Kevin grasped Raina's upper arms in his hands and gently rubbed them, his gaze locked with hers. "We can talk about what happened when we get home. But for now, I need you to leave here looking as frightened as you feel."

"Alone?" she asked, eyes wide.

"No, I'll already be in the carriage. Watch for the carriage from the sitting room window. Whoever is watching the house will assume Sean sent for one. Can you do that?"

While Kevin regretted keeping her in a state of fear, chancing on someone not believing her condition was real was worse. Kevin suspected Sean had kept fairly silent since his arrival, purposefully increasing Raina's anxiety. He didn't want to undo his friend's plan.

Raina took a deep inhale and nodded. "Okay. You promise you'll be inside, waiting?"

Cupping her cheeks tenderly in his hands, he pressed a gentle kiss to her lips and whispered, "I promise."

Her hands grasped his forearms, a faint tremble in her fingers. "I'm terrified."

Kevin rested his forehead against hers and sighed. "You should be."

14

Raina fidgeted at the window, staring out into the dark, rain-soaked night. Sean had disappeared up the stairs carrying his sleeping wife what felt like an hour ago. Of course, Raina knew she exaggerated the time, her anxiety making every-thing seem more than it was.

She tried to hold tight to the relief that had rushed through her when Kevin had walked through the door. Alive. Healthy. But in the endless black of night, fear slithered back in.

Where are you, Kevin?

Not a single light burned in the downstairs. The chill of darkness settled around her. More nervous than cold, Raina rubbed her arms and pulled the cloak tighter around her trembling frame. In the distance a faint glow of an approaching carriage pushed through the misty air. Raina pressed her hands to the cold glass, her heart pounding.

If Kevin's suspicions were correct, somewhere in the night, someone watched the Wintersfall house. Knowing she was being spied on only added to the growing fear gnawing in her belly. The hired ride came to a slow stop in front of the house. The horse shook water from his long, ragged mane and pawed at the brick street.

Raina took a deep, courage building breath and exited the house. She ran like fire burned under her feet to the awaiting carriage. The door stuck when she attempted to open it. Imagined visions of silver flashing through an open window as a gun barrel pointed her direction had her crying out and yanking with all her strength. The latch released so quickly she stumbled back.

Shadows blanketed the interior and for a second she hesitated. Rain drizzled down the opening of her gown causing her to shiver. Ignoring her panic, she leapt up. The second the door closed, a loud bang sounded on the roof. Raina squeaked and pressed herself into the rough wood bench.

"Relax, you're safe now," Kevin said.

Raina went to move across to him.

"No, not yet. We're still within viewing range and there are no curtains."

Frozen by his words, she glanced around. She'd never ridden in a hired vehicle before. The lack of luxury became immediately apparent. No carpet, cheap wood, and an odd odor made her nose wrinkle.

"What is that smell?" she asked.

"You don't want to know."

Raina rested her hands on her lap and sat straight enough to keep her back and shoulders from touching anything. "Will someone be watching at the house?"

"It's possible. But riskier to let you walk in alone."

"You already took care of the maid and changed the locks. No one has the new keys except Mrs. Taft and us," she felt the need to point out, unable to stop the tremble the small amount of water she'd collected settling a chill over her.

"True. But do you really want to walk in alone simply because I'll risk maybe being seen?"

The carriage bucked and shook over every slight change

in the brick road, a testament to the cheap labor that went into building the vehicle. Raina fought motion sickness. The stench inside and constant jerky sway was almost more than she could tolerate. Coupled with too many recent threats, she wanted to disappear into a hole. She realized with shocking clarity she'd taken her programmed life for granted. Everything her father did, he did to keep her in a bubble she now wished she hadn't been so eager to pop.

Releasing a shaky breath, Raina focused on the passing streetlamps. "Does it get easier?" she had to ask.

Kevin didn't pretend not to know what *it* was. He sighed. "Yes and no. Danger is funny that way, its relative. The more you're exposed, the easier it is."

"Familiar."

"Yes."

Raina hated the burn of tears she blinked away. "I don't want fear to become my normal."

"I know, and I wish—"

"That I had made different choices."

"Informed choices, yes. No one can fault you for wanting some freedom."

Raina rubbed her forehead. "My father will definitely fault my stupidity."

"Well, we both know I care less than zero how much Synintel *feels* about anything."

Raina wished she had the same luxury. But she didn't. Nor if she were perfectly honest, could she afford to. The Arch Guardian Synintel was not only her father, but held an authority in Sziveria Raina had been birthed into obeying. The short stint of rebellion she'd managed was now coming at a high cost. Dread rippled through her when she stopped to consider how much the defiance may hurt her father, and hoped Kevin had managed to help catch her mistake in time.

The carriage slowed to a crawl and then stopped completely. Kevin glanced out the window, confirming they'd arrived where they were supposed to. He reached for the handle, carefully opening the door into the foggy night.

Raina accepted his hand and breathed in deep the moment fresh air swept around her. Kevin released her long enough to the pay the driver before returning and guided her to the locked gate. He pulled keys from his pocket, then found the correct one. He released the large lock. The metal hinges creaked in protest, but swung open. The gentle clop of hooves slowly eased out of range until only rain pelting on leaves and ground sounded around them.

Within the house only a single lamp burned on the landing of the stairs. Silence descended like a blanket. Kevin listened, a tight hold on her arm. Raina held still, hating the hide-and-seek game her life seemed to have turned into.

Kevin locked the front door and then made her wait on the stairs while he checked the additional doors at the back of the house. Sitting on the stairs alone, in the quiet, Raina realized she never once checked the locks when she'd arrived home. Mrs. Taft had always waited up for her, leaving when Tabby did. Raina figured Kevin would check again after her stylist left for the night. If her housekeeper or stylist didn't remember to secure the house, Raina was alone and vulnerable to intruders. How had she never considered that before?

The jingle of keys preceded Kevin's return. "You can head up now, I know Tabby is probably ready to go home."

"What about what happened tonight?"

"Get cleaned up and comfortable, we can talk after, I'll be in my study."

At the mention of washing, Raina caught a whiff of the carriage stench and blinked in shock at the unpleasant odor. *I will* not *disagree with that suggestion.* "Very well."

Upstairs, Tabby made quick work of the gown, only making a face twice as she peeled away the gossamer layers and an unexpected, pungent aroma hit her. Raina took her time in the shower. Sitting on the cool tile floor with her shoulders hunched, the hot beat of water flowed over her back, easing stress away. She turned the flow off when the water began to cool, wondering if Kevin had showered too.

Her nightgown and robe were laid out for her, with her hairbrush. Tabby had vanished. Frowning, Raina quickly pulled the long cream silk nightdress on and then stared down at the brush. In the years Tabby had worked for Raina, she'd never left before making sure she was completely ready for bed. Had they been so late?

The mattress sank beneath her weight. Raina stared at the brush before attempting to pull it through her hair. The bristles caught in a tangle, causing them to twist and stick. When she tried to pull it free, the mess intensified. Appalled, Raina sat frozen, the hairbrush hanging from her head.

She'd been so intent on trying to figure out how to get the brush free without going bald, when Kevin's words broke her concentration.

"Please tell me you know how to use a hairbrush."

If THE SHOCKED expression Kevin's question had created hadn't told him the truth, the flush of heat across Raina's cheeks would have. No, apparently his wife was clueless about how to do something as basic as brush her hair. Great.

Sighing, Kevin went to inspect the damage. The thick bristles were so tangled the brush dangled sideways from the back of her head. "Do you have a comb?"

"Um…" Her lips pressed together until they disappeared. "Maybe in my dressing table?"

Kevin glanced around, noting a desk, a small dresser and a nightstand. "Which is where?"

"In my dressing room, through that door." She pointed to the door kitty-corner to her bedroom door across from the bed.

Using only the faint light spilling in from the bedroom,

Kevin quickly searched the dressing table and found a wide-toothed comb. Back in the room, he regarded Raina, knowing he had no other choice than to sit behind her on the bed. He wondered if he should convince her to put a robe on. The thin layer of shimmery silk did little to hide the feminine curves beneath.

"Scoot forward a little," Kevin ordered, climbing onto the bed behind her.

Raina stiffened, but did as requested. Kevin settled his thighs along her hips, careful not to press too close. Already the temptation to do much more than comb her hair plagued his imagination. Taking a steady breath, Kevin began to undo the knot around the brush.

"How is it you don't know how to brush your hair?" he asked after several quiet minutes.

The stiff bristles finally released the last of their silky hostages and Kevin went to slow work drawing the comb through the shoulder blade length strands. Fire light from the woodstove glinted off the paler tresses mixed in with medium shades of brown.

Her narrow shoulders shrugged. "I've always been told to sit and have my hair brushed and braided, or styled, or whatever needed to be done. The only place I put my foot down and insisted on privacy was my shower or bath."

Kevin placed his sole focus on the wide teeth smoothing through hair and not on the thought of her under the hot spray of a shower. He resisted the urge to bury his face and breathe in the sweet fragrance of her still damp tendrils. Struggled even harder against reaching around and seeing how hot her skin was beneath the silk. To learn if her breasts would respond to his touch the way the rest of her seemed to. A simple, basic chore would *not* turn into a form of seduction.

"Aside from bathing, everything is done for you?" He lightly swept gently curling locks away from her neck and over her shoulder. His fingers brushed along her smooth, pale skin. He ignored the heat that coursed along his arm and straight to his groin. Gritting his teeth, he breathed through the desire to once again test how she'd feel beneath his touch.

"Well, yes, I suppose it is. From the moment of my birth I've had attendants. I never really thought about it."

And why would she? Everything she ever needed was provided, right down to never worrying about what dress to wear, or how tangled her hair became while she slept. Someone handled the everyday little details of her life. Kevin's hand slowed halfway through his task as he closed his eyes. Raina would never be able to comprehend what life outside wealth was like. Where every choice made was yours and basic skills were necessary for functioning, let alone in some cases, surviving.

Pushing aside the reminder of all Synintel was poised to take from him, Kevin finished ridding her hair of tangles and then loosely braided the strands.

"Where did you learn how to do this?" she asked.

"My mother. She loved having her hair brushed and braided. She taught me how the moment my fingers were big enough for the job," he said with a smile at the memory.

Kevin grasped the thin ribbon lying on the bed and expertly wound it around the ends of her hair before securing it in a bow. "All finished."

"Thank you." She rose swiftly and put some much-needed distance between them. The delicate fabric of her robe billowed around her as she slipped it on.

Kevin remained sitting, pulling his feet onto the bed. Even though he already knew the answer, he asked, "Does Tabitha often leave you alone to do things yourself?"

Raina frowned, her attention on tying the sash around her waist. "No, this is the first time."

"How did you get the necklace?" Kevin kept his focus on her face, and not on how the wisp of fabric holding her robe closed accentuated the slenderness of her waist. Or how easy it'd be to simply tug the edges back open.

She wound the thick length of cream silk around her hands. "Tabby found it on my bed, in a box."

"You saw the box on your bed?"

Her tongue darted out and touched her full bottom lip, leaving it moist and far too kissable. "No, not exactly. She had it in my dressing room."

"Is it still there?"

"Let me check." She disappeared into the dressing room and then reemerged holding a small box.

Kevin accepted the container, looking over the simple design. "Not much for a fortune in jewels."

"Well, I suppose if you were handing something off for delivery, you'd not want to draw attention to the contents."

"And does someone usually open your packages for you?"

Raina blinked and wrapped her arms around her waist. "No… actually no one does."

Kevin turned the box over in his hand thoughtfully. "How long has Tabitha worked for you?"

"She's Mrs. Taft's daughter, so she's always been a part of the house. Mrs. Taft has worked here since before I was born."

Coincidences weren't something Kevin liked, but he accepted them. Tabby leaving Raina early for the first time, on the night she'd placed a stolen necklace around her employer's neck, seemed too calculated. "And the girl is happily married?"

"Newly married, so yes, still happy," Raina said with a hint of laughter on her voice.

Kevin grunted. The woman standing before him sadly had no idea *why* her stylist was still in the blissful phase of early matrimony. "Okay, so what happened at the theater when Sean found you?"

Raina quietly retold the events from the party, her skin

growing pale and face tight the further she went with the recollection. Before Kevin could stop himself, he'd tossed the box aside and had grasped her wrist, pulling her to the edge of the bed. He grabbed the knot of her robe, tugging on it until her thighs bumped the mattress.

"That's enough," he whispered when tears gathered in her eyes.

"I'm sorry, I'm not normally so cowardly."

He tugged again, until she acquiesced and climbed onto the bed with him. Knowing he shouldn't, playing with fire was always a dangerous pastime, he urged her further into an impossibly intimate pose. Her knees slid to either side of his hips, her rear resting between his crossed legs. He kept her positioned over his ankles, knowing just a slight tilt forward and she'd be over the one part of his anatomy far too desperate for her.

"You are not a coward, princess. Someone threatened you, twice, and made you believe something horrible had happened to me." His fingers caressed up her back in a soothing trail. Two layers of silk only intensified the heat of her skin, sending little whispers of hunger along his nerves. Oh, could he be a bigger fool with himself?

"And the necklace? Was it really stolen from Guardianess Wintersfall, and did she almost die?" she asked.

The muscles of her back tensed beneath his touch and he applied deeper pressure. "We were able to get to the injury before she bled to death on Sean's dining room table."

"You were there?" she asked softly, her eyes searching his.

"Yes, I was there."

The same night Sean had realized a life without Katria wasn't one he wanted to exist in. The moment when everything had changed for the couple, so used to working together for years, deciding to work as one to build a marriage neither had asked for. Kevin then watched in fascination as the two, having fought their attraction, embraced their union with a ferocity that wouldn't be contained for anything. He'd wondered if the same were possible with Raina. Only to realize with sinking clarity it certainly was, and he couldn't allow their union to fully evolve into the love-filled desire threatening to consume him.

"So whoever stole the necklace," she mused, drawing him from his depressing thoughts of their lack of a future together. "Must have had a plan for it all along. Do you think it always involved me?"

"Perhaps. Sean is of the opinion someone is trying to drive a wedge in our team. So whether you, or another woman close to one of us, I think he's right. The necklace was used in an attempt to cause discourse."

Her brows furrowed. "But it didn't work... did it?"

Kevin chuckled, he couldn't help himself. "Not even a little."

Beneath his touch, her frame noticeably relaxed. He wanted to ease her forward, closer, until her chest and her hips settled into his. But he didn't dare. Whatever thread of self-control he managed to hang onto would snap the moment she became too close to completely push away. He wanted her with a passion he'd never experienced before, and knew he wasn't likely to again.

Damn you, Synintel, and your authority over me.

"I was worried. Primary Guardian Wintersfall didn't even speak to me when he arrived home," she whispered.

Kevin sighed, more in regret to easing her off his body, than to Sean's approach to keeping Raina in a state of panic. With a gentle push on her thighs, he forced her to settle back against her pillows. He put distance between them and forced the yearning controlling his body away.

"Only one of us doing something really stupid will cause a rift on our team. And even then, we forgive," he said, then amended, "In time, anyway."

"I'm glad you have such a strong bond with them. I don't

think whoever is doing this realizes how formidable you can be."

Kevin smiled, though he wasn't feeling nice. "That would be helpful."

Settling further into the fluffy wall of pillows, Raina pulled her knees to her chin and hugged them close. She seemed so small, fragile. Kevin resisted the compulsion to climb in behind her and wrap his arms around her.

"I wish I knew if everything that happened at the theater was connected to the necklace. Or if the necklace and the terrible fake memorial pamphlet was for you."

"Someone went to the trouble to ensure we'd be separated tonight."

Her arms tightened around her legs and she buried her face until only her eyes peered at him. "An attack meant for both of us... done through me." A visible shudder wracked her delicate frame.

Kevin stood before he did something he wouldn't be able to stop. "It's over, we're both safe. They accomplished nothing." He paused at her door, hand on the knob. Her worried gaze washed over him and Kevin's grip tightened. He didn't want to leave her. "Get some sleep."

Then with a strength he didn't know he possessed, he somehow managed to close the door.

RAINA STARED AT THE DOOR, flexing her jaw. She knew she hadn't missed the unmistakable sign of desire as Kevin had walked away. The knowledge made the heat growing in her from the languid, seductive way he'd cared for her almost unbearable. So why then, did he leave?

Huffing in frustration, she kicked at the thick, downy blanket covering her bed until her feet slipped under. Honor of course. Because for some odd reason, Kevin truly believed they'd live life as paupers if her father had his way. Foolishness, but was she prepared to call Kevin's bluff on it?

Pulling the blanket up to her nose, she still stared at the door, willing her husband to walk back through. What would he do if *she* went to *him*? Oh the thought was deliciously wicked. Until she considered the repercussions. What if he threw her out?

She raised a brow.

But what if he didn't?

Her imagination wasn't complete enough to consider the ultimate outcome of acceptance. Sure she knew he'd kiss her, and a faint pleasurable shiver of remembrance at the way he'd surely touch her again. But what else? The not knowing brought a trickle of fear. Despite what Kevin said, it seemed she was indeed a coward, as she'd admitted to being.

Burying her head under the blankets, she groaned in frustration. How many more weeks did they have? Two, no three, at least. Maybe a few more days beyond. Once the matter of his rank was settled, he wouldn't be able to deny her any longer.

Eventually fitful sleep found Raina. Having fallen into slumber with her husband on her mind, she'd dreamt of him. Of his mouth, hands and strong body. She'd awoken with a burning need, frightened by the intensity and unsure what to do about it. If anything was to be done. She had a feeling if she asked Kevin, he'd avoid her for the day.

A gentle knock preceded Tabby opening the bedroom door at the same moment Raina's feet touched the cold floor. Raina tried not to glare at her stylist, but she must not have done a great job, because Tabby gave her a bashful smile at the woodstove.

"I'm sorry I left early last night. I... I had to see my husband, I just couldn't wait." Tabby loaded cut wood into the stove, digging the fresh tinder into the smoldering, glowing coals.

Raina realized she'd slept in her robe and tried not to roll her eyes. Had she been so distracted? The ribbon Kevin had tied had come free at some point during her restless night. Her hair fell in a tangled mess around her face. "I was a little surprised. Is everything all right?"

Excitement burned in Tabby's bright blue eyes. "Everything is so perfect." She rose, her hands clasped to her chest. "I'm pregnant!"

Raina gasped in surprise. "Oh Tabby, that's wonderful news! Was he excited?"

"Yes, very much so. I haven't told Momma yet. I knew for certain yesterday."

"I won't spoil the surprise," Raina promised, her hands reaching for Tabby's. At least now she knew why one of her most trusted employees had been so scattered lately.

Tabby uttered her thanks and then set about preparing Raina for a day full of clients. Raina tried to ignore the unexpected ache in her heart at her stylist's joyful news. Tried to ignore the sliver of jealousy over the life the woman's seemingly perfect marriage had created.

Taking a deep breath, she shed the robe. The silk fluttered along her back and puddled around her ankles. Raina closed her eyes and attempted to put the flashes from her dream out of her mind. Her dreams seemed to be the only place her husband would accept a union with her.

At the dressing table, Raina wondered why she suddenly felt so compelled to push for the completion of her marriage. Sure, she was curious, but examining herself in the mirror, she realized curiosity wasn't the strongest reason. She wanted to *know* Kevin, all of him. The kind of knowing that only happened when two people could look at each other and discern the secret no one else did. How very much they loved each other, mind, body and soul.

Loving Kevin Merrick wasn't a hard thing. She was quite certain the moment she'd seen him she'd fallen hard with the emotion. Not only had he been the most handsome man she'd ever met, and the most dangerous, but there'd been a gentleness to him, an authenticity no one else in her world displayed. And he'd looked at her in the moment of their first meeting the way no other man had ever looked at her. With desire. As if she alone belonged to him, would only ever belong to him.

Then she'd made the mistake of saying she'd be a dutiful wife, that her bed was his whenever he wished to claim her. She'd been dispassionate, formal, the daughter of an Arch Guardian making sure the man once beneath her station understood she knew the rules of society. With the signing of a contract, they'd become equals. At least, to Raina they had. Apparently to Kevin, they never would be.

Raina frowned, toying with the comb now back on the dressing table. Kevin's intense words to her that day crept in like a shadow.

When I come to your bed, it'll be because you want me there.

He'd spoken those same words over her prone body weeks ago in what she'd thought had been a dream. Worst yet, she *did* want him in her bed, had since he'd returned to her life, yet she didn't know how to make her desire any clearer. Beg maybe? Growling a sigh, she shoved the comb away. No. A Guardianess did not *beg* for anything.

Tabby hummed merrily, adding to Raina's sour mood while the stylist flitted around and made her presentable. Dressed in a simple flowing cotton cream skirt, a navy blue silk blouse and rich brown wool, open vest, Raina inspected her appearance in the full length mirror beside her dressing table. Her hair was styled in a professional bun with a few curls around her face to keep her looking feminine. She'd allowed Tabby to put some gloss on her lips and a little blush on her cheeks, but nothing more. After the situation with Enbrackon, Raina didn't want to inadvertently have a client think she was anything more than a logistics expert.

The house was silent downstairs. Her first patron wasn't due to arrive for over an hour. The first three appointment files would be waiting on her desk, laid there the yesterday afternoon by her assistant for Raina to review before the day started.

Raina almost missed Kevin leaning against the doorway into the breakfast room. Light filtered in behind him, casting the edges of his frame in a golden glow. He held a steaming cup of coffee in his hand. Barefoot under dark brown slacks, with his sleeves rolled up his forearms, the first two buttons undone on his white shirt, he looked his usual self. Carefree and completely *un*-wealthy. And so utterly delicious Raina's heartrate picked up.

Unable to stop herself, she paused on the stairs and raised a brow. "Do you have to think about it when people refer to you as Master Guardian Raiventon?"

He took a slow sip of coffee, dark gray eyes never leaving hers. "Since I've been Raiventon for eleven years while home, and Merrick or Kevin while away, all the names get my attention."

While she'd remained simply Guardianess Raiventon. Only her father or Enbrackon ever referred to her as Lorraina. Staring at Kevin she realized with a knot of unease, her formal first name had always been Synintel's means of asserting dominance over her. How had Enbrackon known to do so as well?

Kevin straightened from the door frame. "What's wrong?"

Raina took a deep breath and smiled away the apprehension. She saw no need to draw attention to something that was likely her putting more credit than was due on Enbrackon. "Nothing."

His stormy gaze narrowed. "Are you sure?"

"Yes, of course." She brushed her fingers across her forehead. "I'm still a little nervous about last night is all."

"I don't believe you." She went to open her mouth to

argue, but he held up his hand and spoke first. "But I'll let it slide. When you trust me enough to tell me, I'll be waiting."

"I trust you," she said before she could stop herself.

The small smile he offered didn't reach his eyes. "Then when you trust yourself."

Raina once again went to disagree, but snapped her teeth together. He'd already spotted one lie, judging by the annoyed way he regarded her, somehow she didn't think he'd tolerate another. So, she nodded and glanced away from the gaze observing far more than she wished.

"I'll be gone for a while this morning. Don't leave the house until I return home."

Had anyone else given the order, Raina would have been bothered. But Kevin hadn't tried to control any part of her life, and she knew he only cared about her safety. If Raina did too, she needed to obey. "Where are you going?"

"Mason's. He had some questions about the map project."

"Shouldn't I go too, then?"

He shrugged. "I'll see what he needs and if so, we'll go back tonight."

Mrs. Taft appeared from the formal dining room door, a tray heavy with hot tea, scones and breakfast meat in her hands. She rushed past them both on the way to Raina's study. Kevin broke away from the doorway once the head housekeeper was clear. He stopped at the bottom step and Raina grabbed the banister to keep from meeting him at his level.

"Remember, don't go anywhere until I return."

"I have clients to meet, no plans on leaving the house."

"Promise?" he asked, a smile dancing in his eyes.

Raina submitted to the temptation and stepped down the three steps until she was at eye-level with him. "Promise."

Kevin traced her jaw to her lower lip. The pad of his thumb smoothed along before being replaced with his mouth. Sugar, vanilla and the faintest hint of bitter coffee lingered on his lips. Raina closed her eyes, savoring the flavor and sensation of his mouth moving against hers. Her body, already humming with far too much awareness of him, longed to move closer with an almost frightening need.

"Thank you," he whispered into her mouth and then moved away.

Cold air shifted between them and Raina blinked. Only the lingering scent of coffee and Kevin's soap let her know she hadn't imagined the entire exchange. How in the world did the man move so fast?

Sighing, Raina trailed her fingers down the bannister and around the edge, jumping from the last step in a juvenile hop. She smiled, deciding her husband's small act of intimacy would be the official start to her day.

Four hours and seven clients later, Raina set the latest file aside with a weary huff of breath. Janice retrieved the record and set five more down.

"Mr. Bentonmore is in ten minutes. He has yet to arrive," Janice stated, tucking the folder into the crook of her bent arm.

Raina reached for the top of the stack and pulled the paperwork forward. After a cursory glance, familiarizing herself with her next appointment, she nodded. "Yes, he's usually five minutes late. Take a break if you'd like."

Janice inclined her head in acknowledgement before swiftly vacating the study. Raina reviewed the files her assistant had delivered. She'd made it through three when a timid knock sounded on the door. She closed the folder and looked up, smiling, expecting to see Mr. Bentonmore. Instead Mrs. Taft stood in the entryway looking grim. Raina's smile faltered.

"Is everything okay, Mrs. Taft?"

"Footmen have arrived from Arch Guardian Synintel, my Guardianess."

Raina's heart lurched into her throat. She grasped the edges of her desk until her fingers ached. No, this wasn't happening. Not yet. Licking her dry lips, Raina took a deep breath to stay calm. "Master Guardian Raiventon isn't home, you can tell them to leave. I'm not sure when to expect his return." *And if my father wants my husband, he can arrive himself to collect him.*

Mrs. Taft glanced over her shoulder, her hands clenched at her sides. "They aren't here for Master Guardian Raiventon."

Raina stared at her housekeeper, unsure she'd heard correctly. Never, in her four years of being gone from the Arch Guardians house, had he personally sent men to escort her. Synintel always requested Raina's presence with a note, *if* he asked at all. Usually Raina went to him. "Excuse me?"

"They've asked for you."

"You're certain?"

"I asked twice to make sure." Mrs. Taft glanced over her shoulder again, her hands locked together over her generous stomach. "Would you like me to send them away?"

Raina bit her bottom lip and glanced down at her desk. Whatever reason her father had sent the men for must be important, or Raina knew he wouldn't have done so. Disobeying his wishes was sure to get her a lecture the likes of which she hadn't had since childhood. She couldn't think of a safer place to be than with her father's personal guard, other than in her husband's protection.

"Master Guardian Raiventon did insist you stay home until he returns," Mrs. Taft pointed out.

Uneasy by the housekeeper's concern, and the uncharacteristic method of her father's request, Raina opted to turn the footmen away. "Yes, that's a good idea. I can explain to my father, or Kevin can. We will both go see him later tonight. I'm sure he'll understand. Thank you, Mrs. Taft."

Relief washed across the older woman's face. "Absolutely. I'll inform them immediately."

With a swish of her plain black skirt, Mrs. Taft left the

room. Raina relaxed for all of thirty seconds when the rustle of fabric made her look up again. Mrs. Taft frowned and shook her head.

"They won't leave without you. They said your father insists."

Well, that answered that. Raina huffed and stood, hands pressed firmly on the desk. "Very well, but please send word to Primary Guardian Kynhaven's residence to the care of my husband where I am."

"You could just wait upstairs, they can't exactly kidnap you."

Raina raised a brow. "I don't need the drama. If Arch Guardian Synintel is so insistent, then I'm sure there's a good reason. I'll be fine."

But the moment she walked outside, she came to a stop. A footman wearing her father's livery grabbed her elbow and forced her along the walk.

"W-what are you doing? That's not my father's carriage," Raina argued, trying to pull her arm free.

"He didn't want to alert anyone, or cause attention. It's his carriage, his personal carriage he uses for work."

For work. Raina looked over the simple vehicle, reminiscent of the one she'd ridden home in last night with Kevin. A hired carriage. Ambiguous, untraceable, poorly built like the hundreds it'd pass on the streets. She tried to pull free again, not believing the lie for a moment. No matter where her father went, he'd do so in comfort, even incognito.

"Let go of me!" she screamed, hoping to capture the attention of anyone within hearing.

The door swung open and she was shoved inside. She hit the floor with a cry, her hands skimming along the rough wooden floorboards. Her feet were pushed in until her knees bent, and her skirt came flying over her back. Cold air brushed her exposed legs. Curling into herself, Raina quickly scrambled onto her side. The door flew closed, shaking the small carriage with the force.

A faint tsk sounded and Raina looked at the shiny booted feet attached to legs wearing expensive gray wool slacks. She slowly pushed upright and met Enbrackon's dark gaze, black in the low light.

"I tried to make this so much easier on you, I really did. But you seem determined to make everything so hard, Lorraina." His voice was soft, laced with regret.

She pushed herself up, brushing fallen hair from her face. Panic threatened to choke her voice. Remaining calm, she regarded his clasped hands between his knees and the calm way in which he regarded her. "You tried to make it easier to kidnap me?"

"I tried to not resort to this at all." He sat back in the seat, his hand reaching into the shadows.

Fear tightened Raina's throat. The carriage hadn't moved yet, which meant they were still in front of her house. She launched herself for the door. Sharp pain exploded across her scalp followed by a fiery pain in her hip. The flash of a syringe barely registered in her mind. Suddenly weak, she made a grab for the door, which faded from her vision.

"Wha..." The floor rose to meet her face. Enbrackon's voice echoed in her mind, but the words were lost. Then everything went black.

15

"And see this here?" Mason's hand smoothed along the map of Westica Raina had given for reference. "I don't have any of these rail lines on my version."

Kevin leaned over the two maps. Mason had laid them side by side. Not only did Raina's map have more rail lines, but shipping docks along beaches in the Sea of Mexico that were located in uninhabited zones. Everyone assumed the land was still barren and hostile from the cataclysmic event that had nearly destroyed the world almost a thousand years ago. Only islands, and coastal land around the Atlantic, Black and Indian Oceans seemed to have survived enough to sustain life. At least, that's the only place humanity existed anymore.

Pulling a second map down, he tapped Mason's Westica map. "Where's your South American continent map?"

"I don't really know how what's left that the Pacific didn't claim can still be called a continent."

"Yeah, well, last I knew there were outlining islands and a large enough chunk that humanity didn't want to relinquish continent status. Raina has a rail line running almost the entire length of the coast here. Do you have that?"

Mason pulled a huge sheet of paper free from one of the dozens of wide, thin drawers off to the right of his desk. He laid the map out, smoothing his hands across the expanse while examining the details. "I have docks, and a short rail line from Perazil to New Columbia."

"Interesting," Kevin muttered. "How much older are your maps from hers?"

"Six months, maybe. I have to keep updated maps for strategy planning. I'm pretty useless if I don't know all the routes available to us, or our targets."

"Copy that," Kevin said with a sigh. "Okay, so if your maps are accurate, and hers are accurate, which ones are right?"

"I don't see how it'd be in their interest to give her access to nonexistent routes. I'm going with hers are the correct renditions. The question is, why do laymen have knowledge of these rail lines and port cities?"

Kevin drummed his fingers in thought, pulling Mason's map closer. "Maybe they don't. Maybe someone has been keeping this information secret."

"It takes years to build rail lines. Docks can be done faster. But the resources needed for the rails, especially the iron or steel, is expensive." Mason leaned over, his elbows dropping to the table. He shoved his fingers into his long black hair and growled in a manner that matched his rather wild look. "If someone has been keeping logistics of this magnitude secret from the highest echelon of not only our government, but the allies we work with, this is bigger than we could ever imagine."

"And my wife is part of it." Kevin wanted to shove everything off the desk in a fit of anger, but he knew the action would do little good except to make him feel better. And piss off his friend. He stood and jammed his hands into his own hair and turned his back to the sheets of paper that spelled mounting danger. "She can't walk away from this, they'll never let her. Damn it! And Synintel… he's known this entire time and said *nothing*."

"Well, we always figured him for a scab, now we know."

Kevin wracked his brain, tried to figure out how he could learn more information sans his useless father-in-law. "Sean went to Voklane when Kat was in trouble, yes?"

"Voklane was directly involved in what happened with Kat. Sean wanted to know just how much."

"Which means Voklane may know as much as Synintel."

"Likely he does, yes. But he told Sean he won't speak without the Arch Guardians permission."

Kevin flexed his jaw. "He'll speak to me."

Mason snorted. "I suppose if anyone can convince him to ignore the boss's orders, it'd be you."

A sharp knock sounded on the door and Mason straightened. Kevin turned while Mason swiftly pulled his version of the map they'd been looking over to cover Raina's.

"Enter," Mason called.

"A message has arrived for Master Guardian Raiventon," Tybalt said, a folded paper in his hand.

Kevin rounded the desk and met the butler halfway, accepting the note. "Thank you."

Tybalt left them.

Kevin quickly read the message, his stomach falling. "Raina's housekeeper says her father sent men, insisted she go to his house."

Mason propped a hip against his desk, arms crossed. "Is that like him?"

"I have no idea." Kevin rubbed the stubble under his chin. "But I'm going to say no. They show up to collect me, but I've never seen them arrive for her, and she's never mistaken who they want."

The knot in Kevin's stomach increased. He met Mason's silver eyes. "Find out every piece of property Enbrackon owns, no matter how inconsequential. I'm going to see Voklane."

"Not Synintel?"

"Why? So he can tell me to find his daughter and dismiss me? No, this isn't going to end well. I need to know Jonathon Hunter won't be showing up at my door with a certificate for custody."

"I'll find what you need on Enbrackon, and notify Sean and Kat." Mason walked to the door. "Go, we both know she doesn't have a lot of time before he does something stupid."

Kevin fisted his hand. "He's already done something beyond foolish."

SHARP POUNDING pain deep in her head pulled Raina from drug-induced sleep. Groaning and catching a sob in her throat, she tried to roll from her back onto her side, curling into herself. A sudden jerk on her ankle stopped the motion. Again, she tried to shrink into a ball, the pain in her skull causing her stomach to pitch, but her leg refused to budge. Hurt and confused, Raina blindly felt around her feet. Her fingers caught around a thick cold link of chain.

Swallowing against the dryness coating her mouth and throat, Raina forced herself upright. A wall was at her back, something pliable, yet firm beneath her. She waited until her head stopped spinning before carefully opening her eyes.

Enbrackon sat in a seat across from her. Dull light filtered through high windows. Dust danced in the weak beams. With a shiver, she realized they were mostly alone in a vast empty room. A warehouse maybe. The echo of something being dropped somewhere told her others were present, just not where they were.

"Don't look so distressed, my dear Master Guardianess," Phipps said gently. A thin cigarette rose to meet his lips. Tendrils of smoke drifted in the air, mixing with the particulate floating around him. "Your husband is quite good at finding lost things. He'll find you."

Raina couldn't stop the trembles wracking through her frame. She grabbed at the blanket beneath her folded legs. When she attempted to speak, the words hung in her throat. Closing her eyes, she took a deep breath and tried again. "You want him to?"

"Yes, I do. I've tried three times to get rid of him. I've tried more times than I can count to make it unnecessary." He took another long, slow drag from his cigarette. The end glowed brilliant orange before fading into ash. Smoke escaped from his lips and nostrils while he looked her over. Every inch of her. "But you'd have none of it. So, you could say, Raiventon's death will be on you."

The words were spoken with such calm, as though he discussed nothing more than the recent rain they'd had. Raina's teeth chattered. Another shiver raced up her spine and down her limbs. "Y-you've tried to k-kill my husband?"

"Tried. Failed." He shrugged, looked at the end of his cigarette, and then brought it back to his mouth. "And if I believed raping you would equate to that ridiculous infidelity clause you put in your marriage contract, I'd simply take care of things now, no death necessary. But, Raiventon is sadly too noble for that, and you my dear are too noble for seduction. Therefore, death for him it is."

Had Enbrackon lost his mind? "What are you talking about?"

He looked at her like a parent regards a child. "Your marriage contract, Lorraina. There's only two ways out of it."

Raina glared, her mind clearing enough for her to realize she needed to assess her very foreign situation. Daughters of Arch Guardians did *not* find themselves prisoners of Shield Guardians. And a prisoner she definitely was. He'd chained her ankle to the wall. She sat on a palette of some kind. Padded enough to keep the hard floor from becoming painful. A shallow loft took up a quarter of the upper part of the warehouse. The building was completely empty except for a few small crates stacked in a far corner.

"Why do you care about my contract?" she asked, giving a gentle tug on the chain, watching the bolts in the wall. Not even a hint of movement. She could jerk until she bled, it'd do her no good. Great.

"What do you know about the inheritance clause in ranks?" he asked.

Confused and annoyed by the question, she blinked and snapped, "The what?"

He pulled a drag on his cigarette and regarded her with uncontained frustration. "The inheritance clause. For ranks."

"Not much." Other than one was the reason her husband kept a frustrating distance from her.

"Did you know you, or your husband, can take over your father's rank providing your husband assumes the family name?"

Raina stared at him, unable to hide her shock. "No, I didn't."

He nodded and released a lungful of smoke. "Oh yes, it's always been that way. If the daughter wishes to assume her father's role, or the son-in-law, it's possible if it's approved."

Unsure what to make of the information, or why it held relevance to her being chained to a wall, she remained quiet.

Her silence didn't deter him. In the muted light, his dark eyes were black, holding a hard edge she'd never noticed before. Or never wanted to. "Raiventon has no desire to be the next Synintel, nor could I see him giving up the Merrick name. So much pride in that name. Or do you not know just who his father was?"

Heat climbed up Raina's cheeks. She looked down at her hand bunched in the dark red blanket beneath her, knowing the action told her shame the way she didn't want her eyes to. She knew next to nothing about Kevin's past, nor had she asked more than a handful of questions. Granted, he hadn't given her much of a chance.

Phipps's low chuckle forced her eyes closed. "Ah, you don't." He tsked. "Oh well. Remind me to show you some of the articles written about him. I think you'll be impressed."

"Why are you telling me all this?" She tried to keep her voice steady, but tears threatened. She wasn't chained to a wall for nothing. Nor was he speaking about Kevin in any manner except for threatening.

"I want you to understand I had no other choice." Mock sadness entered his gaze. He sat forward, the cigarette poised between two fingers even as he clasped his hands between his knees. "Your father won't be controlled. Raiventon would be no different even *if* he wanted your father's power in society and within the First Intelligence Office. That position is key, and I need it."

He pointed the smoldering cigarette at her. "*You*, my beautiful Lorraina, are *my* key to the kingdom. Literally. All that stands in the way is your wretched marriage contract."

Raina stared at him in repulsion and horror. "You think to have me?"

"I know I'll have you." He straightened. The smug gleam in his eyes raked over her body, forcing another shudder from her. "You've already signed the necessary documents. The second Kevin Merrick is dead, you're mine. All that will be left is disposing of your father once I've made the necessary steps to procure the Arch Guardianship. Others have failed in the past to secure such a vital ranking for us. I won't be one of them."

Fear and denial welled in her stomach. She didn't have time to wonder about the *us* he mentioned. No, she had bigger issues to worry about. She pressed her back into the wall, searching in her memory for when she could have possibly committed such a colossal mistake. "I have signed nothing."

The spent cigarette dropped to the floor, smoldering faintly near his boot. "You did, the first month we worked together, in one of the many piles of documents I had you sign for your *clients*. A little trick the FIO has been doing to operatives for years." He pulled a fresh smoke from his shirt pocket. "Don't believe me? Ask Wintersfall."

"You've lied to me from the beginning." She shook her head, the tears finally falling in a wet streak to drip off her jaw. "Everything... one terrible lie."

A match flared next to his thigh with a swift strike against the wood. He lit the cigarette in his mouth before shaking the flame out. "Everything was going quite well until Synintel had to bring Raiventon back into the picture. I could have figured out a way to dispatch of him on one of their many, many dangerous missions. But, no, Daddy had to keep his precious little Arch Guardianess safe. Not that I mind, really, except he's protecting you from me." He took a long, slow pull. "And I have to say, it's been rather annoying. I'm done with the games. So here we are."

"I'm not an Arch Guardianess. I never have been."

"You are, just not officially. But soon. Soon you will be higher ranking than even the daughter of the queen." His dark brown eyes gleamed. "Why would you not desire that again? You were after all so intent on working in those circles. Everyone in the country and beyond will flock to you, want to be seen with you. Just stand in your presence and *say* they spoke a word into your ear."

Something dark and unpleasant settled in Raina's stomach. She pulled her legs closer to her body, ignoring the uncomfortable bite of the metal shackle around her ankle. "I don't care about power. I never have. I just want to be free of my father's influence, nothing more."

And now I see the terrible cost of my whining and ungratefulness. She closed her eyes to shut out the unwelcome truth.

"No matter, you'll have it anyway. And I know Synintel

trained you well. You'll be a dutiful, gracious wife. You'll host all the perfect parties, and dinners, and entertain all the foreign dignitaries I desire. We'll be an unstoppable team."

Raina could see no point in spewing the venom on the tip of her tongue. Restrained, subdued and at a disadvantage, angering him would be worthless. Instead, she opted for information. "You said you've tried three times to defeat Raiventon. How do you think you'll succeed this time, if he manages to find me? I don't even see how that's possible."

He laughed, a sharp unpleasant barking sound. "So little faith in your man. I wonder if he knows you feel that way? No matter. Yes, I failed the first three times. I underestimated him. This time, however, I've made sure the odds are completely in my favor. I've hired Cairoen Sentinels. Brought in on a shipment of, oh what was it again? Ah yes, cotton. I believe you wrote out the manifest for it two weeks ago."

Raina gasped. Even she'd heard of the feared Cairoen Sentinels. A force of Cairo slaves, born for no other purpose than to be trained as elite warriors for trade or hire. They had one task, they learned one single thing. How to annihilate an enemy, either single or in force. Cairo had worked hard for its place of power in the inhabited world. Their Sentinels held that influence and, when the price was right, offered it to others.

"And do not fear, he *will* find you. You must remember he's an Intel Guardian. Between him, Wintersfall and Kynhaven, they'll know where you are before the sun even sets."

Raina had everything to fear. She was bait to trap her husband for his demise.

16

Within two minutes of walking into the First Intelligence Office building, Kevin had *borrowed* an identification badge, a clipboard, a hat, and a set of files. He strode to the seventh floor without a concern. The key to belonging in a building was making sure he looked like everyone else. So he did. While the FIO wasn't near as chaotic as the Haven City Enforcement Services divisions, it had its own level of crazy he had to contend with.

Ryan Voklane, assistant to the Director of Operations, the Arch Guardian Synintel, was high enough on the food chain to merit his own office. However, to get to said office, Kevin had to not only go through a maze of endless corridors, but two cubicle bays. Sneaking in through the fire escape had been so much easier. If the sun were anywhere but almost vertical, Kevin would have seriously considered doing so again.

Kevin didn't bother to knock, walking into Ryan's open office and quietly closing the door. Voklane scribbled something inside a folder while reaching for a document. The afternoon rays spilling through the window behind him was so bright his hair appeared more white than golden. He didn't look up, simply motioned with his pen.

"Set the folders there on the corner, I'll get to them when I'm able."

Kevin carefully set the paperwork that didn't belong on the man's desk on the corner requested. "The Shield Guardian Enbrackon has my wife."

Pale blue eyes snapped up, shifted to the door and then back to Kevin. His broad shoulders straightened, a frown flattening his mouth. "Merrick."

Kevin returned the greeting. "Voklane."

Ryan tapped the pen against the desk, thankfully not one to dwell on polite exchanges to get to the heart of matters. "You're positive?"

"Yes."

"How?"

"Synintel's footmen. At least they were wearing his uniform and claimed to be from him."

Voklane grasped a fresh sheet of paper. "Have you had reason to suspect a man within Synintel's employ?"

"As of last night, yes."

Ryan's gaze met his again before focusing on the paper. "Report."

With clipped words and years of training to isolate only necessary information, Kevin reported the suspected incidents, along with a few other pertinent encounters concerning Enbrackon. "Blackbain and Dandridge are gathering the information for a possible location now."

"Have you gone to Synintel?"

Kevin crossed his arms over his chest. "For what purpose?"

Ryan's frown deepened. He set his forearms on the desk, shifting the pen between both his hands. "I suppose that's a fair question."

Their Direction of Operations Liaison sat back in his desk

and regarded Kevin for silent moments. Kevin remained calm in the space of time, knowing Voklane was processing, planning, assigning. Doing everything required of him for a mission he usually had weeks to organize instead of minutes.

"I'll need to know where so I can have clean up handled," Ryan finally said.

Kevin nodded. "I won't have time to assess involvement. Whether it's Enforcement he's pulled in, or even Intel Guardians who've joined the ranks, I won't be able to tell you."

"Understood. But I don't think it will be."

"What do you mean?"

Voklane shrugged, sitting back in his seat. "Just a feeling. Be careful, and make sure if Mrs. Blackbain can offer cover, she does so."

"How deep is Enbrackon in?"

Ryan took a long, profound breath. "Too deep. I don't think we'll be able to overlook this particular grievance. He was lucky with Katria, lucky I allowed you and Dandridge to handle it instead of going to Synintel. Now, we don't have a choice, which means we'll have to let on we aren't in the dark anymore."

"Maybe it's time."

"There's never a good time for the other side to know more than you wish." Ryan tapped the pen against the edge of the desk. "You should know we suspect he's after Synintel's position."

Kevin shifted his weight and drew his brows together. "As Director? That's a bit of a step from leading city Enforcement, isn't it?"

"Yes, and no. Sons can inherit after just training. Enbrackon at least has leadership experience. If you can call his showing up at work experience. After all, he's in his current role thanks to his father."

Kevin mulled the information over, not liking the direction it led. "He'd have to be appointed."

"Or marry into it."

Everything became startling clear in that moment and Kevin had to dig his toes into his boots to keep from flying out the door. "She's bait."

"Likely, yes."

"Do you have anyone else in country who can help?"

Ryan shook his head. "No, Survaine is half a world away, literally, in some country barely grasping this side of the Primal Years, ensuring they actually stay in this century. My other interceptor as capable as you is in Westica, saving some Master Guardians daughter who thought it'd be cute to play bandit and ended up being the bounty."

"She didn't get left to her stupidity?"

Ryan rolled his eyes. "Sadly no. She's not alone in the kidnapping, they took a prominent member of the government too, and made an international incident of it. Don't you read the paper? She's been front page news for the last two days. We had no choice but to rescue her sorry butt. While there are others, they aren't at your team's level. I fear you'd get annoyed with them versus being thankful."

Fair enough. When you worked with the best, below standard wasn't acceptable. Kevin let out a deep breath, expelling uneasiness. "Very well. Save the girl, don't die in the process."

"It's pretty imperative you don't die. Let Dandridge know Katria is to keep *you* alive when he's plotting the strategy, whatever he manages time for."

"How long have you suspected Enbrackon's goals?"

Voklane shook his head. "Not so much his goals, rather whoever is running around in the shadows causing conflict that we can't seem to pin down. *They* are setting big goals."

"They want to place Enbrackon in a power position? Why?"

"Not just Enbrackon. They're slowly replacing leadership roles in all the branches of government."

Kevin's already uneasy nerves made his fingers twitch and his shoulders roll. "They've succeeded in these attempts? How many so far?"

"We don't know for certain, and we don't know how many have been coerced and how many are voluntary, either. I've managed to gather some intel that says some of the men and women were forced into compliance. Synintel is working hard to infiltrate what he can, but progress is slow."

"That's why Blackbain's team is still here. You need us to keep picking up the fragmented pieces we're able to find."

Voklane gave a little weary shrug. "Yes and no. Synintel is fixated with his daughter's safety. He has been since… since just before what happened to Nachemir. Then, after that incident, he became fairly obsessed. I don't know what happened almost five years ago, but it was enough to spook the Arch Guardian. He seems to function on two levels now. One handling his job, through me, and another handling his daughter, through you."

A little over four years ago something happened. My father acted strangely for weeks. He wouldn't come out of his office for any reason except to sleep and bathe.

Raina's words came back to Kevin, fitting another piece into the puzzle forming a complete picture. "He needed to make sure Raina didn't become a pawn in *their* game."

And made sure by keeping Kevin a pawn in his.

However, he couldn't really begrudge the man anymore, not when Kevin had to admit the squeezing pain in his chest was likely something he had no choice but to admit to. Somewhere along the very unemotional journey of his marriage, he'd had a very emotional response.

He'd fallen in love with his wife.

Losing his rank suddenly became the least of his concerns. If Enbrackon managed what Voklane feared,

Kevin would be dead and Raina would be an Arch Guardianess. And while the rank certainly suited her better, Kevin couldn't imagine the new husband would. He couldn't envision any man in that role besides him now. No, another man touching, kissing, loving his woman in a manner he hadn't even been able to experience was definitely *not* acceptable.

Kevin flexed his fist and took a calming breath. He'd have to ensure such a fate didn't happen.

A GENTLE EVENING breeze teased the grass around Kevin's thighs. The sun hugged the horizon, leaving dying tendrils of warmth spilling over the field he waited in. He pulled in a deep, calming breath. In his ear Mason's composed, controlled voice relayed information through the bulky, yet necessary magnetically powered radio communicator clipped to his belt.

"I have six on the east side."

Katria replied in an equally clipped tone. "I count four at the south entrance. Sean counts at least five in the loft."

Fifteen visible targets. Meaning there were at least that many unseen, if not more.

"I'm seeing a strange marking on their left sleeve," Katria's soft, female voice crackled over the air.

"Copy, I see it too," Mason replied.

Kevin kept his eyes closed, his emotions grounded. He pressed his com button down. "What does it look like?"

Katria answered, "A pyramid with a sword going through it."

The information made Kevin open his eyes and focus on a bird bouncing between blades of grass. "Cairoen Sentinels."

Mason cursed. The next voice that came over the line was his leader.

"Are you positive?" Sean asked.

Kevin raised a brow. "Did you really just ask me that? Give the com back to your wife."

Katria's laughter arrived before her words. Kevin couldn't help but smile at the easy trust in his team. "Do I need to worry about a counter marksman?"

"No, they're ground force trained," Kevin answered.

"Copy that."

They'd faced bad odds before, but not on this level. The last time, they'd had a building to clear, which meant foes on floors, not all together. Kevin figured he'd have to hold his own for a bit before Katria would be able to leave the safety and necessity of the height she and Sean waited at. The roof of another warehouse. Mason was ground level, and a decent shot, but not nearly as quick or accurate as Katria.

Mason relayed instructions based on what they'd discovered in the short time. Kevin stood, stretched fully, and then went to Eadric, his Icekutian stallion. Large saddle bags hung from either side of the beautiful slate gray beast, packed with necessities Kevin had made Tabby fill for Raina. They'd not be returning to Haven City if he managed to make it out alive.

He mounted the horse, ruffling a hand through Eadric's silky mane before commanding him to move forward. They were a quarter mile from a small collection of warehouses situated barely outside the city. The rail line ran along the western side of the property with a docking line curving away from the main line to load or offload cargo without blocking other trains needing to get to their destination. According to the schedule for that track, a train would provide sound cover in exactly thirty minutes. For how long, they didn't know. Kevin hoped to be free of the building before the last car cleared the property boundary.

Not that Kat needed the cover, her rifle was made with a built-in silencer. But, the fall of bodies couldn't be silenced. The train would help with that. In the distance the loud, blaring horn called to the approaching buildings and anyone within proximity that a charging mass of steel advanced. Kevin urged Eadric into a gallop, in a race now with the oncoming train.

"South entrance clear," Katria's voice called over the com.

"No awareness from the east side," Mason relayed.

"Approaching the south," Kevin said, sliding his mount between two warehouses.

"We see you," Katria confirmed. "Opening a window and clearing the loft."

Kevin tied up Eadric, informing Mason of the stallion's location so he could move him to the east entrance. He sprinted to the warehouse, looking up at the broken window. Time to get his wife back. And hopefully not lose her at the same time. If she didn't despise him after learning his true nature, he'd be shocked.

Ignoring the massacre at the south entrance, Kevin prepared a rope to swing into the window Katria had shot out for him. Before the night was finished, he'd likely have a higher body count than the team's markswoman. He always did. And he always tried to bury the guilt of wasting a human life, no matter how necessary.

GLASS TINKERED to the floor in the loft above. Raina snapped her head toward the sound. A man fell limply from the second story edge, landing in a heap of flesh and bone on the cement floor. She swallowed a scream, her fingers grasping the chain holding her hostage. A diffused pop sounded, another body tipped over, landing not far from the other. Two men rushed the stairs, their focus on the shadowy space above.

Raina yanked on the chain with her hands, ignoring the pain of the metal shackle biting into her ankle. Enbrackon departed hours ago. The sun's dying light had left her with a sense of hopelessness. Kevin hadn't been able to find her like the Shield Guardian had believed he would. Three more rapid, muted pops echoed from the upstairs. The faint accompanying *thump, thump, thump* told her three more bodies had likely fallen.

Who was killing these men and was it a new threat to her? She had no way of defending herself against a bullet. Not that she'd be able to even if someone put a gun in her hand. She'd never held one before Katria had handed her one so many nights ago. She'd been as useless then as she would be now. If someone in the FIO learned of Enbrackon's plan, Raina might be better dead to them than alive, regardless of who her father was. His position was certainly more important to some than her life.

Biting her lip until the pain rivaled the one grinding along her ankle bone, she squeezed her eyes closed in her fear and willed her pounding heart and rolling stomach to calm. She took in several slow breaths through her nose when her head spun. Though, perhaps if she were going to die today, it'd be better if she *were* passed out and didn't see it coming.

A shout followed by running feet forced Raina's attention back to the gruesome scene unfolding in the warehouse. Men sprinted from a short corridor to her right. Their booted footfalls on the concrete echoed all around the empty space. A shadow launched from the loft, landing in graceful arc, taking two men down in the process. When the dark figure rose to full height, Raina gasped.

Kevin.

Fear swallowed her whole and this time she couldn't hold in the scream. Severely outnumbered, she couldn't see anyway for him to walk out of the center of the men who seemed twice as big as him physically.

Then an explosion of motion happened. The expression on his handsome face wasn't Kevin. He wore a mask of indifference, his gray eyes luminesce, almost silver with an inner fire.

Virtually too fast to perceive, he caught, deflected and returned every punch or kick. One assailant lunged with a knife. Kevin caught the man's wrist, twisted and sent the knife blade up through the bottom of the attacker's chin. With a swift yank, the blade jerked free in a fountain of blood and was imbedded in the chest of a man across from him before Raina could blink.

No.

Air refused to enter into her lungs any way other than too quickly.

No.

Her husband did *not* just murder two men... make that three. A man landed on the ground at Kevin's feet, his neck at an unnatural angle. The crack of bone, a scream, followed another body to the floor. Stars danced on the edges of Raina's vision. Every one of her muscles trembled.

The flash of blade preceded another sickening snap. A new body joined the ranks. Blood seeped along the floor in dark puddles. Raina's stomach lurched. Panic tingled along her skin and she jerked harder on the chain, moving her attention to the bolts, wanting to be far away from the nightmare her life had moved into.

"You're in a bad dream. Any second now you'll wake up, when nothing more is wrong than you can't figure out how to brush your hair." She repeated the words over and over, tears burning and flowing down her cheeks.

When the bolts didn't budge, despite her bracing her feet against the wall and yanking with all her strength, a sense of hysteria threatened. A guttural cry formed deep in her throat. The chain rattled and clanked uselessly in her hands. Still she attempted the impossible, refusing to believe she was locked in a warehouse with dead men and a maniacal man she thought was her husband.

Bloody fingers grasped the chain near her ankle. Raina screamed until her throat burned, twisting onto her knees, her only thought to escape. The chain pulled tight, digging the shackle into her upper foot and heel. She didn't dare look to see who was after her. Or if her husband had survived. Terror filling her that he hadn't. Not wanting to know if the gory hand belonged to one of the many Sentinels who may have been ordered to retrieve her.

The binding on her ankle released. She didn't contemplate how. It didn't matter. The only thing that mattered was getting free.

A powerful arm snaked around her waist and hauled her up against a solid chest. A second arm banded around her torso. Strong thighs locked alongside hers, giving her no chance or means of escape. "I need you to calm down. I know you're scared, but I can't be worrying about your emotional state. Later, yes. Right now, I need you to be the very in control of yourself daughter of an Arch Guardian. Do you understand?"

Kevin.

Raina focused on the calm familiar deep timbre of Kevin's voice. Not the cold lethal predator sending men to their death seconds ago. She forced herself to relax in his embrace, slow her breathing, swallow the bile still a burning threat in her throat.

His arm around her upper body tightened. "Do you understand?"

Not trusting her ability to speak, she simply nodded. Slowly he released her, but kept a hand wrapped around her wrist. Raina tried to ignore the sticky slide of his fingers on her skin. She forced herself to look straight ahead at a wall.

Later she'd analyze the strange, weakening relief at knowing Kevin survived, mixed with the warring sense of fear of *who* he was. Now, she'd do exactly what he asked. She'd be Synintel's daughter, pulling on the regal training she'd received since birth. Using the memory of a stiff rod against the back of her thighs when she hadn't obeyed her Mistress of Etiquette as a reminder.

Yes, she might give in to moments of childish emotion, more so in the presence of Kevin than she cared to admit. Even she had to concede her lapse of sanity, in her opinion, was warranted in this particular moment. But the moment had passed. If getting out alive meant reining in her emotions, so be it.

Forcing a sense of calm her pounding heart betrayed, and a breath that continued to be a bit too shallow, she straightened her back and ran to keep pace with Kevin's long strides. Her hips and knees hurt from sitting too long, and little pin pricks danced along the bottoms of her feet. Graceful she was not, but somehow she managed to match his speed.

They sprinted toward the short corridor the group of men had come from earlier. Raina closed her eyes for a second and hoped there weren't more lying in wait. She slammed into Kevin's back so hard she lost her footing. A faint *swoosh* went over the top of her head. The knife meant for her missing by a hair's breadth. Kevin had already released his hold on her wrist, and she landed firm on her rear, bouncing and sliding. A sickening *crack, pop* forced her eyes open, looking upward at the battle raging a few feet away.

Kevin ducked, his fists pounding into the stomach of a Sentinel in front of him before he twisted, yanking a knife free from another assailant whose arm hung limply at his side. The knife flipped in Kevin's hand. In a flash of steel against the dying rays of light, the blade disappeared into the chest of the attacker nearest to Raina. The man slumped to the ground near her thigh and she scrambled away, swallowing a scream.

Looking anywhere but at the blank dark eyes staring into nothing, Raina focused on her breathing. When Kevin's fingers motioned behind himself, she rose, but didn't accept his outstretched hand, still caked in drying blood and gore she didn't want to consider.

At the door he pressed his arm into her chest, forcing her behind his back and into the wall. "Are we clear?"

He must have heard something he approved of, for he eased the door open. Golden light spilled into the darkened interior. The rumble and clank of a train filled the air, drowning out any sounds of nature. Raina found the noise fascinating. She'd only ever heard the hiss and swish of a MagnaRail flying by, never the harsher, grittier steel wheels on track. A powerful commotion fitting for her terrified condition.

"Where are we going?" she asked before she could stop herself.

"To the right."

In another time, Raina would have strained to see as they dashed between a set of buildings to catch a glimpse of the train. Now, however, she was too busy watching for moving shadows that would send Kevin into another battle.

Hours of adrenaline poured through her veins, saturating her system. A squawk overhead made her flinch. Looking upward, she expected an army to be repelling down after them. Only the glide of wings on air and a flash of white as the creature banked greeted her. A tremor raced down her spine and her teeth clamped together.

"Are you still with me?" Kevin asked.

Raina met his concerned glance over his shoulder and nodded. The loose gravel under her feet bit into the weak bottoms of her shoes, meant for little more than fashionably walking around the house or to and from a carriage on bricked paths. She ignored the pain and suppressed the complaints.

Kevin kept at a pace she'd never had to manage before. Her legs burned, and a curious stitch ached in her side. They rushed past building after building, twisting and turning through a maze of wide paths just large enough for a cart to pass through.

"Anything?" Kevin asked and it took a second for Raina to realize he hadn't been speaking to her. A few moments later, he said, "Acknowledged."

They rounded another building and Raina slid to a stop. A beautiful, huge gray stallion stood regal and proud, tied to a post. Kevin spoke a low command. The horse immediately responded, lowering his head. Long silvery hair fluttered as he shook his mane. Kevin unhooked the leather leads from the post and motioned for Raina to come closer.

"He won't bite," he said when she hesitated.

Raina eyed the beast warily. "He's huge."

Kevin was huge too, at six-foot-five-inches, yet he barely reached the back of the stallion. "Eadric is an Icekutian."

Raina had heard of the breed, normally used in the Northern Boundary, where temperatures rarely reached above fifty even in the summer months. The large, stocky class of horse was utilized for its resistance to below freezing conditions.

Cautiously, she neared the beast. Kevin grabbed her waist before she could realize, lifting her with ease. Her skirt fluttered around her ankles and she squeaked when her butt landed hard in front of the saddle on a mass of solid horse muscle. She grabbed fistfuls of mane and held tight. Kevin swiftly mounted behind her.

The heat and strength of his thighs pressed in around Raina. His thick forearms slid along her sides, brushing against her ribs and hips as he guided the steed away from the warehouses and onto a narrow trail leading into woods.

His hand touched her back a second before he spoke. "We're safe, heading north. Thanks again for everything, no way I could have done this alone. Sean, be sure to brief Voklane. Watch your backs, Enbrackon is going to be more than upset. Radio contact out."

Raina sat tense through the exchange. "H-how are you speaking to them?"

"A magnetically powered radio. Doesn't your father have one in his office?"

"Yes, it's quite large though."

"That's because his will broadcast across an ocean if he needs it to. Ours only go a half a mile or so."

Raina pondered that statement for far too long, her hands clenched in the horse's mane. When she glanced up and realized the sun was nothing more than a glow beyond the horizon. They rode through a field. She looked behind them and couldn't find any sign of the forest they'd marched into. Eadric's steady gate clopped along the trail. An edge of trees hugged the meadow to their right.

They'd escaped, and judging by the daylight left, they'd been traveling long enough to put a good deal of distance behind them. Whether enough to keep from being caught up with, she didn't know, and suddenly she didn't care. The whole affair, from being thrown in a carriage, stabbed with a needle, chained to a wall, being told she was basically contracted to two men (one just had to die first), witnessing her husband's lethality and almost being on the sharp end of a knife had her mind rebelling.

She fought against Kevin's arms holding the reins. "Stop," she ordered. When the horse continued to trot along, she lost it. "Stop!"

Raina didn't wait. She shoved at his arms and squirmed free. Eadric made a sound of protest, but had come to a halt when she slid down his muscled flank and landed inelegantly on the uneven ground. Nausea swept through her system. On wobbly legs, she tore across the field toward the forest, her only thought to put space between herself and Kevin before she lost what little she had in her stomach. When her foot caught on a rock and she fell to her knees, she didn't bother to rise. Bracing her palms on the rough grass, she gave in, vomited and sobbed.

17

Kevin dismounted slowly, keeping a wary eye on Raina. He knew better than to chase after her. Knew better than to attempt to offer any comfort. Fully in the throes of adrenaline let-down, she'd fight him with claws she didn't know she possessed.

Everyone reacted differently, and he had his stories, having dealt with the situation nearly every assignment with those he rescued. His lovely wife became detached, panicked, ill, and likely would reach the angry phase shortly. Since he knew from a couple days ago when she managed to get him on the floor, she packed quite a lot of energy in her small frame. She'd come at him with all her anger, fear and confusion. After that, she'd probably crash. He'd wait her out.

Sighing, he reached into the saddle pack, dug around for clean clothes and a medical kit. His right thigh burned from the lucky swipe of a blade. His right shoulder, left side and right hip would be bruised tomorrow. He'd chosen this route for its efficiency to get them to the last passenger rail-line stop this side of the Northern Boundary, and the creek they'd have to cross over. The narrow, flowing body of water was hidden by the tree line.

Walking with Eadric trotting behind, Kevin made his way to the shelter of the trees, keeping Raina well in sight. On her hands and knees, her shoulders shook. Everything in him went to not rushing to her side. He took another calming breath, tied off his mount and disappeared into the trees. He had to be free from the blood of those he'd killed before he touched her again.

After checking on her once more and ensuring she hadn't moved, Kevin stripped and waded into a deep section. The cold water rushed around his aching body, soothing tired, sore muscles. Diving under, he contemplated which Raina would hate more – what she'd seen of him, or where they were going.

Under the water, he scrubbed his hands over his face and then rose. He did a quick assessment of his injuries. The slice in his thigh was concerning. While the bleeding had slowed to a trickle, the cut was deep enough to require stitches. He had some wound strips and iodine to use for adhering and disinfecting from Sean. They'd have to be enough.

Rising from the water, he assured himself Raina was still safe and found a boulder to sit on. He searched through the med kit for what he needed. A loud, soul-wrenching wail sent birds flying from the trees and field in a flutter across the darkening sky. The anger phase had finally hit.

Naked, Kevin moved quickly. He brushed iodine on the stab wound, clenching his jaw against the fresh wave of pain the antiseptic brought. Then, as carefully as he could, he held the edges together while applying strips to the wet iodine. To make sure they stayed stuck, he brushed on a top layer. He dressed swiftly and then headed for his wife. A rock arced in the air away from her, followed by a handful more. He stopped, waited until the throwing of pebbles became weak tosses away from her.

Kevin approached her slowly. She turned on her knees. Her pale brown eyes narrowed as she launched herself upward. Anger danced in her gaze. Knowing he had to weather the storm, he stood his ground.

Raina's fists slammed into his chest with her full hundred and fifteen pounds behind the action. "How could you keep that from me? Why didn't you tell me?"

Kevin caught her hands, holding them firm near his heart. He wanted to crush her to his chest, dig his fingers into her now wild hair and comfort himself that she was alive. Healthy and safe. Somehow, he managed self-control. "Would it have made a difference, honestly?"

She sagged into him with a sob. "I would have known more."

"You would have imagined and still lacked faith in my ability," he answered softly. "What I can do… it's rare."

Tears glistened in her eyes when she lifted her face to him. "And my father uses that ability, doesn't he? That's why you have so many scars. What are you?"

The fear was gone from her expression, replaced with something he didn't want to recognize or acknowledge. "Yes, he does. I'm what's called an Interceptor. Have you heard of one?"

Slowly, he put enough distance between them to guide her to the creek, knowing she'd appreciate the cool, clean water as he had.

"No, I've never heard of one. Do you intercept things by fighting?"

"Fighting is never something I wish, but yes, I intercept people, or documents, or whatever else needs to be kept from falling into someone's hands it shouldn't be in. Sometimes people aren't willing to let it go."

A tremor raced along her muscles beneath his hand. He fought to pull her into an embrace. "Like Enbrackon."

"We'll talk about that later. Right now wash up. We have a bit longer and we need to hurry so we don't miss the last train."

"The last train to where?"

Kevin took a deep breath. "New Hampton."

She worked her bottom lip, stepping over protruding rocks closer to the edge of the creek. "Where is that?"

"The Northern Boundary, past the Tabrias."

"The Tabria Mountains?"

"Yes." He guided her closer to the water, onto a high rock she could kneel on to cleanse herself and not get soaked.

"I've never seen the Tabrias. I thought they were impassable."

"No, there's a pass, always has been. They are intimidating I will admit, so many *consider* them impassable. They shelter the rest of the country from the harsher Atlantic winds, especially in the middle of winter when the arctic airstream shifts, but without a pass, we'd all still be stuck on the other side and someone else would have claimed the southern half of Sziveria."

She gave a little snort while she splashed in the water. Droplets fell on her dust covered skirt and ran down her arms. "Every child learns the lessons. I know about the Tabrias and early colonization after the Primal Years."

Careful of his injured thigh, he eased down on the rock beside her. "Then you should have known about the pass."

"Yes, should have." The distant note in her voice told him she'd rather be discussing something other than geography.

Kevin let her have a few more moments. "Deep breaths," he reminded when she'd stiffen and stop moving. She'd inhale and go back to using the water to try to wash some of the horror of the afternoon away. Nothing but time would ease the fear, and even then not all.

When only faded gray light remained, he forced himself to rise, careful to keep his face neutral despite the pain flaring through his muscles. He offered her a hand. For a moment he waited tensely, thinking she'd refuse, her gaze moving over his fingers. Then she slid her cold hand into his and allowed him to help her rise.

"I have a blanket if you think you'll get cold on the rest of the trip. The temperature is going to drop quickly."

Kevin tried to keep his heart calm as she threaded her fingers through his on their walk to Eadric, not wanting to hope at what it might mean. "How long do we have?"

"Just over an hour."

"I should be fine."

All the same, Kevin did his best to shelter her smaller frame in his larger one on the ride. She burrowed close and he swore she'd fallen asleep when he reined Eadric in at the train depot. Her spine straightened with a gasp when he went to dismount.

"It's okay," he said, placing a calm hand on her hip. "We're at the train stop."

"That didn't take long."

"I think you fell asleep."

A small street lamp burned next to the quaint porch of the rail station. Shock registered on Raina's face. She blinked down at him and held out her hands when he reached for her.

"I can't believe I slept."

"It's been a hard day."

She cast him a stare that said, '*Really?*' complete with a raised brow. Kevin couldn't fight a smile. In the pitiful light, with the biting cold cutting through their clothes, her hair a wild, tangled mess around her shoulders, and her cheeks wind-burned, Kevin wanted to kiss her so badly his chest ached. Instead, he brushed his bruised knuckles along her jaw and then grasped her trembling hand.

The building was small by their standards, more of a shack or shed in appearance with a small porch barely a step from the ground. Kevin pulled her into the slightly warmer interior. Rows of benched seating faced a low burning cast-iron pellet stove. Dust covered the edges of a warped wood floor, worn in places by years of walking.

Raina found a seat near the heat while he bought their tickets. The bleary-eyed old man in the ticket box moved with a speed Kevin had come to expect this far north, away from the rush of civilization. Leaning against the rough wooden counter, his gaze wandered to his wife's form. Shoulders hunched, hands clasped between her knees, she couldn't have pulled more into herself unless she curled into a ball on the bench. A knot fisted in his gut. Damn Enbrackon. She looked so fragile and worn, and the worst hadn't even hit her yet. He clenched his teeth. Nope, she wasn't done figuring out if he was the enemy and someone to hate.

The slow, drawn out *click-click* of a stamper drew Kevin's attention back to the ticketing agent. Two passes and a stable-loading ticket for Eadric slid across the counter to him, along with the stern point to the time on the clock hanging off to the left of the wood stove. Kevin nodded his acknowledgment of the unspoken warning. He was responsible for catching the train on time. As if they had anywhere else to go or wait.

Kevin went back outside, taking a slow deep inhale of cold, clean air. The train was due to arrive any moment, but the lack of a distant deep reverberation told him it was running late. He checked the ties on Eadric's reins before returning inside, joining Raina. She didn't glance his direction, or even recognize his presence, staring blankly at the tiny dancing flames behind the small panel of glass.

"How much longer?" Her voice was thin, weak, so low he almost missed her words.

Glancing at the clock, he answered, "Hopefully no more than fifteen minutes. There shouldn't be any ice on the tracks to slow them down."

She nodded, her fingers clenching together.

Twenty minutes later, the train rolled to a screeching stop. Kevin removed the pack from Eadric, handed his trusted

Icekutian over to a traveling stable-hand with the horse's ticket and then went to collect Raina. She jumped when he touched her shoulder and then stood without a sound.

Kevin grasped Raina's elbow and guided her onto the train and down a narrow, dark corridor to a private cabin. Small lanterns flickered every third door, producing enough light to make out the brass unit markers beside each folding door. Though small, the suite had two benches that fitted together into a bed, and a small corner bathroom. Opting not to assume she'd wished the bed made, he sat on the smaller bench across from her. The conductor came around, punched their tickets and then left, folding the door closed behind himself.

Raina stared at the closed door, frowning. "Why didn't he ask if we needed anything, or even light the lamp for us?"

Kevin braced his feet along the edge of bench she occupied. "Because this isn't a MagnaRail. It's a regular railed passenger train. We're lucky they even offer a private accommodation. If you want anything to eat or drink this far north, you bring it yourself. You do everything yourself."

In the silvery shadows, she continued to stare at the closed door, her frown intensified. "Why?"

Kevin took a deep, bracing breath. "What do you remember from your lessons about Sziveria and the Northern Boundary?"

"Not much, sorry." She fussed with the fabric of her skirt, brushing and smoothing her fingers along the soiled folds.

"Beyond the Tabrias is sovereign land, but ungoverned by Sziveria. As a result, there's little to no national support. The land belongs to our country, but isn't maintained or governed by it. The three prisons that run along the northern coast are the only organizations that receive anything from Sziveria. Everyone else exists at their own risk, or their own freedom, many would say."

She twisted on the seat and shifted until she was in the

corner next to the window. Pulling her legs up onto the seat, she wrapped her arms around them and rested her chin on her knees. "What does that have to do with attending to us?"

"Money. The cost of this suite was the same as a coach ticket on the MagnaRail. He doesn't earn enough to see to anything other than punching tickets and throwing stowaways off."

"There's no money past the Tabrias?"

"Not like you think. Most of the economy runs off trade. Actual currency is rarely used within city limits, and only for things that come or go over the Tabrias."

She shifted uncomfortably. "If I needed a new skirt, I'd need something to barter with?"

"For the fabric yes, and if you can't make it yourself, then for the seamstress, yes. No readymade clothing where we're going."

Raina picked at the hem of her skirt. "I guess fashion isn't important."

Kevin's lips twitched and he was thankful of the darkness surrounding them. "Not particularly, no."

"And you're taking me up there because no one can find us?"

"Properties aren't registered with The Record's Department, so no one knows where we're going."

"Except your team."

Kevin didn't stop the smile this time. "Except my team."

SEAGULLS CAWED and floated on the constant winds above. Raina squinted, glancing up at the bright, yet cloudy sky, noting the hundreds of drab gray birds diving around or at each other when another dared to intrude on their air space. The train ride had taken most of the night, stopping at the last city before continuing on with the next work shift and cargo for the maximum-security prisons.

Eadric picked his way over a rocky, deeply rutted dirt road. Despite the poorly maintained route, the beast of a horse seemed perfectly at home, keeping a steady pace. Dawn had broken hours ago, though Raina wondered if color ever graced the sky that seemed endlessly ashen. A steady cold wind carrying flecks of snow, smelling of salt and brine, teased her tangled hair. She fit right in with the few people they'd passed, dingy and road weary.

They'd ridden through two areas she'd hardly consider towns, consisting of a few ragged, drooping buildings clumped together. Kevin had said nothing, but she'd caught the staked in signs naming the area as an official settlement. The town the train stopped in had entailed a few stores, a radio communications building, the rail depot and what had looked like a large community greenhouse. That'd been the last true mark of civilization.

Raina tried to remain calm. He wasn't taking her to one of these six-building towns where there'd be no means of procuring basic necessities.

He wasn't.

She took a deep breath, tried to focus on the cold, the sorry excuse for a road, the strong man at her back, anything but the unknown they headed for. Evergreens rose high above them, somehow finding purchase among boulder outcroppings and tall, golden grass. Sand blew across every surface, building thick in the ruts carved into the road. Patches of snow and ice dotted the landscape, adding to the colorless feel of the land.

The tree line broke, revealing a high cliff face and a field of tall, swaying grass. Beyond a dotting of buildings, some nearly to the edge of the cliff, others almost appearing to be built into it, rose on a gently sloping hill.

"New Hampton," Kevin stated.

"How many people live here?"

She felt his shrug along her back. "I don't know, maybe three hundred?"

"It's a real town then, not a settlement of fifteen or so people."

"It's a real town, yes. Those settlements are usually families that have either been forced out of a town for whatever reason, or no longer wish to remain among a population, but need to remain on the road for ease of travel."

"Are there some who settle off of main roadways?"

"Sure. Anywhere out here there could be families making their own way. It's one of the calls of the Northern Boundary."

"But Sziveria isn't the only country north of the boundary line."

"True, but our country has come to think of this as simply Boundary land."

Raina chewed on her bottom lip. "So… are there a lot of outlaws up here?"

"No more than near the docks in Haven City, waiting for a ship to take them somewhere new."

She considered the information and then looked out over the now visible ocean. White capped waves churned in the blue-green water. Little boats bobbed along, some with bright poles sticking off at odd angles. The ever-present seagulls hovered over the top of each craft, or outright dared to perch on the edges.

A low mist drifted along the ground as they neared the town, seeming to soak up any shades of life the buildings may have managed to maintain. Flecks of red, yellow, blues and greens remained on a few signs or clapboard walls, but most were old graying wood, or wind worn brick. Sagging porches, boarded up windows and crumbling walls made up most of the buildings, repaired only where people seemed to dwell or use the space for any useful purpose. The rest left to the elements. Little grass patches and saplings grew out of rooftops, wide windowsills and abandoned building windows.

Kevin continued on, past what Raina figured was the main street through the township and down the other side of the sloping hill. The cliff slowly leveled out until they were almost ocean level. The buildings became further apart. He turned down a narrow, switch backing pathway lined with grass and boulders, some so large she couldn't see over them. The trail ended into a waist high fenced-in lot on a huge stone outcropping. No other buildings in sight, and when she looked up, she couldn't see the main road anymore, which meant, they couldn't see them either. The house was completely isolated except from the ocean, whose angry waves crashed on the beach thirty feet below. An overgrown foot trail led to the private beach, closed off on either side by a gently curving inlet.

"Welcome to Merrick Cove," Kevin said, dismounting.

Raina took in the two and a half story, rectangular building. Three stories on the side facing the ocean, two on the land side. Built into the sloping terrain, the cinder block building was unlike anything she'd ever seen before. Large rectangle windows divided into small panels took up the top story, while smaller square windows dotted the ground level floors. Gray streaks covered the once cream, or perhaps gray, painted exterior. A porch came off a door from the second floor, stairs leading up to it from the ocean side. From the land side, she noted a ground floor door.

"It's pre-cataclysm. One of the only remaining buildings from before. My family has lived in it since the first migration to this land."

Raina stared at the drab building with renewed interest. It was likely a thousand years old, or older. Somehow his family had managed to keep it in one piece and still livable. "Where was your family from, before?"

Kevin shrugged, leading Eadric with her still riding

through the gate. "No one can remember, just that it was a long ocean ride and colder than here."

She knew that story well, her own family had a similar one. "Seems to be the same for most."

"The Primal Years cost most families their history. We're lucky anything, let alone anyone, survived."

Raina looked over the simple building. A worn wooden sign hung between a window and the door of the first/second story that read Merrick Cove, the letters carved deep into the wood. At one time the words had been painted yellow, the sign red. Enough remnants remained to help her visualize what the sign must have once looked like.

"You grew up here?"

"Yes, my entire family once lived out of this building. Then slowly they ventured off, past the Tabrias, until only my father's parents remained. He inherited it, and then I did."

She blinked back a longing for the sense of family his heritage brought. A connection to something as far back as anyone could remember. Her own family had nothing like that. Yes, Synintel had his ranked property, which had been passed down to him from her grandfather, but beyond that, there had been a prior Synintel. And after her father, there would be a new one, who'd take over the rank, responsibilities, and the property. They'd have a new history, a new story. She realized with a little wonder, as a Merrick, she was part of this property's history now.

Kevin helped her down and walked away before she could ask any questions or even touch him for longer than a second. She'd spent the entire train ride at war with herself, alternating between wanting to crawl into the safety of his arms and despising what he was capable of. Hating that on one side, she *needed* the knowledge of the safety he provided with his skill, and on the other, the knowledge he used that same talent to kill. Had done so for years. How many? How often? And what had it cost him? Did her father even care?

And would Kevin eventually hate her for the price he'd pay?

So she'd kept her distance, kept quiet, and tried to block out the memory of Kevin's fist driving a knife through another man's skull. Of the blood, the screams, and the impassive expression he'd worn the entire time.

He unlocked the door up the stairs, then returned to Eadric. Raina drew her brows together at the uneven way he walked.

"Did you hurt yourself?" she asked before he could disappear around the side of the building.

"No, I'm fine. Go on inside. You're cold enough. I'll join you a bit."

Raina went up, using the wall for support, lifting her filthy skirt to keep from tripping. Inside, the house was dark. The little square windows provided minimal light. The musky scent of dust and disuse permeated the air. Open stairs led down to the ground floor, a quick peek showed a kitchen with a large wood stove and a small round table. She couldn't make out all the space, but wide wooden counters, a sink and cupboards lined at least one wall.

She ventured further, noting a huge fireplace, and a section walled off with two doors. Stairs leading up were near the front door on the other side of the living space. There were only two rockers in front of the fireplace and a huge, bench style table in the center of the room for furniture. A large grand piano took up the space beside the stairs.

Kevin entered, dropping a load of wood on the floor next to the fireplace, where a small stack was already neatly built. He tossed dry tinder into the hearth and then used a steel fire starter to create sparks and bring the fire to life. Raina sat on the bench nearest the fire and glanced around.

"When will someone arrive?"

"What do you mean?" he asked without looking her direction, feeding small pieces of wood into the blossoming flames.

"To prepare our rooms and food."

He was silent for a moment, building the fire. "No one will be arriving."

Raina blinked, thinking she must have heard wrong. "Excuse me?"

Kevin slowly stood, brushing his hands together to clear them of sawdust and dirt. "It's just you and me, princess. No one else."

Her father's words from weeks ago slammed into her like the train they'd departed from. *I think the question dear daughter, is would he really do that to* you? *Make you live well outside your comfort or station?*

The words hadn't made any sense to her then, nor had Kevin's reluctance to allow anything to progress beyond the passionate moment of weakness he'd shown her weeks ago, because of what would happen *if* he lost his rank. She'd be here, at Merrick Cove, in an unknown city so far from what she considered civilization and the luxuries she had never lived without.

Panic that she'd somehow managed to keep at bay flooded inward. She gasped, tears burning. A heavy pain blossomed deep in her chest.

"Breathe," Kevin ordered gently, but made no move to come near her. "Raina, breathe."

She took a gasping inhale as she shot up and paced. Tears spilled over and coursed down her cheeks. "Kevin… I can't do *anything*. I am completely useless to you here. I can't cook. I don't clean. I can't even brush my own hair! How am I supposed to live here without any staff? Not even one person? H-how could you do this? What were you thinking?"

His expression remained neutral, but his hands fisted at his sides, his frame stiff. "I was thinking you'd rather not be with Enbrackon, or see me dead. If you'd prefer, I can send you back on a train to your father, and I can stay here. But the last time I left you for any length of time, you were rather angry with me."

He was right. Angry didn't begin to describe how she'd felt living life without him. Lost, abandoned, lonely… No, she didn't want to go through that again. She also had to take a moment and realize her selfishness. His only thought was to keep her safe. He wasn't to blame for her inability to manage basic tasks.

"No, I-I don't want to go back. I'm sorry." She swept her hands in front of her in a motion to self-calm, forcing the residual panic attack away. "But what are we going to do? I wasn't kidding when I said I am more than useless to you here."

His gaze softened. "I cook, I know how to clean, and I can help you with your hair until you figure it out on your own. Tabby was supposed to pack you things you can manage to dress yourself in. They're in the saddle bags by the back door."

Raina swallowed the lump in her throat. "Where's my room?"

"You can choose between those two."

She looked at the two closed doors, only a few feet apart. "Is one of them normally yours?"

"The one on the left is the room I grew up in."

She swallowed, wanting the comfort of his space, knowing it'd likely smell of him and be surrounded by the personal belongings he'd never bothered to collect in her home. But she wouldn't. "Then I'll take the one on the right. Thank you."

With a straight spine, she managed to make her way to the room without looking over her shoulder. She knew Kevin watched her exit the living area, and when she opened the door, she immediately knew the room had belonged to his parents. A large bed, with simple square posters and a frame connecting between, stained a rich, dark reddish brown, took up most of the room. A sweet floral quilt covered the bare mattress. Drapes in matching rich floral colors hung from the frame, able to close off the bed to trap in warmth in the winter. Sheer fabric draped around the bed now, likely to keep the dust out with no one living in the space.

Little keepsakes boxes lined a long, narrow dresser. An armoire was situated in the far left corner. A wood stove with a beautiful stone hearth occupied the corner on the right, near the small window. Raina walked along the edges of the room, trailing her fingers along the dusty wood surface of the dresser and a small desk beside it. A door connected the two rooms. Her fingers brushed the cool brass knob, but she made no effort to turn it.

Floor-to-ceiling shelves held books, rolled maps, and loose sheets of paper. She picked up one of the papers. Dust trailed off, revealing musical notes. A music composition. One of Kevin's parents must have played the piano out in the main area. She set the paper back and continued on, focusing on her surroundings and not the days to come where she'd be beyond useless.

There was no one to impress, to be polite to. No one to gain as a connection or an ally. There was also no one to do all the things she'd taken for granted in her daily life. She wanted to be angry, but she knew Kevin had made the right choice. Here they were safe. She couldn't be used against her father, and Kevin couldn't be killed. She closed her eyes as a new wave of tears broke free.

"It's not forever," she whispered into the empty room. "Not forever."

18

For five days Kevin did his best to help Raina adjust. He went to town for supplies, getting what he could that Tabby had been unable to pack. Ordering extra silk slips for her to wear, an extra skirt, shirt and two simple dresses. He kept their wood supply well stocked. Showed her how to start and keep a fire going.

They went on a tour of the property, taking a narrow foot-path to the stables, the small green house, and a storage shed, as well as the way to their private beach. When he cooked, she sat in the kitchen with him. But through it all, she rarely spoke, doing little more than staring off into nothing. Kevin knew if he were to coax her out of her shell, she'd likely indulge him, because he knew the best way was to kiss her. But doing so would mean forcing her to make a choice he knew she wasn't ready to make yet. Maybe she never would be.

By the fourth day he knew he had a bigger issue than what kind of future his wife wanted. His thigh was on fire, and he was positive he had a fever.

At dinner that night he set fried chicken coated in a spicy drizzle, along with roasted potatoes and jar preserved green beans on the table. Raina took a bite of the chicken and made a moaning noise that left him frozen with a bite halfway to his mouth. Eyes closed, she moaned deeply again and the chicken fell from his fingers back to his plate.

"This is so good. Everything you've made so far has been good, but this… this is amazing," she proclaimed, eyes still closed. "What is it?"

All he could do was stare. Damn if he didn't want to haul her across the table and taste the seasoning from her mouth, experience it as she had, but so much more. He attempted to speak, but nothing came out. Clearing his throat, he tried again. "Fried chicken."

She held up her fingers, wiggling the ends, showing off the red grease. "And this stuff?"

"Spices mixed in some of the cooking oil and drizzled over the top."

The tip of her tongue touched to one of her fingers. Kevin blinked and shifted his focus back to his food, trying to ignore the sudden uncomfortable situation he found in his pants. Incredibly thankful a table was between them and she couldn't see the havoc her physical enjoyment of his meal caused.

"It's really wonderful. Where's the recipe from?"

"The Westican south. It's a cultural food from my under-standing."

She took another savoring bite. "And they taught you?"

Kevin took a deep, centering breath, attention still on his own plate. "I learned, yes. Many cultures are excited to teach cuisine. It allows you to take a piece of them with you to your home. A reminder that a world exists beyond our own shores."

"I have lived with chef's my entire life and have never tasted anything with so much flavor."

Kevin smiled, thankful her more vocal expressions seemed to be over. Food, he could talk about. "You should try some of the foods from Italyssa. They have many fish dishes that they cook with olives, citrus and this unique cheese. Flavor is an understatement."

"Maybe someday you can take me."

Something close to hope blossomed in his chest. He met her stare, her light brown eyes soft with a shy smile. "Sure. When this is over, we'll go."

"Without telling my father." She grinned, popping a potato chunk in her mouth.

Kevin chuckled. "Well, how about the day we depart. I can't just disappear."

"Deal."

After dinner she surprised him by helping with the dishes. She didn't speak much, and he didn't initiate, his thigh hurting so badly he kept most of his weight on his left leg. Concentrating on the pain allowed him to keep his attention away from her, where it needed to be.

For the first time in their relationship, she knew everything now, who he was, where he came from, what she'd married. Kevin desperately wanted her to accept, but he'd not force the situation by asking. She knew the stakes, and she'd be the one to decide in the end. Four years he'd waited, he could wait longer.

Once they finished, she disappeared into his parents' old room, her room now, and he let go of the pretense of being okay and limped to the piano. As he did every night since their arrival, he sat before the keys, but never played. Notes floated through his mind, forming a melody his fingers itched to bring to life. But then Raina would hear. Part of him became overly concerned with her opinion of how and what he performed. Another part simply didn't want to share the only piece of himself he had left that was his alone to own. No one else could dictate or make the calls on how he wrote or played his music. No one else could have an opinion.

Giving up, he went to bed. Sleep never found him, the

throbbing in his thigh and fever kept him awake. An hour before dawn, he went outside, allowing the cold air to slip over his heated skin.

He knew he was in trouble. Knew he needed to wake Raina and make a plan on what to do next. But when he went to return to the house, dizziness swept through him. Blackness stole across his vision and he fell to his knees. Slicing pain shot through his thigh. With a grunt he landed face first in the dirt. After several failed attempts to rise, he stopped trying and simply let the darkness overtake him.

SILENCE BLANKETED THE HOUSE, oppressive and alarming. Concerned, Raina eased from her room, checking in Kevin's before searching the kitchen. She called for him, venturing up the stairs. Usually, she found him in the kitchen in the morning, using their leftovers from the night before to create some delicious morning meal. But, the upstairs proved fruitless as well.

The near week they'd been in the house had come as a shock to her. Aside from helping her learn her way around the house and property, he'd taken every effort to care for her. From showing her how the shower worked in the only bathroom in the house, a little room off the kitchen, to how to make her bed and fold her clothes, he'd helped her adjust.

Yes, she desperately missed hot water, and someone to clean up after her. Remembering to pick up her clothes, and dishes, had taken a few days. However, the horror of her abduction had begun to fade, and Kevin's nature broke through her fear. The simplicity of their life allowed her to focus on the things her father had waved in front of Kevin's face, what he'd threatened to take away and leave her stuck with. Leave him feeling guilty over.

None of it was fair, or acceptable.

And that her husband had kept not only a solid arms'

lengths distance between them the entire time, but seemed to have an emotional barrier up as well, had her plotting on how to break through both. Raina was positive they no longer had any secrets between them, everything was fully out in the open for her to see. He no longer had his *you don't know what you're getting into* excuse. A few more days living like normal people might actually convince her she was one, and *she'd* take the initiative and climb into his bed. The idea had merit and she found herself smiling.

Not finding him anywhere inside, she ventured out. Biting cold greeted her, but she ignored it. Hopefully she wouldn't be out long. Hands on her hips, she surveyed the trails and outbuildings.

"If I were Kevin, where would I wander off to?" Her words left her mouth in icy puffs, twirling and disappearing in the frigid morning air.

More wood? Check on Eadric? He let the horse meander around the grassy areas in the late morning, maybe he'd decided to let the stallion have his freedom a little earlier today. She rounded a corner and immediately spotted Kevin, face down on the trail. Her breath stuck in her throat and she screamed his name.

No response.

Faster than she thought herself capable, she sprinted to him, terrible scenarios racing through her mind.

He'd fallen and hit his head.

They'd been found and he'd been shot.

But when she reached him, there wasn't a bump on his head, nor was there any blood from a gunshot wound. Pressing her hand to his cheek she hissed at the heat radiating from his skin. Fever. She shook his shoulder and said his name again. He murmured something unintelligible, but made no effort to move.

Little flakes of snow drifted on the constant breeze. By late afternoon the temperature would reach into the mid-forties, high enough to turn the falling wisps of ice into misty drops. But now, the air hovered in the high twenties. She shivered and knew if she didn't get Kevin back inside, a fever would be the least of her concerns.

Wrapping her elbows under his arms, she hefted him upward with a groan of protest at his bulk. He didn't make a sound or movement. His head flopped forward, his chin nearly touching his chest. Damp hair ruffled in the breeze and pressed into her stomach when she heaved him forward, her feet digging into the loose dirt path. On a grunt, with her thighs burning in exertion, her stomach muscles tight and arms trembling, she managed to move him three whole feet. Weighing at least twice as much as she did, Raina had no idea how she'd manage to get him all the way to house, let alone inside, but she had to. There was no one else.

"Must you be all muscle, warrior of mine?" she breathed out, taking a few seconds to shake her aching arms loose and catch her breath. "Have to be all hard man and heavy. Have to be able to take out all those stupid bad guys."

Bracing her hands on her trembling knees, she tried to slow her breathing. Mucus coated her otherwise dry throat, and she coughed when cold air aggravated her already objecting lungs. "Had to have something wrong with you. Couldn't tell your wife you were sick because oh no, that'd make you some weak warrior." She heaved him up again on a groan. "Can't have that, just wouldn't do, would it?"

Somehow, she managed to get him to the front door. Dripping with sweat she collapsed on the wall beside the door. "How's that plan working out for you, keeping to yourself? I bet you'd trust your *team* if they were here. You and me," she said on a rough breath, motioning at the empty space between them. "We're going to have to talk about this complex you have trusting me."

Gathering strength from a reserve she didn't even know she had, Raina shoved open the door and steeled herself for another hard-fought battle. The distance from the door to the nearest bed, his, seemed somehow further than the path she'd dragged him up. She had nothing left. Every muscle in her body trembled, ached and protested even her straightening from the wall.

The flakes drifting along the ocean breeze had finally given way to mist, cooling her heated skin. But Kevin, despite his fever, had developed a definite gray to his complexion. Steeling herself against the difficulty ahead, she hefted him up once more and dragged him over the threshold. She slipped on the dusty wood floor and he landed on top of her, hard, his head bouncing in the hollow of her shoulder, his hips settling along her upper thighs.

Raina closed her eyes. Her tired arms wrapped around his wide shoulders. She shifted her fingers into the damp, short locks of his hair, her other hand splayed across his solid back. The labored, shallow rise and fall of his chest moved beneath her hand and pressed into her. Tears burned behind her eyes. For a precious moment she allowed herself the luxury of simply holding her husband, catching her breath even though his weight made it difficult to pull in much more than a gasp.

She needed to get up and move him. She needed to find yet another burst of strength. She needed to get him into the bed, out of the cold. She had to do all this because she *needed* him. The rest she'd worry about later. One obstacle at a time.

After easing out from under him, she sat. His feet were still out the open door. A cold draft billowed into the house, sending dust rolling along the floor. Papers fluttered on the piano. Raina waited until her heart didn't pound so hard it hurt before forcing herself to rise and attempt the impossible yet again.

Going up and down stairs throughout her day and *maybe* partaking in a dance or two on social evenings was the extent of her physical activity. Hauling her six-foot-five, two-hundred-and-something-pound husband was well beyond her capabilities. When this was over, she'd make Kevin teach her a thing or two about how he kept so in shape, that way if he needed saving again, it wouldn't kill her.

Twenty minutes and what she knew were several strained muscles later, she managed to pull Kevin onto his bed. She didn't care about the dirt covering every inch of him. Didn't care how sweaty she was, or how much grime she dragged onto his bed. He was in. End of concern. Gasping for air, she stumbled into her room, yanked off the comforter, and dragged it back into his room. The effort of covering him was too much, and all she managed was to toss it over his legs before she collapsed onto the floor beside the bed.

Then, with his hand flopped over the edge, and one foot dangling an inch from the floor, she rested her head back and allow the tremors to consume her. She covered her face and gave into her inner princess and sobbed.

What was she supposed to do now?

19

Raina alternated between numb, terrified, and angry. She succumbed to temper tantrums, screaming at her unconscious husband to wake up. To come around. To tell her what was wrong. To help her fix it.

He hadn't.

He couldn't.

She'd given in to panic, screamed at nothing in the living area, rocked back and forth on the floor in helplessness, and finally fell back in defeat and stared at the ceiling.

Which was where she found herself, hours later, watching little dust motes dance in the shifting light of day. Tears had long since dried in salty streaks on her face. Kevin hadn't so much as twitched. The gray of his skin hadn't improved even with a fire burning in the wood stove. She knew without a doubt if she didn't get him help, he would die. How long he had, she didn't know, tried not to even think about. She didn't even know what was wrong.

Taking a bracing breath, she slowly rose. "Okay, you are the daughter of an Arch Guardian. You're smart, and a Gen-Heir Logistics Expert. Synintel didn't hire the best personal tutors and see to your education only to find out you'd sat like a ninny while your husband died.

"What does Kevin need and how do you get it to him? That's what you do. You get things places," she said to herself, pointing at nothing. Her mind raced as she glanced into the room harboring the other half of her heart, a very sick half currently. "He needs help. He needs his Medical Science Officer. Get him Wintersfall."

Raina blinked and then whispered, "Get him Wintersfall." Excitement bubbled in her chest. Adrenaline rushed forward. On a braced squeal she shot to her feet. "Yes! Get him Wintersfall!"

She ran into the room she'd been occupying and pulled out every rolled sheet of paper on the shelves. The first two she unrolled were of areas she didn't need. The third one had her slamming her hands on the table in triumph. "Yes, okay, here we go."

With precision, she became orientated with the map's layout, quickly deciphering what lines were roads, water, and rails. The map was at least twenty years old, but she doubted much had changed besides new settlement locations and the small numbers beneath, which recorded altitude and population. All the cities remained the same, with likely the same resources. Rail stations, radio dispatch locations, mail carriers, they were all clearly marked on the drawing.

Raina slid her hand along the route she'd need to take, making sure she charted the fastest way. She had to return before dark. A woman traveling alone in regulated Sziveria was dangerous. Traveling alone in the lawless land known as the Northern Boundary was incredibly risky. But she didn't have much of a choice. She had to get a radio communication to Sean, hours ago… rather days ago if Kevin had been thinking clearly. They'd run out of time and she had no more to waste.

In Kevin's room she found coins and took more than she

hoped she'd need. She also grabbed a bracelet Tabby had packed, in case the fee for a transmission was trade only. Wrapping herself up in a long black cloak she'd found in the armoire, with an extra scarf around her head and neck, she left the house.

At the stables, she calmly led the Icekutian from his stall. Raina knew she didn't have the strength to saddle Eadric. She managed to convince the horse to stand next to a large boulder so she could climb on his back. Thankfully he was as loyal to her as he was to his master and allowed her to mount without complaint.

"Okay Eadric, I know you love him as much as I do. Let's go get him the help he needs."

Four hours later, Raina found herself in a little community known as Rails End. She located the radio transmission center. Much to her relief, nobody paid her much attention. Deep in her mind, she knew she over-exaggerated her fear, but having been kidnapped and forced to watch her husband kill in cold blood had her thinking everyone was watching.

She tied up Eadric, taking a moment to make sure no one eyed the large horse. Two dark brown Icekutian's ambled by and Raina breathed in relief. The cold-weather mounts weren't uncommon up here. Made sense, since the average nightly temperature dropped into the teens for all but two months a year. Hitting well into the negatives in the winter.

The line inside the small, narrow building was short. She composed her message at a private table, looked up Haven City's code and used a worn copy of the *Directory of Ranked Guardians* to find information on Sean. The Directory was outdated, almost fifteen years old. Dog-eared and torn pages showed its age. A Joel Blackbain was listed as the Primary Guardian Wintersfall. A man who only marginally resembled Sean was sketched in a rectangle frame. He had a cruel scowl etched on his face, and hard eyes. The image made a shiver race up her spine. She didn't like him. Raina surmised the man must have been Sean's brother. The name seemed somehow familiar, but she couldn't quite place how. Since houses rarely changed from one heir to another, she wrote the address listed and hoped.

Then, because she couldn't seem to stop herself, she flipped the pages until she found the Master Guardian Raiventon. The book would have been released either the year of or only a year or two after Kevin's father had been named. A handsome man with a kind smile the artist managed to capture in his eyes stared off the page at her. Dustin L. Merrick. Kevin favored his father. The line moved forward and two people walked in. Raina wanted to tear the page out so she could read about him. She wondered if the family kept one of the old books at the house. She'd have to check. Snapping the book closed, she left the desk for another patron and took her place in line.

The operator, a skinny man with squinty dark eyes and tuffs of hair sticking out from under a hat took her message. He gave her a droll stare, snapped the paper open, and proceeded to transmit. Nervous, Raina glanced over her shoulder and smiled faintly at the person behind her. A little girl with short brown hair and big brown eyes waved from her mother's arms. A dirty stuffed rabbit clutched tightly in her hand. A threadbare dress hung off her thin shoulders, the color having long faded to little more than gray.

The operator told her the fee, forcing her attention back to him. He slid the message back across the counter. Raina dug into her cloak pocket and produced the coin. Looking over her shoulder again, she asked the man if she could pay for the next transmission. He squinted at her, but nodded. She slid two extra coins across the counter. She nodded to the young woman holding her daughter, and offered the little girl a special smile and wave. The child delighted with a giggle and a shy turn into her mother's chest.

Knowing she'd done what she'd set out to do, Raina

returned to Eadric. She walked the horse out of town until she found a high enough boulder to use to climb atop him. By the time she returned to the house she was exhausted and starving. She took care of the Icekutian, made sure he was safe, fed and watered and warm for the night, and then stumbled up to the house.

The last of the sun's rays faded beyond the endless horizon, a faint glow of light in an otherwise colorless sky. Standing at the door, she leaned against the frame and stared out over the water. White caps gently rolled toward the shore. The calm rush of waves breaking far below made her want to close her eyes and become lost in their lull.

Scared, she didn't want to go back into the house. Didn't want to know what she would find. Didn't know how to handle whatever came next. A tear slid down her cheek. She took a deep breath and steeled herself.

Inside the silence felt like a tomb. She closed her eyes again and shook her head. No, not a tomb. Empty, cold, but not because of death. Closing the door, she called out to Kevin with a thread of hope that he'd answer. Nothing. Every muscle in her body protested her slow shuffle to his room.

Kevin lay exactly as she'd left him. Half sprawled on the bed, pale, unmoving. Raina approached with her gaze fixed on his chest. A slow, faint rise almost had her crying. Kicking off her shoes, she crawled onto the mattress near his feet. Using the last of her energy, she managed to remove his boots. On a sigh, she dragged her aching frame along his. She collapsed on the pillow and pressed her face to his bicep. The heat of his fever radiated through the thin fabric of the dust covered shirt.

Raina searched out his hand and then threaded her fingers through his. Sweat dampened his palm, his hand lied limp along hers. "Don't you dare get any worse. Help is coming, warrior mine. Just hang on for me… just hang on."

• • •

HELP ARRIVED before the first glow of dawn in the form of three big men and one accusing woman. Raina stepped aside and let the team enter. Katria's icy stare, made worse by the vivid blue of her eyes, was the last crack in Raina's carefully constructed façade. Exhausted, hungry, terrified and feeling ten times useless, Katria's condemning glare had Raina breaking like glass.

"You can stop looking at me like that," Raina snapped at the woman, slamming the door closed on the frigid air wafting into the house. "I didn't do anything to him. It's not my fault he kept whatever is wrong with him to himself."

Katria turned, her long black hair arcing out behind her, blue eyes flashing. "And how does a *wife* not realize her husband is getting sick?"

Sean's hand wrapped around Katria's upper arm. He gently tugged her into his side. "That's enough."

Her beautiful face scrunched in displeasure. "She—"

"I said enough." While low, Sean's voice carried enough warning to make his wife's mouth clench shut. Sean's amber gaze shifted to Raina. "Where is he?"

Raina pointed at the sectioned off part of the large room. "Second door."

Sean marched to Kevin's room, and Raina took in the other two men who followed. Mason Dandridge wasn't someone she was going to get used to anytime soon. With his long black hair, barely managed beard and piercing silver eyes, a shiver of unease raced up her spine as it had the first time she'd met him. His massive size alone left her weary. Mason reminded her of a bear. She wondered if he were handsome under all the fur. Jonathon Hunter in contrast was clean shaven, with neatly cropped dark brown hair. His size was similar to Kevin's, more athletic than bulky, though shorter, probably closer to six feet, maybe an inch or two over. He also, she noted, had kind eyes, like he was used to having to comfort people.

Hugging her arms around her waist, she trailed behind them. Katria followed with a bag slung over her shoulder. In the room, Raina made sure she was completely out of the way. Jonathon and Mason pulled, cut and tore at Kevin's clothing. Sean checked his eyes, pulse and breathing.

"Why all of you?" she found herself asking before she could stop.

Sean glanced over his shoulder before continuing. "When Katria was stabbed, it took both Kevin and I to hold her down. She weighs half what I do. If wh—"

His words were interrupted by Mason's sharp curse. "Sean…"

The team leader's jaw worked and Raina leaned over until she could see between Jonathon and Mason. An angry red gash rose from Kevin's thigh, the flesh around it risen and enflamed. She covered her mouth on a gasp. Sean snapped his fingers to wake everyone out of their shock.

"Kat, hot water. Raina help her. Jonathon, find me a small table. Mason, get everything out of the med kit," Sean delegated, and then clapped his hands when no one moved fast enough for him. "Now!"

Raina jumped. She rushed out of the room ahead of everyone else, leading the way for Katria to the kitchen. She took the short set of stairs down too fast, and tripped, catching herself on the wall before she face planted on the tile floor.

"The pots are here, I'll fill one if you start the fire," Raina said, grabbing a pot on the way to the sink.

Katria frowned, opening the hatch on the woodstove. "This is completely cold. When was the last time you ate?"

Raina blinked. Her hands trembled. From anxiety or the lack of food Katria brought to her attention she didn't know. "Um, I'm not sure. The night before maybe?"

A match struck and flared, casting a brief warm glow around the spacious room. "You can't cook?"

The pot filled and Raina quickly cut off the water. "No. I can't do much of anything. I'm the daughter of an Arch Guardian. We don't learn self-reliance, except where it comes to how people view us emotionally."

Sadly, she knew she'd failed at keeping the bitterness from her voice when Katria gave her a contemplative look.

"You aren't very emotionally stable right now." Katria took the pot from her. She adjusted the stove to what Raina assumed was maximizing heat.

"Well, no. Kevin is very sick and there's nothing I can do to help except fill a pot of water." A hot tear streaked down her cheek and she brushed it away, hating the weakness the perfectly composed woman witnessed in her.

A loud bellow echoed through the house. Raina rushed up the stairs. Chaos reigned when she skidded into Kevin's room. Naked, he thrashed, barely missing a punch at Mason, who laid across his chest. Jonathon attempted to hold down his legs. Sean was failing at calming him down.

"What happened?" Raina demanded, appalled, terrified and if she were honest, bordering on angry.

"I touched the cut," Sean said between clenched teeth. "It's so infected just brushing it brought him out of unconsciousness."

Kevin shouted again when Sean prodded his leg once more, and shockingly managed to throw Mason clear off the bed. Sweating from fever, his eyes wild and shiny, Kevin lurched for Sean. Raina didn't think about the consequences, she leapt onto the bed. She ran across the mattress, avoiding Mason's attempt to scramble up off the floor using the blankets for leverage. Sliding in behind Kevin, she wrapped an arm around his shoulders and her thighs around his waist and pulled.

"Shh," she whispered in his ear. Gently, she threaded her fingers into his hair. "You're okay, it's only Sean. They're trying to help you. Calm down."

Kevin stilled and the room froze when he did. His arms lifted, wrapping around her waist as his weight shifted back. Raina found herself pinned to the headboard, but she didn't care. Continuing to stroke his damp hair, her head bent over his, she murmured encouraging words, nodding to Sean when their eyes locked. He returned the gesture and carefully went back to work. Kevin stiffened, but made no further effort to go on the attack.

"And she tames the wild beast," Mason said on a huff, rising from the floor.

"For now." Her heart beat wildly. She knew she'd taken a great risk, having no way of knowing if he'd respond to her. That he had made her hold tighten. He was hers, and whatever he needed to suffer less, she'd do.

Jonathon sat on Kevin's calves at Sean's order. "You weren't kidding when you said he would fight, and win."

"Nope. Even sick he's quick, and strong. Learned that lesson the hard way," Sean said with a grim frown.

Mason threw a sheet over Kevin's waist and then held him down below Raina's clasped ankles, controlling involuntary twitches. Moments later, Katria arrived with a pot of steaming water. Kevin remained silent. Except for the occasional tremor, or flexing of his fingers deep into her flesh, she'd have thought he passed out again. Every time he did, she knew he was hurting and she responded by calmly speaking to him, stroking his hair.

What seemed like hours, and painstaking work on Sean's part, the exhausted MSO finally rose from a chair Katria had brought from the kitchen. "Okay, easy part is done. Infection is cleaned out and I've sewn him up. Now we have to fight the infection and get a handle on the fever."

Raina's arms burned from her long hold, as did her thighs. Had it not been completely inappropriate to let her legs relax at Kevin's sides, she'd have uncrossed her ankles over an hour ago. Even though she figured no one would care, she couldn't bring herself to. "How will you do that?"

"Lots of liquids, herbs and shots." Sean accepted a long, thin syringe from Katria when she handed it to him. He held up the needle. "Twice a day for three days."

Raina worked her bottom lip between her teeth. "Are you going to be here for three days, then?"

Sean carefully injected Kevin's arm. "At least. We'll stay until he's awake and lucid."

Usually someone else handled guest situations, Raina simply made sure everything was running smoothly and in order. She approved menus, what linens would be used in what rooms, and if anything social would happen, such as games or teas. At this house, not only couldn't she cook, but she had no idea where anything was kept.

Sean must have noted her panic, for his hand covered her forearm with a gentle squeeze. "It's okay. We're used to doing things on our own. We can handle everything. I know how to cook, and it won't be the first time we've had to sort out room situations."

No, of course it wouldn't be. Still… "You and Guardianess Wintersfall can take the room next door. There are rooms upstairs, I don't know if any have beds though."

"I'll check," Mason said.

Raina raised her hand. "Before you go, do you think you could help me?" She looked at Sean. "Is he still awake?"

Sean shook his head. Locks of light brown hair fell across his eyes, giving him a boyish look. "No, he passed out again about a half hour ago."

Knowing Kevin's returning to sleep was for the best didn't stop a wave of disappointment from sweeping through her. She'd wanted to see him, speak to him face to face. Mason loomed over them and Raina hugged Kevin quickly before unfolding herself. With a grunt, Mason lifted Kevin's unconscious torso and Sean had to help her climb off the bed. Her feet were numb and a terrible ache sliced through her back. With a braced hand on her hip, Sean kept her from hitting the floor.

"Easy, take a second to let the blood return to your legs." Carefully he guided her to a chair and helped her sit. "Call if he wakes up."

Raina nodded, and then wiggled her toes when little pinpricks danced along the soles of her feet. Soon she knew they'd feel like ants had erupted from the floor to consume her. Before they could all shuffle out, she managed to find her voice again.

"Thank you, all of you. I don't know..." She couldn't finish her words, tears burning behind her eyes.

The three men, so large they took up most of the available space in the narrow room, stared at her. Katria leaned against the dresser, arms crossed. Raina fidgeted with the wrinkled fabric of her skirt.

"He's our brother. Thank you for having the mind to reach out for help," Sean said simply. "When you can, feel free to get some rest. He's going to be okay."

Jonathon cast her a lopsided grin, his entire face changing from serious to rakish with the action. "I'm garnering so many favors from this group, I'll be able to take over Haven City before the criminals can."

Raina nodded again, trying for a reassuring smile as they filed out. Once they were gone, she didn't bother to stop the onslaught of tears from spilling over her cheeks. Alone, she sat with an unconscious Kevin, who might very well be on the road to recovery, but still looked like death had touched him.

"I WAS THERE. The day he discovered his Gen-Heir ability," Sean said with a nod to the open bedroom door, where Kevin still lay, sleeping off a fever that had broken halfway through the second night.

Raina straddled the wide bench seat of the massive table, the only furniture to sit on besides a piano bench, or rocking chairs in front of the fireplace. She couldn't bear to keep Kevin from her sight, so she made sure she could see him through the open door.

Sean sipped on a cup of tea, having made one for both of them while they waited for Mason and Katria to return from their exploration of the beach. Jonathon had returned to Haven City once the need to possibly hold Kevin down again had passed.

"He wasn't always aware of it?" she asked, wrapping her hands around the warm cup.

"No. He was going to school for music, believe it or not."

Raina raised a brow. "Music? He's never played anything, though he did tell me it's what his mother once wished for him."

Sean shrugged. "You'll have to ask him more about it."

"So, he discovered it during studies?"

Sean traced the rim of his mug, his handsome face tense. "Sort of. Kevin wasn't one of *us*, and that caused him no end of grief at Acadamia."

One of us. Raina didn't have to ask what Sean meant. Privileged. The elite of society. High born. Choose a category to describe a child birthed into a ranked Guardianship family. No, Kevin had been born in a tiny city, outside the legal realm of Sziveria, to parents no one outside of New Hampton knew existed. At least, not at first.

Sean continued, "And, because he inherited his rank at sixteen, he was Master Guardian Raiventon while the rest of us were still family names that carried little weight like a ranking did. They despised him for it."

"But the rank wasn't his, still isn't, not really."

A heavy sigh escaped from him. "Well, it is. He hasn't lost

it, he just hasn't been guaranteed it either. Same situation eleven years ago."

Raina tried to imagine a young Kevin, recently orphaned, having to defend himself against the cruelty of a society that made sure he felt unwanted. Anger and humility over the world she'd been raised in, had been forced to obey, made her fingers clench tighter around the cup.

"A stupid group of boys thought they'd teach him a lesson. Show him how *unworthy* he was to be called Guardian of anything," Sean said.

Raina met Sean's amber eyes. "Bad mistake, I'm guessing?"

"Colossal mistake." Sean smiled, a toothy predatory action that made his eyes almost glow. "He had five boys flat on their backs and writhing in pain before they even realized they'd been beat. Three months later, Kevin was pulled from the school and sent to training."

"At sixteen?"

"His ability is that rare, and that important to refine. Like Katria's, it requires years of fine training, which he'd missed out on because no one knew what he was capable of, including him, until he needed the reflexes."

Another mystery Raina had been curious about. "And what exactly does Katria do?"

Sean raised a brow. "Kevin didn't tell you?"

"He said Katria could."

"Ah. She's a marksman, like her father."

Raina blinked. "She's a sharpshooter?" An assassin.

"Yes," Sean confirmed.

No wonder the woman wore an emotionless mask. She'd been trained to be free of excessive thought to keep herself calm and in constant control. Katria's words the night she'd sequestered Raina in their house came rushing back.

A woman who is very capable of making sure you *didn't walk away.*

"Oh," was all Raina could manage to get out. Blinking, she stared at the tawny liquid in the cup. "Why did you tell me about Kevin?"

"Because I wanted to help you understand. I feel like maybe he doesn't offer enough information for an educated decision. Not necessarily his fault. We deal in the shadows mostly."

Raina shifted uncomfortably on the bench, wondering what Sean had noticed to make him feel he needed to give her a different perspective on her husband. "He's been fairly open about how he feels about choices."

"Yes," Sean said softly. "And now you know why."

Raina considered his words thoughtfully. Did she know? Tilting her head, she looked back into the room. Kevin's sleeping form gently mounded beneath the blankets. He'd hardly stirred for the three days he'd recuperated. Not by conscious choice. His decidedly ill body had made sure he recovered whether he wanted to or not.

Realization dawned and her eyes widened. From the moment Dustin Merrick accepted the rank of Master Guardian Raiventon, the son likely had very little choice in anything. He'd do what was best for the emerging ranked house. Then, once his genetically inherited talent had materialized, and the FIO learned of the unsigned Interceptor quietly studying music at Academia, yet another choice had been taken from him. Enter her father years later with an either-or option, he'd had no other decision then either. At every step of his adult life, choices hadn't been a luxury Kevin had been offered. He'd never do that to her.

He'd needed her to know what life with him would entail, but how could she possibly? Unaware of his true talent, ignorant of what life outside of *princess* status looked like, she'd only had her feelings for him to go by. Now she knew. And she also knew what *he* would be giving up as well. She'd be a fool if she thought Kevin was happy in her world. Merrick Cove, in tiny New Hampton, was home.

Suddenly she wanted to touch him. Wanted him to be in her space. "If you'll excuse me."

Sean inclined his head. "I think I'll go find my wife."

Raina didn't wait for him to leave. She went straight into the room, climbed on the bed and sank onto the mattress at Kevin's side. Fitting her body along his, she took his large hand in hers and brought it to her chest.

"You silly, silly man," she whispered to him. "When you awake, you're going to learn how much I love you and how very unconcerned I am about life outside of my father's sphere of influence. I don't want to live a life without you. And I won't."

Shifting onto her elbow, she leaned over him. Very gently she pressed a kiss to his lips, then whispered against them, "Choice made."

20

———

Upon waking, Kevin became aware of three things immediately.

One, he hurt. All over. But most of all his head pounded
and his thigh twitched from a deep throbbing pain.

Two, he was naked.

Three, he wasn't alone.

Blinking grit from his eyes, Kevin carefully rolled his head
until he peered at the petite, peaceful sleeping figure beside
him. He closed his eyes and opened them again to make sure
Raina remained. Four years he'd fantasized about this exact
moment. She didn't disappoint. Dark lashes swept across her
cheeks, flushed from not only being buried under a mound of
blankets, but wrapped around him as though she were afraid
he'd slip away. The steady rise and fall of her breathing sent a
silky rush of air across his bicep and made him acutely aware
of her breast pressed into his side. Her thigh rested atop his,
fitting her curves along the entire length of his torso.

Desire, sharp and strong, shot straight through him. The
pain in his thigh faded in the rush of heated blood. He
wanted to pull her onto his chest, strip off the layers of
fabric she'd kept between them, run his hands along every

inch of her, and claim what he'd been denying himself for so long. But first, he had to figure out why she slept beside him.

As if sensing his return to consciousness, Raina inhaled deeply. Her beautiful pale brown eyes opened on a flutter. A sleepy smile graced her lips. "You're awake."

Then her brows furrowed and she shot up. "You're awake..." She gasped and before he could react, she straddled him, had his cheeks pressed between her warm palms and her mouth slammed to his. She kissed him hard and then jumped off his chest. "Sean! He's awake!"

Before he could process what happened, she was gone in a flutter of wrinkled fabric and tousled hair. That was the second time she'd managed to be faster than him. *What* in the arctic...

Groaning, Kevin attempted to sit up. Every muscle in his body failed at the same time and he collapsed into the mattress, breathless. Well, this was interesting. What was wrong with him?

"You almost died," Sean said.

Kevin was reminded his Sympath friend and team-leader might as well be a mind-reader for how easily he understood expressions. Sighing, Kevin stopped trying to find any strength. "That explains a lot."

Sean pulled a chair close to the bed and sat. He braced his elbows on his knees. "You're very lucky. Why didn't you send word of your injury when you arrived in the Northern Boundary?"

"I didn't think it would be this bad. I'd cleaned and treated it."

Sean let loose a heavy sigh. "A day or two longer and if you didn't die, you may have lost your leg. Though, with the resources available here, I couldn't have done such a terrible procedure. There would have been nothing left to do but try to keep you comfortable."

And leave his wife to watch him fade away. Kevin clenched his jaw. "How did you find out?"

"What's the last thing you remember?"

Kevin managed to pull his arm up to his head. He covered his eyes with his forearm and exhaled slowly. Memories slowly played out in his mind. "I went outside, I hadn't been sleeping well. I was heading back to the house and then... nothing."

"Raina found you. She dragged you back to the house, and then she went to Rails End and radioed Haven City."

Shocked, Kevin lifted his arm and stared. Guilt hit him fast and hard. If something had happened to him... if she hadn't been able to pull forward a strength he'd never thought her capable of, she'd be left alone in a world she had no clue how to navigate. The level of his stupidity for keeping his injury to himself increased.

In his effort to shelter her, he'd placed her further in jeopardy. Instead of leaving him to fate however, she'd stepped up. Not only rising to the challenge, but staying when she could have hopped a train and run back to her father's safe arms. He wanted to list a dozen reasons why, none of them having to do with how she personally felt about him, but Sean held up a hand and continued.

"And before you go thinking she did all this to protect her father from whatever nefarious plan Enbrackon has, she hasn't left you except to eat. Sometimes not even then. Without her, I wouldn't have been able to help until you did a ridiculous amount of further damage to yourself. You threw Mason off. *Mason.* And you'd been unconscious for almost a day at that point."

Kevin considered Sean's words. He didn't want to focus on Raina, or what her actions meant. "Have we learned exactly why Enbrackon kidnapped her?"

Sean shook his head. "I think Raina knows though."

"She's said nothing." Kevin heaved another sigh. "Voklane had his suspicions."

"What were they?"

Kevin shook his head. He didn't want to contemplate the complicated conspiracy or Raina's lack of volunteering information. Enbrackon liked to talk, to brag. Kevin *knew* the man had laid out his intentions to Raina. Why she'd kept them to herself so far, he didn't know, didn't really want to think about. He'd purposefully avoided discussing anything related to her abduction, hoping she'd adjust on her own and come to him with anything she felt relevant.

He was filthy, exhausted, thirsty and hungry. Anything else could wait. For now. "Help me up, please. I need a shower."

"You need food first. I'll bring you some, then Mason and I will help you."

After eating and drinking what he could manage, and being helped into a robe, Sean and Mason assisted Kevin downstairs to the small bathroom off the kitchen. Sean kept vigil outside the door, calling Kevin's name randomly while Kevin did his best to not fall on his face in the cold shower. If Kevin didn't answer within a specific amount of time, Sean would barge in. Sadly, it wasn't the first time Kevin had needed supervision after a bad injury, and likely wouldn't be the last.

He made swift work of washing up, brushing his teeth and getting into clean clothes after Sean did a quick check of his thigh. At least, clean pants. He didn't bother with a shirt, he'd be crawling back into bed.

When he had yet to see Raina again, he asked on their way back to the bedroom, him hopping on one foot while Mason and Sean guided him back to the room, "Where are the women?"

"Raina is seeing to Eadric. Kat is… wherever she is," Sean muttered.

"She's bored," Mason said with a chuckle. "She was shooting at driftwood and whatever else that was large enough to annihilate on the beach yesterday."

Sean grimaced in embarrassment. "The beach is pristine now."

Mason grinned. "She's been moping about since. Said the *one* fun thing she'd found to do won't come back until the next tide."

Kevin stopped and looked between the two men, aghast. "How did Raina handle that?"

Sean shrugged and urged Kevin to move again. "She didn't leave your side. If the sound of Kat's rifle and her equally enthusiastic responses when she succeeded bothered her, she kept it to herself."

"Wouldn't you if said woman came waltzing in with a smirk and a BACR-18 in her hand?" Mason asked Sean, leaning forward.

This time it was Kevin's turn to frown. "Well, I suppose she's had a crash course in an Intel Guardian team now."

They helped him to the bed. Kevin handled the rest, situating pillows behind him so he could comfortably sit. "Anything new while we've been gone?"

Mason straddled a chair. "I've noticed something else odd with the maps. But until Raina can look over them with me, I'm not a hundred percent sure what it is."

"Did going over Enbrackon's properties produce any yields on where the missing cargo, or what it might be, is being stored?"

Sean shook his head. "No. Asherwick discreetly looked into them over the past week. I'm sure they made sure Enbrackon isn't associated with the shipment once Raina was rescued and they realized how badly their plan failed."

Mason scratched at the underside of his bearded chin. "Will he be in trouble with Cairo since none of the Sentinels will be returning?"

Kevin shook his head. "No, he paid for them. When you purchase a Cairoen Sentinel, you're paying for the life. Any returned alive are reimbursed, minus a small fee. It's in the purchaser's best interest to keep the Sentinels alive."

"We took out at least thirty. That couldn't have been cheap," Sean noted.

"No," Kevin agreed. "And the way he lives, he may not have had the assets to lose."

"I can't see Synintel letting his daughter's kidnapping go unpunished," Mason said with a shake of his head. "I think it's just a matter of time before orders show up in Sean's hand for Katria."

Kevin ran his hand over his face. "Maybe we can get something that will give him a little more incentive. Raina and I can't stay here forever, and by now he'll be daring enough to pull a Wystone on me."

They all frowned at the reminder of the homicide Enbrackon had made to look like a suicide. As the First Prefect of HCES, he had easily made the witnesses murder disappear. Making Kevin disappear in the same manner would be extremely difficult, but not impossible. And the Shield Guardian was likely desperate enough to attempt the feat now.

"You have two weeks," Sean ordered. "Don't go to the house when you return, unless it's with Synintel personally. Go to my house, or Mason's. We'll go over any new information with Voklane and Asherwick."

"We have lots of room. I can give you your own wing," Mason said with a bit of a smile. The man had claimed the smallest downstairs room for himself. Space wasn't a luxury he basked in.

A little weight eased off Kevin's shoulders. They had a plan, and he had two weeks to heal. He wouldn't be completely ready to take on another Sentinel force, but he wouldn't be useless either.

When they both went to rise, Kevin asked, "How long was I out for?"

"Almost four days," Sean answered.

Kevin's mouth fell open.

"Don't worry, we won't leave until you can walk to the kitchen on your own. I've been trying to get Raina comfortable in the kitchen, but she has as much passion for cooking as this one here." Sean hooked his thumb Mason's direction.

Mason held up his hands. "Hey, I like my food to taste like something other than burnt. Or salt."

Gratitude and affection formed a lump in Kevin's throat for the small group of people who'd become his family over the years. He swallowed against it and tried to find his voice. "I'm…"

Mason shook his head. "Nope. We aren't doing that. You keep all of us out of trouble, so don't go thinking we were selfless in showing up here."

But Kevin knew they were. He nodded and closed his eyes against the fatigue pulling him under. He felt a firm hand squeeze his shoulder, and Sean quietly said, "You're welcome."

21

Three more days passed before the team felt confident enough to leave Raina in charge of the rest of Kevin's recovery. Sean left her specific instructions, which the MSO had been adamant about writing down. Knowing it was his love for Kevin, and not believing her incapable, Raina had gladly obliged.

The moment they were gone, Kevin reverted back to his in-control self. With a growl of frustration, Raina figured the only reason he hadn't convinced her to return to Haven City was due to him knowing he still needed a little help. Thankful for small concessions, she'd been unruffled about his attitude.

Until now.

Waking up in his parent's room, alone, she'd almost hurled whatever she could reach at the closed adjoining door. Apparently, the moment he could draw his line again, *this is your side, and this is mine,* he'd done so, while she slept, so she couldn't argue. Well, she wasn't going to have any of that. The only reason she'd bided her time on keeping her hands to herself was because she didn't want an audience. From the moment of her marriage, a silent house, free of ears and eyes had been her life at night.

Rich, muffled piano notes had her stilling. Throwing off the blankets, she slid her feet to the floor. The far too large nightgown she'd found in one of the dressers swam around her small frame. A thread of nervousness made her heart beat wildly.

"You can do this," she whispered. "You dragged him up hill, rode a massive horse bareback, rode hours to an unknown city, and helped keep your husband alive. Seducing him will be easy after all that."

Every night, lying in bed next to him, his hard, vital body spread out next to hers, she'd been thinking about seduction. Thought about his touch, his kiss. The way he fitted his body along hers when he'd shown desire. She tried to reverse engineer the memories, wondering how to turn them all around on him. The thought of reaching between *his* legs had sent her face on fire and her hands fisting. She couldn't do it. So, she had to think of something else.

The idea to simply be undressed had been an idea several times. If he awoke to her naked, he'd probably lose his mind. In a good way. But a lifetime of forced modesty, and the chance of rejection, made her scratch the notion. No, she needed a failure-proof plan. One that hinged on emotions, and choice, because that's where Kevin had placed their relationship.

Cold wood creaked beneath her feet. The floor beyond the bedrooms was stone. The extra layer of insulation on the floors helped keep the bedrooms warmer. Over the near two weeks they'd been in the house, she'd explored. In her snooping she'd discovered most of the boxes on the dressers had belonged to the former Guardianess Raiventon.

At the dresser, she pulled forward a small, yet ornate wooden box. Her fingers caressed the simply carved, unstained wood. Slowly she opened the lid, revealing two interlocked bracelets. The Merrick's promise bands. The bands were as simple as the rings she and Kevin wore. Thick silver, with two thin risen intertwining silver strands in the center. Sziverian tradition called for the couple to remove their bands at the contract signing, linking them together and storing them for future generations if desired. Other cultures, such as Westica and Italyssa, continued to wear the bands, a reminder of the promises given. Raina always appreciated those traditions.

When she'd found the bands, she'd known in her heart she and Kevin needed them. She fancied the former Guardianess had somehow known her son would need them and had made sure they were readily available, easy to find. Taking a deep breath, she removed the thick silver bracelets, carefully sliding them free of each other.

Holding them tight in one hand, she used her other to shimmy out of her underwear. She kicked them across the floor. In the morning, when she wandered around while Kevin chopped wood, cooked, or did whatever else she was incapable of handling, she'd pick them up like she did every morning. With a little smile she admitted she was rather proud of how good she'd become at keeping their floors clean.

There, now she was as close to naked as she dared become. Only a thin cotton nightgown stood between her and Kevin. Enough to keep her courage, but hopefully not enough to stop her from claiming her husband.

The perfectly balanced, emotional melody grew louder when she opened the door and padded to the large table. Climbing onto the top, she braced her feet on the bench and let the bracelets fall into the fabric hammock her nightgown created between her thighs. Then she waited, and watched, and listened.

Light from the huge fire behind her cast long, heavy shadows across the room. Heat rolled along her back and helped her relax. The alcove Kevin played in had one small lamp burning, enough to illuminate the keys, but not much more.

A dark shirt, the color lost in the fall off of light, hung open over his torso, brushing the bench with each flowing move he made, swaying to the music he created. Eyes closed, face a mask of concentration, his hands danced along the ivory keys. His hair, always more of a mess, was controlled chaos, finger tousled and a little longer than he usually wore it since they'd been away from civilization. A lock had fallen across his forehead, brushing his brow with every movement.

Handsome didn't come close to describing how he looked in that moment. Devastatingly sexy, beyond what a man had a right to look like, she wanted to straddle his lap, slip the shirt off his shoulders, and remember how those very capable fingers had felt on her skin. Soon, she reminded herself, soon. She didn't dare interrupt him now.

His head bent faintly to the piano, his avid expression of concentration shifted into one of almost pain. Brows furrowed, lips tight, jaw set, his fingers fell harder on the keys. The notes shifted from melodious to angry in the space of a heartbeat. Raina's pulse picked up. The music changed the environment to one of danger.

A quick flash of lightning strobed through the windows. Unfazed, Kevin's onslaught continued. Rain pounded heavily on the windows and exterior. The close roll of thunder made Raina jump. Awed, she stared at her husband, wondering if he'd somehow detected the approaching storm and switched emotions accordingly.

The song flowed through every cell of her body, wrapping her in a story of her imagination until her eyes drifted closed and she swayed, tapped her fingers to the lone higher notes floating in the wild mix. The cadence shifted again, almost blending in its simplicity to the falling water outside.

Like a breath of warm air after a cold gale, she inhaled the wistful, airy change, a smile flitting across her lips. She had no idea music could not only be so personal, but so emotional. She'd been to concerts, but none had played like their very heart was invested. Rather they played as they'd been taught, instructed, creating masterpieces pleasing to the ear. This, what he did, was something else entirely. Almost like… the notes faded to silence.

Startled, Raina opened her eyes and found Kevin staring at her. A flush crept up her cheeks and she smiled. "I… I had no idea music could sound… like that," she admitted.

He rubbed his hands on his slacks, pushing the bench away. "Yeah, well, I haven't played in a long, *long* time."

"Since I've never heard you play before, I can believe that. However, if you play so well getting back into the feel of things, I'm beginning to doubt your genetic inheritance isn't music."

For a moment he simply gazed at her, his face an impassive shield. "My mother wanted me to be a musician. I had a natural ear for it. But, things change."

Yes, they certainly did, and she was counting on it.

"Couldn't sleep?" he asked, looking her over.

"Someone put me in a cold bed."

He had the good sense to look away from her, guilty. "Raina—"

"Come sit with me," she said quickly, preventing him from spouting whatever nonsense he felt she needed to hear.

He sat stiff for so many silent seconds, she thought he was going to deny her. Then, on a heavy sigh, he stood and slowly crossed the distance. The table was huge, so she didn't bother to move, knowing he'd decide where to sit. He slipped onto the bench near her feet. His forearms brushed her outer thigh as he situated himself.

"I found something," she began, pressing her knees together. The cool metal bands made a melodious *tink-tink* sound.

"Doesn't surprise me," he said, having to look up slightly

to meet her stare. "There's a lot of *somethings* to be found in this old house."

The firelight played off the angles of his face, and danced in his stormy eyes. She wanted to slide her fingers along his bearded jaw, trace the shadowed planes of his cheeks, and lean in and kiss him. Collecting her thoughts, she quickly looked away.

Before her nerve could desert her, Raina pulled the promise bands free. The warm glow of the flickering flames caught the silver, accenting the soft arches. "Were these your parents?"

He slowly took the smaller one from between her fingers. "I'm not sure. Maybe. Mom was a bigger woman, this looks too small for her wrist. Then again, she may have been smaller when they met."

"How long were they together before you were born?"

Another drawn out breath escaped from his mouth. "Around twelve years, I think. I was their fifth child."

Raina blinked, confused. "Fifth? I thought you were an only child."

"I am." The silver bracelet flipped between his fingers, catching the light in little flashes. "But, they had six total. I'm the only one who survived to adolescence. The last child, a girl, died when I was three. She was two months old, if I remember."

Heartache fisted in Raina's chest. "Why?"

Kevin shrugged. "There's no medicine this far north, or Medical Scientists to administer it. No money even if there was. No means of getting anything beyond basic herbs, which most communities grow in a communal greenhouse."

"You're telling me they buried five children due to illness because there wasn't access to medicine?"

"Yes. It's cold here, it's a hard life, and even harder still when an infant catches something. A fever can, and often is, deadly for a child."

And treating a fever south of the Boundary was a simple, everyday occurrence. Call for a Medical Scientist to make sure nothing serious is going on, get the medicine to control the fever, and wait for healing. Well, that was a new twist, though not all too surprising. She had after all had to send for Sean to save Kevin.

"I guess if we end up living here, your Logistics Expert of a wife will have to open the lines of communication and trade for MSO's to make it this far north, hmm?"

His shocked gaze snapped up. "What?"

Raina took a deep breath. *Here goes…* She twisted the larger promise band between her fingers. The dancing light caught Kevin's attention briefly before his questioning eyes moved back to her.

"We were forced to skip this part," she said, sliding her hand along his forearm to his wrist. "The promises."

When he remained silent, his gaze searching, she found the courage to continue. With shaky fingers, she slid the band onto his left wrist. She wrapped her hands around the cool metal and held tight.

"I think they're important. They help set the stage for expectation. For what a future with another personality, another view on life, might be like. I want to give you my promises, Kevin. Will you let me?"

His wrist shifted until his fingers found hers. Threading their hands together, he allowed her to still keep hold on the band while holding her hand. He replied on a whisper, "Yes."

Raina took a deep breath, partly to build her nerve again, and partly to keep from crying. "I, Lorraina Melody Merrick promise you, Kevin Joshua Merrick, that I *choose* to be your wife. I promise to be content regardless of what our home looks like or what city we reside in. I promise to accept every scar I can see, and all the ones I can't. I promise to remain faithful when you're called away. I promise to listen and be patient with what I don't understand. I'm not perfect, and I won't ever be the perfect wife. But I'll be yours."

He stared at their intertwined fingers. "Mine." The single word left him on a growl.

Chills ran along Raina's skin. A tremble raced up her spine. "Yes."

Slowly, he caressed from her palm to her wrist. The band, warm from his heat, slid onto her wrist. "Do I have to say all the name stuff?" he asked.

Raina couldn't help but smile and chuckle. "No."

"I promise to honor your decisions. I promise to only be yours. I promise to keep you safe." He slid closer until his side rested along her leg and his free arm slipped across her thighs and curled around her hip. Dark and full of emotion, his eyes stared deep into hers. "Most of all though, I promise your father won't be able come between us ever again."

No. Synintel wouldn't. And not simply because Kevin promised, but because Raina wouldn't allow it either. Their life was to be of their own making. No more meddling, or making choices neither of them had any say in when their lives were the ones being affected. Raina found something in these weeks locked away from all she'd never known. She'd found she had a spine, and strength she didn't know she possessed. She wasn't useless, or incapable of handling the hard situations life might throw her way.

Synintel had a new daughter. Raina couldn't wait for him to meet her.

Pulling her hand free, she slipped her fingers along his jaw. She didn't dare hesitate, didn't dare give Kevin the opportunity to deny her. She brushed her lips to his. A sense of triumph filled her with courage when his arm tightened around her waist. He shifted, making her lift her foot and part her knees to give him room to sit between her legs. On a growl, he slid her closer.

Raina straightened her spine. Everything in her wanted to

slide down onto his lap. Somehow sanity reigned and she remembered she'd hurt him. Her mouth opened at the gentle probing of his tongue along her bottom lip. Then he was over her, his chest pressing to hers, urging her back onto the surface of the table.

Desire shot through Raina, heady and drugging. Every muscle in her body tightened in expectation. Her breath fought to be free of her lungs. The sensation of him settling between her thighs made her back arch. Their tongues tangled together, tasting, exploring, memorizing. Raina dug her fingers into his short hair, her other hand slipping beneath his shirt to find his shoulders. The heat of his chest burned through her nightgown, an annoying barrier between them.

She tore her mouth free and with shaky fingers tried to undo the small buttons running down the front of nightdress. When she couldn't even get one free, she rumbled in frustration. "Help me."

"Slow down," he breathed out, his fingers brushing hers aside.

"No." She caught his face between her hands and brought his mouth to hers again, picking up the aggressive kiss where they'd left off.

Kevin didn't bother with the rest of the buttons, he simply yanked. The little pieces of shell bounced around the table and onto the floor. His hands cupped her breasts and she gasped, pulling her lips free and pressed into his touch. The warmth of his breath teased a second before his mouth swirled around her nipple and pulled the sensitive bud into his mouth. A gasping groan escaped her. On their own, her hips pressed into the evidence of his desire jutting into her low stomach.

He paid gentle attention to her other breast before moving lower, his hands sliding the fabric up her thighs to her hips. The moment he realized she wore nothing underneath he gave another short growl. She couldn't stop from glancing up.

Dark with desire and need, his gaze met hers as he lowered his mouth between her legs. Raina didn't have a chance to be concerned or embarrassed about his intentions. Sharp pleasure stole her breath, and her hips bucked as his tongue teased her center.

"We should move," he whispered against her sensitive flesh.

Raina sucked in air, her fingers searching for him. She dug into his scalp, her hips moving against his searching mouth. "N-no. I-I can't... please."

The rush of her climax took her by surprise. An intense, building pleasure that exploded through her body in a wave. Before she could contemplate it, Kevin was *there*, his hard length pressing into her opening, stretching and filling her with a gentle thrust. She cried out at the short-lived burst of discomfort, accepting him, rising to meet his controlled moves. His arms wrapped around her, holding her close to his chest. She held on to his shoulders, her head falling back. Raina shifted, spreading her legs wider to accommodate him, her heels braced on the edge of the table, taking more of him.

A new sensation formed, coaxed by the friction of his moving within her. Slowly, he eased her back onto the table, thrusting deeper, faster, until strange little cries she had no idea she could make rose from her throat. She wanted so much more, needed more. Digging her nails into his shoulder, she tried to form words, but failed. Kevin's quick breaths ruffled her hair, caressed her neck and shoulder, adding to her enjoyment of him, of their moment.

White-hot lightning flashed and Raina couldn't tell if it was outside, or within her body as she screamed and arched into the climax that tore through her. Kevin's fingers dug into her hip, holding her down as he pumped furiously into her, sending another wave of an intense orgasm coursing through her blood. His shout mingled with the corresponding rumble of thunder. On a hard thrust that stole her breath, he poured into her. Her heart felt near to exploding with love as he took his pleasure in her body.

The house vibrated from the explosion of energy outside. Panting, Raina hugged Kevin close, her ankles locking around his hips to keep him in place. She never wanted him to leave. His face buried in the crook of her neck.

"Are you okay?" he asked on a huff.

She tightened her hold. Breathless, she replied, "I should be asking you that, I'm not the one with stitches in my thigh."

He rose enough for her to catch the firelight in his eyes. "Is that a yes?"

"It's a yes." She lifted enough to give him a quick kiss. "Though I'm really, *really,* upset we wasted four years."

A tender smile graced his face, softening his features. He brushed a damp strand of hair from her forehead. "It wouldn't have been like this."

Frowning, she drew her brows together. "No?"

"No."

She wiggled, testing the feeling of him still erect and deep within her, and then gasped when another tendril of pleasure whispered through her body. "Why?"

Gently, he rocked his hips and she groaned, closing her eyes. "Because, love changes everything."

The admission made her freeze. Her eyes flew open and she found him still staring at her. "What?"

Still moving in unhurried strokes, he brushed his lips across hers. "I love you."

If her heart hadn't already been beating to the point of pain, his words would have done so. "You love me?"

Before she could squeak a protest, he had her lifted off the table. She wrapped around him and held on for dear life. Knowing he was strong and wouldn't dare drop her, didn't stop her from squeezing her eyes closed while he crossed the short distance from the table to his bedroom. With a faint grunt, he dropped them both to the bed, his good leg breaking the fall. They bounced on the mattress faintly. Raina's giggle turned into a sharp intake when he moved again, though this time in disappointment as he pulled free.

His fingers traced her cheek to her jaw and along the side of her neck, then he followed the trail with his lips. "Yes, I very much love you."

Tears brimmed in Raina's eyes. Her heart swelled. "I love you so much."

"Good, now that we've settled that, how about we get this out of the way." He tugged on the now ruined nightgown and Raina couldn't help but laugh.

"Yes, let's."

"WHEN WERE you going to tell me what Enbrackon said to you?" Kevin asked, his fingers drawing a lazy trail up and down Raina's naked spine. In the quiet aftermath of their passion, the question he'd been keeping inside kept surfacing. He decided why not ask? There wasn't much left between now they hadn't shared.

She propped her hands on the center of his chest and rested her chin on them, her eyes meeting his. Unabashed, she lay sprawled across his torso, her knees against his hips, her stomach pressed to his. The small mounds of her breasts brushed against him with every movement, driving him slightly crazy. A storm still raged outside, pelting wind swept rain and ice into the windows.

"You really want to talk about this now?" she asked.

His gentle caress paused while he considered the question. She didn't sound upset, only curious. Good. "Yes."

"Very well, but only if you agree to answer a question or two for me."

"Deal."

She wiggled and Kevin pressed a hand onto her back. A teasing smile curled on her way too sexy lips. Kevin had so many reasons to be thankful they'd moved their relationship into the physical. For one, he could now afford to give into temptation. Leaning up, he forced her body forward and claimed her lips for a passionate, open-mouthed kiss.

When she pulled away, her mouth was swollen and pouty from his assault. "Well... I don't know how you expect me to talk about much after that."

"Try."

She settled back onto his chest. Her fingertips thrummed a delicate beat under his collarbone. "I didn't keep what he said from you because I have anything to hide."

Kevin's gaze swept over her face, taking in the tangled mass of hair framing her face and drawing attention to her beautiful mouth. No longer innocent, wholly his. He closed his eyes, recalling the day he'd seen her for the first time. All young virtue and everything he never thought he'd be able to have. A delicate flower of a woman who had yet to know her true beauty or potential. He'd never wanted a woman more in his life.

Forgetting for a moment the direction of their conversation, he confessed, "The first day we met, if we'd been anywhere but in Synintel's office, I would have had my way with you."

She propped her chin on her overlapped hands and regarded him curiously. "What do you mean?"

"I mean," he said, grasping two handfuls of her very nice rear in his palms and kneading. "I would have tossed you on that desk and claimed every inch of you right then. I wanted to. Badly."

Her pale brown eyes widened. "Are you serious?"

"Very"

She rose, her knees pressing into his sides and slapped his shoulder. "You should have, it would have been the only good memory I had in that office."

The weak dancing light caressed her skin in flowing shadows. Small, yet firm, her breasts were perfect mounds. She was all gentle curves, from a narrow ribcage, to a flat stomach, to the delicate flare of her hips. He wanted to follow each smooth plane with his tongue, but settled on sliding his hands up her silken thighs to her hips. Unconsciously, she rocked against his stomach when his hands ventured low into the sensitive skin inside her legs.

She gave him a seductive glare. "You tease."

"You tempt," he whispered, skimming one hand to the curls still damp between her legs.

Kevin knew she was in no condition for much more, but couldn't stop himself, sliding his index finger along the tender nub still swollen. He was rewarded with a low moan and a sensual roll of her head back. She'd shocked him with her passion. Unashamed and unrestrained, she'd given him all of her, and he hadn't been able to deny how deeply in love he'd fallen.

Raina was everything to him. His entire world. She always had been, always would be.

And now he'd started something he had to finish, feeling the liquid heat of her desire. Her weight shifted onto her knees ever so slightly when he ventured lower, sinking a finger deep inside her. She shuddered a groan, her muscles clenching inside and out. Her hands massaged and dug into his shoulders. Using gentle finesse, he let her set the pace of his touch by her breathing, the slight twinges of her muscles, and the sensual little noises she made deep in her throat.

By the time she came apart on a trembling cry, he was gritting his teeth and counting himself all kinds the fool. Tomorrow night, and not a minute before, and even then he'd need to be gentle. He'd waited four years for this moment, he could wait another night for a repeat. After that... He caught her spent body in his arms when she collapsed onto his chest. After that, they had the rest of their lives to indulge in their passion.

"We won't be able to have a coherent conversation if you do that again," her words fanned across his chest.

Kevin smiled, trailing his fingers along her spine again. "I'll try to behave."

A faint shiver followed the path of his touch. He swiftly tossed the sheets and blankets over them. She snuggled against him and sighed comfortably.

"So," he asked, situating a pillow behind his head so he could see her better. "If you weren't keeping anything a secret, why stay silent?"

Her face, still flush from excursion, lifted, poising elegantly on her hands. She worked her chin, her gaze settling on his mouth. "Because you refuse to see things from any angle except bad usually, and I didn't want to risk *us*."

Kevin drew his brows together, smoothing her hair back from her face, tucking the tangled mass behind her ears and over her shoulders. "What do you mean?"

She lifted a hand and trailed a feathery path along his bottom lip to his chin. "I mean if I told you what he said, what he's done, you'd have decided anything I said or did was for a single-minded purpose and could not possibly be because I love you. But now you'd better know how honest my feelings are, or I'm going to kick you in your injured thigh."

What he's done.

Alarmed, Kevin stiffened and forced her face to rise and meet his stare. "What do you mean, Raina? What has he done?"

Working her bottom lip between her teeth, she rose slightly, pulling the sheet with her. "Deep breath, okay?"

Kevin pushed up into a sitting position, helping her adjust when she shifted down his body. "Why do I have a feeling nothing is okay?"

Her fingers twisted in the sheet clutched her chest. A frown pinched her features. "Enbrackon wants you dead."

"I know." That information wasn't new. "He won't come after me with men again, he'll likely try to find a marksman, or another means, like poison in my food."

She gasped and stared at him in horror. "Are you serious?"

"Of course. Losing the Cairoen Sentinels wasn't only embarrassing, it was expensive."

Slowly, she shifted off him and onto the mattress, her gaze thoughtful. "Not necessarily expensive, not to him personally anyway."

"What do you mean?" Unable to keep from touching her, he slipped his hand under the sheet until he found her thigh. She scooted closer, making the contact easier.

"That shipment of medicine he forced me to reroute, I bet you anything that was payment for the Sentinels."

Made perfect sense, and wouldn't cost him a personal coin. Kevin cursed under his breath. Once again, he found himself completely awed by Raina. Quick-minded and beautiful. He was a lucky man. "I'd forgotten about that."

"Yes, well, you've had lots of other things keeping you occupied." She shifted closer until their hips touched. "Like remaining alive."

"Something that should never have happened. I'm sorry."

She leaned into his chest and kissed him. "I know, but I can't really be too sorry. I learned a lot about myself because I had no one else. I'm just thankful I was strong enough."

His heart squeezed. "Raina…"

Shaking her head, she pressing a finger to his mouth. "Wait, I have more you need to hear before we get sidetracked again."

She inhaled long and slow and then released the breath on a huff. "He's after my father's position."

"Voklane figured as much. And with me out of the way, it leaves you open. All he'd have to do is threaten your father.

Except *if* you marry him, they'd likely kill your father once the rank exchange was approved."

"If it was approved."

"I don't think they'd have such an elaborate plan unless they were positive they could execute it."

She nodded and sighed again. "Yes, I suppose that's true. But threatening my father wouldn't guarantee my compliance. They needed a plan for that too, which they've already implemented."

A heavy sensation settled in Kevin's chest. The worry in her eyes and the way she moved closer, seeking his hand told him she didn't want to speak aloud what had to come next.

"What?" he urged when she remained silent. "Tell me."

Tears shimmered in her eyes. "I want you to know I didn't know. I *swear* I didn't know."

Kevin slipped a hand around her waist and pulled her forward until her knees nearly touched his bicep. He squeezed her small hand in his. "Hey, it's okay, it's all right, just tell me."

Two tears spilled fast and raced each other down her cheeks. "He said they often hid marriage contracts among other documents in FIO and SNID that Guardians sign." She sniffed, pulling her knees into her chest. "He did that to me."

For a moment Kevin stared at her, unsure if he understood correctly. "Enbrackon had you unknowingly sign a marriage contract?"

"Yes," she whispered and then buried her face.

If Kevin died, all Enbrackon had to do was file the contract and Raina would find herself another man's wife within hours. Rage boiled dangerously within him, but Kevin stayed composed, keeping his touch light on her hip, caressing her tense muscles. The revelation wasn't exactly new either, but knowing all Enbrackon's little pieces were so close to falling into place was concerning.

"I see. Voklane assumed Enbrackon was after the Synintel

rank, but he hadn't figured out how he'd accomplish taking over. Now we know," Kevin stated, keeping his voice calm.

"You aren't upset?" She lifted her gaze. The tears coursing down her cheeks caught the light, reflecting every trail they'd taken.

"Oh, I'm beyond upset, but not at you."

Her gaze searched his. She sniffled. "How do you do that? Remain… almost emotionless?"

"Self-preservation. What the enemy can't see can't be used against me."

She dropped her knees to the bed and leaned forward. Her fingers slid along his jaw. "I'm not the enemy. You don't have to hide from me."

Kevin closed his eyes, appreciating the tender touch he never thought he'd be able to claim. "Some parts of me you don't need to see." He caught one of her hands, holding it captive to his face. "You didn't tell me because you thought I'd question your motives toward me."

"Yes," she whispered.

A painful lurch jumped in his chest. Shame hit him like a punch in the gut. "I'm sorry. I never…" He took a deep breath when the words caught in his throat. "I never should have made you feel that way."

Her fingers curled into his short beard. "Mistakes are part of any relationship. We've both made our fair share, and we'll both continue to. I love you. As long as we work on what matters, the rest we can let go of."

Kevin pulled her across his chest and caught her mouth. Kissing her with all the emotion swirling through his system. He forgot his unspoken promise to keep his hands to himself, dragging her across his hips. She moved without hesitation, settling over his growing erection with a needy moan.

"How did I get you?" he asked. He trailed his tongue from her bottom lip to her chin and lower to her throat.

"Obeying an order? Preserving your future?" Breathless,

she wrapped her arms around his neck, pressing her breasts into his chest, her mouth seeking his jaw.

"Yes, you are definitely my future."

Before he could tell her no, she grasped his hard length and slid him inside. Slowly she rocked. Kevin lost all logical thought at her warm, wet heat surrounding him. Her shuddering breath fanned across his throat.

"I-I'm not sure what to do now," she admitted, gently lifting and rocking, setting her own rhythm.

Possessive and so humbled by her giving body, Kevin wrapped his arms around her small frame and held her close, lifting his knees to give her better balance. "You're doing everything perfect."

"Really?"

She shifted, taking him deeper and he groaned, his head falling back, pleasure snaking and building within him. "Really."

Their heavy breaths mingled with faint *tink-tink* of rain on glass. Kevin resisted holding her hips still and pumping into her. Instead, his held tight to her shoulder blades and focused on the flutter of her breath along his collar bone. On the tantalizing way tiny cries escaped her throat, and on the gentle coaxing of her inner muscles along his shaft, dragging him deeper into the intoxicating seduction of her body.

With a keening cry, her body tensed, her nails dug into his scalp and shoulder. He held her through the rush of her climax. Kevin surrendered to his own, mindful not to push too hard into her, but unable to stop the jerk of his hips as he joined her.

"Perfect," he whispered into her hair when he could speak.

"Yes," she muttered sleepily. "Perfect."

22

———

Two weeks later, Raina shielded her eyes against the sun setting beyond the ocean and frowned. She wasn't ready to return to Haven City. The admission took her by surprise. To her complete shock, she'd adjusted to the simple way of life. Kevin still helped her dress in the mornings. She'd learned how to brush and even braid her hair, though the result wasn't elegant or even pretty, but it kept the mass out of her face and from getting tangled.

The privacy they'd be giving up returning to the city was almost more than Raina could bear. So, instead of dwelling on what she couldn't change, she focused on the memories they'd made. Held them close, and dear.

Kevin stopped at the back porch on Eadric. The horse's incredible height paired with her tall husband brought him almost eye level with the floor. "House locked up?"

"Yes." She dropped the keys into his waiting palm. "Do we have to leave?"

"Yes. I thought you'd be happy." His gray eyes searched her face.

She sighed. "I did too."

He angled in the saddle, still regarding her. "What's wrong?"

Sitting on the edge of the wooden deck, she held her arms out for him to help her down onto the mount. "I don't know, I guess... I guess I'll miss the privacy. I never realized how very public my life is."

"Ah, now maybe I'll have some sympathy when I disappear into my study."

Eadric dug his hooves into the sandy ground, acknowledging her additional weight in his very horse way. Raina patted his mane. Long tendrils of gray hair tangled between her fingers. "I think I'll join you."

Kevin nuzzled her neck, placing a gentle kiss over her pulse. "I won't complain."

Raina sighed into the intimacy. She enjoyed the new expressions of their love, and how openly Kevin embraced the change between them. "Will we be able to be so affectionate in our Haven City home, do you think?"

He urged Eadric forward into a slow gait up the winding path, away from the house. "I think the bigger question is, will you want to be?"

She considered the inquiry, realizing it had merit. Would she mind if her staff, and possibly her clients, witnessed what some may consider an inappropriate display between the spouses? "I'm not sure."

Another kiss landed on the back of her neck, exposed by her braid sliding over her shoulder. "At least my princess didn't completely disappear. I don't know what I would have done."

Raina stiffened and slapped at his good thigh. "Don't make me feel bad about what's been trained into me. I'm trying... I am."

His arm slipped around her waist, pulling her close to his strong chest. "You mistake my teasing. I fell in love with a princess, I'll have you anyway you decide to be."

All the frustration left her and she relaxed. "You've never really teased me before."

The flutter of his lips against her ear made a shiver race up her spine. "There's a lot we've never done before a couple weeks ago."

Heat fanned across her cheeks. How could so much change so quickly? She laced her fingers through his, still pressed possessively to her belly. She knew the answer. They'd trusted each other not only with their bodies, but with their hearts. They had a battle ahead of them still, one she didn't want to return to, but knowing they'd be in it together made the fear easier to accept.

The cool, gentle wind off the ocean teased her bound hair and ruffled the fabric of her peach skirt. A gift from Kevin, along with two more. Something easy to take on and off, she simply slid the skirt on, pulled a thick matching strap tight around her waist and tied the whole thing off. A feminine tail of fabric hung from her left hip to past her knee. She rather liked the simple, elegant style, planning on having more made upon their return to the city. The warm finely spun wool sweater kept the chill in the air from settling on her skin.

They reached the outskirts of the small New Hampton community. Off in the distance on a hill, Raina recognized the tall wooden arch marking the town's cemetery. She squeezed Kevin's hand. "Can we stop there?"

"At the cemetery? Why?"

Raina drew her brows together. "I don't really know, I feel like we need to."

He urged Eadric into the new direction, but remained silent.

"Do you ever visit?"

"No."

Raina chewed on her bottom lip. Maybe they shouldn't go. But yet, she couldn't stop the compulsion to do so. Eadric waited at the gate for Kevin to tie his reins and then went to exploring the rocky ground for edible grasses. Kevin jumped down first before helping Raina. He eased the creaky gate open, his hip braced against the rough wood.

"Where is your family?" she asked, grasping her hands together in nervousness.

"Over here."

He gestured to the right of the cemetery, picking his way through closely packed headstones. Raina followed carefully. Large expanses of rock separated meticulously spaced markers, the residents using every available space of diggable land to bury their family members. They eased over several huge boulders, reaching a squared off plot with a large *MERRICK* family memorial. Names were etched into the slate with dates, taking up the entire left side and half the right. Probably close to fifty names if she had to guess. The small plot had been in the family for generations.

Taking a deep breath, Raina sat cross-legged before the grave. Most families chose cremation, making a burial site possible for near infinite generations. Behind her, Kevin leaned against a huge boulder, shading the area from the last warm rays of the sun. Raina read the names and dates until tears burned. So many children lost to one family.

The last two names caught her attention. Listed together with the same date.

Dustin and Angela Merrick – August 17th, 823

"What happened to them?"

"You don't recognize the date?"

Raina stared at the carved stone and shook her head. "No, should I? I would have been eleven that year."

"The Great Derailing of 823," he said.

A gasp escaped before she could contain it. Now she remembered. Over a thousand people died in the only recorded mega-accident of a MagnaRail. They never discovered what actually happened, and the resources to repair the line, and replace the train, had been immense. The economy was still recovering from the loss. Not to mention the population. In a world where life was cherished by most, the pain of losing a thousand people at once had been felt across the entire country.

"I'm so sorry," she said.

She felt more than heard his presence shift behind her. The warmth of his body spread across her back as his arms wrapped around her upper chest. His thighs slid along hers, locking her into the strength of his form.

"Why are you sorry?" He whispered the words against her temple. A feather light kiss lingered on her cheek. "I have everything I need right here."

Her heart nearly burst. "But they're your parents, and I know they loved you."

"They did. I was their only survivor of six. Saying they loved me is an understatement. I couldn't have had parents who treasured me more. And yes, I miss them. But I still have family. I have you, and we'll build our house. And I have Sean, Mason, Kat, Cora and now Jonathon is being folded into our hectic little family. We will do almost anything for each other. Family is who you make it, Raina, not only who you're born into."

"I know."

His arms tightened around her chest. "Do you?"

She grasped his muscled forearms and squeezed. "Of course. I'm still heartbroken for you, for your parents. It's not fair."

"Never is."

They sat in the still peacefulness of the cemetery for a few more minutes before he stirred behind her. "Are you ready to leave my bleak family history now?"

Raina nodded and accepted Kevin's hand when he helped her rise. On their way out, she paid careful attention to the family lots, noting some parents hadn't been able to simply list their children, they'd given them individual, personal little stones. Raina's heart clenched. No, none of this was fair.

Looking over the uneven resting grounds, she figured children occupied over half. If Kevin's family was the average, most families experienced an eighty percent mortality rate beyond the Northern Boundary. Did the Sziveria government know? Did they care they lost entire generations due to lack of medical care? One way to find out.

"Is a census conducted up here?" she asked.

"Here as in past the Tabrias?"

"Yes."

"Yeah." He helped her over a jutting rock and uneven ground. "Around every five years."

Once they returned to Haven City, she'd visit the Records Department and get copies of the census and see what exactly everyone appeared to be ignoring. She also decided on their way out, to make Kevin stop so she could order the additional skirts from the young woman who made them. If the residents of New Hampton couldn't earn a living, nothing anyone did would help in the long run.

They arrived at the train depot well after dark. A thin layer of frost coated every surface and glittered in the low light of street lamps. Inside people sat huddled under cloaks or blankets on bench seats, drawing them closer when the air swept across the room from the open door. A small woodstove barely took away the chill.

Raina noted a man moved from the counter and dropped two pieces of wood on a small pile. Kevin followed her in, stomping dirt off his boots. He carried an armload of wood to the pile and dropped it, before continuing on to the ticket counter. Raina raised a brow and hurried after him.

"You have to supply firewood?" she asked.

"Yes, it's customary since we all need to stay warm, to help provide. Wood is more expensive here. The trees are smaller and closely guarded to keep the environment intact.

Most wood is cultivated further up north by the prison inmates and shipped down."

While Sziveria supplied a lot of its own wood, it was a major import from several nations. She knew, she handled the logistics of shipping and distribution, and she also knew there were several companies always looking to offload a surplus. Why did none of it make it north? The more she glanced around, the more she felt like she looked at a forgotten people.

Kevin purchased their tickets, and then they settled in for the wait, which wasn't long. The train outbound for the mainland, returning the last shift change for the prisons and picking up anyone leaving the Northern Boundary, arrived minutes later. They took care of Eadric before finding their small private suite. Once the thin folding door was secured, Raina let out a long exhale. They were heading home. Sort of.

After much discussion they decided staying at Mason's house would be best. Not only was it larger, offering them more of the privacy they'd grown accustomed to, but Mason needed to converse with Raina about the maps. Until they knew what they were up against in the city, traveling had to be kept to a minimum.

Kevin settled in the smaller bench seat across from her, resting his head against the wooden wall. The train lurched forward. Under them, the metal wheels squealed and ground on iron tracks. Within moments, the gentle sway of momentum rocked their cabin.

"Why does this place feel like some forgotten realm?" Raina mused aloud, watching the dark landscape roll by. Shadows of tall trees and glistening patches of snow.

"I thought you paid attention in Geography lesson?" Kevin bumped his foot playfully into her thigh.

Raina shot him an annoyed glare at the reminder of her snappy words to him when he'd tried to explain Northern Sziveria's precarious situation. "I did. But you're not allowed to hold my attitude against me. I wasn't exactly in the best place when I said them."

"Very true. Does that mean you're ready to listen now?"

She glanced back out the window again. "Consider me completely at your mercy."

"Dangerous words to say to a husband."

Raina slid her attention back to him. They'd moved well past any hope of light beyond the faint glow of the moon. He sat in the shadows, but she knew the look he'd have if she could see his eyes. The same look that had landed him between her legs anyway she could get him over the past two weeks.

A sliver of desire raced through her body and she took a slow breath. If the little door meant to be their gate to privacy weren't as thin as the walls likely were, she'd be closing the distance between them. She'd learned something else over the last few weeks however, she wasn't quiet.

"Indeed," she whispered. "How about we save *that* particular lesson for another train ride?"

He chuckled. "Coward."

"Princess," she corrected.

"Very well, for another ride. Back to geography then." He leaned forward and clasped his hands between his knees. "It would help if I had a map, but you know enough of the land to get an idea.

"The Tabria Mountain's divide the top third of our country from coast to coast. There's only one useable pass, and it's barely wide enough for two trains. An in-going and out-going, nothing more, nothing less. We have a small military tower station at the base of the mountains near the pass, that *should* something happen and we're invaded, the pass can be blown up and the top half of the country closed off. Whether or not it's taken back will depend on a lot of things, and many people have varying speculations. In the end it doesn't matter right now.

"The reason for the land being sovereign versus incorporated is because if anything *does* happen, the response time would be too slow. Also, when thefts, murders, assaults, arson, or any other crime happens, it takes too long for an investigator to arrive to handle the issue. The population is too small to assign a unit to the area, and the taxes too few to account for the cost of paying people. Most disputes are handled by a town Marshall and local judgement by a group of peers who are voted on yearly. People run for the Judgement Committee and, like in Italyssa, can't run more than once, keeping people from being bought by criminals."

"Or that's the idea," Raina mused, relaxing back in her seat, taking in everything he said.

"Yes, that's the idea. Anyway, the economy is, you could say, purposefully kept weak."

Raina drew her brows together. "I don't understand."

"Say it were to become strong, protecting it would then become a priority and everything I just said would need addressing."

She sucked air in between her teeth. "And the logistics behind that would be a nightmare."

"Yes. Plus, with three maximum security prisons holding the most violent of our criminals on the northern shores, they don't exactly want a population bloom a rising economy would bring."

Disgusted, Raina shook her head. "So everyone suffers because our government doesn't want to inconvenience itself. Everyone north of the Tabrias has to deal with burying five out of six of their children because, so sorry, you're just not worth the effort it would take to keep you safe and allow you to afford a Medical Scientist."

"This has become important to you," he said softly.

Anger at the reminder of how close he'd come to death crept like a dark monster into her mind. Seeing his sibling's names, precious lives neither he nor his parents had the time to know or love, made the fury grow.

"I almost lost you." She took a deep, steadying breath. "I would have lost you if I didn't know Sean's role in your life. If I didn't know with absolute certainty he'd come the second he was able. No one else has that, Kevin. They bury their sick who could be saved with medication we consider basic. Yes. It's become important to me."

He slid down to the floor at her feet. Resting his arms on her thighs, he dropped his chin and looked up at her. "Well, instead of getting mad at the people I work for, who mostly do the best they can in the interest of all, how about your incredibly smart self thinks of a way to improve their lives, and give others the opportunity to step up and help small communities."

Raina smoothed her hand along his jaw and into the short length of hair at the back of his neck. Her heart fluttered and swelled. He heard her rant, let her have it. Then he supported her need, and trusted in her ability to see it through. "I love you so much."

His arms wrapped around her waist and before she could protest, he yanked her forward, forcing her knees apart to accompany his large chest. "Good, because I changed my mind about dangerous husbands and train rides."

"Here we are, Master Guardian Raiventon, your quarters." The housekeeper pushed a tall door open and stepped aside. Raina tried to peer inside, but the woman swept her arms forward. "And if you'll follow me Guardianess, I'll show you to yours."

Raina wanted to say no thank you, she was fine with her husband. However, social traditions dictated they have separate sleeping quarters, usually for their possessions and attendants. Dutifully, Raina followed. She caught Kevin's bemused smile on the way past and wanted to glare. She knew exactly what he thought, *back into princess mode.*

Squaring her shoulders and ignoring the annoyance at falling so quickly into her old self, she walked into the lavish suite. Decorated in shades of rose, sage and cream, the elegant room held a large pine bed on a dais draped with rose and cream silk, a sitting area, and reading nook. Huge double doors led out onto a balcony. Satiny sage curtains rustled in the wind, sweeping the floor with each inward gust.

"The bathroom is joining and shared, right through there." She pointed to the right. "Your closet is over here. Miss Cora was unsure how long you'd be joining us and has already sent for your Stylist and wardrobe."

Shocked, Raina barely kept her mouth from falling open. "Thank you."

"Of course. Primary Guardian Kynhaven said Master Guardian Raiventon will be handling dinner, so I'll leave you to it then. Ring if you need anything." She bowed her head and then disappeared, closing the door behind her.

Raina rushed to the joining bathroom, flinging the double doors wide. Kevin stood in the center of the large room and grinned at her.

"Look," he said.

She followed his hand to where a massive tub was recessed in the floor. Beyond the tub, a shower took up the entire back wall, closed in by glass. Warm water. A hot shower. A sigh of longing escaped her mouth. Raina gravitated to the shower, slowly shedding clothes from her body each step. She would have stepped right into the tub if Kevin hadn't redirected her. The cool glass swept aside with the faintest touch. Raina frowned, unsure how to work the knobs.

Kevin reached around, pushed and turned. Water fell from three different areas, steaming and glorious. Cold stone tile met her toes along with a rush of warmth. She moaned and tilted her head back, soaking in the heat. Kevin stood in front of her, doing the same.

"This is amazing." She held out her hands and caught random drops in her palms, reveling in the sensation of hot water flowing over every part of her body.

"Yes, you never take a hot shower for granted again after returning from the Northern Boundary."

On a happy sigh, Raina dropped her forehead to his solid chest. "We will have to scheme how to remedy that."

His strong arms pulled her against his body and she complied, sliding her hands up his slick back. The flesh of her belly pressed into his growing erection and she smiled. Her smile quickly turned into a squeal when with a growl he hefted her upward. Hard, cold tile met her back the second his mouth found hers. Raina wrapped her arms around his neck and her legs around his waist and held tight. Desire shot through her like lightning. Then her talented husband showed her how *amazing* a shower really could be.

"I HOPE you like your rooms, because you're never leaving." Mason dropped a rib bone on his plate and Raina kept from laughing at the almost pitiful expression on his face. "I haven't eaten this good in months."

"Still no cook?" Kevin asked, wiping his fingers on a dark blue cloth napkin.

"No." Cora wasn't as polite. She licked sticky sauce from her fingers. "I haven't found anyone I liked."

"You know your problem?" Mason asked, fork pointed at Cora. "You're too picky."

"I'm *selective*. There's a difference, dear brother. Learn it."

Mason glared at his twin. "And I have no opinion?"

Cora's smile mocked. "That's right, you don't. You'll make a good husband one day. You always know when to defer to a woman."

With a groan, Mason's head fell to the table. His long black hair flared out around him on the cream table cloth. "Why me?"

Cora patted his wide shoulder. "It's because you love me, nothing wrong with that."

"You are the bane of my existence," he muttered, his words barely intelligible against the wooden table.

"I do try."

Raina glanced at Kevin, who watched the exchange with an amused smile. "Are they always like this?"

"Mostly," Kevin answered.

Cora's silvery eyes found Raina. "Do you like your room?"

"It's very nice, thank you. And for sending for my wardrobe and Tabby."

Cora waved the praise away with a graceful flick of her wrist. "Nonsense. I know you've been living in savage conditions up there in New Hampton. I'd have gone crazy in your place for that long, it was the least I could do."

Raina set her fork down on her plate. "You've been to the Northern Boundary?"

"One time for a story. Dreadful place. I don't know how people stand it. No hot water, unpaved roads that are more like ditches than travel worthy. Not to mention the primitive living conditions."

Intrigued, Raina braced her forearms on the table and leaned forward. "What was your story about?"

"Prison escapes." Cora popped a piece of biscuit into her mouth. "With three major prison facilities up there, and most of the Wolven Guard being primarily based either out of Haven City or along the southern shores, I wanted to know how the population handled the threat."

Raina drew her brows together. "There aren't any Wolven Guard teams beyond the Boundary? Or even positioned at the tower station at the foot of the Tabrias?"

Cora shook her head. "No. The escapes are fairly infrequent, and depending on the convict determines which Wolven Guard team is called upon to go on the hunt."

"The escapee has several hours lead on anyone searching for them?"

"Pretty much. That's why I did the story. It was exciting and dangerous to consider."

Raina sighed. "What did you find out?"

"What I found out wasn't quite as exciting. Turns out the prisons are, at the nearest, a solid day's walk from any inhabited town. In the ice and snow, most prisoners only make it halfway before they're found. And then it's a toss whether they survived the elements. The towns also know anyone sentenced to those three prisons isn't anyone they want around, so the escapees really have no hope of help."

Raina considered the information and focused on the people left to deal with yet another danger on their own. An idea formulated in her mind, spurred on by the whispered reminder of Kevin's suggestion. *Give others the opportunity to step up and help…*

"Do you think you'd be willing to do another story on the Northern Boundary?"

Hours later, Raina learned two interesting facts. First, Cora was smart, too smart to be running around gaining the reputation she so carefully cultivated as a woman with loose morals. Raina wanted to know why, but couldn't ask, not without overstepping social boundaries she'd been taught *never* to overstep. Which left her to muse, glancing up at the woman over a map, who curled comfortably on a seat in Mason's cramped study, idly turning pages in a book.

Second, Mason wasn't scary. Not even a little. The man was big, no question, but with a large presence and even larger smile. He picked at his sister, and held an air of polite aristocracy toward Raina that allowed her to slide into the professional role she'd become content in.

After pointing out the discrepancies between her maps and his, they'd set about determining which were fact. Raina was shocked at the vast differences.

Kevin lounged against the wide windowsill behind them, his legs stretched out. "You built these over the course of four months?"

"Yes. I was given information on rail lines and trade routes with some of the shipments, to help plan them accordingly. Some ports ended up being closer than one I would have used due to the updated information, cutting transport length." She sighed, pulling a map of South America closer. "This doesn't make any sense. Why would they have access to different information than everyone else?"

"Several reasons come to mind, but the two making the most sense are they either stole the information from the governing bodies, or they built the lines, roads and ports," Mason answered.

Raina looked over the borders of several touching South American countries. "It's the entire continent." She slid her finger from New Panama to Perazil in middle of the continent. "And these two nations have been bickering with New Columbia over border issues here in the middle for over a hundred years. Little skirmishes break out along all three borders. There's no way New Columbia would share this rail information willingly. It could give New Panama and Perazil advantages."

Kevin rubbed at his beard under his chin. "Isn't there an Italyssian colony in Floradesol?"

Raina nodded. "Yes. Cairo has a large colony on the western side, but only Graecily is recognized. Both countries help protect the borders for Floradesol, and in return the colonies are left alone for the most part. I think Cairo is looking to secure the land wholly for themselves though, and be recognized like Graecily is. They're capable military wise."

"A new Cairo." Mason shook his head. "That's a scary thought. They'll attempt purchase and treaties first."

"Of course," Raina agreed. "But, if they want the land, not much will stop them from securing it. They just have to have the right pieces in play."

Cora straightened. "How many of the new features run through Italyssian and Cairoen land?"

Drawing her brows together, Raina surveyed the maps. "All of them have differences from what Mason has."

"Interesting. Cairo would definitely not part with that information if they're planning on separating their land from Floradesol," Cora surmised.

Mason nodded. "I agree completely. It would hurt them *if* a war broke out."

"So," Raina began with a sigh, "we're likely looking at thefts?"

Cora tapped her index finger to her bottom lip. "Or carefully constructed alliances built on lies. A do-this-for-us-and-we'll-do-this-for-you scenario."

"There's a way to find out." Mason stood and crossed his arms over his chest. "We happen to know an Italyssian shipping heiress who probably deals a lot with the colony. I bet she can get the information for us at least on what pertains to their land."

"Unless it was given in secret, then no one will admit to it," Cora argued.

"Then we'll know one way or another it was stolen," Kevin stated.

Something about the position of the lines and roads, and even some of the ports bothered Raina. Tapping her fingers on the map, she chewed her bottom lip. She pulled Westica's map to the top. "Where is your map of Westica?"

Mason searched through the sheets and pulled a huge

map to the top. He carefully laid it out, smoothing the corners down. "I updated it six months ago based on information they sent us."

Raina slowly nodded and compared the two. "I was given this map when Enbrackon first hired me. I didn't make it."

"He gave it to you, or one of the people he was working with?" Kevin asked, coming to stand behind her.

"He did." The urge to lean back into his strength had Raina fisting her hands until the desire passed. Carefully, she analyzed the maps, her heart pounding with each little discovery. "I don't know how this is possible, but I think I see what they've been doing. I bet if we check against the other countries with differences, it'll be the same."

Kevin's chest brushed against her back. His hands rested on her hips as he looked over her shoulder. Raina took a deep breath and sank her weight onto her heels, pressing closer to him. He whispered into her ear, "What do you see?"

"Look at the interior edges of Westica on my map compared to Mason's." She pointed to the jagged lines that separated known safe land from unsafe.

"They've ventured into Uninhabited Zones," Kevin stated gruffly.

Cora leapt to her feet. "What?"

"Look," Kevin pointed to a section of land that swept deeply into a partitioned off line. A railroad followed the new edge. "All this is unclaimed territory, deemed unsafe."

"Deemed by who?" Raina asked, never quite understanding the zones. Sziveria didn't have any, but most nations either had borders with them, or had areas quarantined off.

"By the local governments. Something about the land, either the water, soil, air, or some other factor makes it unlivable. How often it's reevaluated is determined by the country the land borders," Kevin explained.

"Either these roads and rail lines are entering into

dangerous territories or someone has decided the land is no longer a threat and is utilizing the resources," Raina said.

Cora let loose a long exhale. "If this land is being resourced without the knowledge of the country, the profits would be enormous."

"Where are they getting the laborers do you think?" Mason wondered. "They couldn't use men from the country, there'd be too much talk."

"Bringing in large groups of people would cause an issue too," Kevin surmised, his fingers clenched and relaxed on her hips in a thoughtful massage.

Raina thought about all the shipments she'd arranged for the group of men Enbrackon had brought to her. Knowing how they worked now, a notion formulated. "Unless they were smuggled in and forced into some sort of work camp."

Cora shook her finger in thought. "There would be evidence of that in the country. If I could—"

"No," Mason bit out.

"But—"

"No," he snapped at her again. "Absolutely not. These are dangerous people who have already killed to keep their secrets. You'll be nothing against them, especially out of the country."

"He's right, Cora," Kevin said. "It's too risky."

Her pale gray eyes glimmered with determination. "Do you realize what kind of a discovery this could be? What I could do with the information? The stories I could write?"

Mason leaned forward, his hands splayed on the desk. "Do you realize no one will ever know if you're dead?"

Cora braced her palms on the desk and copied his action, coming inches from her glaring brother. "Their entire network, all their plans, could be unraveled with one story, Mason. Think what Synintel could do with anything I'd be able to learn."

Raina stilled at her words. Would her father risk one

woman against an entire organization for the chance at information? While Raina figured the answer was probably a resounding yes, the problem here wasn't whether Synintel would agree or not, but whether Mason would. Since the twins were mirrors of each other's personality, Raina didn't see the argument resolving any time soon.

"Maybe we can find out some information a safer way and still ask Asherwick's promised to check with the colony's leadership," Raina suggested, hoping to ease the spike in tension between the siblings.

"Sure, fine," Cora bit out, but didn't back down. "But we all know Westica is the most stable country to investigate the Uninhabited Zones along its borders. Everyone else is either a hostile culture, or on the edge of war with someone. Due to Westica's isolation, like us, they're remarkably stable and don't have any colony's vying for emancipation."

"Still a no," Mason said.

Cora shoved away from the desk and huffed. "I'm twenty-seven years old, fully grown, with my own career. I don't need, nor did I ask, for your permission. If I want to go to Westica to chase a story, I'll go. If I wanted to go to Westica to chase a flock of birds, I'd go, and you'd have nothing to say about that."

"Birds don't shoot or kidnap people, now do they?" Mason snapped. "As you said, you're a grown woman, now start acting like one and make better decisions."

"Always comes down to my decision making." Cora waved a hand and flopped into the chair. "Hard to believe I'm still alive."

"I do stare at you in wonder," Mason said with all seriousness. Then he sighed and straightened. "As a Master Tribunii, Asherwick likely has a radio at his house. We can ask Miss Seartavos to make the communication where no one else will overhear."

Raina looked over the map. Kevin had yet to move away

from her and she resisted the need to thread her fingers through his still gripping her hip. They'd only been around people for a couple hours now and already she missed him. How silly could she be? Forcing her focus onto the map, she traced a long rail line that bordered a Perazil UZ and ran through Italyssa's colony.

"I want her to ask about this. It runs through both Perazil and their territory," Raina said to Mason.

"I'll draw it up. Do you think she should mention Perazil's sharing?"

"I'm not sure. I'm not involved in politics to know what asking that could mean."

Mason nodded and started sketching. "Have you had any luck with the records for Asherwick, Cora? Since it looks like we'll be going to see him soon?"

"Yes, I have actually, but I've been a little worried about that," Cora admitted with a frown.

"Why?" Raina asked.

Cora shifted in the chair, her frown growing darker. "Well, of the ones I've reviewed, your name and signature has been on all of them."

Behind her, Kevin stiffened. "On all the imports or the exports?"

"Both," Cora admitted. "I'm hoping I missed something and maybe a few of the original manifests are buried. But, I have a strong feeling someone else has them."

Panic seized Raina. Her breath caught in her lungs. "That must be plan B. If they failed to kill you, they had an alternate means of getting rid of my father."

Mason slowly turned and looked between her and Kevin. "What do you mean, *if they failed to kill you?*"

"Me," Kevin specified. "Which we already figured out, but Raina confirmed."

Raina couldn't breathe. Her legs became useless and had Kevin not still had hold of her hips, she would have sunk to the floor. His arms wrapped around her waist, easily supporting her weight.

"Breathe," he whispered, giving her a soft shake and gentle squeeze. "Breathe."

She sucked in a lungful of air. "He's going to frame me, take the evidence to the E&R meeting, and have my father thrown out of office."

"The E&R meeting was already supposed to have happened," Kevin stated.

Cora shook her head. "No, it was postponed."

Raina didn't hear any of it, she was fixated on the catastrophe waiting to become her life. "They'll arrest me. Oh no, no." She turned in Kevin's arms and grabbed the front of his shirt by the fistful. "You'll be married to a criminal."

"Why was it postponed?" Kevin asked, his hands on Raina's shoulders.

"I'm not sure," Cora said. "There was an article about it. Let me see if I can find the paper, hopefully they didn't use it for tinder yet," The rustle of fabric sounded as she rose.

Closing her eyes, Raina considered every bad decision that brought her to this point. "Oh sweet summer sun, you *are* already married to one. I *did* do those things. No one forced me. I willingly let them do this. I'm going to jail. I will be stuck in a prison cell, tattooed with a felony stamp..."

Kevin dropped down to his haunches before her. Since she still held his shirt, the fabric lifted. He swiped in a quick downward motion, forcing her to release and redirect to his shoulders if she wished to maintain contact. Taking hold of her chin, he urged her to meet his stare.

"You aren't going to prison."

"But—"

He shook his head. "No. Listen to me again. You aren't going to prison."

"But they have..."

Kevin no longer looked at her. His attention shifted to

Mason and he stood. "We're going to Blackbain's. There's too much planning involved now, and new information he needs to know."

"Agreed."

"I can take the map to Jonathon," Cora volunteered, returning with a paper in hand. "I have to bring him the records anyway."

"We need him at Sean's," Mason told her, rolling up the copy he finished.

"I can tell him that, too."

Mason tapped a coal pencil against the desk. "We shouldn't be seen arriving together."

"Raina and I will dress down and take a hired coach," Kevin said.

Dread filled Raina at the idea of sitting in a rough, smelly carriage again. But, she also didn't want to worry about an assassin's bullet finding her husband.

23

So far past tired, Jonathon wasn't sure how he managed to see actual words on the papers in front of him. He scrubbed his hands down his face and sniffled. Yawning, he reached for an empty coffee cup. If he didn't find something interesting in the case files he'd spent the last few hours searching through soon, he was going to call it finished and head to bed. His day started around three am, and he was feeling every one of the missed hours of sleep.

"Jonathon, go get rest," Sylphine ordered, slipping the cold porcelain cup from his fingers.

"I will in a little while." Forcing his back straight, he shifted through the mess of information spread across his desk.

She propped a hip on the only spot free of documents across from him, both hands wrapped around his empty mug. "What good are you doing any case like this?"

Jonathon forced himself to focus on her, looking her over. Uneven layers of cream lace and delicate rose beaded fabric draped from her shoulders to her elbows. Small pale pink silk roses formed a swoop neckline over the rise of her full breasts, and despite the chaos of the design, somehow form fitted to her torso. Random layers of the lace and silk pooled on the wood near her hip and cascaded beyond his view to the floor beyond. Thin metal and beaded bracelets adorned her wrists. The wild array of beads, feathers and ribbons were expertly woven into her soft, golden curls. She looked completely exotic and wholly her nationality.

"Where are you going?" he asked.

"I was invited to a diplomatic dinner as an honored guest. Countries seem to like to stay in the good graces of Sun and Wind Trade. I couldn't say no."

Jonathon frowned. Under normal circumstances, as her promised future husband, he'd attend such events with her. "Why didn't you tell me?"

"Jonathon dear, you are…" she waved her hand searching for a word and sighed, "*kasustostasi*, what is your saying for this, ah, in no condition. You're tired."

No point in denying the obvious. "Yes."

"I have convinced Ramsey to go with me. Since everyone believes she's soon to be my sister, no one will think much of her appearance with me. It's in my interest to bring anyone I wish."

"It's your choice, not your interest," Jonathon corrected with a chuckle.

She waved her hand again and stood. "Interest, choice, it is what I wish, so same thing."

"Very well, if you say so."

"I do." She nodded curtly. "And I will fill this up if you promise to go to your room when you are finished. I've accomplished the impossible with one of you, I wish to do so again."

Jonathon braced his forearms on the desk and grinned. "Only because you wish it, I'll do as you ask."

Sylphine did exactly as he hoped. She graced him with a brilliant smile. His stomach clenched and he forced himself to keep breathing. "You make it so hard to forget I will never be your bride."

"I am trying."

Her beautiful tourmaline eyes sparkled and she shook her head. "What am I to do with you?"

"I'm not answering that."

She laughed and sashayed from the room in a flurry of lace, silk and jingles. Jonathon dropped his head to his desk and groaned. Moments later he heard the warning of her approach and quickly straightened. The last thing he needed was for her to truly know how badly she affected him. He accepted the steaming cup of caffeine when she handed it to him.

"Thank you."

"Of course. Now promise."

He took a small sip. "I thought I already did."

"No, you hinted, you did not speak the words."

Jonathon raised a brow. Ramsey appeared at the office door. Her riot of black curls were swept atop her head, held in place by purple flower pins. A gray silk gown with a full skirt, fitted bodice and sheer, long loose sleeves, adorned with intricate silver beadwork from the bodice to the hem spoke of the latest Haven City fashions. Her ivory skin seemed somehow paler. Sylphine clicked her tongue to the roof of her mouth. Ramsey frowned.

"What, do I not look all right?" His younger sister glanced down at her attire.

Sylphine looked Ramsey over. "The gown is truly beautiful, Ramsey. But you are stunning in your coloring, and the dress hides you."

Ramsey raised her chin. "Perfect. I don't want anyone to notice me."

Sylphine looked at Jonathon in desperation. He shrugged. She sighed and crossed the room, holding out her arm. "Very well, your goal shall be accomplished."

The women locked arms and disappeared. "Have fun!" Jonathon called out and then waved his hand. "Don't mind me, I won't miss you, and I don't care when you'll be home."

Sylphine's face appeared and she winked. "I will miss you, too. We won't be home late, it's a dinner."

"I'll be up."

"No—"

"I'll be up, I need to know you both are home safe. Unless you're going to come to my room and…"

Her cheeks flushed. "I'll see you when we get home."

Jonathon grinned. "Coward."

"Yes," she breathed out and then flashed him another heartbreaking smile and disappeared.

Jonathon waited a few minutes to let the coffee start to work before diving back into the files. The caffeine soon let him down and he was awoken by a murmur in his ear. A delicate touch smoothed hair away from his forehead. Jonathon turned into the touch and exhaled slowly. Soft lips skimmed across his. Subtle feminine floral notes invaded his nostrils. The kiss was timid at first, then more aggressive when he didn't move away. The tip of her tongue traced along his bottom lip.

Still fighting sleep, Jonathon slowly opened his mouth, touching his tongue to hers. She moaned deep in her throat, her fingers sinking into his hair. Jonathon's eyes fluttered open. Ivory skin and a curtain of shimmering black hair greeted him. Sucking in his breath through his nose, Jonathon tore his mouth from hers and sank away.

Her silvery eyes opened slowly and a cat-like smile curled across her full lips. "Oh yes, that was everything I thought it would be."

"Cora."

"I suppose you're going to lecture me now about how I shouldn't attack a sleeping man." She slid onto his desk until her feet dangled above the floor. The folds of her pale blue gown swayed between her knees and around her ankles. "I still had my way with you."

He sighed. "There are worse ways to be woken up I suppose."

She tugged on her bottom lip with her teeth. "I'm proud of you, you're not even acting like you're angry with me."

Jonathon tried to pinpoint exactly how he *did* feel. Anger wasn't it. Annoyance… maybe. "What did you need?"

"Besides you?"

He crossed his hands behind his head and leaned back in his chair. "I am not a need you get to have."

Wrapping her hands around the edge of the desk, she leaned forward. The fabric across her breasts strained and pulled, revealing the full curves. "Now that I know the best way to you, perhaps I'll just sneak in your bedroom window."

Jonathon stretched his neck and shoulders. "If you can sneak in my house, I'm not much of an enforceman."

A teasing smile toyed at her lips, still glossy from their kiss. "Maybe I'm that good."

"I'm sure you are." When she went to open her mouth, he held up his hand. "But not for me. Again, what did you want?"

Lifting a black brow she heaved a heavy sigh and then reached beside her right hip. Brandishing a stack of files with a folded slip of paper on top, she handed them across to him. "The manifests from the records department. The top page is a map of Graecily. Guardianess Raiventon was given maps that contained roads, rail lines and ports that aren't on maps Mason was given from First Intelligence. They're wondering if your promised would be willing to reach out and make some inquiries."

Jonathon set the files down before retrieving the map. "Only Graecily?"

"Oh no, it appears to be worldwide, mostly around UZ's interestingly enough. Graecily can maybe be easily tested."

"More puzzle pieces, yet none are fitting together."

"They'd also like you to return with me to Sean's house."

Jonathon shook his head, flipping open the first couple files. "Not tonight, I'm not much use to anyone. Let me review these, see if I can find anything, and ask Sylphine about the map. Once I have something useful to contribute, I'll reach out to Wintersfall."

Cora reached for him and before he could censor his reaction, he jerked away. Her hand fell to her lap. "I think I've already told you I don't bite. At least not usually."

"And I *know* I've already told you nothing is going to happen."

Slowly, she slid from the desk. The tips of her ballet style shoes touched the floor and then flattened in an elegant slip along the hardwood. "I feel I should warn you, breaking her defenses won't be easy. She went the exact opposite direction I did when faced with betrayal and heartbreak."

"Who are you talking about?" Jonathon rubbed the bridge of his nose, sitting forward in his chair.

"Miss Seartavos."

Every muscle in his body froze. Cora knew what happened to Sylphine? Part of him wanted to demand answers, while the other part cautioned Sylphine deserved her privacy. To tell him her story in her own time, if she ever wanted to. She owed him nothing. There weren't any stipulations on their arrangement, only they could call it off whenever one of them wished. So far, five months in, neither of them were in any hurry to be *single* again.

Jonathon relaxed and turned his attention back to the files. "I don't need to work on her defenses, I'm happy with her just the way she is."

"Well no wonder I'm so obsessed with you," Cora declared on a huff. "You're perfect!"

Rolling his eyes, Jonathon reached for his empty coffee cup and stood. "I'm not perfect, I'm practical. What good is hounding a woman about her past when she's obviously wishing to forget?"

"Because her past destines her future."

"No." Jonathon rounded his desk and strode from the office.

The swish of fabric behind him made him groan. Cora's footfalls echoed his own across the foyer. "Yes it does," she argued.

Jonathon swung around. She slammed into his chest and he steadied her with a firm hand on her upper arm. "Why are you here causing trouble?"

Her pale gray eyes widened. "I… I'm not."

"Yes. You are." He turned and headed to the kitchen.

"I don't want to see you make a mistake."

Clenching his teeth, he rounded on her again. Thankfully this time she was ready and she stopped, hands up in defense. Jonathon a dropped a frustrated arm at his side. "Then please, tell me, what mistake could I possibly be making? She's beautiful, funny, and smart. She managed to get my sister out of the house tonight. Do you realize no one, and I mean *no one* has been able to get Ramsey to leave this house in four years except to maybe go shopping or out to eat. Being seen in society? Forget it. Sylphine will *never* be a mistake in this house."

Cora's normally playful, seductive gaze turned sad. Her shoulders drooped forward. "She's not who you think she is… at least not anymore."

"Why are you saying all this?"

"So that when she walks away, like you seem to think I would do, you won't be surprised. Trust me."

Disgusted, Jonathon shook his head and turned his back to her once more. "I can't believe you. Will you stop at nothing to be a distraction for a man?"

"Who said anything about me being the distraction?" She snickered. "You have it all wrong. *You* would be the distraction for *me.*"

Jonathon snorted in disgust. "Well, we both deserve better than that. I'm not anyone's distraction, and you shouldn't be either."

A now thickened pot of coffee sat on the back of the wood stove in the kitchen. Jonathon poured what he could manage until grounds started leaking out with the liquid.

She crossed her arms over her ample chest and braced a hip against the counter where he headed with his cup. "Well, you won't have to really worry about it anymore. I think I'm going to Westica."

Jonathon's cup clanked to the counter. Dark fluid sloshed over the rim. He stared at her, positive he'd misunderstood. "What?"

"It's safe, really safe compared to most places, and I want to see for myself some of these road and rail lines. I'm good at investigating, and I can't really investigate much here right now, not safely. Over there, no one knows me."

"And your brother is okay with this?"

"Arctic no, he's not okay with it. He flat out told me absolutely not."

"But you're still going."

"Yes."

Jonathon sighed and reached for a covered bowl of sugar. "Of course you are. Why are you telling me this?"

She shrugged. "What can I say, if one method doesn't work, figured I'd try another."

Jonathon leaned back against the counter, crossing an arm over his chest and resting his other on top. Slowly he sipped at his coffee and considered her. The light from a single oil lamp next to the kitchen door barely threw enough light in the room to chase away shadows. A sad, almost lost expression flickered across her beautiful face.

"Do you want me to talk you out of it?" he asked gently.

Her lips parted and for a moment she remained quiet. Slowly she shook her head. "No, I don't think so."

She swallowed and stared down at the floor, her fingers twisting in the fabric of her dress. For the first time, Jonathon realized she was allowing him to see the real Cora.

"I don't have many friends. One really, and she'll likely try to talk me out of it, too. I just..." She took a long, deep breath. "I need to do something. I can't... I can't keep living like this and I know it's going to kill me one day."

"Going to Westica could make that happen sooner. What's so wrong with waiting for love, Cora?"

Tears glistened in her silver eyes when she raised her head. "I already did that. Didn't work out too well for me. I'm not willing to go through it again."

24

"The Verdict Council? That's Synintel's answer?" Kevin asked, wiping sweat from his face. Sean had cleared him for training three days ago, and Kevin hadn't wasted any time returning.

Voklane nodded and sighed. "Yes, he feels any other route would lead to too many questions and very likely incriminate Guardianess Raiventon."

Kevin glanced Raina's direction at Ryan's words. Curled up on the bench near the stairs, she'd remained quiet and watchful during the training session. Now she continued to keep to herself, reading. She flicked her attention up from the book laying in her lap, but remained collected.

Sean shook his head, swinging a towel over his shoulder. "The evidence against Enbrackon is tied up in Raina's name. How will he manage to remove her from it?"

"As you know," Voklane began, "names aren't utilized with a verdict session, only evidence. The accused is listed simply as subject and any evidence dealing with others is listed as victim and a letter. Guardianess Raiventon's name will be stricken and likely replaced with Logistics Expert or something like that."

Kevin flexed his jaw. "What are they hoping to gain with a guilty verdict?"

"The course of recommended action will be removal from Guardianship. The motion will be heard at the rescheduled E&R meeting if the action is approved."

Kevin glanced at Sean, who stared at Voklane in outright shock. Kevin took a deep breath. "He'll retaliate."

"Synintel is hoping so, yes."

"Why?" Raina asked, her soft voice making everyone turn toward her. A faint flush rose on her cheeks at the sudden attention, but she didn't look away.

"Because, if Enbrackon retaliates, it'll be a provocation against an Intel Guardian team, which they can meet without fear of repercussions. He'll no longer be a peer of the realm, and he'll likely be acting on his own, without any support from those who were using him for his pretty face and charisma. No one will concern themselves with his death at that point," Voklane explained.

Synintel was handling the situation the only way he knew how. Strategically and diplomatically, ensuring limited means for error and maximum outcome in his favor. Kevin scrubbed the towel across his face again and sighed.

"There's only one problem," Kevin pointed out.

"I know," Voklane said with his own long exhale. "The evidence."

"Right now, even with the manifests and the Cairoen mess you cleaned up, there isn't enough to present. We need a shipment."

"And the original manifest," Raina stated. "Not the doctored ones they had me create. You need the originals."

Voklane turned to her and Kevin crossed the space between them. Despite his being sweaty, she leaned in close when he sat beside her.

"Do you think they still exist?" Sean asked, stepping

closer, snaking the towel around his neck to hold on to both ends.

"Logically, it makes sense," Raina said. "Without either the manifests, or files, they'd have no way of keeping track of their cargo. Since I'm assuming the purpose of falsifying the manifests was to keep the actual cargo a secret for whatever purpose, *they* still need to know what their cargo is and a way to keep track of it, either by location or sales, perhaps both."

Sean made thoughtful clicking noises with his tongue, glancing up at the high beams of the basement ceiling. "Did you ever meet any of the men you were supposedly working for?"

"No, I was only told of them. Enbrackon acted as a liaison."

Sean turned his attention to Kevin. "Did you verify their existence?"

"I haven't, no. I handed everything to Mason. What are you thinking?"

"I'm thinking," Sean began, "that there isn't anyone else. Enbrackon was acting in the interest of the group and needed to keep Raina in the dark, so they fabricated clients. Everything is actually under one company or individual. We just need to find out who."

"Would also ensure everything stayed contained. If he's discovered, only he takes the blame, he can't bring anyone else down with him," Voklane surmised.

Sean stretched his neck. "Unless he turns chatty."

"That's doubtful," Voklane stated with a frown.

Unable to keep from touching her, Kevin slid his hand along her foot to her ankle, his fingers brushing the hem of her skirt until he reached skin. "Did you arrange any shipments that will be coming in soon?"

Raina shook her head. "Not that I remember. Anything I may have managed would have already come in. It's been well over a month, most arrangements occur within three to four weeks, very rarely do they take longer."

"How would they take longer?" Sean asked.

"If the shipment is coming from a farther distance and has a lengthy trip to the docks. Then, the cargo may sit in storage until the ship arrives to carry it to the next location. If the cargo has to change hands again, it can be a slower process."

"Does that happen often?"

"No, I try to avoid multiple companies handling one product. Too much output, makes margin too thin for the product. There's only so much a customer is willing to pay, regardless of how *rare* a commodity may be."

"Anything they've needed recently they'd have to go to someone else," Voklane said.

Raina sighed, closing the book in her lap. "Actually, chances are they never stopped using whoever handled their shipments. I've only been working with Enbrackon for six months or so."

Sean rubbed his brows with his thumb, his face scrunched in a grimace. "They needed evidence themselves, against Synintel, an alternate route in case their other plan failed. They used you."

"Yes." The single word was spoken without infliction. Kevin tightened his hold on her ankle, giving a squeeze of support.

Ryan chuckled. "You all are acting shocked, like the group we're dealing with couldn't possibly be as smart as us. You forget, they've been at this at least five years now, and haven't been caught. Their only mistakes have been utilizing loyal people with a conscience, who were brave enough to come forward and give breadcrumb warnings. We have to assume their grand master plan is well devised and won't be easily unraveled."

"Then we have to be equally smart," Sean said with a grin.

"What are you thinking?" Kevin asked.

"I'm thinking the Summer Honorary for the HCES is at the end of this week."

Voklane crossed his arms over his chest. "It is, but why is that important?"

"We need evidence, and only Enbrackon knows where it's at. I'm also predicting he doesn't want it somewhere out of his sight. It's at his house. As the Shield Guardian Enbrackon, his home is owned by Haven City and must be utilized for all city-wide social functions, especially those solely for Enforcement. The Honorary will be held at his mansion, same as every year."

"It's for HCES though, not just everyone," Voklane reminded him.

"True. However, the Arch Guardians usually attend, and the enforcers can bring a guest. I'm sure Asherwick can find us invitations," Sean said.

Kevin drew his brows together in frown. "What good is showing up at the event?"

Sean grinned. "We're going to play him at his own game, and when we're done, he'll walk you right to the evidence."

FRIDAY EVENING CAME FAR TOO QUICKLY for Raina. After much debating, and on Raina's part arguing, the team had decided she was safer at her father's house than anywhere else. The plan was beautifully simple, but required a timed execution. Pacing in the spacious foyer between the stairs and the pillars of the open ballroom, Raina chewed her bottom lip. The folds of her rose skirt flowed around her ankles with each rapid turn.

Synintcl appeared at the top of the stairs. Taking them down at a clipped pace, he fussed with the cuff of his left sleeve. The long black jacket, silver vest, light gray shirt and the onyx encrusted blood red ruby the size of her thumbnail at his throat in place of a tie, made his tall frame and fit form stand out. A power outfit if she ever saw one. She wondered if the others dressed equally authoritative.

"You're going to be late," Raina chided, hating being left out.

He stopped at the bottom of the stairs, his pale brown eyes settled on her. "Even in a simple skirt and shirt, you look beautiful."

Raina sighed, pulling on the edges of his jacket and then tugged on the bottom of his vest, making sure the buttons where all centered. "You never compliment me. Are you that nervous?"

His larger hands closed over hers, stopping her fussing and forcing her to meet his stare. "I'm not nervous. Black-bain's plan is sound and your husband is like a ghost, he's never seen, let alone caught. We'll be home before you have a chance to worry about either of us."

"I'm already worried."

"Don't. The entire event is for enforcement, Enbrackon won't do anything stupid tonight. He won't even know what's happened until the E&R meeting. When he returns from checking on his files like Blackbain predicts he will, he'll think he's still safe. He'll smile and charm like he always does."

Forcing a smile, she patted his chest. "I'll take your word for it."

Still holding her hand, he guided her to his office. "I told you, you'll be able to listen to Voklane and Merrick while they conduct the operation, if you want."

Part of her wanted to, while another part cautioned the rising anxiety churning her stomach would only get worse. "I'll think about it. Thank you."

"It's behind the desk. I've already programmed the station, you just need to switch it on when you're ready."

"I'll figure it out, I'm sure. You need to get going."

"I need to be late. If Enbrackon hasn't made a move for the files, my presence is supposed to force him to check."

Raina sat in his padded leather desk chair and faced the radio. The glow from the fire and a few burning lamps around his desk cast the room in shifting shadows. She leaned forward and tried to make out all the little dials and knobs on the blocky radio unit. Twisting, she met her father's sober stare. "Is the Honorary happening now? They're engaging in the plan right now?"

"They should be, yes."

On a quick inhale, she faced the radio again. "Do you want to know how it's going?"

"Lorraina, if you want to hear, turn it on."

She ignored his sharp tone, used to his sudden shifts from patience to annoyance. "They can't hear me?"

"No, and I'm not telling you how to speak to them."

"You mean they could?"

"Yes, I can transmit as well. But I'm not telling you how. Your husband's life is worth more to me than appeasing your desire to speak to him."

Raina resisted the urge to glare at her parent. "I wouldn't speak to him when it mattered."

Synintel fussed with his cuff again, shaking the sleeve down to fully cover his wrist. "Actually, you'd be unable to resist if you heard even the slightest indication he was in danger. You aren't trained to understand the importance of complete focus. It's the reason you're here safely in my house, and not at the function, or even locked away at Dandridge's."

"I thought I was here because security is better."

"Dandridge has no security."

Raina opened her mouth to say that was her point, but realized the words would fall on deaf ears. She gave a closed lipped smile and nodded. "I will listen only if I wish to."

"Very well. I'll return with Merrick once he has the files in hand. If you're listening, you'll know when we're headed your direction."

If that wasn't motivation to turn the radio on, she didn't know what would be. When he turned to leave, she stood and braced her hands on surface. She wanted to run around the desk and give him a hug, tell him she loved him. But Henry Edmond, Arch Guardian Synintel, wasn't a man for affections, physical or spoken. Unable to let him leave without any words, Raina said warmly, "Be careful, Daddy."

He stopped in his tracks and glanced over his shoulder. The faint light caught at the streaks of silver in his styled, short dark brown hair. "I'm always careful, my dearest."

The sting of tears welled in her eyes and she took a deep calming breath. "I need you both to come home to me. Not just one of you."

"I know. We will. I promise."

With those words, he strode from the office. A steady clip of boots on marble informed her of the procession of footman who followed him out and would accompany him to the Honorary. Breathing out a long sigh, Raina faced the radio and chewed on her bottom lip. Did she want to know, or not? One of the plush chairs situated before the fire looked inviting, and a book from the vast collection along the wall across from his desk could keep her occupied. If she were able to stay focused. Which was unlikely.

Everything hinged on Sean's plan working. On Enbrackon suspecting they knew of the evidence, had somehow managed to sneak it out from under him. As a result he'd check to make sure, leading Kevin right to the hiding location. If the plan didn't work, they were back to the beginning, with her being framed for smuggling, and her father dishonored due to her crimes.

Raina braced her elbows on the table the radio rested on and dropped her head into her hands. How could she have been so naïve? The weight of her actions bore down heavily on her shoulders. Whenever alone she found herself dwelling on what she couldn't go back and change.

Taking a deep breath, she reached for the switch on the radio. A second before her finger touched, she stopped. Her father's biggest mistake was always underestimating her intelligence and willpower. A cursory glance told her everything she needed to know about the magnetically powered device, including how to transmit. If she truly wanted, she could speak to both Kevin and Voklane. However, the assumption her father had made concerning her inability to keep quiet should Kevin be endangered was also correct.

Curling her fingers into her palm she knew she couldn't pose such a risk to the team. She wasn't trained, and didn't know their dynamic. Intruding over an airwave would have the same disastrous results. Decision made, she quickly rose from desk chair before she changed her mind.

Instead of sitting in front of the fire, she paced the long expanse of her father's office. The ornate wooden clock above the fireplace ticked time away far too slowly. Her gaze kept shifting back to the silent radio. Maybe if she switched it on and then put distance between them, she could keep from intruding on their conversations. Squinting at the radio in thought, she flexed her jaw. Nope. She'd mess it up, she knew so. Sighing, she went back to the safety of marching back and forth.

Her stomach in knots and her heart racing, she tried to take deep calming breaths. But after several, her vision wavered. Anxiety quickly took over. Raina rushed to the nearest chair, barely collapsing before her lungs refused to cooperate. Bracing her head in her hands, she stared at the low, dancing flames in the fireplace. Her gaze drifted to the beautiful bronze calendar placard hanging from the wall beside the pale brick.

No...

Blinking she straightened her back. Surely that wasn't

today's date. A new uncomfortable sensation swept through her. Tapping her toes on the carpeted floor, she chewed on her bottom lip. Despite knowing she'd never actually know how long ago she'd left their Haven City home without looking at her desk calendar, she began counting on her fingers backwards. The distraction was most welcome, even if it did prove to be useless in the end.

The sound of voices drifting from beyond the office made her jump from her seat. Kevin appeared first. Unharmed, with not even a fiber out of place on his black, skin tight outfit, she almost crumpled to the floor from relief. Grabbing the back of the chair in support, she pressed a hand to her stomach to squelch the butterflies still fluttering.

"You found the files?" she couldn't stop from asking.

He nodded. A grin slowly spread across his handsome face. "Yep, he led me right to them just as Sean figured he would." He held up a sheet of paper. "Also found this."

Raina stared. "What is that?"

"The fake marriage contract. No longer a threat."

"Oh, thank goodness," she breathed, touching a hand to her still pounding heart. The relief was quickly replaced in her preoccupied mind. She waved her hand. "We need to go to the house."

Kevin drew his brows together. He tossed the contract into the fire. The edges curled as flames engulfed the paper. "What house?"

"Our house. Right now."

"But—"

"No, right now." To show how urgently she needed to get to her desk, she rushed around the chair and reached for him.

Synintel came into the office, flipping through the top folder. "I'll need you to verify these documents, Lorraina."

"I will, later. Tomorrow, okay?"

Her father's head snapped up. "Tomorrow?"

"Yes, tomorrow. I need to get home now." When he still

continued to stare at her as though her head had rolled from her shoulders and came to rest at his feet, she added, "It can wait that long, right? Just until morning?"

"Um…"

"Okay then, thanks Daddy." She air blew him a kiss and pulled on Kevin's arm in the direction of the office door.

"I think you broke your father," Kevin muttered, glancing over his shoulder.

Raina did the same, noting her father hadn't moved from his position in the center of the room. He even still stared at the place she'd been standing with Kevin. "He'll be all right."

"I don't think anyone has ever told him no before."

"Maybe not, I can't imagine who would, except maybe the Queen-Elect."

Kevin raised her hand to his mouth and brushed a gentle kiss across her knuckles. "You did."

Raina paused at the stairs and peeked into her father's study. He shook his head, moving slowly toward his desk. As an Arch Guardian, Synintel had not only earned her respect, but demanded it. However, he'd been her father tonight, not a high-ranking government official. "I shouldn't have."

"Is getting home that important?"

She took a deep breath. "Yes."

25

The delicate rustle of pages filled the still, dark room. Only the silvery moonlight illuminated Raina's office. She'd been too intent on getting to her calendar to worry about stopping to light anything.

A faint chill hung in the air. Not expecting them to be home, Mrs. Taft hadn't lit any fires in the house. Kevin had run upstairs to get the woodstove in her room burning. Since they were home, he figured they might as well stay. They'd been away long enough for most threats to fizzle out.

Raina touched a finger to the current date on the calendar and then flipped back through the weeks. Almost seven in all... Sitting back she swallowed against the sudden dryness in her throat. Carefully, she eased the desk chair back and stood. In a bit of a daze, she somehow managed to get to her room.

The curtains in her room where drawn tight. Only the faint glow from the woodstove Kevin knelt before, gently working the budding flames into life cast any light in the space. He glanced at her for a second, continuing to encourage the fire.

"Did you find what you needed?" he asked, setting the poker to the side.

Raina's spine stiffened. "Who said I needed anything?"

"You did, when you blew off your father to get here so quickly."

Raina tugged at the fabric of her skirt nervously. "Oh, yes, I found what I needed."

"And?" he prompted, leaning a hip against her footboard and crossing his arms over his broad chest.

She licked her lips and stared past him to the headboard. "And… I'm late."

He cocked an eyebrow. "Late for what? I imagine you missed a lot of appointments while we've been hiding."

Sighing, she crossed the distance between them. Taking his hands, she led him to the bed and forced him to sit with her. He was going to make her come right out and say it. Why was she so nervous about that? Would he be excited? Angry? No… he'd never be angry. She released a slow calming breath.

"I'm pregnant."

Silence followed her announcement. At first Raina wasn't sure he'd even heard her. Then his fingers slid from hers and shifted to her jaw. Before she could ask how he felt, Kevin's mouth moved across hers. The slow, sensual glide of his lips and tongue silenced any words she could coherently form. Opening her mouth, she lost herself in the depth of his kiss, barely registering when he shifted her onto his lap, until he forced her knees apart to straddle his hips. The thick bulging proof of his desire pressed against her center. She let out a shuddering gasp of pleasure, unable to stop herself from moving her hips to feel more.

Raina wrapped her arms around his shoulders. Her fingers grazed through his short hair along his scalp. He swiftly removed her clothes, while she fumbled with the buttons of his shirt between freeing her arms from her sleeves. Not quick enough for his liking, Kevin took over the task, breaking their kiss long enough to shift her onto the mattress beneath him and remove his pants. Impatient for more, Raina lifted her hips and ran her toes along his thighs.

"Slow down," he breathed into her mouth, his hand slipping between their bodies to search out where she so desperately needed him.

"No," she exhaled, bucking as his finger glided along her slickened flesh, heightening her desire. How could he make her want so quickly?

But he left her no other choice. Loving her with slow, leisurely strokes. First with his touch, then with his mouth, he coaxed her to climax twice before finally sliding deep inside her with equally drawn-out strokes. He loved her like they had forever, his lips whispering kisses along her throat, jaw and temple. When the delightful friction of his body moving above and inside her mounted into an intense eruption coursing through every cell of her being, she screamed and arched off the bed, her nails digging into the flesh of his hips.

Still, Kevin didn't stop. "You are everything to me," he whispered into her ear, pushing her closer to another earth-shattering orgasm. "Everything."

Raina could only reply with a cry of pleasure, tears burning as she held him close, shaking from the power of her release. She held him when he finally allowed his own release to claim him. Despite being breathless and spent, she clamped her legs tightly around his waist when he moved to roll from her.

"I'm too heavy, you know that." He kissed her cheek and then shifted his weight, forcing her to relax so he could.

"I like you where you are."

"I know, me too, but I don't like the idea of squishing you, especially now."

Raina smiled and hugged him tight. "I don't think you can hurt either of us."

He helped her stand so he could pull down the sheets. She crawled onto the supple mattress. Thankful to be in her bed, she sighed, gliding her fingers along the finely spun cotton sheets as she laid on her belly. Kevin joined her, but instead of covering them, he urged her onto her back. His fingers laced between hers, he laid his head on her stomach. With her free hand, she stroked his damp hair.

"What are you thinking?" she asked.

"What if our son or daughter is like me?" His arm tightened around her hips. "I don't want this life for them, Raina."

Raina's hand froze mid-stroke. Uncertainty tightened in her chest. "You're unhappy about the baby."

His fingers unwound from hers. Laying across her abdomen, he gripped her ribs, making her feel tiny. "Never." He kissed between her breasts, his short beard tickling and teasing.

"But you're anxious about the future?"

The rough texture of his whiskers brushed the insides of her breasts as he gently nuzzled her flesh. "You aren't?"

Raina relaxed and went back to smoothing her fingers through his disheveled hair. "Not really. We will love our children, both of us, and make sure they're given a future *they* get to choose, no matter what the choice is. Whether they decide to become a Guardian, or wherever else their passions lie."

On a sigh, Kevin shifted until he once again laid across her belly. His large hand spanned the distance between her hips. "I don't know how I'm going to be able to go on my next assignment."

The confession was spoken so softly, Raina barely heard it. Her fingers clenched in his hair. With a gentle tug, she forced his attention back to her face. "Only you can do what you do for your team. And when you come home, we'll be here. Waiting. Safe where you left us."

"I'll be leaving you with your father," he muttered.

Raina stiffened. "This house has always been safe enough, and I'm sure my father will send guards if you ask."

He pressed a kiss above her navel before easing away, dragging the blankets with him. "Synintel lives in a virtual fortress. Until this, whatever it is that's happening in this country, cycles through, you aren't safe like you used to be. You know too much, not to mention *because* of your father, you're a target. One they've made very clear. You have more to think about than yourself now."

Sighing in aggravation, she rolled onto his chest. Propping her chin on her hands, she met his concerned gray eyes. "That's true enough. Fine, *if* you get called away, I'll stay with my father."

"Not if, princess, but when. When I'm called away."

A fist clenched around her heart and she dropped her cheek to his chest, her hand smoothing along his firm stomach. She didn't ever want to think of him leaving again, especially now. Everything had changed between them. They had a real marriage, with love, hopes and dreams. The moment her father's men, or Sean, arrived with their orders, she'd have to say goodbye. Not knowing when she'd see him again, clinging to the hope a next time would arrive.

Kevin yanked her attention away from their somber future by asking, "How did your mother die?"

Confused by the change in subject, she met his stare again. "What?"

His hand stroked up her spine, causing a delicious shiver to race through her. "Your mother, how did you lose her?"

Raina swallowed against the painful memory, and the sense of betrayal that always came when she recalled *how* she'd lost her mother. "She... she poisoned herself."

"Suicide?" Kevin asked gently.

Taking a deep calming breath, Raina rubbed her chin along his pectoral muscle. "No, I don't think she did it on purpose. Then again she may have. I was only eight. The only reason I know how, is I overheard the Medical Scientist telling my father what he believed happened."

"How did she poison herself then?"

"Alcohol. They also found a half-smoked cigarette laced with halioke on her nightstand, too. They didn't know if she'd smoked it or not, but if she did, it helped explain why she died. Everyone, including the paper, was told she died of heart failure."

He hugged her tight to his chest, kissing the top of her head. "I'm sorry."

"I've never been able to touch alcohol."

"I know."

Of course he knew. Even before he knew every inch of body more intimately than she did, he knew *her*. Not an Arch Guardians daughter. Not a pocket of wealth to reach into. Not a pawn to be utilized. Simply Raina Merrick, his wife. Who mattered to him enough to know when she needed to act her station, and when it was okay to simply be herself.

"I love you," she whispered, rising enough to reach his mouth.

With a growl, he tugged her across his chest. "I know."

MUTED LIGHT FILTERED in from the wall of windows into Synintel's office. The rustle of pages accompanied the occasional pop of a log in the fireplace. Cup of coffee in hand, Kevin stared out a tall window, watching rain pelt the leaves on the many plants lining the curving driveway.

"I think it's all here," Raina said with a note of wonderment. "I even think the warehouse locations are noted on the manifests."

Kevin raised a brow and turned. "Wouldn't that make everything easy."

"I know." She sighed and sank back into the chair. "A break, finally."

"What's a break?" Voklane asked, strolling into the office and taking a bite of a pastry in his hand.

A server followed closely behind, clasping a tray filled with fruit, sliced ham and muffins. She set the tray on a table before the fireplace, bowed swiftly, and then exited. Raina's spine straightened, her eyebrows lifted as she peered over the desk and licked her lips.

Kevin grinned. "Would you like something to eat?"

A pretty flush spread across her cheeks. "Yes, please."

Setting his cup on the corner of the desk near a bronze dragon, he asked, "Something of everything?"

She nodded and went back to looking over the documents. Kevin loaded a small plate with food. Voklane polished off his pastry looking over Raina's head to the papers spread across her father's desk.

Raina twisted in the seat and glared up at Ryan. "If you get crumbs in my hair, I will be upset."

The man had the good sense to take a step back. "What was the break you think you caught?"

Kevin placed the food in front of his wife, barely managing to keep from laughing as she attacked it before he'd completely released his hold. "She thinks they wrote the warehouse locations on the original manifests."

Voklane's pale brows rose with interest. "Really?" He leaned over Raina again and she waved her hand above her head in annoyance until he shifted to the side. "Where do you see that?"

Raina searched through the sheets. Kevin went to the side of the desk and braced his hip on the edge, crossing his arms over his chest, unable to take his eyes off her. Her glossy light brown hair was in a sloppy bun atop her head, something she never would have dared leave the house with before their Northern Boundary escapade. One of the simple skirts with a long ribbon tie for the waist fell over her legs in crimson ripples. A billowing cream peasant blouse completed the comfortable attire she'd dressed herself in this morning. Pride swelled in his chest. She'd taken her newfound freedoms to heart, not caring what anyone else thought.

If it'd been up to him, they'd still be in her bed, doing more of what had brought about the miracle currently growing inside her. He figured now it was *their* bed actually, since she'd told him before the sun rose she'd only be sleeping alone when he wasn't around. Which was more than fine by Kevin. He couldn't get enough of the woman. His woman.

Voklane took the paper Raina held up and Kevin sighed in annoyance. Too bad the man was here, or Kevin would have shown his beautiful wife how much he loved her again. In her father's office, like he should have done all those years ago. The thought made him smile. Raina caught his smirk and raised a brow. He shook his head and her little giggle told him she'd figured out *exactly* what had been on his mind. Ah well, maybe next time.

"Where is my father?"

Voklane shifted, reaching for the radio behind the desk. He adjusted the dials and flipped two switches. "At the FIO, no doubt seeing what his little internal spies have found out."

"Are you over them, too?" Kevin asked.

"No, that'd draw too much attention if I was seen too often with more than Synintel's Guardians. The only input I had was who I determined to be loyal enough to carry out the task."

Kevin had always wondered how the man established loyalty. But looking over Voklane's intense expression as he adjusted the radio, he knew he wouldn't get an answer. "Who are you calling?"

"Asherwick."

"Why?"

"Isn't he the one you all have been working with?"

"Yes."

"Then he's the one who needs to make one of the warehouse discoveries. He already knows the stakes, and I know he can be trusted. Also, if HCES is involved, it'll make the papers, and I definitely want that."

Nothing says 'This round goes to us, maggots' like reading it in the paper, Kevin mused. He picked up his coffee and took a slow sip. "You sure you don't want us there?"

Voklane slowly shook his head. "I don't want any of you near that place when a shipment is confiscated. This is a very intense game of chess. We take a pawn, I don't need them taking one of my knights over it."

Kevin conceded the strategy. "Very well."

The radio beeped, signaling an out-going transmission. Ryan let it continue for a full minute before cutting the feed with a growl of frustration. "He's at Enforcement Services."

"Doesn't he have a radio in his office?"

"Yes, but I'm not risking someone else overhearing this particular conversation. I'll go find him."

Raina twisted in the seat to face Ryan. "Are you taking one of the manifests with you?"

Voklane nodded. "Would have been handed to me anyway."

"Are you going to see my father afterward?"

"I'll be going to the FIO, yes. As for seeing your father, I can only go to his office if I'm summoned."

"Will you be?"

His lips twitched into an almost smile. "Very likely, why?"

"I need you to deliver a message for me, I wrote it already."

"Why can't you tell him in person?"

A frown pinched between her brows and Kevin's stomach tightened, knowing what she was going to say. "Because he'd have to schedule time for me, and I don't want to worry about when. I'd rather he know what I need to tell him now. If he wants to speak to me, he knows where we live."

Voklane grimaced. "And this is why I'm perfectly happy simply being a Guardian without a ranking."

"Do you mind?" she asked.

"No, of course not. I'll make sure he gets it."

Raina dug around underneath several pages. She flourished an envelope and handed it off to Ryan's waiting hand. "Thank you."

He inclined his head and then turned to Kevin. "Do you have anything?"

"No, he knows pretty much all I have to say to him."

Ryan did laugh at that. "All right then, I'll see you two later."

Raina let out a long exhale after Ryan left the room. Kevin set down his coffee, and went to close the door. Once alone, he disregarded the pretense of propriety, scooping Raina out of the seat on a squeal and carried her to one of the plush chairs in front of the fire. She settled across his lap without protest, wrapping her arms around his shoulders.

"They won't leave us alone too long," she warned.

"Then we better be quick." He nibbled at her collar bone, smiling at the tremor and breathy sigh he coaxed from her.

"Do you think it'll really work?"

Kevin leaned back in the seat and took her worried face between both his hands. "Synintel will make sure, you can trust in that."

Her hands covered his, her frown deepening. "It doesn't excuse what I did."

"You didn't do anything wrong."

"Yes, I did!" When she attempted to untangle herself from his lap, he wrapped his arms around her waist and held her still. "My ignorance does not excuse my involvement in what amounted to what is looking like treason."

"Raina, they used you. At no point did you knowingly participate in their scheme. The forged manifests will prove that."

"But *I* helped forge those manifests. My innocence hinges on my word against theirs, should they be caught and tried. Barring a full confession from Enbrackon, or whoever else is involved..."

"And we handled the situation the moment we became aware, we didn't hide it, or try to play it down. No council member in their right mind, or on the right side, will believe you were tied to the group, whoever they are." He pressed a kiss to her tight lips. "Please trust me."

"I do. But..." She bit her lip and looked away from him.

"What?"

"What if I do something so stupid again?" she whispered.

Kevin pulled her into his chest, hugging her. "You won't."

Her fingers bunched in the fabric at his shoulders. "How do you know?"

"Because you aren't the same person they took advantage of."

She gave a little sniffle and sat back, her eyes searching his. "What do you mean?"

Kevin traced the pout of her lower lip with his thumb. "You aren't Raina Edmond, daughter of Arch Guardian Synintel pretending to be Raina Merrick, wife of Master Guardian Raiventon. You *are* Raina Merrick, Guardianess Raiventon. And no one is going to tell or treat you otherwise."

Pride and love shone in her gaze. "No, they aren't."

"See?"

In a single blink, her eyes filled with tears. "How did I get you?"

Kevin smiled. "I keep asking myself that very same question about you."

She burrowed against his chest. "You know, when Patricia first met you, she asked me how I wasn't pregnant."

Kevin laughed. "Oh really?"

"Yes. She'll be most happy when I tell her I am."

"Shouldn't we tell your father first?"

Raina shrugged. "If he wants to know first, he'll come to the house tonight. I told him I have something to share and I won't do so in writing."

Kevin slid a hand under her shirt to caress her back. "What did you write to him about?"

"I told him I made the decision for you, and now you're honor bound to me."

Kevin raised a curious brow. "What decision?"

"About whether we would be normal people should the E&R meeting not go in your favor."

"Ah." He'd almost forgotten about that unhappy scheduled event. "And what did you say?"

She rose on her knees, taking his face between her hands, her answer feathering against his lips, "I chose you. Any way I can have you."

HAVE YOU REVIEWED THIS TITLE?

First, thank you! Second, I love to hear from my readers and send a special gift as a personal thank you for taking the time to leave a review. For authors, reviews are the best way for others to discover us and know that you, our awesome readers, love our work. Please email me at authorsarahwestill@gmail.com to let me know about your review.

Look for Mason's book next!

Kynhaven
GEN-HEIRS: The Guardians of Sziveria

An unimaginable tragedy sends Mason Dandridge, Primary Guardian Kynhaven, to Westica, on the hunt for Jessalyn Silverna, the only surviving victim of a sadistic killer-for-hire. What he finds is a broken woman, emotionally and physically scarred, unable to see her beauty or power as a woman. Needing answers only she can provide, Mason is determined to persuade Jessi to return with him to Sziveria. When she refuses, and with his life in ruins, Mason has no choice but to find refuge in Jessi's small Westican home.

Learning the kidnapping she barely escaped from wasn't a random act, but a calculated move meant to strike at her Sziverian father, turns Jessi's life upside down. Going to a foreign land is out of the question, especially when Mason reveals someone might want her dead.

But Mason is convincing. He shows her a side to herself she didn't know existed.

Suddenly, life outside her sheltered reality doesn't seem so terrifying. Jessi begins to dream of the partnership he offers, the chance for something bigger than the both of them. At his side, as his wife, she could have a family, an opportunity to love, and a passion she can only imagine. If she's willing to take the chance…

KYNHAVEN - AVAILABLE IN ALL FORMATS JAN. 6TH 2022

Want to know how it all started? Be sure to check out the Prequel:

Levkaseon
GEN-HEIRS: The Guardians of Sziveria
Available Nov. 4th 2021

My dearest reader,

Thank you for turning the pages until you reached this small message I've written only for you. The main theme of this book you may have noticed was choice. To make one, not to make one, to have the ability *to* make one. Every day we have decisions. Some are small. What to wear, what to eat, what type of coffee or tea am I going to have today? What shade of eyeshadow or lipstick? Some are really difficult, and we may even find ourselves putting them off. Should I take that job? Should I still be her friend even after what she did (or said to me)? What if I follow this dream and… I fail?

My twelve-year-old son (at the time I'm writing this) was watching a silly show on the History Channel, where an industry expert commented that sink holes may hold the secret to life. Still in his pajama's, eating a bag of chips (don't judge us!), he scoffs and says, "The secret to life is to live it." I blinked. Wow.

The secret to life is to live it.

What choices can you make, beautiful or scary, that will see you living, not just existing, in this beautiful world? What dreams will you follow that leave you dancing and laughing after you see what your hard work has accomplished? What can your blank canvas become, even if you've never taken a brush to one before? Who else will sing the song you write because you finally decided to put your pen to paper? Who will smile because you chose to smile first? Who will feel so strong because you chose told them they had the ability when they struggled to see their value? Because perhaps you spoke up, you spoke out, you made the choice to be the voice they needed to hear. Or maybe you needed to hear this, too. To take a deep breath, again, and know living is so amazing because LIFE is amazing. Because YOU are amazing.

Untitled

With love,
   Sarah

But you are God's chosen treasure – 1 Peter 2:9 (TPT)

ABOUT THE AUTHOR

SARAH WESTILL lives in Alabama with her US Army-retired husband. They have two sons – one they've successfully raised to adulthood – the other is still a work-in-progress, navigating middle school. As a full-on creative, Sarah lives to write, paint, teach, and meet amazing people while doing portrait photography. A veteran in the publishing industry working as a cover artist under the name Elaina Lee, she has been blessed to help hundreds of authors to achieve their own publishing goals for over a decade. To learn more about Sarah as she blogs her adventures, and about her Guardians, please visit her at sarahwestill.com or follow her on Instagram @authorsarahwestill

9 781955 293037